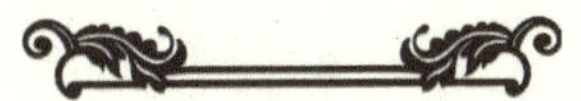

Tears into Thy Bottle

The Chronicles of Alice & Ivy, Book 7

a novel by Kellyn Roth

Published by Kellyn Roth, Author

Wild Blue Wonder Press

ISBN: 978-1-962222-08-2

Scripture quotations are taken from the King James Version (KJV).

Cover design by Carpe Librum Book Design

Copy Editor: Katja H. Labonté

admin@wildbluewonderpress.com

www.wildbluewonderpress.com

Contents

Dedication

For Janelle, a true friend who never fails to point me toward the unfailing love of Christ through both mentorship and the lived example of a godly wife and mother.

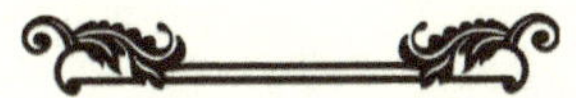

Character List

Alice Strauss — our heroine.

Peter Strauss — our hero.

In England & Scotland

Ivy & Jordy McAllen — Alice's sister and brother-in-law who live in the village of Keefmore in Scotland; parents of twins, Molly and Letty.

Mr. Philip and Mrs. Claire Knight — Alice's adoptive parents. Owners of Pearlbelle Park, an estate near the village of Creling in Kent, England.

Ned, Caleb, Jackie, and Rebecca Knight — Philip and Claire Knight's children.

Nettie Jameson — Alice's biological mother who served as her childhood nanny and governess for many years.

Tom Jameson — Nettie's husband.

Malcolm, Ella, and Deborah Jameson — Nettie's children.

Mr. Steven Parker — Alice's biological father, who is no longer allowed at Pearlbelle Park due to his behavior.

Kirk Manning — Alice's biological half-brother.

IN PHILADELPHIA

Mr. Christopher "Chris" and Mrs. Lillian "Lilli" Strauss — Peter's parents.

Cassie Hilton — Alice's dearest friend. Wife of Patrick; mother of Aidan.

The Baldwins — Patrick Hilton's employer and his family.

Caroline and Barnaby Webster — Peter's sister and her husband; parents of Barnie, Maudie, and Howie.

Elias and Dahlia Thorpe — Peter's younger sister and her husband.

Andrew Strauss — Peter's brother, who is married and lives in Boston with his wife.

IN CINCINNATI

Juno — Alice's dog

Ophelia and Cassius — Peter's cats

Riley, Maddie, Polly, and Susie Farjon — Peter's cousin and his family.

Mr. Terrence "Terry" and Mrs. Felicity "Flick" Tappet — childhood friends of Riley Farjon.

Essie Farjon — Riley's younger sister who lives with Terry and Flick.

Dr. Brett and Mrs. Sarah Engall — a doctor and his wife who attend Peter and Alice's church in Cincinnati; parents of Annabelle and Cecelia "Cece."

The Tremains — an older couple who own a dress shop in Cincinnati.

In Virginia

Mr. Colin and Mrs. Georgiana Farjon — Riley's parents who live in Eleanor, Virginia, on a former tobacco plantation, Clairdelune.

Mrs. Eleanor "Nora" O'Brien — Riley's older sister who lives in New York with her husband and children.

Miss Ruth — the Farjons' elderly cook.

Content Warning

Some readers are uncomfortable with certain types of content in the books they read. Though my novels are all closed-door romances with no gratuitous content, contain no swearing, and handle all topics discussed biblically, I have a brief list of content warnings for each of my books on my website.

kellynrothauthor.com/content-warnings

Some of these may contain minor spoilers. Read at your own risk!

"Thou tellest my wanderings: put Thou my tears into Thy bottle: are they not in Thy book?"

~Psalm 56:8~

Chapter One

February 1886
Keefmore, Scotland

Alice's eyes followed the path of packed earth that wound between dark shop windows. The village of Keefmore rested serenely under a blanket of snow. Early morning sunlight caught facets of ice until the surroundings glittered as if dusted in gold. "It is a lovely place, isn't it?"

"It is." Her husband, Peter, placed his hand on her waist. "We'll be back someday, but perhaps not in the winter." He shuddered. "It's entirely too cold."

"If Ivy can take the cold, so can you, darling." Alice smiled as she turned away from the road to face her sister. "Now, remember what I told you, Ivy. Don't shy away from asking for help. Your family here loves you, and you know that Mother would come running back, too, if you were to write her."

Ivy nodded. Like Peter, she was trembling from the early-morning chill, but the weather wasn't so bad, really. Alice just happened to be surrounded by weaklings. Of course, she would never acknowledge that her tolerance for snow far exceeded her tolerance for rain. She tended to hide inside when it rained, while Peter acted like a fool over a "good spring shower," as he called it.

Alice turned last to her brother-in-law. He'd risen early with Ivy, gathered their four-month-old twins, and scurried over to the inn where the coach was set to arrive.

It was awfully kind of him; Alice knew the immense work required to get two infants bundled into so many layers and out the door this early. It was nearing five now, but Alice had been up for almost two hours, packing and repacking her trunk and then pacing the room they were staying in while Peter slept until about ten minutes before they had to go.

Now the coach was late, which put rather a damper on leaving.

Ivy shuddered again, and Alice started forward to offer comfort then changed her mind. She could do better than that. She collected little Margaret Alice—*Molly*, the baby was called—from Jordy and nodded toward Ivy, silently encouraging him to take his wife in his arms.

Molly fussed in Alice's arms then settled. It had been such a joy to see "wee Molly" and her sister, Violet, delivered safely and then to spend those precious four months here, helping Ivy settle into motherhood. Alice had woken up every morning before dawn to make the trek from Aunt Daphne's house, where she was staying, to Ivy's small cottage over the hill behind the village. There, she'd helped in every way she could—cooking; cleaning; doing all the laundry babies seemed to create, from nappies to soiled blankets; and sometimes watching the twins so Ivy could sleep.

Ivy was always needed. With her own empty arms, Alice sometimes struggled with that—there was one thing she could not be for these babies, and that was "Mother." She hoped she had made the burden less, but she had certainly not removed it entirely, for keeping two babies well-fed and cared for was a full-time job.

However, she was confident it was time to leave. Jordy would have to manage—for he must—as would his family and the other citizens of Keefmore. Everyone loved Ivy, naturally, as she was all sweetness, so everyone would be happy to help out.

And Alice needed to go home. Back to her own house, in America, with her own people—Peter's people. And she needed to make herself let go, even of this bonnie child who along with her sweet new sister had so effortlessly stolen Alice's heart.

Ivy adjusted "Letty" in her arms. "Is that the coach?"

"Finally," Jordy mumbled, the word half-breathed into Ivy's hair. She had forgotten her hat—Alice had already half seriously scolded Ivy for that. She couldn't risk her sister catching cold.

"Oh, they're only a little late." Ivy always gave anyone or anything grace without question, an excellent habit that Alice would probably do well to cultivate.

The stage rumbled its way down the dirt road and swung to a stop in front of them. A person or two hopped off, and the driver shouted. Men unloaded luggage from the top and then replaced it with Alice and Peter's trunks.

Alice embraced Ivy cautiously around the two babies, then gave Molly over to Jordy and charged him to take good care of her nieces and sister. Jordy agreed to do so, and before she knew it, Alice and Peter were off.

They were the only ones in the coach as it left Keefmore behind, heading north to Inverness and the nearest station.

Peter took her hand and squeezed it. "We're still a long way from home, but this is the first step."

She nodded. "Riley must be tired of Juno and the cats."

"Oh, doubtless." He grinned. "I'd say he's probably more tired of our mail. Did I tell you his last letter confirmed the advance for *In Heart-Wrung Tears* arrived safely?"

Alice gave a small smile. "Thank heavens you gave him power of attorney before we left. I can't imagine trying to manage bank drafts from here."

"I can't either," Peter agreed. "But he'll still give us both a scolding for staying away so long." Riley Farjon, Peter's best friend and cousin, never kept his thoughts to himself.

"First we've my family to see once more. Do you mind?" Alice had been dragging Peter all over England for some time now. A quick trip to keep her friend Cassie Hilton company and perform some research for a book of Peter's had been lengthened by Ivy's impending motherhood and further lengthened when Alice had decided Ivy couldn't be left alone. Peter had soldiered on, cheerful as ever, despite the fact that it had been long since he'd seen his own family back in America. He'd yet to meet his latest nephew, and who knew what else had changed? Certainly, Alice and Peter were in a much different place financially than they had been when they left. Riley's last letter had included a bank statement that made her jaw drop.

"I don't mind." Peter turned and kissed her cheek. There was a luxury to being alone in the coach, allowed to express affection without sideways glances. For other couples, perhaps that luxury meant spreading out, distancing themselves, each taking a bench; but Peter would never allow it. Alice would've been disappointed if he had. She needed him—to keep her warm, to assure her of his affection, to trail kisses down her neck and distract her completely from her plans. She was subtle in the way she returned physical affection, but she wasn't about to reject it, either.

"It'll only be a few weeks, then we'll go home. No more adventures." She lifted her carpetbag from where it rested at her feet. "It'll be a long day, so we might as well do a few revisions."

Peter moaned and drew away from her. "Alice, please."

"You know we're behind."

"We're *not* behind."

"Yes, we are!" He would never admit, on his own, that he had changes to make in his most recent manuscript. At least, not until they were days from the deadline. But that's why Alice was there: to help Peter. And she helped by forcing him to edit—or, these days, practically doing his edits for him. "We'll just do a few pages. Then we can talk about whatever you like."

Peter sighed and resigned himself as Alice settled the papers, tied together with twine, on her lap.

"This is set to be published in May," she reminded him as she handed him the first sheet of paper, a typed copy sent back from his publisher. *In Heart-Wrung Tears* had been written mostly during their stay in England and Scotland, and Peter loved the half romance, half drama he'd constructed inspired by his Scottish surroundings.

"Mm." He held out his hand, and she placed a pencil in it. "I still say I like the way it is now."

"All novels need edits, dear." Even Peter knew that, and he could be terribly protective of his books.

For some time, a quiet rhythm developed between them as they traded ideas, discussed grammar and sentence structure, and considered changes suggested by the publishing company's editor.

At last they put the novel away and sat in silence, Alice's head on Peter's shoulder, as the trip continued—long and dull and cold.

"It was good for us to stay with Ivy for a while. I feel like if we hadn't been, there might have been some strain on her marriage."

Alice blinked and raised her head. She wasn't unaccustomed to Peter saying things like that, out of the blue; however, it always confused her. How could he know? Alice was not naturally talented at understanding people. In her more childish days, she'd deemed it an unchangeable part of her character. Now, she asked frequent questions to expand her knowledge about people. Yet still, she never would be able to observe as he did so effortlessly. "Why do you think?"

He shrugged. Alice always asked; Peter didn't always have an answer. "Something I can't place my finger on. We know Jordy wasn't particularly pleased about his impending fatherhood at the start, even if he did seem to adjust. That might've been worse had we not been there. We both know that sometimes a dear friend can make all the difference in a difficult time."

Alice nodded. After she had suffered a nervous collapse more than three years ago, Cassie had come to stay near them in Cincinnati for a few months, caring for Alice and giving her someone to talk to. It had been an incredible blessing. But Alice couldn't really give her friend credit for saving her marriage—that was all owed to God.

"It must cause a strain to be first-time parents, regardless of the circumstances. It certainly can't be any easier with twins." Alice glanced out the window. "We're passing a lovely lake—or loch, I suppose." She'd had quite a few lectures from her brother-in-law on proper Scottish vernacular, and though generally she was stubborn enough to call a body of water whatever she wanted to call a body of water, Peter found Scottish words charming. Alice would bear a lot of nonsense on Peter's behalf.

Peter moved to the opposite bench so he could look out the small window until the loch passed. "I don't think parenthood is ever 'easy,' no. Besides, being here was good for us, too."

She cocked her head, regarding him as he continued to stare out, plainly fascinated with the rugged countryside, its frozen world so different from the landscape they'd traveled through on their way to Keefmore that spring. "How do you think?"

"I'd wondered if it'd made you think ..." He stopped and glanced at her. Worry filled his honey-brown eyes.

"Tell me."

"I'd wondered if it'd made you think about children again."

She took a deep breath and let it out slowly. She always thought about children. They'd lost two babies early in their marriage—Zebedee, an early miscarriage, and Daniel, a stillbirth at full term—and it had broken them both. Years of seeking the Lord's healing had helped, but it was still a sore subject. It never *wouldn't* be. And yes, every time another woman had a baby, it passed through Alice's mind briefly that she was childless—and she'd think, then, about how old her sons would be, wonder what they'd be like, and eagerly anticipate meeting them again in Heaven. "Of course I think about it. I think about it every day. But I also can accept that it's not a part of our life right now, and, much as that pains me, I know that God's plans are good. I'm not afraid." She hesitated. "Are you?"

"No. Grieved, but not afraid." Peter sighed. "I have a confession, if I'm honest. I hadn't expected to feel so much ... so much *jealousy*, I suppose, over Ivy and Jordy having children while we remain childless. I feel as if I finally have an idea of what you've been going through these last several years since we lost Daniel—watching my sister and Cassie and others have their babies, and raise them, and be mothers. I'm not quite sure I fully understood until now. Something about Ivy becoming a mother—it knocked the breath out of me."

A wave of guilt washed over Alice. She hadn't once thought to ask Peter how he was handling these last few months. Peter's grief was as deep as hers. In some ways, she felt it even ran deeper—that his inability to communicate certain things, so entirely unlike his usually open mannerisms, spoke of a depth of sadness she wouldn't ever be able to touch. Yet she tried, and lately, she'd been succeeding. But no, she hadn't thought that it would be any different for Peter. "I'm sorry. I should've ... Why didn't you tell me?"

A small, pained smile touched his lips, but he kept his gaze fixed on the window—an unusual slight, for Peter rarely spoke to anyone without giving them his full attention. "I wasn't sure what I was feeling at first, and when I was, I thought it better to tell you after we were removed from the situation."

Disgusted with herself and shocked at Peter, she couldn't help but exclaim, "Never do that again!"

He looked at her then, as if surprised by her vehemence.

Softening her tone, she continued. "Tell me these things, Peter. Please, darling. I need to hear them even if they're not sorted and tidy, at the first. Please confide in me. I promise I'll do my best to help. I know I'm not the most ... the most empathetic person—"

"You do just fine. You're a tremendous blessing to me and always will be," Peter protested. "This is my fault."

"Perhaps it is and perhaps it isn't. I still wish I'd been a little more observant, but since I wasn't, I must simply ask your pardon and continue on. What makes you bring this up now? How did you think of it?"

A slight indent in his cheek indicated he was biting the side of his mouth. His shoulders moved again, almost a shrug. "I was actually wondering if you'd ever consider adopting."

Alice's chest compressed. Adopting? They hadn't discussed that in years. At first, the idea had been broached in the depths of their grief, when the longing for a child was at its most acute. However, they'd both decided that it wasn't a healthy desire—just an ineffective way to try to ease the grief—and tossed it aside. "I didn't know that was something you were seriously interested in."

Peter nodded. "More and more, I am, Alice. I want to be a father."

His voice caught. He looked away again, but then turned back to her, his shoulders set as he gave her his full attention. She reached across the coach and captured his hands in hers, determined that not even an impulse would pull him away from her again. "I've never made that a secret, but it seems to me that it's more important now. I believe we would be good parents. I truly do. We can offer a child so much—a stable home, a life without want. We're in a position now we only dreamed of when we were younger. Though God has not blessed us with children, we both know that there are many orphans in this world who need a loving family. Maybe we can make a difference that way."

"Maybe." Alice knew little about adoption. It was somewhat of a taboo in her social circles—orphans were looked down on, and there was the stigma of potential illegitimacy or simply unknown parentage tainting any association with an adopted child. Alice knew that more than anyone—she was the product of a perverted union, one of violence and great evil. Yet that was not always the case, and even if it were, it wouldn't be the child's fault. No one could control their origins—yet it was possible for origins to control a person, to a certain degree.

"You don't have to agree." He tried to lean away from her, as she'd expected, but she wouldn't let him. "I understand if that's not something you'd ever be interested in, but do consider it, Alice. I admit I've never quite shaken the feeling that we ought to have a child. Or many children, honestly. But if that's not a desire you share, except within specific parameters, I will accept it without questioning and consider you to be the voice of God in my life—my helper, the first person I turn to for guidance and input."

She nodded, taking his words in, letting them settle deep in her mind in a way she had only learned to do this past year. Peter chose every syllable he spoke so carefully that Alice felt he deserved the return favor of rumination.

What would it mean to adopt? How would they go about it? Was it simply the matter of visiting one of the orphanages that seemed to exist in every large city and putting one's name forward? She'd heard that some orphanages weren't even looking to have their children adopted—after all, children could be a useful commodity, especially children no one cared about.

She looked into Peter's eyes and saw the hope he struggled to smother, the trust he placed in her. How could he do that when she had failed him so many times? The thought made her shudder. Yet here he was, trusting her. It was a kind of insanity, and it made her want to do something equally mad—a grand gesture entirely foreign to her own nature.

She found nothing within her that protested the idea. Fear, yes. She had too little information. But for now, no true doubt took root. "I ... I am open to the idea."

His expression lightened, though he worked to control the upwards twitch of his lips. "It wouldn't be immediate. We'd want to be home and settled. But I know there's an orphanage or two in Cincinnati."

Alice pressed her lips together. "The one I know of is Catholic."

Peter laughed at that, though she didn't see what was particularly funny about it. "I don't think a baby's religion should matter too much as we make a decision."

"If they even let us adopt," Alice pointed out.

"We'll see when we get home, once we're at peace again. And that's a long way off. Let's pray about it now, and every day, until we hear something. God will determine this for us, one way or another, Alice."

Nodding, she bent her head over Peter's hands, still clasped in her own, and listened to his quiet prayer.

Chapter Two

Pearlbelle Park

It was pouring down rain on the day Alice and Peter arrived. As the carriage pulled up from the station, her large family descended upon them with an almost overwhelming enthusiasm. Thankfully, Alice was accustomed to the violent affection of her brothers, so their enthusiasm hardly surprised her.

Though Alicc had striven over the years to find within herself the true love for her siblings that would allow for no favoritism, Caleb was still the one she understood best. He was a sweet boy, who would be eleven this summer. As always, she was struck by his height as he dived into her and gave her a hug. He was never one to hold back his affection.

Behind him came Jack, who was a year younger than Caleb, and Rebecca, the baby of the family. Ned, now a reserved fifteen-year-old, greeted Alice without the enthusiasm of former years. However, his hazel eyes spoke of a gentle kindness that reminded Alice vaguely of Ivy. He was the only member of the family besides their father who didn't have Mother's blue gaze. Alice's eyes were black; however, no one had commented on this over the years due to their matching Papa's.

Rebecca was the last child to step back from Peter and greet Alice. Her darker curls stood out in stark contrast to her deep blue eyes. She would be a lovely woman one day, but now she was a precocious seven-year-old who gave Alice a fierce hug and tried to tell her everything that had happened—mostly mundane events but adorably exciting to Rebecca herself—in three rushed paragraphs, all while being talked over by her louder brothers.

After the children had given their excited welcomes, Alice's adoptive parents stepped forward. Alice still called them Mother and Papa, but her mind always supplied the unspoken truth. Her real mother was Nettie; her father, unimportant.

Yet to call Claire and Philip Knight "Mother" and "Papa" was as natural as breathing. Alice greeted them with a warm embrace and apologized for not coming sooner, for her delayed arrival, and for the brevity of her stay; she and Peter could only linger at Pearlbelle Park for a few short weeks before beginning the journey home to America.

With Mother's arm circled about her waist, Alice strolled through the mansion's marble pillars and into the foyer with its high ceiling and numerous Rubenesque cupid paintings. Behind her, she heard Peter conversing with her siblings. They all loved him with an affection that Alice herself sometimes failed to gain. Peter had a way with children.

Even as she answered her mother's questions about Ivy's well-being—for Mrs. Knight had spent several months with Ivy but had been forced to leave before Alice, due to her various responsibilities—Alice's mind turned to her conversation with Peter when they had left Keefmore.

She had always known that Peter would be an excellent father—beyond that: he longed to be a father. However, as the gift of living children had never been granted to them, she had long assumed it was simply not to be. Not unless some miracle happened, altering the course of their life.

They had been godmother and godfather to several children. She hoped they were a great blessing to those that they loved and cared for. However, that was not the same as having children of their own.

It would be wonderful to raise a child with Peter. But how could that ever happen? Adoption seemed such a foreign idea, and she was not at all familiar with the process, a fact that made her uneasy.

Mother continued speaking as they walked into the parlor. "I always knew Ivy would be an excellent mother."

"Yes," Alice replied. "She is doing well. Quite well. When we left her, she had settled into the role, and I couldn't be more impressed with her." For years, Alice had thought badly of her twin. She had not given Ivy the credit she so deeply deserved, for Ivy was a great woman. The more Alice came to know of the true Ivy, as an adult, the more she was impressed by her. Now she only hoped she could atone for years of slighting her sister. An apology didn't feel like enough, though it had been warmly accepted.

A small smile flickered over her lips as she considered the word "twin." After all, Ivy was not really her sibling, let alone her twin. Ivy belonged to Mr. and Mrs. Philip Knight; Alice was Nettie's. However, Alice had lived her life believing Ivy her sister, and now how could she think of her as anything else?

Yes, Ivy would always be her beloved "twin," and now Alice must consider Ivy to be her equal in everything. In some ways, her superior, for Ivy possessed great gentleness and love, and Alice hoped she could learn a fraction of such natural grace.

"And what of Jordy?" Mother asked. There was an air of hesitance in her voice. Jordy, upon first learning they were due to have children—though at the time they had assumed it was just *a child*, for who could know it was twins before the babies arrived—had been frightened. He had recovered well enough to comfort Ivy through the last few months of her pregnancy; however, it was clear to all that fatherhood had not been his first desire.

A fact for which Alice might never forgive him.

"I think he's adjusted well to being a father." Alice took a seat on one of the chairs near the window, and her mother joined her. "At least, all involved believe so."

"Good, good. That is all I have wanted to hear. I only pray that he will grow more and more toward the man that God has intended him to be. I believe that was the root of the issue." Her blue eyes were somewhat distant, and Alice supposed there must have been considerable worry on her mother's part. What woman wanted her eldest daughter's marriage to be in potential peril, when parenthood already brought so many new challenges to a relationship? "I pray for them every night."

"As do I." After all, sometimes all one could offer was prayer. For years, Alice had offered her prayers as a kind of barter system with the Lord; however, she had learned as time went on that thinking of prayer in such a way was ineffective and almost sacrilegious. As if she had anything to offer but her heart. Now she involved God in all her decisions and had found that when she listened, she often found a better answer.

"We'll be busy here." Mother glanced out the window at the rainy sky and sighed. "Uncle Charlie will be here, which I don't mind, and he's bringing Posy. Then the Montgomerys are coming for a time."

"Lorelei Hilton and her husband?" Alice asked. She didn't know them well, though Cassie had married the former Miss Hilton's brother.

"Yes, and Mrs. Montgomery's sister." Mother drummed her fingers absently on the windowsill. "Mrs. Montgomery is bringing her baby with her. Odd, to bring such a small child on a journey all the way from Dorset, but apparently she's her parents' pride and joy, and I like having a baby in the house again. We all miss that."

"Yes, well." Alice didn't comment on that. If she were to say, "Of course, Mother, I would give anything to bring a child into the house again, but we both know that lies beyond my power," there would be sympathy with an underlying awkwardness, and Alice couldn't bear that. She had learned long ago that hiding her pain was the safest option. But it could not be hidden forever; eventually, it must be shared with someone who might understand. "I should go see Nettie soon," Alice said absently.

"Why don't you go visit her before tea?" Mother suggested. "That is, if you have time. I'm not sure how rested you feel from the journey, but I'm sure that she would want to see you."

Alice nodded. "I shall do that."

Nettie was working in the kitchen when Alice arrived, but she dropped everything at the sight of her eldest daughter, as she always did. A half-finished meat pie was set aside—"I'm ahead of time anyway, and I'd rather visit with you"—and they settled at the kitchen table to talk of family and friends.

But Alice could not remain silent about her question for long, not with it pressing at the back of her mind—a question she would never discuss with Claire Knight. She loved Mother, yes, but this was something that was an "only Nettie" issue, as so many things had been over the years.

So, in a comfortable silence that rested between them, Alice spoke.

"What do you think of adoption?"

Nettie stilled and slowly raised her soft gray eyes to Alice's face. "Please tell me that's because you're considering it."

Alice pressed her lips together. "So ... you think it would be ...?"

"I think it would be very fulfilling for you, my dear Gracie, to consider allowing a child into your life that way, yes." Nettie leaned forward slightly, and Alice found she couldn't avoid her gaze. Which was an irritating trait Nettie and Peter shared—Alice could never really get away from either of them, even when she sometimes wanted to. "Now, I'm not saying it would be easy, but don't you think that, of all people, you would have the best insight into what a small child might face when living without their natural parents, under the care of another?"

Alice scoffed at this. "My situation wasn't anything like that."

"But you were adopted, weren't you? The former Miss Alice Knight." Nettie raised her eyebrows. "I know your mother would mention that adoption for non-practical reasons is, well, impractical. And you will hear people say things—terrible things—about how adoption is a perversion of the natural order."

Alice stiffened. "I would say that based on my experiences—"

Nettie shook her head. "I shouldn't have drawn that parallel. You're so literal. This would be such a different situation, Gracie. If you adopted, you would tell the child the truth—that though you may not share their blood, you will still love them deeply. I know you'd feel that way because that is how I have always felt. Why, even Ivy ... Or any one of Claire's children, really ... They are dear to me. You know this."

Alice nodded. "And I have been told, at least, that I am dear to Claire."

Nettie smiled. "You are at that."

So they sat still for a time, and Nettie let Alice think. What if Peter was right, and this was God's plan for them?

"I suppose then we only need to consult God's will," Alice murmured.

"Exactly." Nettie cocked her head. "So pray, my girl. Pray and let your heart be open. He'll tell you what you need to know."

"Of course." Alice drummed her fingers on the table and stared into her half-empty teacup. "But you know how bad I am at listening, and I admit my reluctance to adopt. But Peter ..."

"Peter wants this?" Nettie suggested.

"I can tell he wants it very much. He must have refrained from bringing it up sooner because he feared my reaction. We'd talked about it years ago."

"But never when either of you were ready."

"Yes."

"You have time. You'll have to go home and settle yourself."

"Right. There's no rush." Peter and Nettie had both said that, and yet Alice liked to have decisions made. Perhaps she could resolve in her heart to not make a decision until God allowed them to, regardless of how hard that would be, and Peter would hold her accountable to that. He was marvelous about slowing her down. She had once resented this gentle approach to life that felt so impractical, so purposeless—now she appreciated it.

She and Nettie talked on about this and that, until Nettie's children burst in from outside, and Alice realized with a start that she was late for tea.

The next day was frigid, as March in England could often be, especially given the overcast weather, but naturally, none of the children could be deterred from the outdoors. Caleb and Jack, Alice was told, had been begging for weeks to play with the kites they'd received for Christmas, and Peter was their "chump"—a colorful bit of vernacular Ned had picked up at school. Once Peter had summoned them all out onto the lawn, the eldest Knight boy had given up his veneer of adulthood and joined in on the fun.

The boys were a whirlwind of movement on the pristinely clipped grass, darting and shouting as they wrestled their kites into the brisk wind. Rebecca trailed behind them, her small figure determined but struggling to keep up, her own kite dragging in the grass.

Alice knew well what it took to keep up with boys while wearing layers of skirts and being watched by one's mother, but Rebecca was determined—and tougher than Caleb or Jack ever would be.

On the veranda, Alice stood beside her mother, her arms folded against the cold despite the layers of coat and muffler and gloves. Meanwhile, Peter stood laughing with the boys. His hand shielded his eyes—a reflexive gesture though there was no sun—as he tested the breeze before making a series of wild gesticulations.

"I don't know how they dragged him out of the library on a day like this," Alice murmured, half to herself. "It's like they give him another life."

Mother smiled faintly. "I imagine it's one of the many reasons the children adore him."

Alice didn't reply. She didn't know what to say. "I wish my husband had a child of his own, and it's killing me that I can't give him one," perhaps? Or should she answer, "Every time I see him with a child, I can imagine Daniel or Zebedee there with him, and I want to weep"? The more palatable response would be, "Yes, he's so good with children," but even that felt too intimate. Anyone who knew Alice knew how deeply the loss of her children had bereaved her. She did not even have the benefit of privacy in her grief. Everyone knew she had tried to take her own life mere months after Daniel was stillborn.

"Alice!"

Her eyes refocused, and she caught her husband's gaze.

"Come on and help!" he shouted even as he caught Rebecca by the shoulders and reached for the kite she had somehow tangled about her small person.

"It looks like rain!" Alice called. "And it's freezing out there!"

She could see Peter's grin in his posture, though the distance made it hard to catch his expression. "If we get a thunderstorm, I'll introduce the boys to a Philadelphian tradition started by Ben Franklin himself!"

Alice laughed despite herself. "You'd better leave my baby siblings out of any electrical experiments."

Mother glanced toward the horizon. "It does look like rain," she said. "I think I'll go inside before it starts. Join me."

"In a moment," Alice replied, glancing at Rebecca, who had, as Peter worked on the knots of her kite string, plopped down in the grass, pouting with the practiced air of a child who knew that if she only waited, she would be served.

Mother nodded and disappeared into the house, her skirts brushing softly against the smooth stone. Peter caught Alice's eye again, tilting his head toward Rebecca as if to say, "She needs you!"

There were plenty of ghosts at Pearlbelle Park. Alice could still hear her mother's voice in her mind, gently chastising her for not keeping her hands clean or her dress unwrinkled. But then Rebecca's forlorn expression broke through, and Alice took a deep breath. She stepped down from the veranda and crossed the lawn toward her.

"Rebecca," she called. "Get up. We're going to get that kite in the air and show those boys what a lady can do with the proper assistance."

The pout remained for a moment longer, but then, slowly, Rebecca stood. "Really? You'll help me?"

"Of course." Alice lightly touched Rebecca's shoulder, the best she could do in terms of affection unless it was first offered to her. "I bet we can get it higher than the boys ever dared to. Peter'll help us."

Peter handed her the kite string with a quiet smile, then, despite Alice's halfhearted protestations, stepped back to give them space.

Alice had forgotten how exhausting getting a kite up into the air could be. They ran and waited for the wind and ran some more. They tried once, twice—but the third time was the charm.

The kite dipped and tumbled before finally rising into the air. Rebecca squealed with delight, and Alice laughed, her cheeks flushed and her dark hair tugged loose by the wind. She stepped back, shouting instructions, and Rebecca took the spool and slowly let out the string as the kite soared into the gray sky, above the neatly pruned trees.

From the distance, the boys shouted and exclaimed in proper admiration; Rebecca shrieked and laughed in joy.

Peter watched, his hands in his pockets, a smile tugging at his lips. Alice seemed lighter now, unburdened, her usual composure replaced by a rare, unguarded delight. He glanced toward the house, half expecting Claire to appear at the window like a specter observing proceedings, but there was no sign of her.

When the rain began, Peter stepped closer, intending to take down the kite so Alice could run for the house, but she caught his eye and shook her head.

Leave it, she mouthed.

Peter was of the same mind, so he stood by and watched the sky for lightning—he really would make them all go in if there was even a hint of it.

By the time they finally decided to return inside, they were all drenched—especially Alice, somehow. Her hair dripped in tangled waves, her dress was grass-stained, and her cheeks glowed from the cold. He didn't like to see the natural flush of her cheeks turned fashionably white any more than he liked to see the circles under her eyes carefully concealed with powder. Someday, he'd convince her of that—of the value in reality, of the beauty in imperfection.

This was the Alice he loved most—perhaps even the one he'd first fallen in love with, the woman he'd glimpsed beneath the carefully constructed masks, the protective propriety, and the frustrated anger of a thwarted passion. He loved her fierceness, her loyalty, her competitiveness, and her love for those close to her. He even loved her stubbornness and independence, which almost always came from a desire to put things right, to fix the wrongs of this world, and to hold fast to those ideals she held dear.

All right, and sometimes she just wanted to be *right*, at all costs, but then it was all the more flattering when she listened to him, turned to him for advice or comfort, or thought of him first.

He caught her hand when they reached their bedroom and pulled her into his arms.

"Peter!" She pressed her hands to his chest and made a noticeably slight effort to push him away, though there was amusement in her voice. "I want to get out of these wet clothes and get warm again."

"What a coincidence—I can help with that."

She threw her head back and laughed. "Tea is at four," she reminded him, though it barely counted as a protest, especially with the way her hands had somehow moved inside his jacket.

He knew for a fact that the clock in the hall had chimed half past two as they passed it. Yes, four years ago, or even two years ago, he would have released her. He would have felt his affection a great burden, even when she had previously indicated otherwise. He would have politely withdrawn and bashfully apologized for daring to touch his own wife.

How beautiful it was to be free of that worry—to instead be granted kisses and caresses and whispered words of praise. There was surely no worse feeling than being shamed for desiring a lover's touch; there was surely no greater comfort than knowing, with beautiful, holy certainty, that he belonged to her—and she was irrevocably his.

Peter had learned he was better at showing Alice she was perfect in his eyes than he ever was at telling her.

Chapter Three

April 25th, 1886
Philadelphia, Pennsylvania

"What do you think? Too much?" Lilli adjusted her necklace. "This was my mother's, and I forgot I owned it until I was going through the attic at Clairdelune this Christmas. Georgiana gave me a box of my parents' things—at last."

"I don't think it's too much." Standing in the doorway of her mother-in-law's bedroom, Alice gave Lilli a cursory glance. The pearls matched well with Lilli's light-blue dress. "Actually, I have a pair of pearl earrings that would match perfectly. Let me lend them to you."

"Oh, thank you, darling."

They left Lilli's bedroom behind and went to the guest room Peter and Alice were staying in. As they walked down the hall, Alice's father-in-law shouted up the stairs that they were running late. They picked up their pace, and Alice quickly rescued her pearl earrings from her jewelry box, handed them to Lilli, and grabbed her shawl from where she had draped it over the end of the bed.

Lilli clipped one of the earrings on and turned her head this way and that, admiring it. "We'd better run. Relying on Dahlia to drive us means we submit to her timeline."

"Is Elias—?"

"Impatient? How could our dear Mr. Thorpe be, when married to our Dilly-Dally?" Lilli laughed. "You know, they're well-matched—we have been so pleased with them."

"It will always be surreal for me that Dahlia is married. I may never adjust." Peter's baby sister would forever be sixteen to Alice.

"Oh, I know." Lilli smiled, though her mouth wavered a bit. She'd sobbed her way through the wedding, and even Alice had had a few tears in her eyes when Dahlia said her vows. Peter certainly hadn't been dry-eyed.

They hurried down the stairs and soon Chris and Lilli were headed away toward the church in Elias and Dahlia's carriage, while Alice and Peter walked the few blocks hand in hand.

The Easter service at Peter's childhood church was always joyful, and today was no exception. Alice and Peter were eagerly greeted by the congregants, including Peter's other sister, Caroline, and her family. Alice took Maud-Alice—called Maudie—in her lap, though at nearly three, the little girl was no longer interested in being held with the same placid contentment Alice remembered.

"She's missed her Auntie Alice," Caroline murmured as she slid into the pew next to Alice, her flailing youngest—one-year-old Howard Andrew Webster—clutched in her arms. "And a good thing, too! These three have been utterly exhausting this week. You and Dahlia—and Mama—are the reason I'm surviving these days."

Alice briefly took Caroline's hand and squeezed it. She noticed Chris had taken charge of his eldest grandchild, Barnie, leaving Caroline and her husband to manage only Howie. However, if previous patterns were any indication, it wouldn't be long before Caroline and Barnaby added another child to their growing brood.

Alice had perfected the art of guessing when a pregnancy announcement was imminent. It was almost uncanny how quickly she recognized the signs these days.

After the service concluded, Alice and Peter greeted other members of the church. As they were speaking with the pastor, one of the members approached them with his hand extended to Peter.

"Mr. Strauss, a pleasure to see you back with us," the rotund man said in a rumbling voice. "My wife and I were just discussing *Matins* the other evening. A truly thoughtful examination of a clergyman's faith. You gave us a great deal to ponder."

"You're too kind, Mr. Baldwin," Peter said, shaking his hand. "It was a difficult subject to explore—my wife is to be thanked for letting me talk it all through with her. I trust you found the ending hopeful?"

Mr. Baldwin's smile broadened, if that was even possible. "Yes, very much so. A testament to God's grace."

Alice watched the exchange, a scene she had witnessed countless times all over England and America. It was always a little odd to hear strangers speak so intimately of the stories that she'd first been introduced to as barely developed concepts—whose words she herself had carefully edited until they were clear and smooth and without error.

In time, they slipped off, with promises to linger longer the following week. Lilli had planned a family dinner, and with the exception of Peter's younger brother, Andrew, and his bride, who had moved to Boston shortly after their wedding, all the Strauss siblings and their families would be present.

Back at the house in Mt. Airy, Dahlia immediately called Alice to her side, and they talked about Alice's trip, what Scotland was like, and how dear Ivy's babies were.

Dahlia was glowing. It was clear the first year and a half of her marriage had been a happy one—clearer still that young Elias Thorpe delighted in his bride, and Dahlia adored her husband.

Their relationship had been slow but seemed rushed to her overprotective family. There was still a general consensus that Elias and Dahlia were "fools in love" and the scales were sure to fall from their eyes sooner or later. But Alice knew too much of God's strength to truly believe that. Trials might come—they would come—but Dahlia and Elias had as much chance of facing them with courage as any other couple.

Perhaps they stood a better chance than most; Alice had counseled

Dahlia via letter through those early days and knew that beneath a light-hearted veneer, her sister-in-law had a good head on her shoulders.

"Alice, Dally, I need you both," Lilli called from the kitchen, and they went to help, leaving Caroline, her children, and the men alone in the parlor.

"Peter, can I speak with you?" Caroline's tone made it less a question than a command. After relinquishing Howie to his father, Peter followed her from the parlor into the dining room.

The table was set, but the clattering and conversation in the kitchen indicated that there were still a few more minutes until the meal would be ready. He heard Alice and Dahlia both laugh—Dahlia adding "Mama!" and a string of scolding words—and he had to smile. He could almost picture Alice's expression: amused by Dahlia's annoyance with Mama, yet still deeply affectionate toward her mother-in-law. She always was.

"Peter, I want to tell you something, and I promise it's well-meaning. All right?"

He smirked at Caroline's intensity. She was always so serious about everything, a side effect of having two older brothers she felt needed her loving but firm wrangling from time to time. "'Speak the speech, I pray you, as I pronounced it to you, trippingly on the tongue.'"

She held up one finger, a firm expression on her face. "No Shakespeare. This is serious."

His smile faded. He placed a hand on her arm, his frown deepening. "Are you all right? Did something happen?"

"I'm fine, but that's ... Peter, we're going to have another baby. There. I've said it. And we want to announce it tonight, but Alice ..." She paused and pressed her lips together. "Well, Alice."

Peter stilled for a moment then laughed. "That's wonderful! When—?"

"Shh." She grabbed his arm and gave it a slight pinch. "It is wonderful, but Peter, if you aren't quiet about it—"

"I'm so happy for you. Tell me when or I'll be louder still, and you won't be able to tell anyone except me on your own timeline." He didn't laugh again, though, despite his overwhelming desire to do so. This type of news ought to be celebrated.

She frowned. "October, I think. But Peter, you must understand that I have only told you because of Alice."

"Oh. Well, that's kind." Unnecessary, but kind. There had been a lot of babies lately, and most mothers had not had Caroline's foresight. "I suppose you haven't told her in person before. Not with Maudie or with Howie, given how often we've been away."

"Exactly." Caroline closed her eyes for a brief moment. "I wouldn't ever want to hurt her, Peter. You know that. I'm happy for myself, but I hate to think my joy ..."

"It's not. It's fine. I can tell her ahead of time, but I think she'll be all right."

Carolinc sighed. "I imagine she will be, but at the same time ... I would not be. And I would wish that type of courtesy to be extended to me."

"I'll tell her." He pulled Caroline into a quick hug. "But I'm very happy for you, and I know Alice will feel the same." He held her by the shoulders and met her eyes. "I don't want you to curb your joy on our behalf."

"I know that, but ... Oh well." She dashed a hand over her eyes, before Peter had a chance to see if they were even damp. "We want to tell everyone while we eat. If you could—"

"I will. Go back to the parlor."

"Thank you," she whispered, and gave his hand a quick squeeze before slipping out.

After Caroline slipped out, Peter opened the kitchen door and stepped in. Alice was washing a large pot while Dahlia and Mama prepared the serving dishes.

"Alice, can you leave that for a moment? I want to talk to you."

She glanced up, swiping an escaped lock of dark hair from her forehead with the back of her wrist. "Can it wait?"

"I'd rather talk now."

She nodded and picked up a towel to dry her hands, then followed him into the garden. He took her hand and led her to the oak tree that grew near the tall wooden fence. It was as close to a private spot as could be found, with the exception of the bedrooms. But he had always found the outdoors was the best place for delivering news. At least, he preferred it that way—under an open sky, with a soft breeze from the west.

He glanced over his shoulder and put a hand on her arm. "Caroline wanted me to tell you she's with child, and they'll be announcing it at lunch today."

"Oh!" Alice smiled, and he almost melted with relief. He had been right; the wound was not so raw as it once was. "I'd wondered. Honestly, I had a feeling about it at church, but I didn't say because I could've been wrong. Plus she seemed so tired—more so than usual, I mean. It must be so hard to have the first three constantly needing her attention while another little one is on the way." She paused then, and that was the moment her face darkened. "She felt I would not be happy?"

"Not ... well, perhaps. It wasn't so much, I think, that she thought you would not be happy as that she thought you might be ... disappointed. *Reminded*, perhaps, is a better word. Yet we've talked about that, haven't we?"

"Yes, we have. I wonder if I've ever seemed to her ..." She paused and raised her eyes to his face. "I'd hate to think that I've made Caroline feel as if she can't share that kind of news with me. Granted, in the first few years, I might not have been able to hear it without some sort of reaction—and even now I'm never sure of myself. Yet I don't want her to feel I'm so sensitive that ..." She frowned. "Obviously she didn't feel she couldn't tell you."

"In her defense, that's a bit different. She grew up with me—and though she loves you, I think she knew more readily what my reaction would be, regardless of what I felt."

Alice nodded, but the troubled expression on her face didn't ease.

In truth, there had been a moment when Peter's heart protested his own reaction, but he didn't tell that to Alice. He would, later, when they were not due inside to see his family in mere moments. He pressed his lips to her forehead. "We'd better go, but we should talk about it tonight."

As he turned away, Alice caught his arm and stopped him, pulling him back behind the tree. "Do we need to?"

"*I* need to."

"All right." Her eyes were dark with concern, but she said nothing, simply met his eyes for a long moment. She tugged him toward her, fingers threading through his hair. "Kiss me, will you?"

He cupped her face with his free hand and pressed his lips to hers for a long moment before withdrawing and resting his forehead against hers. "Thank you. I needed that."

She laughed softly, the sound soothing him in a way little else could. "A dose of courage, is it? I love you."

"I love you, too. More and more all the time."

"Good." She patted his arm and released him. "Come on. If we stay out much longer, we'll have to endure Lilli's embarrassing comments. She always knows just what not to say and says it anyway."

Alice wasn't wrong, but Peter would rather have a thousand awkward conversations with his mother than miss a single stolen moment with his wife.

Lunch progressed as normal. Peter anticipated the moment when Barnaby glanced at Caroline, she nodded, and Barnaby announced that they were expecting another member of their family in October. Everyone was deeply congratulatory, but Dahlia, being Dahlia, rarely meaning to be thoughtless but never considering the impact of her words, chose that moment to exclaim, "What! You, too?" and even Peter winced.

And then the attention reeled from Caroline to Dahlia, and a confession was pulled from her. Dahlia and Elias' first child was due to arrive in November. They hadn't intended to share the news for weeks, not until things were more certain, but the words were out, and there was no taking them back.

And Peter sat in silence while congratulations were issued, even from Alice, and wondered why he felt so hollow inside. He thought he was past this, yet the thought struck him with unwelcome clarity: he was now the only one of his siblings without a living child. He felt the gentle pressure of Alice's hand on his thigh and reached to take that hand, pressing her fingers in his.

It was perfectly all right. His life was different from his siblings'. God controlled every event, and this was the best path—for if it were not, it would not be happening.

Yet he wanted to be anywhere else in this moment than at that table hearing such news from his baby sister.

Lord, help me. Help us. I need You more than ever.

Peter went on a walk that evening after dinner. Everyone had stayed much longer than intended, lingering over his sisters' news, and Alice understood his need for space. She knew he would come back to her and talk when he was ready, so she didn't begrudge him some time to himself.

She was shaken, too, but in a different way. In an exhausted way. It had been a long day of nothing but baby talk, and she didn't mind—she enjoyed it, even if it meant the selflessness of listening to something that had nothing whatsoever to do with her—but it was tiring.

So now Alice sat on the porch swing at the back of the Strausses' home, the cool spring air raising gooseflesh on her arms. The rhythmic creak of the chains was a lonely sound in the evening quiet, broken only by the distant clatter of a streetcar. She rocked herself—and prayed.

"I wasn't going to say anything, you know. It just happened."

Alice turned and met Dahlia's brown eyes across the back of the porch swing. "It is early."

"Well." She flushed; Dahlia never flushed. "That, and I had wanted to ... Oh, Alice, I don't have words! You know I don't. And I am such a bumbling thing—both to make the announcement and now. You mean so much to me, and I would have warned you, had I just—"

Alice held up her hands. "I don't want to hear a single protest from my dearest sister. Dahlia, I love you so much more than any awkwardness ... which is all on your part, you know. Not mine."

Dahlia dashed around the swing and tossed her arms around Alice. "Oh, I knew you would understand. You always do. Goodness, though, I made Caro cry. Do you think she was angry at me—or just happy? I have never made her cry before, and I have been so awful to her. Practically heathen. Will you come be with me in November?"

"We shall have to see. But I would love to."

Dahlia nodded and leaned back on the seat, keeping one arm looped about Alice. "That's the first time Caro has surprised me since ... oh, since she was a newlywed."

"Oh?" Alice reached up to smooth her sister-in-law's hair. "What did she say? Nothing too shocking for your girlhood sensibilities?"

"I was shocked, but not in a way I oughtn't to be." Dahlia grinned. "We were quarreling, as we always do; and I told her I'd tell Mama how much Caro and Barney had been kissing, and perhaps a little more, before the wedding—I'd seen enough, I thought, to give an accurate account. But she just stared at me for a moment and then said, 'Go ahead.' And I suddenly realized she was an adult, and it didn't matter what I told Mama, and I almost cried. I did, later that night, lying alone in our old bedroom. Seems silly now."

Alice smiled, but the story struck a mournful chord within her. "Now I could say just about the same to you, couldn't I?" She'd heard a lot more about Dahlia's relationship with Elias in those early courting days than Lilli or Caroline had. "What would you say?"

"Oh, I wouldn't want you to tell her. I have a healthy fear of the consequences." Dahlia rolled her eyes toward the ceiling. "Forgive me, but does it matter now?"

"Hmm. That's between you and God."

Another moment of silence, then Dahlia cleared her throat. "I was going to ask ... I can't see my way to asking Mama or Caro or even the doctor ... And Alice, I know you don't like answering those sorts of questions, but ..."

"Go on, Dally."

Dahlia glanced over her shoulder. "Now, with the baby ... Can we ...?" Again, she trailed off into a blushing silence.

"Oh. I believe the generally accepted knowledge is no, but I've heard people say otherwise. My sister, actually, had a midwife say it was a myth—especially if you happen to be in love. Just be cautious. All right?"

Still red in the face, Dahlia nodded. "We're still ... *new*. To this. To everything. You know? And it just doesn't seem fair."

Alice just smiled and avoided eye contact to save Dahlia further embarrassment.

"You'll have to tell Caro I don't need to be told what to do about anything, Alice. You can make her listen." Dahlia shifted and dropped her head on Alice's shoulder. "I know I can trust you."

"I told you, I'm not going to mediate anymore." Alice laughed. "It is time to be a woman grown, as you have so often claimed to be."

Dahlia simply rolled her eyes, but she didn't protest further. The thing was, unlike the other members of the family, Alice did see maturity in Dahlia. Oh, it was hidden under layers and layers of exuberance, difficulty holding her tongue, and petty quarreling with her siblings, but Dahlia was starting to grow beyond those. The process was simply a slow one.

The child would grow her up, doubtless. Alice knew motherhood could mature a woman quicker than anything else. Then again, she thought, maturity could be forged in many different fires.

If Alice had any maturity, it had come from grief, after all.

Chapter Four

Aidan Hilton was nearly two years old, and possessed the rosiest cheeks and biggest grin in Philadelphia. Dressed in a crisp, navy-blue sailor suit with a starched white collar, he sat on his mother's plush wool parlor carpet of rich red and brown tones, blocks scattered about him.

Sipping her tea from the delicate, translucent porcelain cup, Alice regarded her godson with affection as he stacked one block on top of another until the precarious tower tumbled to the ground.

"He's gotten so big." Alice set her teacup and saucer down on the small, beautifully made side table. "He looks like a little boy instead of a baby all of a sudden."

Alice's dearest friend smiled and nodded, adjusting a pillow behind her back, the only concession Cassie made to her rounded figure. Aidan's little sibling would be arriving this July, if he was as prompt as his older brother. "That's what you get for abandoning me in England and running up to Scotland for years. But never mind that. Aidan looks more like his father every day, don't you think?" As always, the slightest hint of an Irish brogue colored her tone under layers of English politeness and Philadelphian practicality, a mix of where she'd been and what she was.

Aidan had gray eyes; auburn—nearly brown—curls; ears that stuck out far too much; and a wide, happy face which was charming but not what one would call handsome. Yes, he was the mirror image of Patrick.

"That was never in doubt," Alice retorted. "He looked like his father when he was two hours old, and that's not changed."

"Patrick says Aidan looks like me." Cassie seemed to bite back a grin as she smoothed her skirts down. Alice felt positively out of style compared to the way her friend dressed now, even with the baby coming. "He's insane."

Alice laughed. "He's at least bewildered, like most men in love. Where is our deluded businessman, by the way?"

Patrick Hilton traveled a lot for his job, and though Cassie went with him when she could, packing up a two-year-old was no easy affair, especially while six months pregnant. With her husband frequently gone, she spent most of her time with Alice's in-laws or Patrick's business partners. Far better than being alone, though at least she was certainly anything but poorly provided for. Their new townhouse, with its tall, sunlit windows and the quiet sounds of a maid working in another room, was a world away from the tiny, drafty flat they'd started in. For all his faults, Patrick Hilton was no slacker, and he had worked hard to give Cassie the life Alice believed her friend deserved.

Cassie waved her hand in dismissal. "Boston. He left early Monday morning. He's navigating a new deal with a railroad company, I believe—I suppose you wouldn't know the Jacksons, and it's rather a long story, but Patrick had some connections. John Jr. is with him, so I've been with Henrietta every morning except today. She's with child again."

"Oh?" Alice stilled, for Cassie had relayed the story—another sad tale of loss and longing for a child, with no known explanation for *why* Henrietta Baldwin always miscarried after a few months. It was heartbreaking. "Do you know how far along she is?"

"Nearly four months, so there's hope." Cassie sighed. "But last year, as you know, she couldn't ..." Cassie made a helpless gesture, as if the full phrase were too dirty to say—and perhaps saying Henrietta *couldn't* carry to term was unfair. She hadn't *yet*. "It was a little girl; they named her after Mrs. Baldwin. I don't know if I ever told you. It doesn't help that John Jr. isn't home right now, but he'll be back soon. This is their fifth pregnancy, Alice. It's killing her." Cassie's face was dark with concern. "I just wish there was something—anything—I could do."

"Right. I understand." Alice sighed. There just never was a thing to do except offer any aid and comfort one could, but sometimes all there was left was to pray ... and to hope. "I wonder if she ever thinks of ..." But she stopped herself, for that was her problem—not Henrietta Baldwin's. "Never mind."

"What?" Cassie's blue eyes softened. "Not trying? Is that what *you* decided?"

"N-no." The stutter was stupid, a symptom of days when this was a painful subject—but Alice was past that. At least with someone as close to her as Cassie. "Actually, Peter thinks ..." She lowered her voice, as if somehow this topic would scream its way past the privacy of the parlor walls into the streets, labeling her at once as a woman who couldn't have her own child. She carefully set *that* thought aside to tear apart later, when her husband could bolster her courage and her God could set her straight. Instead, she focused on what she really wanted to talk about. "Peter thinks we should adopt."

"Oh." Cassie cocked her head. "I suppose I should have thought of that. It makes sense. Have you visited an orphanage or ...? I suppose you'll want to wait until you get home to Cincinnati."

"I'm not sure we will." Alice disguised her frown with a nibble of the raspberry scone from the tiered silver tray that, alongside small crystal dishes of clotted cream and jam, had appeared in the magical manner in which things always had appeared in Alice's youth. "I feel so much fear about it—and a sort of resentment, I think, which makes me feel even worse. I hate that I feel this way. I know Peter desperately wants to have a child. It doesn't matter to him where he or she comes from."

Cassie's lips were pressed in a thin line. "But it matters to you."

"In a way, it does. Or maybe it's only that I must give up the dream I've been cherishing." Alice shook her head. "The truth is, it sometimes feels like not much in this world is a part of me. It's stupid, but finding out that ... that my parents ..." She stopped herself. "You know it all, Cass. I just want something, *someone* ..."

"You want your child to be yours in blood," Cassie said with an understanding nod. "I know. I'm not sure what I would do myself, in your shoes. I love my son, yes, and a part of that is that he's mine and Patrick's. Heavens, he is absolutely Patrick's!" She gestured to Aidan, with his towering blocks and his auburn locks. "Yet I can't help but think I would love him even if he were not, because regardless of where his features come from, he is ours."

That sounded good—in theory. Alice hated working off theories. "Yes. I hope I would love our baby, regardless of how we came by him or her, but that doesn't stop me wishing it would happen the way *I* want it to. Now does that make me a little person? I feel as if it would be so noble of me to accept that we could give a needy child a home." Her eyes fluttered closed as she took a deep breath. "Otherwise, what are we doing of value in this world?"

"So many things." Alice heard rather than saw Cassie shift in her seat, followed by her hand being placed on Alice's arm. "Don't you ever say to me that you don't have value, Alice Strauss. You do so much for me—and for others."

Alice opened her eyes and stared down at Aidan, still content with his blocks. "Perhaps, yet I can't help but feel that all we're doing is ... is having fun. We enjoy being alone together. I like to travel with Peter, to spend time with our families—and then to go home alone. Much as I want a child, I can never quite admit to myself, let alone to him, that I'm growing content—and while I would do anything for a child of my own, I'm not sure adoption would fill that place."

Cassie hummed softly to herself. "Perhaps you're right. After all, it would be better to remain childless than to adopt a child whom you wouldn't love completely."

Alice bit her lip. "I'd like to hope—"

"I know, I know. You hope you'd love any child given into your care, and I believe you would, but your hesitancy could indicate that it's not God's will for you—at least right now. I know this is a terrible thing to hear, but it's nonetheless true: you have time. Don't be afraid of waiting—of listening to God before acting. Does Peter … Is he pushing you to …?"

"No." Alice shook her head. "No, he will wait until I'm sure."

"That's good." Cassie smiled. "But even if you make the decision not to adopt, your life is impactful. Think of how you have blessed me, and Ivy, and so many others. Besides, if you and Peter are just 'having fun,' as you put it, I'd like to point out that you're simply enjoying the biblical command and strengthening your relationship. That's not a bad thing."

Alice rolled her eyes. "That's not what I meant."

"Oh, sure." Cassie's eyes fluttered down to Aidan. "I know you won't be here when my little one arrives, but should I keep updating you as I have been? I can say less if it's painful. I don't talk about the baby with Henrietta—mine or hers. It makes our interactions easier."

"Oh, don't worry about that." Alice leaned back in her seat and drummed her fingers along the embroidered armrest. "I'm quite accustomed to it by now."

Cassie nodded. "Caroline …?"

Alice's fingers formed a fist before she forced her hands to relax. "And Dahlia, but don't tell I said that. I'm sure she wants to announce it to you on her own time—she let it slip over dinner last night."

"How exciting. I know she was hoping it would be soon. But that can't have been easy."

Alice reached up to massage her temples, the beginnings of the headache she'd developed during last night's conversation with Peter returning full force. "I'm fine. Peter's the one who's struggling with it. He was … emotional about it last night. Said some things he hadn't in years." Or ever, for that matter. "I realize how much adoption would mean for him—how it might help soothe the wound. It's different for him than for me—he's now the last one of his siblings to be childless."

"Oh, that makes sense." Cassie frowned and was silent for a moment. "I know it must be hard to have the man who is such a rock in your life break down."

Alice glanced down at Aidan, who had moved on to stacking blocks on top of the incredibly patient dog. "I want Peter to feel it's safe to tell me anything."

"Oh, I'm sure he does. I only mean ... Never mind. It doesn't matter. I'll pray for him, too. I'm sure that God has it all under control. Whatever He does next in your life will be perfect, whether that is opening your heart to adoption or giving you the child you and Peter both want. Because that is what's at the root of it, right? In your own ways, you both want to be parents. God knows about that pain, and He's not going to let you sit there, whether it means you do have a child or you learn to have a life that doesn't include parenthood."

Alice sighed. "I know that. We both do. It's the trusting that's hard. It's strange; I find myself 'learning' the same things again and again. Do other people find this easier?"

"No. I think there are many who handle it a lot worse than you—and some who handle it better. But God knows your heart, Alice—it's His, after all."

"Right. There's another prayer to add to the growing list—my faithfulness, my trust. I'm trying—we're both trying—but there are times when it's harder." Alice rose. "Come. Let's not worry about this more today. Aidan, can I help you?"

Aidan eagerly assented, and Alice settled in to play with the toddler, who soon found himself in stitches over Alice's feigned offense every time he knocked over her tower of blocks.

While Alice was at her friend Cassie's home, Peter spent the morning with his parents—who, as far as he could tell, were just delighted to have people in their home now that all their children were grown.

The Strauss home had never been empty before—but he was happy to hear his mother talk excitedly about all the things she could do with his father "now that they had the time." Granted, Papa pretended to be utterly tortured by these activities—and even Peter couldn't imagine his father "helping with the garden." He could see his parents reading together, though, and that thought made him smile.

"You two will be fine alone if I run for a few things, won't you?" Mama asked after breakfast was cleared and they'd lingered over too many cups of coffee. She rose and set her mug in the sink. "You won't sit in silence or wander off in opposite directions?" When neither of them replied, she said, "Chris?"

Papa very deliberately picked up a spoon and stirred his coffee, which certainly did not need stirring, given that he took it black. "Are we not owed a little peace and quiet?"

"Talk to your son." Mama stepped forward and kissed Papa. "We don't know when we'll see him and Alice again."

Papa made grumbling sounds, but after Mama left, he rose, slowly, and caught up his cane with his remaining hand. The other had been lost in the War Between the States. Papa didn't like to talk about it.

"I feel I must stretch my leg. Let's go on a walk," he said.

Peter would have protested, knowing his father sometimes pushed himself too hard for the leg that had been mangled enough to remain permanently stiff; but he knew his father was far too stubborn to heed his advice.

Minutes later, he found himself rambling down the Germantown street with Papa. The brisk spring air nipped at Peter's cheeks, and the rhythmic sound of their shoes against the cobblestones was almost comforting, though it did little to quiet the thoughts swirling in his mind. Philadelphia had always been home—but it wasn't anymore.

Peter glanced at Papa, who seemed lost in his own thoughts. The loose sleeve of Papa's overcoat was pinned neatly up, as Mama had carefully and inconspicuously done with all of his shirts and coats. Peter noticed today, for the first time, that his father's hair had gone almost entirely gray, but he was still getting around all right, leaning on his cane and swinging his injured leg along at a decent gait.

Still, it was strange to think that his parents were getting older. They had been so young when Peter was born—they almost felt more like his peers than his elders.

But then, Peter wasn't exactly a young man anymore. Unlike his parents, he hadn't gotten an early start on marriage and fatherhood—when he married Alice, he'd been twenty-seven, which was eleven years *older* than his father had been when Peter was born.

His parents' marriage had taken place between six and seven months *before* that date. They didn't talk about that much—the story had become more of a warning his father had impressed upon him from childhood: do things God's way, not your own, and you will never regret it. So no, his parents hadn't had an ideal start, but they had had an *early* start. When Papa had been Peter's age, three of his children had been born.

And now every single one of Peter's siblings would have a child before he did. If he ever did at all.

Peter was *not* bitter. He wasn't. He'd never been bitter a day in his life.

"I'm sorry you and Alice don't have a child."

Papa's gruff voice breaking the silence that had settled between them was the last thing Peter had expected.

It took him a moment to blink through his surprise and also reassure himself that his father couldn't read his thoughts. At last, he managed, "Thank you."

"I know it was hard on you for Caro and Dally to announce they're expecting the same night—unintentional though Dally's announcement was—and then I know you had to pretend to be happy for them." Papa shrugged. "It's bittersweet—and sometimes the bitter outweighs the sweet. It's not right to think God doesn't understand that, that He doesn't give you grace for those wholly human emotions."

"I know." Peter smiled, but he looked away from his father—he felt it wasn't a true smile, and he didn't feel like sharing it. "I'm happy for them. Dally deserves to be a mother—and we know Caroline and Barnaby want a big family. Mama has always talked about having a house full of grandchildren, so they might as well. It's not anyone's fault that Alice and

I can't be a part of that." *Oh. I do sound bitter.*

"But it still hurts that those grandchildren aren't your children. I understand that, son. You know I do. Now, we didn't have to wait for you—perhaps we should have, but God worked miracles through our sin. We hardly knew what to do with you, but we knew we wanted more children—so when twice we had hoped and then lost a child as you did, so early on and so needlessly ... I won't compare it to your pain—but I do understand a little." Papa exhaled, as if exhausted from all that talking. Which, with as little as he generally said, was probably true. "Your mother was devastated. I didn't know what to say or do to comfort her. I didn't even know where our next meal was coming from. The midwife said your mother couldn't bear the strain of a pregnancy—that she might have lost her ability to carry a child to term, because she was so young the first time. We were told it would be best not to risk another baby—ever—and that if I ... The details don't matter. Suffice to say, I was angry and guilty, yet I was terrified of revealing how much the loss hurt. Your mother was suffering—and you know how much she expresses every emotion. I was overwhelmed. So I do understand the depth of grief for a child one never gets to meet."

Peter fought to straighten his shoulders—they kept hunching, as if trying to protect him from the feelings that continually rose to the surface—and nodded. "I think of them, you know. My siblings who I never got to meet."

"Yes. They are safe in God's arms. Your mother and I now have the benefit of knowing that God did let us have your siblings, too. We can look back so easily and think, 'yes, but only a few years later, we had Andrew, then Caro, then Dally.' At the time, it felt like an eternity. I remember going to see my family and watching your mother yearn for another baby. You've seen how prolific your aunts, uncles, and cousins are. Then there were the questions and comments. 'When will you give Peter a brother?' and 'you know you will spoil him if you don't have another' and 'you should have another child before he's too old to play with him.'" Papa scowled. "I hate to think what your mother endured."

"And what you endured," Peter said. His father often needed prodding to remember that he, too, had a heart that could be broken.

"Yes. Yes, what we both endured. I wish I could tell you I have now learned to find joy in all things, but we are given a time to mourn as well as a time to rejoice. We do not always have to 'move on' as quickly as possible. We can let God comfort us as we confront grief in our own time."

Peter nodded. "Alice and I have been talking about what comes next. If we can't have children of our own."

"What did you decide?"

Peter hesitated. "There are so many children out there who need homes. It seems like the right thing to do—even the Christian thing. We have the space, and we could afford to support a child. But Alice ..."

Papa filled the silence Peter left. "That's not what Alice wants."

"No. It's not. At least, not yet."

Papa was quiet for a moment, the only sound between them the shuffling of his feet along the road. Finally, he sighed. "She's borne a lot, son. More than she should have had to, in a perfect world. But it isn't a perfect world, and she's suffered much from it."

"I know."

"As have you."

"I know. But I know how I feel about it." Peter just didn't understand why Alice couldn't feel the same. "There's an emptiness in our life. I know she feels it, too."

"You won't fill that emptiness with a child, Peter. We love our children's souls. You can't replace a soul."

Peter's chest tightened in frustration. He knew that. "But you can give that love to someone else."

Papa was quiet again for a few steps. "This pain is a part of you," he said at last. "You can heal, but you can't stop loving the children you lost. You can't. Grief is love we can't express, but we can't truly give that love to someone else. We don't have a limited amount of love, which is good in so many ways. Any way you become a father, you'll love your son or daughter deeply—but not as a replacement. The child wouldn't fill the hole in your heart, for he or she cannot. You know the only healing you'll find for that is in Christ. Don't let yourself seek it elsewhere."

And then Peter wondered if he was more bitter than he thought. There was an anger in him, he knew—a frustrated, horrible feeling that seemed to get worse the more he ignored it.

He was supposed to be a father. He was supposed to have two healthy sons running around, exhausting him and Alice. He was supposed to *love* those boys—to pour his heart into them—to raise them carefully and thoughtfully.

He had been so ready to be a father—had anticipated it for so long, had so carefully planned it. Now, it seemed impossible.

"I feel helpless." He shoved his hands deep in his pockets. "I feel so helpless to do anything for her. For us."

"I know you do. I wish I knew the secret to finding peace in our helplessness, but the only answer I know is to give that helplessness to God. I pray for you—your mother and I do constantly. We pray that you will have a child of your own—and now we can pray for clarity on your next step—but mostly, we pray that you can both trust that God's ways are best—are higher than what we can ever know. He knows your heart, and He sees your pain. Don't give up on Him."

Peter didn't know what to say, so he didn't say anything. He just nodded and kept walking.

They walked on in silence for a few more minutes, then Papa mumbled, "I wish you lived closer."

"Hmm?"

Usually, Papa didn't express many wishes that couldn't be fulfilled. It wasn't his way. He was fundamentally a practical man, and he held his adult children loosely as a result.

"I wish you lived closer so we might have these talks more often."

This time, a genuine smile found its way to Peter's face. "I wish so, too."

CHAPTER FIVE

May 1886
Cincinnati, Ohio

THE HOUSE WAS JUST as they had left it, only quieter and filled with the scent of dust and stale air. Their train had come in late at night; Alice had dozed as Riley's carriage bore them home, hardly hearing Peter's quiet conversation with his cousin about the final property tax payment Riley had made on his behalf, and the confirmation that the last—apparently substantial—royalty check from his publisher had been safely deposited in the bank.

This morning, not long after breakfast, Peter tucked himself inside his office with yet another pressing deadline. A formidable mountain of mail awaited him—months of royalty statements, business letters from his publisher, and invitations he would never accept, all of which Riley had stacked in disorganized piles that covered every surface.

Alice offered to help, but Peter waved her off for once, so she tied her hair back, put on one of her older dresses, tied an apron over it, and slipped out the back door into her small garden.

Honestly, they should have been home far earlier in the spring if Alice wanted to maintain her garden in any sort of order. As it was, the area had become overrun by weeds and in need of much help in general. Thankfully,

Alice was at her leisure to attack said weeds.

Behind her trailed, as always, her faithful black dog. The cats were in Peter's study—Ophelia and Cassius liked to watch him write, which was fair, as sometimes Alice enjoyed the same.

However, today she had work to do.

Juno sat beside her, brown eyes keenly fixed on Alice's face. She'd been left alone far too long, poor thing; and though she seemed to enjoy the company of Quip, Riley's dog, Juno was much too faithful to tolerate long stints away from Alice.

It was gratifying, in a way, to have a dog so wildly obsessed with her. If Alice were honest, she would admit it to be rather exhausting, too, but she could bear being loved to the point of exhaustion. The intensity of it matched her own love—at least, once she allowed herself to feel it as intensely as she wished to.

"Auntie Alice!" On the heels of the cry, a small body fell onto Alice's back.

Laughing, she set down the trowel and turned to pull the giggling Polly Farjon into her lap, pressing kisses to the six-year-old's rosy cheeks. "There's my Dolly Girl!"

Polly wiggled to an upright position and placed her hands on Alice's shoulders. "You've been gone for *forever*!" she said. "Will you stay home now?"

"At least for a long while. Did you go see Uncle Penn?"

"Can I?" Polly's blue eyes were full of delight at the thought. "Mama says he might be busy all morning—he's writing a book, you know."

"I know, but he'd want to see you, darling. Go on in."

Polly giggled, dashing off, and Alice rose and dusted her hands on her apron. Weeds could wait—children were far more precious.

She walked toward the door, already hearing Peter's delighted exclamations and laughter within. A welcome interruption indeed.

Maybe Peter's right. It's time.

But there were so many more factors at play there than only what they wanted. The primary one was God's will. "Oh, Lord, help me know what

You want for us," she murmured. "It would be so easy to just say yes, to just plunge in ... to make him happy. He certainly deserves happiness, to get what he wishes for. What I couldn't provide."

Yet those were old thoughts, and the old thoughts never helped. She knew they weren't of the Lord, for the tightening in her stomach and the tears pressing behind her eyes were laced with grief and shame, a deadly combination.

She would never give in to them again. Not for long, at least.

"You give—and You take away," she whispered, still staring at the back door, hearing Peter offer the gift they'd bought in London for his goddaughter. "So help us make this decision and fulfill Your will through us. If our home and our hearts must be open, You're going to have to open them. I'm not ready. But for You and for Peter ... Oh, God, You know I'd do anything."

Polly dashed out of the office, holding the picture book high. She ran back to Alice and crashed into her skirts, giving her a firm hug with the present crushed between them. "Thank you so much for my gift." She tilted her chin up, beaming at Alice. "I love you."

"I love you, too. Did Uncle Penn go back to his work?"

Polly nodded.

"Can you help me with my garden?"

"Yes! Until Mama needs me, I mean."

"Naturally." Alice turned back to the flower bed. "Get the watering can. We're going to rescue these roses—if God helps them out a little, because they need more than just being pruned and watered. You're a big help to Mama, aren't you?"

"Yes—because Susie is *not* much of a help." Polly shook her head as she lugged the heavy metal can over to Alice. "Mama says Susie makes her tired all over."

The words were said without malice, yet Alice couldn't help but smile at the casual sibling rivalry. The girls were as different as night and day—Polly sweet and malleable, Susie fierce and stubborn.

After helping Alice trim back the rosebush and assess the damage, Polly put her full attention toward watering the plant—and then every other growing and not-growing thing in the garden—while Alice cleared away the weeds.

"Oh, there you are, Polly!" Maddie's ever-chipper, somewhat high-pitched voice broke the gentle rhythm of birdsong and soft conversation. She stood at the gap in the fence, dressed not for a morning of work but for an afternoon of calls in a day dress of brilliantly striped muslin, a fabric almost too fine to be near a garden. An ornate cameo brooch was pinned at her throat. "Good morning, Alice. Thank you for watching her. I confess I lost track."

Alice nodded. "Oh, she's been a great help to me. Hello, Susie." She made a point of waving at the younger child. Susie was coming up on four this June—Alice always knew the girl's age without thinking about it, as her second son would have been only two months younger than Susie. It always pierced her with a familiar sadness—though the pain grew easier with every year that passed.

Susie ran to Alice with the same fervor as Polly, though her hug was fiercer and her chattering less coherent, more focused on random things she'd done throughout the morning. Alice knelt to hear Susie's bubbly rambles, which were at least partly a form of English, with a heavy dash of "Susan Farjon" thrown in; and Maddie spoke softly to Polly about the picture book which her daughter proudly displayed to her.

"Susie has a present, too," Alice said when a rare break occurred in the younger girl's rambles. "Shall we go see what it is?"

There had to be yet another pause in the garden work, then, for Susie to see Peter and receive her stuffed animal—a rabbit—and be delighted in it. Then once Peter had disappeared once again, with Alice silently praying that this would be the last interruption of the morning, Maddie offered to help finish clearing the flower beds.

And Alice wanted to turn her down. She had never really gotten along with Maddie—even now, after five years of marriage to Peter, whose best friend was Maddie's husband, she couldn't truly like the woman. Yet Alice knew better than to turn down an offer of help—and more than that, her ability to tolerate Maddie made it easier for Peter to spend time with the friend who seemed to fill his soul in a way few others could.

Peter Strauss and Riley Farjon understood each other, having one of those rare male friendships that provided both amusement and encouragement. She knew some of their conversations in the dark months after Alice and Peter's son died had sustained Peter when she had been unable to rise above her own demons. Alice would be a fool to do anything that might risk such a bond.

Yet she didn't like Maddie ... not really.

They worked in somewhat companionable silence broken by Polly's sweet comments or Susie's rambles and questions. Alice efficiently pulled weeds, while Maddie, more hesitant in her fine dress, made small, careful piles with a trowel. Her laughter was frequent, and Alice found herself not minding the other woman's perennial joy. She didn't seem authentic, usually, but today, somehow, Alice believed in the glow on Maddie's cheeks and the soft light in her eyes.

The girls must be behaving themselves. *Or perhaps Riley is making good on his reputation*, Alice thought wryly. Riley liked to tease her because he knew she found some subjects too private to be discussed, but either he'd mostly toned down his innuendos or she'd learned to tolerate them. However, about three years ago now, Peter had had a chat with Riley about the practical details of marital intimacy. Physical love had become awkward and painful in the aftermath of ... *everything*. The problem had begun after the miscarriage and grown over the series of tragedies that followed, and it had seemed impossible for Alice to relax or find comfort in Peter's arms. So she had agreed that he could seek out advice, as had she.

Despite having given permission, Alice was wary of Riley now, if only because she worried that, through implication at least, he knew more intimate details about her life than she was comfortable with.

She trusted Peter to have been appropriate. He was a man who could keep secrets, and he prized the sanctity of the marriage bed more than anyone she knew. But all the same, it unnerved her that Riley had heard anything about her private life with her husband, even if it was vague and respectfully shared.

Maddie leaned the rake against the tall board fence and wiped a hand across her forehead. "It's warm for May, isn't it?"

"Mm." Alice had little else to add about the weather save that.

"Riley says he wants to get out of town this weekend—a picnic, maybe. He brought home a new hamper—you should see it, Alice; it has a full set of silver cutlery and little porcelain plates inside, all strapped in with leather. I think it's darling, and he's just dying to use it. He'd like to take the girls to a swimming hole he heard of and make at least Polly learn to swim. Though I'm not sure she'll like to—she's not nearly as venturesome as Riley thinks she ought to be." Maddie clucked her tongue. "That man needs a son."

Alice added to her pile of dandelion plants—roots uprooted after a mighty effort. "Right."

"Did I mention we're hoping to have another baby? We were always going to have four—Lord willing. You can pray it happens soon. Susie came along quickly, so I am not too worried, but I don't think I'm expecting yet, and it has been a little over two months. It's always so hard to wait!"

Alice stiffened, briefly closing her eyes as she uttered a silent prayer, then nodded. "I'm happy for you." Her voice was soft and even—that much could be said for the Holy Spirit's work on her.

"If we'd started earlier, we might have had more, but I'm thirty-two now, and my energy isn't what it used to be." Maddie gestured toward her daughters, who had left behind the travails of gardening in exchange for an indecipherable type of game played with two dolls and Susie's new stuffed animal. "I'd have done better to marry young, as you did, but I was waiting for Riley. I'm not sure I knew I was waiting—but I was."

Yet marrying early did not guarantee a healthy child. Nothing did. And Alice was reminded again *why* Maddie was a hard woman for her to get along with, for through no fault of Maddie's own, she represented exactly what Alice most craved.

To be thought of as soft and innocent. To build a household and make it feel like home. To have and raise children. To think of pregnancy and childbirth without near-paralyzing fear.

And, as if to compound Alice's guilt, Maddie realized what she had said—she always did, eventually.

"Oh, Alice, I didn't think." Her wide eyes and the rosy blush on her cheeks confirmed the statement. "Of course you ... you're still grieving the fact that ... that it hasn't happened yet. Children, I mean. I'm so sorry; I shouldn't have mentioned it."

It was the same predictable pattern—the thoughtless chatter, whether practiced or accidental; the dawning horror; the potentially earnest or at least outwardly kind apology. Alice felt a familiar wave of exhaustion wash over her; it was simply easier to grant the absolution than to endure the fuss. "Never mind it, Maddie. I'm fine. I should probably go in and make sure Peter gets some lunch, though."

"Right—and I need to feed those little ones." Maddie smiled and disappeared through the fence, calling to her daughters.

Alice only had to call for her dog.

Peter had been so deep in a troublesome scene that he hadn't paid Alice much mind most of the afternoon or evening, taking both lunch and dinner at his desk. He almost never did that—eating meals with his wife was usually the highlight of his day—but he had an inkling of an idea, and chasing it down was worth some small sacrifices.

He emerged from the office around 8:30 with a clearer idea of his novel's direction than he'd had in months. Alice wasn't in the kitchen, so he turned toward the front of the house—only to hesitate when he heard a light knock on the back door. Juno, who lay stretched in front of the stove, perked her ears but didn't sit up, leading Peter to believe that whoever was at the door was no stranger.

The door opened to reveal his cousin and best friend.

"Hey, Penn."

"Good evening, Riley. Need something?"

"No." Riley slid through the door, confident and suave. He slumped onto one of the kitchen chairs, his long legs stretched out. Blue eyes twinkled at Peter. "Came over to ask you to dinner tomorrow night. We need to get everyone together." He grinned. "Plus your wife promised me a chess match she never made good on. Don't think I forgot in the last couple years. She can't escape."

Peter chuckled. "Not sure she wants to, given how soundly she bested you last time."

Riley brushed this off with a flippant wave of his hand. "I was being easy on her, but I'll give her no quarter this time. I tried to be a gentleman, Penn, but that lady won't let me."

"Whatever you say. She's competitive—you know that." Alice liked nothing more than trouncing Riley at anything she could. "As far as I'm concerned, though, she's one in a million—and you're the one who doesn't stand a chance."

"Hmph. Well, tomorrow night all right? Chess or otherwise?"

Peter shrugged. "I'll ask Alice and tell you in the morning, but I think that'd be just fine."

Riley grinned. "Henpecked, as always."

Peter laughed. "Happily. Though not really—I'm just incompetent when it comes to scheduling. God must have made her for that purpose; she keeps my head attached. Anyway, why shouldn't she have a say on where she spends her evenings? Would it really be good leadership to drag the troops into battle without so much as a by-your-leave when a high stakes chess match is in the offing?" Peter smirked. "When strategizing needs to happen, no less?"

"'The troops' probably don't care—but I get your point." Riley stood. "It's late. I should get back."

"Night."

Once Riley disappeared, Peter turned out all the lights, locked the doors, and ascended the stairs to the bedroom.

"There you are." Alice smiled, putting down her Bible and rising from the chair by the window. "I was starting to worry."

"I got the chapter finished—and Riley poked his head in. He wants us to come to dinner tomorrow."

"All right." She moved about the room, drawing the curtains and turning back the bedclothes while Peter put away his shoes. "I was thinking a lot about adoption today."

Peter blinked. That felt off topic. "Oh?"

"Yes. I prayed about it." She worried her bottom lip between her teeth. "I'm not sure I feel at peace."

"Oh." That was ... disappointing. "I said I would take your conclusion as a word from God, but I admit I feel differently." Yet he couldn't push her, couldn't voice the torrent of thoughts within him. *I am so ready to be a father, Alice, but I don't know that I can risk losing you again. I have fought to keep my selfishness at bay, to tend to your needs, to acknowledge how deep you grieved and how desperately heartbroken you were. I know you saw this differently—I know you have had to reframe your thoughts about yourself, motherhood, and God around this new life where a child is not a guarantee. But we are ready to move on ... and I just want to raise a baby with you, any way God lets us. Please, darling—please. Give us a second chance.* But he didn't say any of that. He couldn't.

She placed her hands on his shoulders, her gaze meeting his, then reached up to cup his face. "I love you so much that it tears me apart to see you hurting. Don't think I don't know. I listen to what you tell me, and I listen harder to what you don't. So much that I find myself returning to old thoughts, so afraid I have denied you the family you want and deserve."

"No." He shook his head firmly. "No. It is not in your hands, and even if it were, you don't owe me anything. It's enough to have you. I just ... I want *everything* with you. Every bit of life." Even if it wasn't perfect—as long as it was God's will, he was ready to dive forward.

Alice sighed. "I know. And I want the same. Let's keep talking about it.

Truly, I would be willing to let you make the decision. You might know better than me. Maybe it's your job to lead me where I am afraid to go." She glanced away for a moment then dropped her head on his chest. "I can see our sons so vividly—I never had much of an imagination, but suddenly I see Zebedee and Daniel at every stage of life, looking just like babies we created through our love ought to look, and I want that. I want a strong, healthy boy like Cassie's Aidan or ... or the son Maddie is sure to give Riley. I want to hold him in my arms, and I want him to be alive, and screaming, and I want the labor pains to disappear and my heart to fill with love for him. I want to feel that rush that everyone tells me women experience after birth—I want to weep from *joy*. And more than anything, I want to see the look on your face when you hold him for the first time. I want that, Peter—I crave it so keenly." The catch at the end of her voice almost undid him. "I desire that experience of womanhood. And I pray every day that God gives me the grace to accept that I haven't had it yet, that I may never have it, that if we raise a child together, it will not be our flesh and blood. I am at peace with it sometimes—and other times it's like someone's taking a knife to my heart, and I'm screaming and screaming for it to stop ..." A soft sob. "It never stops. When does it stop?"

"Oh, my darling." He lowered them both onto the bed, pressing kisses to her hair. "I know. I feel like someone's stabbing at me, too. I would do anything to take that pain from you, but I can't. I feel like there's such an ache in both of us, and I believe God placed it within us for a reason. I want us to be parents, and I would rejoice over a child not my own, too."

"Yes. Just ... give me some time." She nuzzled into his neck and sighed. "Pray for us."

He nodded. "Lord, comfort Alice and me tonight. We know our sons are safe in Your arms, and we know that You do not withhold a healthy child out of malice but out of love. Give us the strength to follow You in faith, to praise You in the midst of our pain. Guide us in the path You have for us, and give us hope while we wait on You. Amen."

She echoed his "amen" softly, and after a few quiet moments, she rose and went to her chest of drawers for her nightgown.

Peter sat up and swiped a hand across his eyes. "I feel lighter."

"Right. I hope we'll feel better and better as we seek God's will in this. He makes all things new, darling."

"Absolutely. And He gave me you. What a gift!"

Alice laughed as she stepped out of her dress and draped it over a chair. "A bit like getting coal in your stocking."

"No." He, too, rose, and began preparing himself for bed. "You are precious to me. My greatest blessing."

She cast him an affectionate look then continued her toilette.

By the time Peter was ready for sleep, she was already on the edge of the bed, intent, as always, on completing one last task before laying down her head. This time, she was fiddling with the twisted bridge of his spare spectacles. He smiled; it was so entirely Alice to think of such a thing, even now.

He knelt before her and cupped her face in his hands. "I have a confession. I'm in love with you."

The spectacles were set aside, and her hand came up to slip through his hair, gently caressing the back of his neck. "And I, you."

He pressed his lips to hers, a featherlight kiss for a moment before he deepened it, delighting in her eagerness as she returned it. She made him shaky sometimes—always—and he wanted to tell her that, and that he loved her—so much—and that she was everything—*everything* to him. "Alice, I—"

"Shh." She silenced him with another kiss, drawing back just a shade to whisper, "No more talking."

Chapter Six

Maddie Farjon had always been the type to host regular parties at her house. It was a skill Alice herself technically possessed; but she'd rarely had the time to do so, nor much reason, given that the Farjons' house was better suited for hosting than her own, and Maddie genuinely delighted in having a crowd sample her cooking—and yes, it was still largely *Maddie's cooking*, no matter how many servants Riley hired.

Alice and Peter crossed through the garden that evening, Juno trailing after them only to drop onto the back porch next to Riley's own dog. They proceeded through the kitchen door. Already, a stout woman with flushed cheeks—Mrs. Cooper, the Farjons' new cook—was pulling a roast from the oven, while Riley's younger sister, Essie, was at the sink, washing a dish. She lived with friends of the family, while she worked at a local library and embraced life as an "old maid," as she very cheerfully called herself—whether or not that was true, much less charitable, was up for debate. At thirty-one, though certainly not too old to marry, Essie seemed to have given up her hopes of it—if, Alice mused, she had ever held them to begin with.

Maddie stood at the main worktable, intensely focused on whisking a sauce, a smudge of flour on her cheek. Peter greeted her then slipped through the door, heading toward the parlor.

Alice lingered, a small smile playing on her lips. It was just like Maddie to hire a cook and then refuse to leave the kitchen. For all her recent talk of new dresses and society teas, this was where Maddie felt most in command, proving her worth with every perfectly seasoned dish.

"Are Terry and Flick already here?" Alice asked, referring to the couple Essie lived with. Terrence and Felicity Tappet were both longtime friends of the Farjon family and had moved to Cincinnati not long after Maddie, Riley, Peter, and Alice had. Terry worked on the railroad and was seldom home, always traveling back and forth; so moving Flick to where she could be close to friends seemed like a natural step—especially as both of them were practically alone in the world.

"Yes, in the parlor. I think Riley was showing Terry something, and Flick will have found a corner to rest in. She's never one to get sucked into Riley's nonsense."

"I can help, if you need anything," Alice offered. But whether through politeness or past knowledge that she wasn't good at domestic tasks unless closely monitored, she was refused and shooed off. This was just as well, as she would far rather be with Riley, her husband, and the girls than stay in the kitchen. Polly and Susie instantly monopolized her time, and though Riley threatened her with the upcoming chess match, she knew he would not truly insist until after dinner—or "supper," as Riley blithely referred to it.

The Engalls, a family who went to their church, came not long after. They had two children—Annabelle and Cecelia, who were five and one respectively. Annabelle ran off with Polly and Susie immediately, and since Sarah Engall was a dear friend of Maddie's, she disappeared into the kitchen with her baby on her hip, knowing that was where she would find the hostess holding court.

As Flick remained absorbed in a book in the corner, Alice sat with the men, a position she had become more and more comfortable in as her life in Cincinnati progressed. Oh, she attended a regular women's Bible study—at the Engalls' home, actually—but her relationship with those women was surface level at best. She might share an occasional distant prayer request, attend dinner at their houses, and greet them kindly enough at church. But she was not otherwise inclined to share much of herself with them. Her closest friends in America were living in Philadelphia.

They had been so rarely in Cincinnati that building a community there hadn't made much sense. Perhaps they should now, especially as it was clear that they would be here for some time to come. Alice had noticed, in spending time with Ivy in Scotland, that her sister knew how to create and serve a community. Though perhaps that might be easier in a little village than in a growing city like Cincinnati, it would be in Alice's best interest to at least try. What Ivy offered to and received from Keefmore was infinitely valuable.

The men were chatting about some experience Terry had had on a recent trip to New York, and Alice paid it some small attention while mostly allowing her mind to drift to what she might need to undertake in the following weeks.

She felt eyes on her and turned to meet the blue gaze of Felicity Tappet.

Perhaps building a community should begin with the moment she currently lived in—not some distant someday. Alice stood from her chair by Peter and walked to the window seat where Flick sat.

"May I?" Alice gestured to the place next to Flick. Hopefully she wouldn't expect Alice to maintain the polite distance they'd never broken since they first met.

Flick looked up from her book, her expression unreadable for a moment. Then, with a small, almost imperceptible nod, she shifted on the cushion to make room. "Yes, you may." Her soft southern drawl dragged the words out in an almost friendly way. From what Alice knew, Flick wasn't the most social person in the world. Other than Essie and her husband, no one seemed to know her well. Granted, she and Riley had been childhood friends, but Maddie spoke of that with an unusual tightness in her voice which indicated that at one point the relationship had been a little too close. Riley was now a dedicated Christian, whereas Flick and Terry refused to have anything to do with religion, which created an obvious distance. The friends were too devoted to leave each other, perhaps, but the Tappets were too different to truly feel a part of the group where shared faith was a clear part of life. Even Flick and Terry must see that.

Yet the group had failed Flick and Terry if this had left the couple feeling excluded.

"What are you reading?" Alice asked, despite not really caring about the book in question whatsoever. She knew it was the polite thing, the right thing, to say.

"*Hard Times* by Charles Dickens." Flick set the book to the side on the windowsill. "I see you were not welcome in the kitchen."

Alice stilled but forced herself to relax. She knew better than to allow offense to color her relationships. Too long had she shied away from the brusque honesty of some while continuing to be abrasive herself, a double standard she could ill afford to maintain. Not anymore. "I was told not to help—and to be honest, I'd rather hear the men talk than the women."

Flick inclined her head. "Fair enough. I simply don't make friends easily—not with women, at least. And I'm all right with that."

"I see. I suppose that can be a struggle of mine, too. Peter is at ease anywhere, but I haven't been that way, not since I was quite young. I used to be brave and uncaring—I've become more cautious. I'll not say that's a good thing, though."

"No. I'm sure it's not." A slow smile slid across Flick's face. "Yet I am accustomed to it—and there have been times when I've benefited from it. I am often alone, but I have always been content with that in the past."

"In the past?" It couldn't be that easy, could it—that Flick was now ready to open up at the exact same time Alice was ready to reach out?

"Yes." A firm, slow nod. "In the past."

Alice started to ask why, but Essie appeared in the doorway, calling them to dinner.

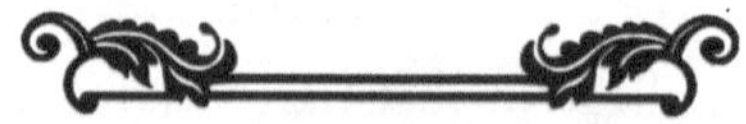

Peter's conversations that evening had been easy, mostly listening to everything his friends hadn't written him during his long absence.

Riley waxed eloquent about Peter's newfound success as an author, saying that everyone was talking about both *Matins* and *Katie Grace*—that he saw them everywhere, both in bookshops and in peoples' hands. Peter answered questions about *In Heart-Wrung Tears*, which would come out in a few short weeks and which he believed had an even wider appeal, as a romance inspired by the Brontës. Yet he didn't say that. It seemed strange to brag about his success—stranger still to have what could be generally referred to as "success."

Through this, Peter watched Alice out of the corner of his eye. She had spoken with Flick for a time, so it wasn't as if she were alone—but Peter would have to ask her later if she had chosen to stay out of the kitchen or if it was a deliberate exclusion. Sometimes Alice preferred to hear the men talk, he knew, but he didn't want her to do that if it wasn't her choice.

He had no idea that she *ought* to stay in the kitchen—no idea of where Alice "ought" to be at all, as long as she had followed God there to begin with—but he knew there was a tension between Maddie and Alice, whether or not either of them admitted it openly. If there was cattiness involved, he would have to mention it to Riley. Peter had never been able to take a firm tone with Maddie—a holdover from his youthful infatuation—but Riley suffered from no such ailment. If anything, he could be so blunt as to be hurtful.

Peter almost found it amusing that he had once been so obsessed with Maddie. He'd believed for many years that they could be happily married. Oh, they might have gotten along all right, but they were ill-suited in so many ways. Maddie praised his flaws, flattered his pride, and made him melt into a puddle of agony whenever her emotions took an unpredictable turn—which he had thought a sign of great love at the time.

Now, given what he had with Alice, he rolled his eyes at his own naivety. He was done romanticizing pain in a relationship. Alice wanted him to be happy—and though they'd had their share of dark moments, and she had certainly shown herself as capable of inscrutability as Maddie, he had always known she didn't want to manipulate him through those feelings. Maddie had always exhausted him. She was fine in small doses, but at seventeen, he had been willing to be worn down by her; he wasn't anymore.

Maddie might claim otherwise, might not even know this was true, but there wasn't a chance on earth she respected him. Alice did, even if sometimes her impulses were hard to tame.

Peter turned his attention back to Alice, who was watching Riley with a somewhat amused expression as she nibbled at one of Maddie's rolls. At least she seemed to have taken to Flick this evening. He hoped she wouldn't mind the chess match Riley was sure to force on her after dinner. She couldn't hope to escape, not with Riley so determined.

Halfway through the meal, Terry cleared his throat and leaned forward in his seat, an indication that he would like to speak. It was so rare that he or Flick chose to say anything that everyone stilled and stared at him.

"I thought y'all would like to know that Flick is expecting."

The silence lasted far too long. Across the table, Flick stared intently down at her napkin, twisting it into a knot in her lap, her shoulders hunched as if expecting a blow. It was Mrs. Engall who quietly said, "Congratulations to you both."

A soft round of good wishes circled about after that—but Terry had made it more than clear that he didn't want a child. Based on his somewhat somber expression, the same was still true. The Engalls didn't know, and Maddie might not either—but Riley and Peter, and of course Alice, to whom Peter told everything, knew exactly how unpleasant this announcement must be for the expecting parents.

There was a look of pain in Flick's eyes that Peter wished he could address. It was not his place—not simply because he didn't know her that well, but because she was a woman, and another man's wife at that, and he didn't want to get in the way. But oh, how he wished he could tell her that it would be all right—that a child was a blessing—that she would do so well as a mother.

Conversation eventually sputtered back to life around the table. Once the meal was completed, the men wandered into the parlor once more.

On the way, Riley grabbed Peter's arm and mumbled, "This is *not* a good thing," under his breath. Peter knew at once what he was referring to, but Riley wouldn't bring up the situation to Terry in front of Brett Engall. In front of Peter, maybe, but Dr. Engall was a near stranger, especially to Terry, and the man deserved some privacy.

Yet Peter felt confident Riley would speak with Terry about it soon. More and more lately, Riley had spoken about reaching out to the Tappets and finding ways to minister to them. Perhaps this was a good entry point.

Peter certainly prayed so.

After dinner, while the other women chatted in the parlor, Flick slipped out the back door. Alice followed. She wasn't sure why, only that Flick looked so alone—and so vulnerable.

Flick had taken a seat on the bench in the corner of the garden and was watching Polly, Susie, and Annabelle play over by the two maple trees, Quip jumping around them and barking. Juno, always more austere, circled them in big strides, watching but not participating.

Flick's eyes were slightly glazed over, but she straightened and gestured to the seat beside her when Alice approached.

"I'm convinced we will never be happy again," Flick said in the softest voice Alice had ever heard her use. "Terry has been so downhearted ever since I told him. When we got married, we agreed not to have children—not to risk bringing more lives into this world. Terry doesn't want children to suffer as he did, which I understand, and I never thought I could, so I agreed. No monthlies, you know—or not often. It was always a blessing in disguise. But they started about six months ago. I suppose it was ... during the war, when we were starving, and I ... I was only a child, but somehow it must've ... Apparently everything is in working order now, and I suppose a baby is just about the most natural consequence of that." Her hands, resting in her lap, clenched into white-knuckled fists for a moment before relaxing again. "I feel like such a fool—but I'm thirty-three. I'd thought if it was going to happen ... well. It should have already. Yet here we are."

Surprised by Flick's uncharacteristic candor, Alice could only nod.

"Terry says I won't be happy with a baby. That I won't be a good mother anyway—I've never been much of the maternal type. But we only have until September—yes, that soon; I haven't wanted to tell anyone—and then I *will* be a mother, even if I'm not a good one. So I need your help—and Penn's."

Alice blinked. "For ... what? Excuse me, but we haven't been ... we haven't been parents. Not really. I wish I could help, but I don't know the first thing—"

Flick brushed off Alice's concerns with a wave of her hand. "I know you haven't been. It's not about that. It's about religion." After saying those words, her jaw snapped shut briefly, and Alice saw a flash of anger in her eyes—and pain, underneath it, seasoning the fury Flick felt and driving her to the bitterness that had kept her silent for so many years. "It's a hard world, and I'm used to the pain, but I'll not have a child go through what I did without ... without at least believing *something*. You need something to believe in, or you die when the hard times come. It took me until I was older to be strong enough to do without. I need you and Penn to tell me what to do. I decided it almost as soon as I was sure I was in the family way—after I realized Terry will never love his child. What other choice do I have?"

Alice cocked her head, forcing herself to sit still and think before she spoke. "Of course we'll help any way we can. But how do you know Terry won't love your child? I think most men don't know what to do with a baby until they have one of their own. He's sure to fall in love as soon as he has his son or daughter in his arms."

"No." Flick's eyes dropped. "I know him too well. Anyway, it won't change what I've said. He might not be around forever—or me, either, for that reason. Terry lost his parents young, and I lost my father when I was ten. If I'm going to give my baby a reason to live, it has to be outside of anyone—at least, anyone *real*. And Penn's the best man in the world to give a little thing that reason. I'd have just talked to him, but I want you to be there. I want you to feel ..." She stilled for a moment then shook her head. "I have always had to wonder with Terry, and I've found I don't like it. I wouldn't wish it on anyone. I used to like to make other women wonder, too, but I don't anymore."

"I see." Alice regarded her for a moment, wondering what combination of sorrows had forged such a strange and fascinating woman. Oh, she knew parts of Flick's story ... raised during the war that had left her fatherless, losing her mother at eighteen, marrying Terry right after—a marriage that even Riley didn't seem to fully understand.

Apparently Terry had been offered his education paid for by the Farjons—offered the chance to attend Harvard alongside Peter and Riley—but turned it down and instead began working a backbreaking job at a railroad line out of Philadelphia. And he had married Flick, whom he didn't seem to love—and for years, it seemed that their relationship consisted of a marriage in name only. Peter had made several references over the years that hinted at adultery on both sides—a concept so foreign that Alice struggled to comprehend it. She'd think a woman as independent and opinionated as Felicity Tappet would leave in the face of infidelity—but there had seemed to be no discord between Flick and Terry until today. It was almost as if neither of them cared what happened to their marriage and yet felt bound to each other for reasons unknown.

Oh, Lord, they're in a terrible mess, slaves to their sins and the lies they've been telling themselves. But You, Lord, are the redeemer of terrible messes. Please help them. They need You so desperately.

"Peter and I will do whatever we can," Alice said firmly. "I normally wouldn't speak for my husband, but I know him—he would not turn you away." Or anyone else in need of help, certainly. "Perhaps you could come over for lunch some day, and we could talk. Would that be all right?"

Flick nodded. "Tomorrow?"

That soon? She must be desperate. *Lord, help Peter and me, too.* "Tomorrow is just fine."

Chapter Seven

As promised, Flick was at Peter and Alice's doorstep at the stroke of noon the next day. She seemed to have regained the stride in her step and the light in her eyes overnight, though Alice had no way of knowing if it was genuine—or simply a show put on for their benefit.

They sat at the kitchen table, and Flick asked questions about Peter's latest book and their trip to England and Alice's nieces. She petted Juno's head and talked about a puppy she'd owned as a child. There was a forced brightness in her voice, as if she were now reluctant to begin the very conversation she had come to have.

It was Peter who broke through this awkwardness, dragging the three of them away from small talk and into a harsher reality. "Alice mentioned you were concerned about your child's well-being."

"Yes, well." Flick folded her hands in her lap. "The child will be here in September, and by that time I want to know enough to create a safe place for him or her. You know what my childhood was like, and I'm sure Riley told you what you didn't see for yourself; and you know what my life has been like since I married Terry. Judged it, even—oh, don't shake your head. If anyone was going to judge me, Penn, I'd want it to be you; I know your heart is always in the right place, the place that wants to save and not reject. But I don't need that. I ... I was never going to be saved. But this baby ..." Slowly, she raised a hand and placed it on her abdomen; the loose, artistic cut of her clothes kept the casual onlooker from guessing her condition, but it seemed obvious in that moment. "The baby will be new to the world, and innocent, and should be safe."

"Right." Peter glanced at Alice and then took a sip of his coffee. It was clear to Alice, though it might not be to their guest, that he was mildly flustered and trying to gain his bearings. "And you think the way to safety is through Christ?"

"Yes."

"But surely you know—"

"That I'm redeemable? That Christ makes 'all things new'? Oh, Penn, I've heard it all before. *You* have told me it all before." Flick shook her head. "No, it's too late for me—and I don't need what Christianity offers me. But I need the baby to have that steady comfort. If it weren't for Terry, I'd give the baby to you; you and Alice would do a fine job raising a baby, and I've always thought you not having one was unfair. But Terry was raised in one of those old money families that value honor, and I think he'll stay with the mother of his child." She shrugged. "I can't risk him leaving me."

"I see." Peter frowned. "I just don't know what to say. I'll do whatever I can to help you—Alice and I will, I mean. But I wish Terry would decide to do what is right."

"But he won't. He ... he has a mistress, whom he says he's in love with."

Peter stilled, and his eyes flew to Alice before returning to Flick. "I'm so sorry. That's wrong. Do you want me to—?"

Flick held up her hand. Her expression was pained but her words were soft and firm. "Please don't tell Riley—don't tell *anyone*. Terry and I didn't promise each other fidelity when we married, and he's made it clear that if I started wanting to keep him to myself, that was my problem. I have dealt with it as best I can." She offered a tremulous smile. "I won't blame you if you judge me for loving him. I can't help it, but I don't understand it, either. I can see that Alice didn't like that—she wouldn't stay by you if you betrayed her, Penn; she would leave, she would go home; and perhaps she has every right to do so. But that's not me."

Alice said nothing. She didn't believe Peter capable of breaking their vows, but it was true that they had discussed infidelity as being a harsh end to a marriage. Once that boundary was broken, Alice didn't understand how anyone could have the grace to go on, though she also understood that most wives had no choice but to stay. But Flick wasn't one of them—Riley would have seen she was taken care of. Yet Alice saw in Flick the same proud independence that in a similar case would likely send her running to the Strausses before she went to her own family—if only to feel she had control over something, even her choice of haven.

Peter cleared his throat. "Flick, forgive me, but you can't ... you can't healthily raise a child—"

"I haven't any choice!" Her voice broke, but she pressed on. "Terry is all I have anymore, and a life without him wouldn't be worth living. I know he doesn't treat me right, but I also know he won't leave me alone with this child." Flick took a deep breath and seemed to calm herself once more. "I was heartbroken at first, when I realized the baby was coming, because I knew how much he'd hate me for what I did not expect and could not control. It's a wild coincidence, all of it—he never visits my bedroom anymore, but he did, and at the right time, and he was working near Cincinnati, so he's more than aware that I haven't taken a lover myself—it's his baby. Not that this would've been untrue any other time, as I have been faithful, but I know if he had a way to deny he was the father, he would."

Peter pressed his lips together. "I hadn't realized it was so bad. I thought ... I thought that at least, you were happy together. I mean, Essie never said anything, and surely, she must know!" Riley's sister usually couldn't help but share any bit of gossip she got.

"Essie has her own reasons for keeping this quiet," Flick murmured with a slight shake of her head. "But none of this matters. If it weren't for Terry, I wouldn't have made it—or I'd be in a much worse place, at least. Alice, you may not know this, but Terry offered to marry me after my mother died when I was eighteen—and if it weren't for him, I don't know what I would have done."

"The Farjons would have taken care of you," Peter interjected.

Flick straightened her shoulders. "I'm no one's charity case."

"Except Terry's," Peter countered, his mouth twisting into a sardonic line.

"Perhaps. But I keep his house clean and provide meals when he's around, and I never ask where he is or who he's with. That's about all a man can ask from a wife, if he doesn't want children." She shrugged. "Besides, my father saved his father's life during the war, at the cost of his own, and I think Terry'll always remember me standing at the funeral, dripping wet in the rain and crying because his father was alive."

"But his father also died in the war, didn't he?" Alice asked. She seemed to recall that Terry had been raised by the Farjons because he'd been orphaned as a boy.

"Yes, but that was later. He got to see him one last time because of my father. I don't understand Terry all the time, but that did mean something to him." Flick sighed. "He's not a cruel man, just an unfaithful one. But he never lies, so I've learned not to ask. I just wish he hadn't picked her ... Oh, but it doesn't matter. That's not important. What is important, Penn, is that my baby is raised—"

"With hope. The hope you don't have."

Flick was silent for a long moment, her eyes distant. Alice thought she saw her bottom lip tremble, but then Flick gave a single, firm nod. "Yes," she whispered. "Hope."

"I think I can tell you something about that," Peter said, his tone soft.

Flick didn't leave for several hours afterward. They sat in the kitchen and then eventually the living room and talked about God and religion and Flick's child. Peter talked the most—Alice sometimes forgot that Peter had spent most of his time before meeting her studying theology, had even spent most of his time at Harvard buried deep in dusty Latin and Greek tomes. As always, he had a way with words that Alice lacked. Even when he stumbled or rephrased, she admitted she couldn't have shared the same information with such empathy.

After Flick went home, Peter and Alice sat at the table for a little longer.

"I have hope she'll change her mind," Peter said. "Flick has never been hard to reach—it's Terry who's made her keep so much of herself away from others, and I'm not going to hold back from saying it anymore." He sighed and shook his head. "It's what Riley has always said, but I didn't want to assign blame, and Riley has always tended to assume the best of women in general, so I struggle to know what's real insight and what's some kind of misguided chivalry. But Flick doesn't hold grudges the same way—she hasn't in all the time I've known her. And yet, women who turn away from their husbands ..." His voice trailed off and he ran a hand over his eyes. "I wish Terry would just think, for even a minute, of how much power he holds over her, even if he doesn't acknowledge it. Riley talks to him about how the way he's living, the way his marriage has been operating, will destroy him in the long run. Really, I don't know why Flick didn't go to Riley—unless Terry has never told her how much Riley has been trying to reach him."

Alice shrugged. "Some people don't want to be saved, Peter, and we can't be responsible for that. And I'm not surprised at all that Flick would rather talk to you than to Riley."

"Right. They also have a ... a shared past that I'd rather not go into." Peter grimaced. "Suffice to say, I know that Flick has not been entirely faithful in the past to her marriage. It was a long time ago, yes, but I'm not casting her as a complete victim here. I wouldn't want her put in a more vulnerable position, though."

Alice nodded—she could accept not knowing everything, especially when "everything" sounded like about twenty years of personal sin and worldly disasters ruining relationship after relationship. "Does Riley know about Terry's infidelity?"

Peter pressed his lips together. "I don't think so. Riley wouldn't let Terry around his girls—Maddie or the children—if he knew. He probably just assumes Flick and Terry are unhappy together, and that Terry won't stay home—which is also true. I doubt Riley would permit Essie to continue living with them if he were fully aware."

Alice cocked her head. "Essie is a full-grown woman who probably makes her own decisions," she observed.

"Right, but Aunt Georgiana controls the purse strings. She would never let Essie live in such a household. I have to tell Riley." Peter's decision solidified as he spoke. "I know it was told in confidence, but he'll want to talk to Terry, and Essie needs to get out of that situation—whether she knows what's happening or not, it isn't safe."

Alice cocked her head. "Maybe you should talk to Terry yourself, Peter. He might listen to you."

"I doubt it, but I'll pray about it. Tomorrow we'll go see Flick and ask her a few clarifying questions."

"Yes, we should."

The Tappets' house was nearer to the railroad tracks, in a less savory area of Cincinnati. Peter hoped Alice hadn't been there before, and he had only stopped by once when Flick and Terry were moving their things in. He liked the area no more now than he had then. Without his really meaning to, his arm found its way around Alice as he led her up the path.

He knocked on the door, and Alice stepped slightly to the side. Essie usually went over to Riley and Maddie's house at least a few times a week to see the girls; and Terry was, as always, "out of town"—though now Peter had an uneasy feeling in his stomach as he wondered how often Terry was really out of town and how often he was with his mistress.

After a minute, when no one had responded, Peter knocked again. This time, a few seconds later, Flick opened the door and ushered them in.

"Penn and Alice. I can't say I was expecting you." She reached up and smoothed her hair with one hand as she gestured them toward a few chairs in the small parlor. "I'm not feeling my best this morning—so I can't say I'll be a pleasant hostess."

They took a seat on the chairs by the window, while Flick lowered herself onto a small, battered sofa with fading floral print. "We won't stay long—and I'm sorry for disturbing your morning." Peter glanced at Alice, who nodded, before he spoke. "I have been thinking and praying about what you told us yesterday. I believe Riley needs to know."

What color was left in Flick's face disappeared. "I see."

Alice reached over and placed a reassuring hand on Peter's arm. "Flick, Riley's sister is involved here—he'd probably never forgive Peter if he didn't say something. Besides, if we keep this quiet, we can't help you as much as we could otherwise, and we're sure we want to help."

Flick nodded. "I understand that, but I wouldn't worry about Essie. Riley knowing won't change anything for her."

"But Flick—"

"Penn, it's Essie who's having an affair with Terry. Since we moved to Cincinnati, I think, though it may have started earlier."

Silence swept over the room like an avalanche—sudden, total, crushing.

Peter's mind scrambled to take this information in. Riley's younger sister, Essie, was her parents' darling. Though she kept to herself, Peter had at least been under the impression she was a Christian—but how could a Christian repeatedly commit adultery? Live with another woman and that woman's husband, and presumably take advantage of the privacy that situation offered?

His eyes flew to Alice. She seemed outwardly calm, but he saw she'd stopped looking at Flick—a subtle tell that she was just as shocked and appalled as he was.

"I know it's not good, but I can't get out. I love my husband." Flick's eyes were still fixed on Peter's, unblinking. "And with the child ... Terry will keep up appearances. Maybe someday things will change, but my life would be far worse without him."

After another moment of silence, all Peter could think to say was, "I am so sorry, Flick. What Terry and Essie are doing is wrong. More than ever, we must tell Riley. He could reason with Terry."

"I doubt it. Besides, Terry has no need to genuinely change unless he does it on his own terms. You know he can pretend to be whatever he wants for Riley, and Riley'll be fooled."

That was true enough. For years, Peter had been convinced that Terry and Flick were happily married—it wasn't until the move to Cincinnati that the cracks had begun showing. Though honestly, Peter hadn't given it much thought. It seemed that the move to Cincinnati had affected all of them in profound ways—and he'd been far too preoccupied with himself, and with Alice, to worry about anyone else.

"Flick, I need to tell Riley."

She took a deep breath and looked down at her hands, folded in her lap. "Very well, then. Do what you must."

Chapter Eight

After Peter got Alice back home, he went straight to Riley's offices. Riley worked for a law firm in Cincinnati, but usually took an early lunch, and Peter couldn't wait the whole day to tell his friend, not now that his course was set. Furthermore, Riley would want to deal with this immediately—he was not a man who valued his peace of mind over honesty, a fact which Peter appreciated as much because it was so different to his own approach to life.

As he had expected, Riley was sitting at his desk enjoying Maddie's carefully packed—perhaps even overpacked—meal. If he was fazed by Peter wandering into his office in the middle of the day, he gave no sign, just offered Peter a handful of cookies and an apple.

"I'm supposed to share these, but socializing with my colleagues stops progress more than Maddie knows," he mused. "But you never stop me from working, exactly, Penn. I'm glad you're here. Is anything wrong?"

Peter took a bite of a melt-in-your-mouth raisin cookie. After he'd swallowed every comforting crumb, he nodded. "I'm afraid there is. I just came from talking to Flick."

Riley's pale eyebrows arched over his blue eyes. "Curiouser and curiouser. What is it?"

"Terry is having an affair. He's been doing so for many years."

Riley's lips pressed in a thin line. "Honestly, after their interactions the night they announced the baby ... I'm not as surprised as I wish I was, Penn. I suppose any man would like to be surprised that his friend is a ... a word you keep saying I shouldn't use, and I won't, but I *can* say he's an adulterer. Maybe that's as harsh as any crude word in my vocabulary. How is Flick?"

Peter winced. "She won't leave him. Because of the baby, and I think because she feels like she owes him some blood debt. And Riley, there's also—"

"I'll talk to Terry." Riley drummed his fingers on the desk as he thought. "I know he's not a Christian, but I can reason with him—remind him that this is not the way either of us was raised. I think even he would admit that it's one thing to run around with loose women as a college boy, but at his age ... It's wrong either way, I know, but he'll see it differently if I remind him that he has responsibilities now. At least, he'll take care of Flick—I'm sure of it, Penn."

Peter nodded, but that wasn't the worst of it, at least from his cousin's perspective. He took a breath. "Riley, the woman ... the one Terry's with now ... It's Essie. They've been having an affair since she moved in with him and Flick. Maybe even before that. They're living in sin together, right in front of Flick." The only word Peter had for it was "shameless." It felt so cruel to openly flaunt a lover before the wife—especially when said wife adored said sorry excuse for a husband. Riley was right that some of the less savory words in the English language applied to Terrence Tappet.

For a long moment, Riley said nothing—just stared at Peter open-mouthed and wide-eyed. "Is Flick sure?" His voice shook.

"Riley, it's happening under her own roof. How could she be mistaken? I think Terry told her that was how it would be, and she could accept it or leave, and she had to ... Or she *felt* she had to ... It doesn't matter, except that it's true."

"How could this have happened?" Riley ran his hands over his eyes. "I knew Essie had drifted away from the faith, but to have an ongoing affair with a married man for at least four years—to live with his wife ... I can't believe it of her! But I know Flick wouldn't lie—she'd have no reason to—and I suppose I had thought ..." He shook his head. "But I assumed that a woman of Essie's age ought to be able to make her own decisions, even if I didn't agree with them, and I assumed that living with a married couple was a good way for her to keep her independence while remaining protected. I never thought ..." He stood, beginning to pace the room frantically.

Peter let him—sometimes Riley needed to get some energy out, and Peter didn't blame him for that.

"I'm going to have to send her home to Virginia."

"Given that she's an adult—"

"I'll threaten to tell our parents; she'll not want to be cut off from them. Not when that's where the money comes from."

"But it's more than just removing Essie from the equation. Both she and Terry will have to answer for this, one way or another—especially if neither of them repents." Peter shook his head. "Riley, you can't just run in and shout at her. She must be reasoned with, as must Terry. Though at the end of the day, none of us can do anything to prevent her from doing what she wants—she's not sixteen anymore—we can at least appeal to them in a reasonable manner. Surely Essie will see that Terry ought to be with the mother of his child."

Riley paused in his pacing and frowned. "Maybe that's so, Penn—or maybe it'd be better for Flick to be without the scoundrel. But I wouldn't want to see a child raised with such a father."

"Maybe God can turn this around," Peter said softly. "Maybe He can redeem this situation. I don't know, Riley—but I know we should pray. We should now, and then I can let you get back to work. But take some time to mull it over and consult the Lord before you move forward. All right?"

Riley agreed, though as they bowed their heads, Peter suspected his friend's thoughts were still racing as he prayed for wisdom and guidance.

Alice heard nothing of the situation for a few more days. Peter advised her to give Flick some space, and she begrudgingly agreed. After a few days of prayer and counsel from their church, Riley, with Peter at his side, finally confronted Terry.

They both arrived home late that evening.

"I barely kept Riley from beating Terry," Peter told Alice when they were cuddled up in their bedroom. Something about watching an adulterous affair play out under their noses had made them more clingy to each other—especially Alice. She never doubted either Peter or herself, but she valued him all the more for it, and the safest place in this unsafe world was always in his arms. "Maybe I should have let him—I don't know. But Terry is unrepentant. He told Riley to stay out of his business. Riley will have to talk to Essie about it, but that will require even more tact—and I think he's hoping that something will come up to stop him from having to do so. I can't imagine confronting one of my sisters in such a way. It's painful, and the awkwardness is even worse. Yet who else could he trust to approach her? Maddie won't, and Essie doesn't know anyone else—not really."

Alice nodded. For once, she shared Maddie's great repulsion about a situation ... but if Essie were her sister-in-law, she would certainly approach her. "She wouldn't listen to me, would she?"

"No." Peter kissed the top of her head. "Though I love your willingness. But I don't want you involved—or not more than you have to be."

"But Flick, Peter." Alice had seen so much pain in Flick's eyes and words. It had touched a sisterly spot in her, the one that stirred whenever a woman suffered at the hands of another and felt powerless to act. Alice would never let Cassie go without comfort or support or whatever she needed. The same had come to apply to Flick.

Peter shook his head. "Let me protect you in this way. It's a messy, unpleasant business. It's hard enough to stand by and watch Riley deal with this; I want you out of it."

Alice nodded, though reluctantly. She'd do as he asked her to, but that didn't mean she had to like it.

The next morning, before the sun had made the oil lamp on their kitchen table unnecessary, Alice was at the stove. The smell of sizzling bacon filled the small room—an unusual accomplishment for her, but she'd been up early, her mind too restless to let her sleep. Peter sat at the table, his hands wrapped around his mug, hair still tousled. His attempts to keep up with her early morning hours were appreciated—but he looked frazzled.

"It's not that early, Peter," Alice said as she slid a plate in front of him. "Don't forget to actually drink your coffee."

"It's early," he mumbled.

Alice laughed and returned her focus to the stove. As she flipped a slice of bacon, her gaze wandered out the kitchen window, and the smile froze on her face. "Peter."

Something in her voice must have alerted him, for his next words sounded significantly more awake. "What is it?"

Alice didn't answer. She removed the pan from the heat, set the spatula down, and moved swiftly to the door, untying her apron as she went. Juno started to rise from her spot near Peter, only stopping when Alice muttered "no" in a firm tone.

The sight of Flick on the doorstep made Alice's heart sink. There was no reason she'd have come here this early—not if everything was all right.

Flick's face was drawn and pale, and her posture was stiff. She clutched the edges of her shawl around her. Tears stained her cheeks, but her jaw was set. Sheer willpower must be keeping her on her feet right now, given how utterly devastated she looked.

"Good morning, Alice," Flick said, her voice low and unsteady. "I'm sorry to come so early, but ..."

Alice stepped forward, taking Flick's hands. "Never mind that. You're welcome here. Come in. Have some breakfast."

Peter was on his feet now, his coffee forgotten. "Flick? What's happened?" He gestured to the table. "Sit down and tell us about it."

Flick lowered herself into a chair opposite the one Peter had been sitting in. Alice hastened to pour her a cup of coffee, in case that's what was needed. She had no idea how to deal with Flick's brittle composure—no idea how to offer comfort.

"It's Terry," Flick said after a long, quiet moment. "He's left me. For good."

Peter exchanged a glance with Alice. His expression was dark, angry. She wasn't sure she'd seen him like that before—but she understood. He had every right to be angry. Alice herself felt furious. She sank into a seat at the table and gestured for Peter to join her.

He sat heavily back into his chair. "You're sure of that, Flick?"

Flick swallowed hard, her gaze fixed on the wooden grain of the table. "Yes. He's gone. He and Essie ... they're running away together. I suppose they've been planning it for weeks. Maybe since I found out I was pregnant. He left a note. Said he doesn't want me anymore, doesn't want the baby. That marrying me was a mistake."

Alice swiftly placed her hand on Peter's under the table. It was pressed in a fist against his thigh. Yet other than that, he gave no outward reaction—just waited, as Alice did, for Flick's next words.

"He said he doesn't want to be tied down," Flick continued, her tone bitter now. "Essie understands him better; she 'matches his spirit.' I'm not even sure what that means. He'd say anything to justify himself, I suppose, but he was my husband. He knew he was in the wrong."

"And the baby?" Peter asked. His voice was soft, gentle. He might be angry, but there was no world in which he would take that out on Flick—Alice was as sure of that as of the sun rising every morning.

Flick shrugged, attempting a nonchalance she probably didn't feel. "He said he wants nothing to do with it. Or me." Her voice cracked, but she quickly steadied it. "He's left everything behind—his debts, the house, *me*. I'll lose that house in a month. That's why I came here. I don't know where to go or what to do."

Peter and Alice glanced at each other, almost at once. It took only a moment to reach an unspoken accord.

"You'll stay here," Peter said. "Until you find something better, you'll stay with us."

Flick's head snapped up, her eyes widening. "I couldn't—"

"Yes, you can," Alice interrupted. "There's room here, and so it's settled."

Peter nodded. "Alice is right. We'll figure out the rest as we go along—we'll help you—but for now, you'll stay here where we can take care of you. You're having a baby, Flick. You shouldn't be alone anyway, and you can't get a job. You shouldn't have to. It'd be our honor to help you any way we are able."

Flick blinked rapidly and swallowed several times before she responded. "I don't even know how to thank you."

"You don't have to." Peter stood. "I'll go talk to Riley about this, and we'll start working on taking care of any legal matters."

"Penn!" Flick straightened. "Don't let Riley chase Terry down. I don't want revenge, and I don't want him dragged back. If he wants to go, let him."

Peter swallowed. "That'll be a hard thing to convince Riley of. Essie is his sister, and Terry was a dear friend for so many years. He'll want to—for your sake and for his own."

Flick sighed. "I'm done forcing Terry to be with me. Can you convince Riley of that?"

"I can try." Peter's eyes landed on Alice for a long time, then he nodded and slipped out the back door.

Alice returned to the stove. After all, surely everything was more manageable on a full stomach. At least, she wanted to believe so.

A week later, Alice stood by the window of the tiny nursery, her fingers gently brushing over the fabric of the pile of baby blankets she'd set aside. She hadn't gone through them since Cassie came to stay here all those years ago, and that had only been to neatly put them away, crushed dreams set aside for another day.

Even now, the scent and sight of them triggered a rush of memories, all stained with the bitter anger of loss. Daniel would have been four this August—not long before Flick was due to deliver her child.

She could be tucking a little man into the small bed Cassie had slept in when she stayed with them. This room could be full of his clothes, his toys, his noise.

"We wouldn't be able to help Flick then," Alice murmured to herself as she set a few of the blankets on the freshly made bed, turning back to the chest of drawers that held the few items she'd made, purchased, or been given for her baby four years ago. The first drawer was full of white and pastel clothing—including a tiny pair of knitted booties. The note Nettie had pinned to them upon shipping was still there. Phrases flashed out in the familiar, carefully elegant handwriting of a former lady's maid. "I'm so excited for you. A child is a blessing. May God give you comfort during the delivery. I wish I were with you. You will be such an excellent mother." The words swam before Alice's eyes until she was forced to set the paper aside.

The sound of footsteps from the hallway snapped her out of her reverie, and she turned to find Flick standing in the doorway, a small bag in her hand—the last of the few possessions Peter and Riley had packed for her. Flick had decided to have furniture and most of her and Terry's belongings sold or donated to charity. She'd only taken with her some personal articles, her clothes, and a few sentimental items, which already rested on every flat surface of the small room.

She had nothing for the baby yet, which was just as well. Alice had everything she would need.

Flick's eyes met Alice's, and for a moment, there was silence between them—perhaps an unspoken understanding of the weight both carried, albeit for different reasons. Alice never bothered to get to know the other woman, but now every glimpse of her revealed something new that Alice understood deeply. The reticence around other women due to feelings of inadequacy, the desire to be independent even when it didn't make sense, the mistrustful bitterness that came from being wounded by a man who should have been a protector.

But despite her many failures, Alice had learned a thing or two about inadequacy and independence and bitterness over the years.

Flick stepped into the room and set her bag down. "You don't have to go through all of that for my sake," she said, gesturing to the chest of drawers. "I wouldn't want to, either. I can live out of a box."

Alice straightened her posture and smoothed down her skirts. "I'm fine. Really. I've gone through all of this before. I decided then that I could be sad about our baby without avoiding the things we got for him entirely." She glanced back in the drawer. "Anyway, I want you to have them." There was another long moment of silence before she cleared her throat and continued. "Why don't you help me go through these things? I'd like you to choose what you want for your baby."

Flick's eyes widened slightly, and she immediately took a step back. "You shouldn't have to do that."

Alice shook her head, reaching into the drawer and pulling out the first bundle of tiny clothing. "Please, Flick. I want to do this for you." She smiled. It might have trembled, but it was a smile. "I don't need these things right now. If I ever do, and your child is grown, you can return whatever is left of them. But only God gets to decide that. I trust Him—even with this pain and this loss. Perhaps more so because I didn't always."

Flick hesitated, clearly uncomfortable, but Alice scooped up a second bundle and set it on the bed then gestured her over. "It'll be easier with you here," she continued. "I'm not much for being alone with my thoughts."

With a resigned sigh, Flick sat down on the bed, her gaze falling to the tiny clothes. She picked up one and played with the linen. "You have a lot of nice things."

Alice nodded. "My mother sent me more than I could ever use, when I told her I was expecting. Anything that looks distorted and mangled is of my making—and anything that looks carefully knitted was probably given to me by Lilli, Maddie, or Nettie—um, she was my governess growing up, and we're … close."

"That's sweet." Flick set the long dress down. It was the type babies would wear until they were old enough to be clothed like tiny adults. "I wouldn't have had anything this nice, so thank you."

"You're very welcome."

For a while, they worked in companionable silence, Alice pulling items from the drawer, and Flick inspecting them. Some brought faint smiles to Alice's lips as she recounted their origins—a pair of mittens from Lilli, so small it was hard to believe a human hand could ever fit inside; a yellow bonnet Maddie had insisted on knitting. Honestly, Alice thought the color was hideous.

"I never liked that one," she admitted. "Frankly, it makes me a little ill."

Flick laughed. "Then why keep it?"

"I don't know. I knew she'd want to see the baby wearing it."

"Oh, no!" Flick held up the bonnet by its strings and then dropped it to the floor and kicked it under the bed. "We won't be petting Maddie's fragile vanity."

Alice gasped and glanced toward the door. "Flick!"

"Well, and why not, Alice? She's never done a thing for either of us except to please Rye or Penn. I can't stand a catty woman. You know, there's a few things we'd say about a girl like that where I come from." For a moment, Flick's southern accent deepened, and she winked. "I won't say them because that's too much gossip to waste on Maddie. But I'm awful sick of pandering to her pride. She can fall off that high horse for all I care."

Alice laughed. She couldn't help it. She knew better than to be cruel or read an insult where there was none, but sometimes it felt like Maddie, in the guise of kindness, poked and prodded at all of Alice's tender places. She couldn't help but feel the other woman wasn't as innocent and harmless as she pretended. It seemed just when Alice was feeling most happy and content, Maddie would make a tactless, condescending comment about

Alice's inability to give her husband children—all while disguising it as pity and prayer.

As Alice kept working, she mulled over Flick's words. Honestly, they weren't half wrong. Maddie wasn't a bad person, but perhaps her sugar-sweet persona wasn't the full story.

Alice knew sugar-sweet. She'd feared and even hated it in the past. It felt weak and vulnerable. It felt open and approachable, though, too. Ivy was like that—always thinking the best of people, kind and gentle and ready to pray for anyone who needed it. Yet as Alice had grown up and leaned toward God rather than relying on her own fragile strength, she had come to appreciate her sister. More than that, adore her. Respect her. Seek to emulate her in little ways. Ivy was a force to be reckoned with. Her loving heart contained a fierce loyalty to those she considered her own.

Flick set aside a blanket she'd just finished folding and sat still. Her brows knit together, and her lips pressed into a thin line. "Alice," she began, her voice quiet, "I need to say something."

Alice noted the serious expression that had slid over Flick's face as she thought. "Of course."

Flick's hands tightened in her lap, and she kept her gaze fixed on the blanket. "I think you know I'm not sure I'll make much of a mother."

The words hung in the air, and Alice felt a familiar answering pang. She had never let herself wonder that specific thing, but it had tugged at the back of her mind, taunting her whenever she examined her own future goals. She had pressed it aside, so sure she must have babies for Peter, and after Daniel died, she'd not had time to think about it again. The years that had intervened since had taught her much about herself ... and one of those things was that she *did* have the tenderness for children that she considered a prerequisite for motherhood. She'd been an adoring auntie often enough now, by blood or affection, to know that. "That's not true. Everyone thinks that—or, mostly. But it'll change."

Flick shook her head, her throat working as she tried to find the words. "It's not just that. I don't know if I'll ever feel like this baby is mine. Not in the way it deserves."

"You don't know what you're saying." Alice was sure of that. "Someday, someday soon, it'll become more real. It's hard at first, I know. Especially since you were so unprepared and with everything that has happened!"

Flick managed to raise her eyes to Alice's face. They were dry and lifeless, but otherwise, no emotion showed in them. "What I know I'm saying is that you and Penn should take my baby. You've already lost a child, and I know you wanted him. You'd give this baby a better life than I ever could. You have everything here for one already. I don't think I'm suited for this, and anyway, I don't even know what the next year will bring."

The words struck Alice with the force of a physical blow. Only years of practiced self-control, a holdover from her youth, kept her standing. She stared at Flick, her heart pounding in her chest as conflicting emotions swirled inside her. A part of her was tempted by the idea—achingly so—but another part recoiled. Flick would regret that. Alice was sure of it.

"No," she said firmly without moving or breaking eye contact. "You're going to feel differently once you meet your baby. It's terrifying now, but once you hold a tiny little thing, all yours, it'll change everything. Trust me, Flick. You'll love that child more than you can imagine."

Flick looked away at last. "You can't know that."

"I do," Alice insisted. "I've seen it happen again and again. I know how I would feel. I know how I *did* feel. It wouldn't have been so devastating if I had not loved so deeply, almost against my will. You're stronger than you think. You can do this thing, too."

Flick stood abruptly. "Maybe you're right. Maybe you're not. But I don't want to argue about it now. It's been a long day."

"Neither do I," Alice agreed. Not that she wouldn't argue about it later—after Flick was well-rested and at least a little over the heartbreak of the last week. Not just that—it had been a long, drawn out heartbreak, that of years of rejection and humiliation at the hands of her husband. Flick had suffered too much to make a rational decision right now. "Let's leave it for now. Just promise me you'll think about it some more. Don't do anything rash."

Flick nodded stiffly. "Fine. But I won't change my mind."

Alice watched her for a moment longer, then turned back to the drawer, continuing to sort through the baby clothes as if the conversation hadn't bothered her. It didn't matter, after all. Flick could never do it. She might think she could, but she couldn't.

When Peter hears ...

Alice's hands stilled, and she knew then that Peter wouldn't hear because she could never tell him. He wouldn't understand—no, that wasn't true. He'd understand too well, and that was the problem. She could imagine his face, the mad hope of someone denied too often that might flicker there, followed by the weight of guilt when he realized the cost of even entertaining Flick's offer.

No, it was better to forget the conversation. Flick would change her mind once her baby was born. For now, all Alice could do was wait and pray.

Chapter Nine

"It's just not fair, Penn." Riley kicked the side of the stall, causing his bay gelding to perk up his ears in concern. "They disappeared without a trace. What am I supposed to do?"

Peter was sitting on a hay bale, waiting for Riley to either vent his anger or give up on his endless quest. He'd come to meet Riley here after he saw him riding back from yet another (of course unsuccessful) trip out of town to try to track down Terry and Essie. "What would you do if you found them, anyway?"

Riley sighed and ran a hand through his blond hair, causing it to stick up in six or seven spots. "I don't know. I'd punch Terry first. I haven't thought about the next step."

"That's Christian of you."

Riley sent Peter a look and turned back into the stall to remove the horse's saddle. "Maybe I wouldn't hit him. I suppose if they don't want to be found, I oughtn't to keep trying. But Penn, what they've done to Flick—"

"It's not your fault." Peter stood and walked to the stall door. "You can't fix this. Not for Flick or yourself or Essie. Terry and Essie chose this path, and though Flick was their victim, we had no way of knowing what was happening. There was nothing either of us could have done, especially since we didn't know."

Riley dropped his forehead against his horse's back for a moment, then lifted it and marched past Peter to put the saddle away. "I know that with my head, but I want to do something for Flick. With Maddie ..." He paused, facing away from Peter. "She's not always an easy woman to live with, but I love her. I just can't stand by her on this. Not the way she wants me to. But I don't want to upset her, or make her feel like I am choosing another woman over her, so there's not much I can do."

"You don't have to do anything," Peter said as gently as he could manage. He didn't agree with Maddie's cold treatment of Flick any more than Riley did, but it was true that Flick was taken care of. "Alice and a few women from the church are doing their best for Flick, and she's fine. Maddie must be insecure. She knows about your past, and she knows what happened with Flick was a long time ago—but there's nothing you can do to heal her if she feels insecure. Sometimes all you can offer is patience. I have learned it's better to err on the side of not giving your wife anything to doubt you about. Some people are slower to trust than others."

"Right." Riley slowly turned and met Peter's eyes. "So when does the trust kick in, Penn? Another ten years of marriage?"

Peter flinched. There was a bitterness in Riley's tone that he rarely—if ever—heard, and he wasn't sure what to do about it. "It's only been seven years, hasn't it?"

Riley scoffed. "It's been a fair sight longer than that since I've done any of the things Maddie is convinced I *might* do any moment now. I don't drink or gamble or run around with loose women. And it's more than that—I'm the most careful husband there ever was. I never do anything she might disapprove of, but nothing I do is good enough. I don't need it to be enough most of the time—it's not that I don't care, but that I know I'm not perfect, and I don't aim to be perfect—but every once in a while ..." He shook his head. "I wish she could forgive and forget."

Peter nodded and stood there, because what could he really say? Everyone needed grace, but it wasn't like Maddie to easily give it—that much was true. She would forgive, at least verbally, but she never forgot anything, and she had a way of making that clear to anyone who had wronged her, whether that slight was real or perceived.

"If Flick's all right, I won't worry about her," Riley said after a long silence. "I'll let Terry and Essie live their lives, and I'll stop sticking my nose where it doesn't belong. The truth is, Maddie has been better to me than I deserve. I'm not perfect—oh, but you knew that." He winked. "I'm sure she could tell a tale or two that would stand your hair on end."

Peter nodded, grateful Riley wasn't going to force him to come up with the perfect words to make everything right. He didn't know how to do that. "Thankfully, we serve a God who offers grace for our imperfections and salvation from our sins—and from the sins of those around us."

"Yes. And Maddie's trust was broken a few different times when she was barely old enough to understand it." Riley shook his head. "Not sure she knows that, but it's true. The leash has been looser, but I think she sees Terry and me as different versions of the same person. And I know!" He held up his hand. "I know that's not fair. You can pray for her, and for me, because I'll probably have to sit her down and talk this through. She's all wound up about— Well, it doesn't matter."

"About what?" Peter said before immediately thinking that it might be private.

Regardless of if it was, Riley gave Peter a long look then shrugged. "I don't know if Alice told you this, but Maddie wants another baby, and it hasn't been as quick this time. That could be for any number of reasons, and it's not been enough time to worry about it."

"It's still a disappointment, though," Peter said quickly. He didn't want Riley to think he couldn't talk to him about these things. "I'll pray for that, too. Hopefully soon."

The corner of Riley's mouth twitched. "Unfortunately, I doubt a baby would make her *less* emotional. But it'll pass, and things will be good again. Wherever there's a valley, there must be a mountain. That's my 'substance of things hoped for,' and 'evidence of things not seen.'"

Peter squinted. "You mean faith? Faith is—"

"Shh, I thought I sounded intelligent for a moment there. Just leave it." Riley grinned and turned back to the horse. "I need someone to think I'm capable of basic reasoning, even if you just pretend."

Peter opened his mouth to contradict him then shut it. If Riley wanted to let this go, Peter would let it go—at least for now.

July 1886

Peter stepped out of his office, leaving the cats to nap in the sunshine, and was immediately greeted by the sight of a sparkling kitchen. Alice had scrubbed the entire room until it shone, and now she was arranging a platter of cookies on a plate. Her face was flushed, though he suspected it was more from anticipation than exertion. Juno looked on with palpable anxiety, head resting on her paws, ears pricked, brown eyes following Alice's every move. When Alice turned to adjust the tablecloth, possibly not for the first time, she began mumbling something under her breath.

"You know," Peter said, leaning against the doorframe, "for a woman who insists she doesn't need a housemaid, you are working very hard to look like you have one. If you keep fussing like this, the ladies will think you've finally given in."

Alice looked up, her eyes narrowing with mock severity. "If I had, she'd be dismissed for not straightening this hem."

Peter chuckled, stepping into the room. "It'll be fine. You've done more than enough. I thought the whole point of this was to sit about and drink tea. The kitchen shouldn't be involved."

Alice sighed but didn't argue. She wiped her hands on her apron and turned toward him, hands on hips. "It's not about me," she said, though Peter suspected it very much was. "It's for Flick. If things are tidy, I can think about her more. I want her to see how kind these women are, how much they care. She doesn't know what it's like to have that kind of community."

Peter nodded. He didn't say what he really thought: that he wasn't sure Alice knew what it was like, either, except from the outside "She'll see," he said. "Knowing Flick, she'll pretend she doesn't care, but I think it'll mean a lot to her."

Alice stepped forward and reached up to adjust the collar of his shirt. "You're slipping out as soon as they get here, aren't you?"

"Absolutely," he said with mock solemnity. "I must believe the Bible warns against straying into the domain of many women."

Alice raised her eyebrows. He expected her to snark about how he'd certainly never stayed away from groups of women before—but instead, she said, "I don't remember that."

He shrugged. "I believe it's somewhere in the apocrypha."

Alice laughed. "That might be why it sounds so extra-Biblical. But don't go too far. I might need rescuing."

Peter kissed her forehead, savoring the way she leaned into him for just a moment before returning to her tasks. "I won't be gone long."

Things had settled into a happy rhythm in the past two months. Flick and Alice had grown closer, and Peter was delighted to see it, as well as to watch Flick's vibrancy slowly return, despite—or perhaps because of—the child that grew within her. The baby would be here in less than two months.

By the time the women started arriving, Peter was already at the door, hat in hand and Juno at his heels, as she despised large gatherings on principle. But he lingered, watching from the edge of the room as Alice greeted the ladies warmly and ushered them inside. Flick appeared in the doorway to the parlor, her arms crossed and her expression guarded.

It wasn't until Mrs. Tremain, one of the older women, reached for Flick's hand and explained the purpose of their visit—"We intend to bless you, Mrs. Tappet, with some gifts and some encouragement, if you'll let us!"—that Peter saw Flick's mask slip. Her eyes widened, her lips parting in surprise.

"We know life has been cruel to you," Mrs. Tremain said. "A baby is a precious gift, and one that comes with practical needs. Please, let us help—just a little."

Flick blinked rapidly, her head dipping slightly as if to hide her face. "That's very kind of you," she murmured. Her voice wavered, and Peter knew it cost her something to say even that much.

Alice stepped in and grabbed Flick's arm as Peter had often seen her snatch Cassie out of a social situation that had left her speechless. "Come on," she said. "They're here to spoil you, so you have to sit down."

As the women bustled about, chattering happily as they unpacked bundles of small, mostly handmade gifts, from baby items to food to little things for Flick herself to enjoy, Peter caught Flick's gaze. He smiled. Yes, he and Alice could have just bought Flick everything she needed, but they could never buy this—the outpouring of simple, heartfelt generosity from a dozen different hands. This was what Alice had wanted for her friend. Flick gave him a small, almost imperceptible nod, her lips curving into the faintest of smiles.

It was enough.

Satisfied that all was as it should be, Peter and Juno slipped out the door. He would head to Riley's office to help with some proofreading; Riley would be thankful for the assistance.

And he'd tell Riley that things were going well with Flick. That everything was going to be all right. Because it was.

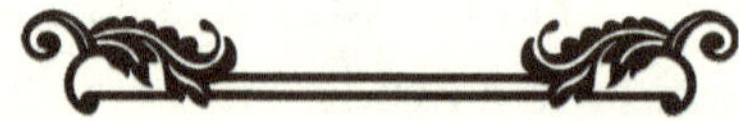

August 17, 1886

The summer heat clung to the air, thick and still. Peter and Alice walked side by side, their steps slow as they wound their way through the cemetery. The silence between them was heavy but comfortable; they both understood each other perfectly about this. There was little to say. Everything that was, simply was.

In the back corner of the cemetery, they stopped at the small gravestone with *Daniel Riley Strauss* etched deep into it. There were lilac bushes nearby, not in bloom now, but they would be in the spring. Peter let out a slow breath, his gaze lingering on the letters. It had been four years since they had buried their son, but time had not dulled the ache.

Alice knelt, smoothing her hand over the soft grass that grew over Daniel's grave. For a moment, she said nothing, simply staring at the stone as though trying to see beyond it.

"Four is such a good birthday for a little boy." Peter knelt next to her and placed his hand on her lower back. "They're still babies in some ways but just starting to be tiny men, and they want to know and do and investigate everything. He'd be chattering like a bird, tearing into his gifts. And finding new ways to cause trouble, I suppose." *I wouldn't mind, though.*

"Yes," Alice said. Her voice was quiet and small. "Yes, he would have had a lot of energy, I think."

"I wonder what he would have looked like now," Peter mused. "If he had my eyes or your nose. That sort of thing."

"He has your nose *and* eyes," Alice said in a tone that brooked no argument. "Your hair, almost, except it might have been a slightly different shade, more light-brown or even golden-brown. He looked a lot like you."

"Mmhmm." Peter gave her a squeeze. He didn't argue with her anymore about that—about her believing she had seen their children in something like Heaven. Alice had been near death at the time, and she swore she was tugged back to earth by the knowledge that her children were safe, and Peter was waiting for her. At first, Peter wasn't sure his theology matched with what Alice said had happened, but he decided he didn't care what his theology was—if this vision or dream or gift from God had comforted Alice, if it continued to comfort Alice, it was a blessing. "It'd have darkened. The hair, I mean."

"Maybe." Alice smiled. "But if I wanted a lookalike, I'd have had Zebedee. He was so handsome."

Zebedee was the name Alice had given the unknown child they'd lost to miscarriage early on in their marriage. They hadn't known the gender. However, Alice insisted his name had been revealed to her in that same dream. Peter had once again let it slide, for oh, it was so tempting, so sweet. Thinking of their sons frolicking together in some idyllic heavenly place, where no pain or suffering could take them, was the best thing he could imagine.

"Zebedee had freckles. Not sure where they came from," she added.

"My mother, possibly," Peter suggested. "Though she keeps out of the sun, so you wouldn't always know it. She had more when she was younger."

Alice nodded her head. "You had never told me that before." Her subtle way of informing him she still believed she had briefly entered Heaven. "Zebedee had big, dark eyes, more like my father's than even mine, and ears that stuck out and a honey-gold brush of hair like yours."

"My ears don't stick out."

"Lilli says they did when you were little."

Peter pretended to frown. "You've been talking with my mother far too much. I suppose they would be short, funny little things like I was, too."

"Maybe they'd get their height from me." Alice was tall for a woman, and her father was tall for a man.

Peter chuckled, though the sound felt a little strange. "And would Daniel be like you in his own ways? Independent and bold and inquisitive? Would he get your smile? Would we always wonder if he was into some mischief?"

"Oh, yes."

They fell silent again. After a moment, Alice glanced at Peter. "And Zebedee," she murmured. "He'd have been the older one, wouldn't he?"

Peter's throat tightened, but he nodded. "By a few months, yes. I know it's impossible—he'd have only been born in the spring; we couldn't have had both—but I always imagine them together. They'd have been thick as thieves, even if they were a year or two apart. Zebedee could have been the serious one, trying to keep Daniel in line, like all older brothers, but Daniel might have dragged him into mischief anyway."

Alice laughed, though tears glistened in her eyes. "Zebedee *could* have been cautious, I suppose, like you: always thinking everything through and seeking a deeper meaning and desiring to know people. Perhaps he would be introspective and calm and rational. Or maybe that would be what Daniel was like. I suppose we'll find out someday."

Peter's hand tightened around hers. "I admit I sometimes imagine their laughter. It's like I can almost hear it." He paused and reached up, brushing a tear from her cheek with his thumb. "We'll hear it one day," he said gently. "Not here, but we will."

Alice nodded, swallowing hard. "I know," she whispered. "It just feels so far away. I wish you had seen them, but I tell myself you *will*. I tell myself they will recognize you at once, and it will be glorious for you. If I had any power to change what happened, if I could spare them for your sake—"

Peter wrapped his arm around her, pulling her close. "No," he said. "We cannot change God's plan. *You* could not. Understand me? This is not your fault—no part of it is. They are with God because He willed it. 'The Lord gave, and the Lord hath taken away; blessed be the name of the Lord.' You were such a good mother, my Alice. You are perfect. I am proud to be your husband. All right?"

"All right," she echoed, almost too quietly to be heard. "All right."

So they sat for a time, the stillness around them broken only by the faint rustle of leaves and the singing of distant birds. Peter still feared he'd never do enough or say enough to convince Alice not to blame herself for things she couldn't control, not to seek her worth in actions only to lose it when inevitable tragedies struck. But she was stronger now, more bold, coming into herself more every day.

God, protect and shield my wife and show me how to be her strongest comfort and defense. Give me the courage to stand between her and whatever pain will come our way, and help me see how I must love her through the suffering I cannot stem.

Finally, Peter spoke again, his voice quiet but steady. "We should go back.

I don't like Flick to be alone."

"Yes."

He rose and helped Alice to her feet, but he could feel her eyes lingering. It was no easy thing to leave. They never visited as often as they would have liked—perhaps, in some ways, it would be ghoulish to do so. "We'll come back sooner next time," he said, "and we'll keep praying. Daniel won't be our last child. We have time."

"You don't know that." She sighed and leaned into him. "We might never have another."

He didn't bring up adoption. Somehow, he knew she didn't want to discuss that possibility yet—or at least, not today. "There's no reason to believe we won't."

"It's been four years. Three since we started trying again, I suppose, but that's still a long time. I know everyone says there's no reason we shouldn't have another child, but if it hasn't happened yet, why should we believe that it will someday?" Alice shook her head. "Of course I hope, but we were able to conceive so easily the first two times. Why would that have changed?"

"I wish I knew that. I only know that God's plans are best, even if we don't understand them. It may feel like it's been a long time, but it hasn't been in the grand scheme of things." Peter took her hand and squeezed it. "We'll be all right, won't we?"

She caught his eye at that, smiled, nodded. "We will be."

It had been a dark afternoon for August, but as evening fell and the cloud-covered sun refused to attempt its shallow illumination a minute longer, a baby cried for the first time—and everything got a bit lighter.

Alice bathed and swaddled Flick's son while Maddie and Mrs. Engall tended to the new mother. Flick had done well—better than Alice had when Daniel was born, Alice thought. The living child was evidence enough of that.

But as she cradled the newborn, she tucked the bitter thought away. It wouldn't do. Now was a time of great joy—to steal from this moment with her own grief would be appalling.

As Maddie whisked past her with a tray of various items, Alice returned to the bedside. "He's a handsome one, Flick," she murmured. "Here—you must hold him."

But Flick turned her head away, her arms limp on the counterpane. Her blonde hair hung, damp and dark with perspiration, about her pale face, and there was agony in her dry eyes. "No, Alice. You hold him. I want to talk to you—about something I've been thinking over. Sarah, could you give us a minute?"

Mrs. Engall nodded and slipped out of the room, leaving Alice and Flick alone.

"Alice, I can't provide a life for him. No father—his name borrowed from a man who doesn't care about him and who plainly would rather be selfishly pursuing his own desires than providing a decent life to his son. I'm not that good with children. I like them, and in another world I would have wanted some of my own, but I'm not *good* with them. I could give the baby love without understanding, and I would still like to offer that, but a child needs a father and a mother. I think that should be you and Penn."

Alice's heart ached, as it had whenever Flick brought up this particular subject. Yet she knew there was no chance of her fulfilling Flick's request. "You don't know what you're saying. You—"

"You and Penn should take my baby. I … I'd like to see him. Maybe I'll find a way to make a place for myself somewhere—I don't know. But the baby should have a life. You and Penn *deserve* a baby. It may be that you can't have one of your own, ever—and if you can, why not give them a big brother? You'd raise him right. Alice, I don't even know how to begin."

"But Flick …" Alice tightened her hold on the child she held, her eyes fastened to Flick's face. "He's your son. You can't just ..."

"He would be your son." Flick's strained voice was quiet now. "You know as well as I do that blood isn't everything. Why, wasn't that what Penn said the other day? That we should fix our eyes on spiritual things, on a spiritual family? He would love this baby as his own. You would do the same. This is the best way for my baby to be safe and loved, raised in the way I want him to be raised—the way I can't raise him myself."

"Yes, but your child should be with his own mother. That's not me. I couldn't ..." Alice turned her eyes back to the small wrinkled face. Flick's son was bald and wrinkled and red and fussy, but he had a wild beauty, like Flick. He was his own small person, all bundled up and new and fresh. He was perfect.

Her heart caught, before she could stop the foolish organ from its typical foolishness, and Alice knew she could love him. A life where she and Peter raised this child flashed before her eyes for an insane moment—and then it was gone.

She caught a slight shift and turned to see Flick's face. There was a slight smile on Flick's lips—but her eyes were full of agony.

"See?" Her tired voice was kept purposefully light, but there was an edge to it. "You want this, Alice. I couldn't imagine a worthier person. I like you; let me give you this. Haven't you suffered enough? Haven't *I*? Keep my baby and spare *him*."

Alice took a deep breath, held it for a long moment, then exhaled through her nose. Flick was emotional right now; it was not the time for a life-altering decision. Temptation bit at Alice, whispering into her ear that she could be a mother—that she and Peter could be parents—that the longing and the desperation and the despair could end, now, if she just said the word—but the choices Flick made tonight might well be entirely different if she were given the opportunity to think it over.

A heavy responsibility settled on Alice's shoulders, and solemn certainty flooded her chest. If Flick were given the opportunity to rest, to live amongst healthy people, to be loved by the body of Christ, and to know with certainty that all physical needs were provided for, would she really not want to be a mother? Or would these circumstances make the difference in how she felt about the baby?

"We'll talk about it later," Alice said firmly. "Unless you truly cannot, you must hold him, and we'll take care of you. That is our only job right now—to help you be this baby's mother. Don't worry about what comes beyond that yet." Then, without asking, Alice placed the baby on Flick's chest.

As Alice had hoped, Flick's arms automatically reached to cradle her son.

Alice turned and walked out of the room. By the time she'd summoned Maddie and Mrs. Engall, Flick was lost in a world that presumably contained only her and her child.

Alice stayed up watching Flick through the night, helping her or the baby whenever they stirred, but when she was relieved in the morning by Maddie, she went into Peter's study, sat on his lap, dropped her head on his shoulder, and cried until she had no tears left.

"Is it because of Daniel?" he whispered over and over again as he rubbed her back and kissed her flushed neck and cheeks.

"She wanted us to take her baby," Alice managed to pant out eventually. "She wanted us to take him and raise him as our own."

"Ah." He changed from back rubs to slow pats. "What did you think about that?"

She pushed back from him. "We can't." She used her sweaty hands to brush the tears from her cheeks; Peter gave her his handkerchief. "That's her baby. Do you think I could take another woman's son? Do you think I could watch her lose him, like I lost my child? Oh, I know it's not the same thing, but she has always loved and wanted her baby, even if she's never been able to admit it to herself. To watch another woman take her place would be torture. She was willing to give him up because she thought we would love him—and we would. That's the horrible thing—we *would*. But we'll do everything we can to help her, and if she can't, if she truly won't be that child's mother, I will beg you to let me keep him. I'll—" A sob caught in her throat, and she dropped her head back onto Peter's shoulder.

His arms came around her, tightly. "We'll do everything we can. Shh, my darling. Shh. You don't have to beg me for anything that lies in my power to give you. It'll be all right. Flick will keep her child. We both knew that, didn't we? That was never a question we doubted the answer to. Oh, my darling ..."

Chapter Ten

September 1886

Three weeks later, Flick decided she wanted to attend church.

Alice wasn't sure what had led to this change. Over the weeks, various members of the small Baptist congregation in their corner of Cincinnati had dropped by, visiting Flick and her baby so perhaps that had had something to do with it.

Flick hadn't mentioned wanting to give up little Allen Peter Tappet again. If the thought had crossed her mind, perhaps she'd decided that arguing with Alice would do no good—which was true.

In truth, Alice would take that baby in a heartbeat if the circumstances were different, but it became increasingly clear that Flick loved her son, and in fact, she'd settled into motherhood with fewer bumps than most women. She was almost unrealistically chipper, up and about only days after the birth despite Alice's best attempts to keep her in bed, and quickly acting like a happier version of her old self. It helped that Allen was very well-mannered for a newborn—he limited himself to a few dissatisfied squawks a night, and these generally calmed as soon as Flick nursed him. Breastfeeding had come easily to Flick, and within a day, her initial reticence to hold her son had given way to a brash confidence.

Alice knew that if she'd had a baby to raise herself, she'd have been jealous of Flick's maddeningly good luck. However, as it was, Alice just watched the series of fortunate events with vague amusement. It was as if God was going out of His way to bless Flick with idealized circumstances.

In Flick's opinion, her renewed energy and newfound confidence had a side benefit: it annoyed Maddie. Alice was learning that Flick, for better or worse, had a number of scores to settle with Riley's wife. Alice hadn't known just how catty Maddie had been toward Flick—she hadn't paid attention, perhaps, or had been too wrapped up in her own woes to care. Whatever the reason, Flick seemed to enjoy anything that made her motherhood experience seem effortless, if it could happen in front of Maddie or be told to her later.

Considering Maddie was a healthy, happy woman with many friends—and that she hadn't always been particularly kind to Alice herself—well, Alice didn't confront Flick about it. It was little of her—petty, perhaps, and a bit ungodly—but Alice liked to see Maddie squirm.

Just a bit.

Besides, Flick wasn't a Christian. Why would Alice expect her to act like one?

Not that I'm acting very holy, her inner monologue admitted. *But I'm* personally *kind to Maddie. Defending her against every person on earth is not my duty, God.*

That said, regardless of Flick's lack of interest in God, she had carried through with one claim: she wanted her child raised to understand Christian values. A strange wish for a woman who didn't want anything to do with Him herself. Peter and Alice had had many long conversations with her about this over the past few weeks, but none had led anywhere conclusive.

However, today, for the first time, Flick's talk was leading to an action: she wanted to go to church with Peter and Alice.

"I think Allen will be quiet during the service." For the first time, there was a touch of anxiety in Flick's voice as they approached the church building. "He is usually such a good baby."

Alice nodded. "Yes, he is. And if he's not, I can slip out with him so you can listen."

"No one will mind if he cries," Peter added. "There are lots of families here, and most of them have little ones."

They stepped into the building. In a moment, Mrs. Engall was at their side.

"I'm so glad you made it!" she said instantly, placing a hand on Flick's arm. "I had to come over and see Allen. How's he doing?"

In the face of such warmth, Flick visibly relaxed. The tension vanished from her shoulders as she began to update Mrs. Engall on the baby. She wasn't even frosty when Mrs. Engall introduced her to a friend.

Eventually Peter guided Alice, Flick, and Allen to a pew near the middle, and as they sat, Mrs. Tremain leaned over from the pew behind them.

"You won't remember me, but I'm Mrs. Tremain—Rose, if you like—and we met at Mrs. Strauss' house. I didn't want to stop by and bother you right after the baby came—but I've been just longing to meet him! Is this your little one?" Her eyes were sparkling.

Flick blinked, seeming unsure how to respond to the warmth in the woman's tone. "Yes," she managed, her voice soft as she tugged back at the edge of the blanket to show off her son's round face. "This is Allen."

Mrs. Tremain clasped her hands. "What a handsome boy! Oh, look at those tiny fingers. I love how plump he is already. My goodness." She glanced over at another woman a few pews down. "Elizabeth, come see!"

In a matter of moments, a small group of women had gathered around Flick, their faces beaming with admiration. They cooed at Allen, asked questions about his birth and his temperament, and assured Flick that he was indeed a very pretty baby.

Alice would have found it annoying—but it was also endearing. Something about Flick's patient, long-suffering, smiling face told Alice that her friend felt about the same. But it was sweet. Clearly Mrs. Engall—who by necessity had seen a lot of Flick in the last few weeks of Flick's pregnancy and first few weeks after Allen's birth—had made sure that her friends were as welcoming as possible.

Maddie, however, was pointedly avoiding Flick, and perhaps as a result, she was avoiding Mrs. Engall as well.

Alice wished that didn't feel quite so vindicating, but she knew even Riley was awkward around Flick right now. Perhaps it was guilt he felt for not "rescuing" Flick sooner, or perhaps it was simply some odd aspect of his personality that Alice didn't care to investigate. She did like Riley, but sometimes he could be a little particular. Peter felt that Riley was more sensitive to betrayal than most people realized, and that Terry and Essie's actions had wounded him in a way he would eventually have to process with prayer.

Until then, he was apparently drinking too much coffee and driving Maddie crazy by pouting around the house whenever he wasn't at work or taking care of things for Flick, which occupation he had thrown himself into with unparalleled energy.

Peter wasn't too worried, though; he felt Riley would figure it out with God and then discuss it with him.

Alice would have probably just slapped *her* best friend if Cassie had acted this way, but everyone communicated differently.

The moment the sermon began, Alice noticed a change in Flick. She sat stiffly in the pew, her arms wrapped protectively around Allen, her gaze fixed on the pastor as though she were bracing herself for an attack.

The sermon was about the prodigal son, which wasn't necessarily applicable in every way, but it was still verging on poignant. Alice would have scolded Peter for putting something so obvious in one of his books where he was inevitably trying to wrap up a character's journey in far less space than he needed. Nonetheless, she glanced at Flick occasionally, hoping to gauge how the story was landing. Flick's knuckles whitened on Allen's blanket as the pastor described the son at his lowest—convinced he was unworthy of love, let alone forgiveness. Nonetheless, with nowhere else to go, the son returned.

"'And he arose, and came to his father. But when he was yet a great way off, his father saw him, and had compassion, and ran, and fell on his neck, and kissed him.' The father in this parable could not wait for his son to walk the rest of the way home—he ran, eager, to meet him. In this same way—"

Without a word, Flick rose and slipped out of the pew.

Alice hesitated for only a moment before following her. She caught sight of Flick disappearing through the side door of the chapel, Allen cradled tightly against her chest.

Lord, help me. You couldn't have sent someone less worthy to talk to her about this.

She found Flick sitting on a small bench behind the church, beneath the shade of a sprawling oak tree, staring at nothing.

Alice came to stand beside the bench; Flick didn't acknowledge her. "May I sit with you?"

Flick's eyes briefly flickered to Alice and then back at ... well, nothing. "If you like."

Alice lowered herself onto the bench. For a moment, neither of them spoke. The only sounds were the distant hum of the pastor continuing his sermon inside and the occasional chirp of a bird overhead.

"I don't know what's wrong with me," Flick whispered.

"There's nothing wrong with you."

Flick shook her head. "I thought I could just sit there and handle it. The problem is, I feel so much whenever I'm in a church. I want to run."

"That's understandable." Alice cocked her head, thinking over everything Peter had said about Flick's life—and things he'd said about other people, too. "People from churches haven't always been kind to you. It was never an option for me to not go to church, but I admit there were times when I disliked the scrutiny." She shrugged. "I'm not pretending it's the same thing as what you've lived through, but my family has known its share of judgment and gossip. And more than that, I've known my share of pain. For me, God is my succor in that, though it was a long time until I could allow Him that place in my life. You probably know that—I'm sure Maddie's said something."

Flick offered a slight smile. "She's tried."

"Right." Alice sighed. "But I'm not here to talk about it—or past grievances or anything like that. Why did you come out here?"

Flick's lips were tucked in a tight line. "I don't know. I just realized that I didn't belong there. With all those Christian people. I mean, Alice, I haven't told you half of the things I did. They'd make any man or woman in that building"—she jerked her head back toward the church—"blush. Even if I hadn't, I've been out of church for so long. I've told you I think it's too late for me, but not for Allen, and yet ..." She stopped and shook her head. "I know the Bible well enough, I suppose. 'Too late' isn't really a Christian concept, you know, or so I understand."

Before Alice could answer, soft footsteps in the grass made them both look up. It was Mrs. Engall. Her eyes were kind and gentle.

"Mind if I join you?"

Flick hesitated, then nodded again.

Mrs. Engall settled onto the bench on Flick's other side. "I don't know quite why I came out," she said. "Brett is going to be struggling to keep those girls from causing havoc. Cece can't sit still to save her life, now that she's learned how to walk; and Annabelle just wants to chatter away the whole sermon long."

Flick nodded. "Allen has been good, though, hasn't he?"

"He's a very good baby," Mrs. Engall agreed jovially. "God has blessed you with him, if you don't mind me saying so. You're going to be all right. Both of you."

"I don't deserve Allen," Flick murmured. "He's perfect; I don't deserve him."

Mrs. Engall nodded, her expression growing more serious. "I'm sure no one deserves anything on their own merit. But you were created by a God Who loves you—and Allen, and all of us." Her eyes turned to Alice, which Alice supposed was her prompt to speak.

"Mrs. Engall is right, Flick." Alice swallowed. "I mean, you don't think I've earned my way to salvation, do you? Even knowing me a little, you can't think that. I can be stubborn and overbearing and even cruel. Sometimes my thoughts are not kind toward people, whether they deserve it or not. I've said and done horrible things—and more than that, I've not trusted God even when I should have known that He was with me even in the pain. I don't blame myself for experiencing grief or anger or desperation, and neither should you. He can't take it away, but He can lighten the load and comfort you. At least, that's what I've found," she ended lamely. This was why she didn't try to give emotional speeches. She thought it was far wiser to leave it to her husband, who always knew how to talk about such things. Alice was not meant to advise anyone. She was destined to be the somewhat distant, frightening aunt, not the comforting mentor, or the loving, motherly figure.

Yet Flick didn't say, "Thank you for all that useless information," even though she could have. She just nodded. "I just feel like God couldn't possibly want me. Some people don't become Christians. Some people go to hell. Some people aren't destined for Heaven. Why would I presume that I'd be one of them?" Flick gave a watery laugh. "If anyone is going to lose it all, it ought to be me."

A thought popped into Alice's mind. "That reminds me of a different parable." She wasn't like Peter; she couldn't reword it, making it infinitely more palatable to the average person or specific to some lost soul. But she could quote it. "'And He spake this parable unto them, saying, What man of you, having an hundred sheep, if he lose one of them, doth not leave the ninety and nine in the wilderness, and go after that which is lost, until he find it? And when he hath found it, he layeth it on his shoulders, rejoicing. And when he cometh home, he calleth together his friends and neighbours, saying unto them, Rejoice with me; for I have found my sheep which was lost. I say unto you, that likewise joy shall be in Heaven over one sinner that repenteth, more than over ninety and nine just persons, which need no repentance.'"

For a time they sat in silence, then Mrs. Engall spoke. "You don't have to do anything, but you are welcome here, and Alice and I will fight anyone who treats you badly. You know that, don't you? Anyway, they'd have no right. God is reaching out for you. I know it; I have thought so every time I have seen you."

Flick squinted. "What an odd thing to say."

"Well, haven't you ever had a feeling about something?" Mrs. Engall grinned. "I have a feeling about you."

Alice nodded. "I know what she means. I feel as if you're my sister and that you belong here. But if you don't want to be, if you can't be at church, then I'm not going to argue with you; and if you don't want anything to do with Christianity, that's your choice. Despite what you may have heard, it's impossible to force someone to believe in Jesus as their Savior; that's something you'd have to decide for yourself. If you don't believe, you don't believe."

Flick nodded. "I know." She adjusted Allen's blanket. "In truth, you have me thinking. I wish I could believe. For Allen's sake, at least."

"I can understand that," Mrs. Engall said. "But at the end of the day, even if it would benefit Allen, it's something you must genuinely believe yourself. After all, though there is great rest and comfort in Christ, it's a relationship you would have to choose to engage in yourself. That involves an immense amount of surrender, which doesn't come easily to any of us."

Flick's laugh was even shakier now. "Surrender." She shook her head. "I've never been good at that. I've held onto quite a few things in my life as tightly as I could. I've had to."

Mrs. Engall smiled gently. "The good news is, God doesn't expect perfection from us at the start—or ever, really. Surrendering to Christ by definition isn't about getting it all right. It's about saying, 'I can't do this on my own, and I need You.'"

Alice nodded, her voice softer now. "And He meets you there. That's what's so incredible. He comes to us, like that shepherd going after the one lost sheep. We don't have to find Him on our own. We couldn't—we need His pursuit."

Flick looked down at Allen, her fingers tracing the edge of his blanket. "I don't know how to let go."

Alice reached out, placing a hand over Flick's. "You can't fix yourself. That's not the concept. It's about giving it to Him. The pain, the guilt, the fear—you can give that to Him. You don't have to carry it alone."

Flick's gaze stayed fixed on Allen. Her shoulders shook slightly, as if under a great weight, but she didn't make a sound—didn't cry or even let her breathing change. Then, so quietly Alice almost didn't hear her, Flick whispered, "How do I begin?"

"You just talk to Him." Mrs. Engall's voice was light and unconcerned, as if afraid of frightening Flick away with great vehemence.

Unable to promise the same lack of emotion, Alice avoided speaking. She'd have been embarrassed to show her complete investment anyway.

"Like you would speak to a friend, I mean," Mrs. Engall continued. "You don't have to be formal, and He won't mind if you aren't perfectly articulate. Tell Him everything. Your fears, your doubts, your hopes. Not that He doesn't know, but every relationship needs communication, now, doesn't it?"

Flick's lips parted as if to speak, but then she stopped, her brows furrowing.

"What is it?" Alice said, nudging her slightly.

"What if it's too late? What if He's already given up on me?"

Alice felt her throat tighten, but she forced her voice to remain steady. *I'm becoming a romance heroine—all shaky and trembly and swoony*, she reflected before she replied. "Flick, if He'd given up on you, do you think you'd be sitting here now? Feeling what you're feeling? He hasn't given up. He's been waiting for this moment—for you to come to Him."

Allen began fussing, and Flick brought him to her shoulder and crooned to him until he settled again. Mrs. Engall intently stared at the quiet, nearly empty road to the right, and Alice watched Flick patiently, knowing that the other woman would reply, eventually, as she always had in the past.

After Allen was settled, Flick laid him across her knees and brushed his face with her fingers. Then she looked up, glancing to either side of her to meet Alice's eyes and then Mrs. Engall's.

"Would you pray with me?" she asked. "I might need a little guidance the first time, but only if you don't make it too dramatic."

Alice pressed her lips together then hastily nodded.

Alice and Flick met Peter outside the church after the sermon. Neither of them said anything, but Peter—who had decided that Alice was more than capable of handling whatever questions or concerns Flick brought to her—could see a subtle change on both of their faces.

For now, he left the issue undiscussed. He'd talk about the matter later, with Alice, in private. Instead, he smiled at the two of them, gesturing toward the street. "Ready to go home?"

Flick nodded, shifting Allen in her arms. The baby squirmed slightly, one tiny fist waving in the air before settling back down. "He's been so good today," she murmured, brushing a kiss across his forehead.

"He's *always* good," Alice protested. As usual when talking about Allen, her voice was full of a warmth Peter generally only heard when she spoke of Cassie's children.

It's going to be hard on Alice when Flick finds a new life for herself, one that doesn't involve her living with us and needing Alice's help. But he brushed that thought aside.

"Mr. Strauss!"

He turned to see Mr. and Mrs. Tremain, a middle-aged couple, walking toward them, their faces alight with warm smiles. The Tremains were familiar to him but not well-known. He believed Mrs. Tremain attended a Bible study Alice had occasionally gone to with Mrs. Engall and Maddie; and Mr. Tremain and he had had the occasional conversation outside of the church. He believed their family owned a dressmaking shop not far from Riley's offices, which he'd passed a time or two.

"Good morning," Peter said, inclining his head as they approached. "How are you both?"

"Quite well," Mrs. Tremain replied, and Mr. Tremain echoed her sentiment in a quieter voice, asking how Peter and Alice and Flick were.

After the usual pleasantries were exchanged, Peter found himself wondering why he'd not had more contact with the couple; they were perfectly pleasant, yet he knew so little about them.

The Tremains exchanged a glance before Mr. Tremain cleared his throat. "We hope you don't mind us approaching you like this, but we had something we wanted to discuss with you." He nodded to Peter and Alice. "Would you mind?"

Flick took a quick step back. "I want to catch Mrs. Engall and ask her a question," she said, clearly not meaning it in the slightest. "I'll be back in just a moment, Alice. Take Allen, will you?"

Alice gladly received the baby, and Flick scurried off.

Peter raised his eyebrows, curiosity piqued. "Go on."

Mrs. Tremain clasped her hands in front of herself and glanced at her husband, who commenced speaking instantly. "We couldn't help but notice how well you've taken care of Mrs. Tappet, and we admire it greatly. But we also know it can't help but be a strain. No young couple is without their own needs, and her own must be so great right now, with no one left in the world to care for her. But—" Mr. Tremain paused and offered a slight, rare smile. "We are not a young couple or just starting out. God has blessed us, and we want to spread those blessings about. We were wondering ... if there might be a way we could help."

Alice tilted her head slightly, her expression unreadable.

Peter pulled his eyes away from her and back to the Tremains. "That's very generous of you."

"Well. It's nothing. It's just—" Mr. Tremain paused again, then continued, "Our last daughter just married and moved out, and the house feels empty now. We've more rooms than we know what to do with. We've always had a busy home." He shrugged. "If Mrs. Tappet were willing, she could come live with us."

Here, Mrs. Tremain—usually the more talkative of the two—couldn't resist speaking up. "It would help me feel more settled, and we'd like to have a baby in the house again. Besides, I could use some help, eventually. When she's rested from the birth—a little more; she seems well, but every new mother ought to have plenty of recovery—we could teach her the trade. Dressmaking is a skill she could carry with her anywhere, if she ever needed to provide for herself and Allen. Not that we'd ever toss her out, but if she wanted independence, this could give her a way to gain that."

Peter glanced at Alice, whose brows had lifted slightly in surprise. It wasn't the sort of offer one heard every day, and he could tell she was mulling it over as carefully as he was.

What if this was Flick's new start? The first step on her path toward a new way of living?

"That's a kind offer," Peter said. "I can see so many ways in which that would bless her immeasurably and give her a second chance at life. But the decision would ultimately be up to Flick—Mrs. Tappet."

"Of course," Mr. Tremain said quickly. "We didn't mean to presume."

"It's just ... We've been praying for a way to put our empty house to good use. And when we saw her today, it felt like perhaps God was pointing us toward an answer. I should have talked to her sooner, but I wasn't sure it would be welcome." She smiled, a little nervously. "But I would correct that error if I could. Mrs. Tappet doesn't deserve her lot in life, and everyone can tell she's done such a good job with her baby."

Peter nodded slowly. Beside him, Alice was quiet but serious, her expression thoughtful.

"We appreciate you bringing this to us. It's certainly worth discussing." He glanced about the crowd of milling parishioners, searching for Flick. "Would you like to approach her?"

"Would you bring it up to her and perhaps allow her to think it over?" Mr. Tremain asked.

"We'd love to meet with her, if she's willing." Mrs. Tremain's eyes were bright. "Perhaps she could come see us—could all of you come to supper? Tonight?"

"I don't see why not," Peter said. After all, even if Flick didn't accept their offer, he would still like to be on friendly terms with this couple and learn more about them. "What do you say, Alice?"

Alice nodded. "Yes. Yes, I think she would appreciate that."

The Tremains bid them farewell and walked off down the street, leaving Peter and Alice, Allen cooing in Alice's arms, to track down Flick. They soon found her, standing near the door by herself—if she had spoken to Mrs. Engall, it had certainly been a brief conversation.

"What was that about?" Flick asked as they began their walk back toward the house.

Peter hesitated, glancing at Alice before answering. "They made an offer to let you live with them, if you wanted. They have the space, and they'd teach you dressmaking so you'd have a way to support yourself in the future."

Flick blinked, her brow furrowing. "I don't know them."

"I know." Peter smiled. "But they want to bless you. There's no pressure, Flick. We're not trying to send you away or anything like that."

For a moment, Flick said nothing. Then she seemed to arrive at an internal decision. "I would like to talk it over with them, at least."

"They invited us to supper tonight." Peter paused and looked at her. "We said we would go—and you were included in that invitation."

Flick nodded. "I'll go."

As they walked home, Peter couldn't help but marvel at how quickly God seemed to be answering prayers. Whatever Flick decided, it was clear to him that she—and little Allen—would have a place in this world.

Peter never doubted that God was at work, but perfect moments showing with clear certainty just how mighty He was could be difficult to spot in the messiness of day-to-day life.

Thank You for Your never-ending love and mercy, Lord.

Chapter Eleven

Early November 1886

Flick did accept the Tremains' offer—perhaps blown away by Mrs. Tremain's infectious enthusiasm, perhaps comforted by Mr. Tremain's steady kindness. But either way, within the week, Flick and baby Allen were settled in a large room, which had once belonged to the Tremains' many daughters, on the top floor of the Tremains' home, and Mrs. Tremain—who had several grandbabies of her own but was no less devoted to any baby she got her hands on—was delighted to have them there.

And Alice was alone most of the day again.

She didn't mind having the house to herself and Peter. Really, she didn't. But it was odd not to wake to the sound of Allen's fussy cries or to obsess over whether the food she prepared for breakfast was nourishing enough for a new mother.

It had given her something to do. And granted, it had been a little exhausting, as Alice's homemaking skills were still a constant work in progress, but she had grown much in the last several months.

With Flick gone, the house had never been cleaner, the laundry more promptly washed and dried and ironed, the meals more consistently warm and well-cooked and timely. Alice's small garden had little to harvest due to the lateness of their arrival home, and her pets could only take so much of her attention, given that she ignored the cats as much as possible, and Juno was a well-behaved dog.

So when, toward the end of the summer, Alice's half brother Kirk arrived in Cincinnati, bringing along a broken heart and an eight-year-old stable boy who was always into some sort of mischief, she didn't turn him away. If anything, she welcomed the distraction he brought, both because she enjoyed scolding Kirk about his broken heart—it was always a man's fault, at least when that man was a brother—and because it allowed her to do something other than sit and think about her life.

She still visited with Flick, and then, because Flick was dragged by Mrs. Tremain to every ladies' knitting circle, tea, Bible study, or other social activity in Cincinnati, Alice also ended up with a wide variety of activities to participate in. Still, she kept running into the same barrier: women fell into three categories.

First, there were those who were single and usually being unfairly pressured to marry. Alice could no longer relate to that.

Next there were those who were newlywed and hopeful and almost sickeningly in love. Maybe a little afraid to admit that there were conflicts—maybe a little terrified of what they could mean. Alice was safely past that stage. She wasn't sure she'd *had* that stage, frankly.

And then there were the mothers. Old, new, it hardly mattered—Alice couldn't participate in their conversations. She had nothing to say when they went on and on about their babies. Her babies were never naughty or well-behaved. She had nothing to brag or complain about. She tried to be supportive, and she asked questions, and she listened, and she was patient and kinder than she felt. She even ignored the occasional thoughtless comment, but at a certain point, she went home, and she distracted herself with what sometimes felt like remnants of a life.

Kirk got a temporary job at a Cincinnati factory, and Tommy, whom he'd brought with him, kept Alice company and gave her plenty to think about with his sometimes harebrained, sometimes overly creative mischief.

And Alice learned again that the best way to take the edge off her own suffering was to serve—not to the point of exhaustion, not as a way to avoid pain, but by lovingly investing in the stories of others.

It was humbling and yet a lesson that God had attempted to teach her often enough that she rolled her eyes at herself and offered a prayer for forgiveness when she realized it.

Toward the end of October, Kirk was given an opportunity to move to Louisville and work in a wealthy man's stable there. He would take Tommy with him, and Alice was already planning how she'd find ways to serve God and others once Kirk was gone.

That didn't mean Alice wasn't taking advantage of his somewhat excessive gratitude for letting him and Tommy stay with her and Peter for a bit. Oh, no; if it had been anyone else, she would have insisted her guests simply relax, but because it was Kirk—and Alice enjoyed making Kirk suffer—she had the boys chopping wood.

Might as well fill the woodshed before they left, and save Peter the sore shoulders, she thought.

She couldn't help grinning to herself as she watched through the window while Kirk showed Tommy—not for the first time—how to stack wood in the lean-to woodshed so it wouldn't topple over easily. Having Tommy "help" meant the job took Kirk far longer, yet he'd still managed to create a significant pile of chopped wood that now needed stacking.

At last, Kirk stepped back, shook his head, pointed at the pile, and seemed to commence a speech that was doubtless about responsibility and how Tommy *had none* and why stacking this wood was an important experience of manhood, a mountain to climb on the path to adulthood, and that Tommy must scale on his own.

Then he stuck the axe in one of the few remaining unchopped log quarters he'd hauled in the weekend before, having borrowed Riley's wagon and taken Tommy on an expedition to a lumber mill near the river, and marched toward the house, looking stormy.

He slammed through the kitchen door and glared at Alice.

"Please tell me you're not being too hard on my nephew," she teased.

The glare only intensified. "He is not my son."

"Oh, be nice." Alice dropped the towel she'd been holding over the edge of the sink. "He tries so hard to please you. You're his hero. He'll learn!"

"If only you could be so charitable with me and my ongoing struggles with 'fatherhood.'" Kirk's tone dripped with sarcasm. In truth, Tommy was more a little brother to him than a son, but Kirk still seemed determined to train up the boy as if he were his own.

In truth, Alice thought Kirk would be a good father, someday, once he figured things out with the woman he loved (presumably by throwing himself at her feet), but Kirk had put an official stop to their conversations on this subject. "Have you left him there to sort out how to stack that huge pile on his own?"

Kirk sat at the table. "I'll go back, but I just wanted to sit down for a moment."

"Tea?" She'd already put the kettle on. "I was going to have some."

Kirk nodded, and in a few minutes, they were both seated at the table with a cup of tea. They sipped in silence, which was only broken by the occasional mumble of Peter from his office and, once, the sound of the woodpile falling over.

Kirk winced but once again said nothing.

"You'll be leaving soon," Alice said finally. Perhaps it was better to just talk about it. "I'll miss you, you know. It's been nice having you around."

Kirk glanced at her, then down at his cup. "Yes. I suppose I'll miss you, too."

"You will?" She grinned. "See, your stoic demeanor has some downsides. How am I supposed to know that you care about me, your sister, if you refuse to say anything?"

"As if you're any better," he said dryly. "I've known cats friendlier than you."

"I will pretend I didn't hear that." Alice leaned forward, resting her elbows on the table. "I suppose it'll be nice to have things settle down around here. We're going to Virginia for Christmas—Peter's family demands it and they pay our fares, plus Peter can work there as well as here—but then I hope we'll have a long rest. It seems ever since I got married, it's been a long string of one thing after another."

They lapsed into silence again, but this time it was Kirk who broke the stillness. "Can I ask you something? It's personal."

"Anything," she said. "I reserve the right not to answer, if it doesn't suit me."

Kirk stared into his tea, his brow furrowing. "Are you all right?"

"Am I ... all right?" she said slowly, trying to avoid squinting, which was an unladylike mannerism. He could confuse her sometimes, though. "I suppose so. Are ... you all right?"

"No, I mean ..." He stopped and seemed to swallow. "I know about your children. I'm sorry I never said anything, but I did pray. And I want to know, before I leave here, that you are all right."

Alice's breath caught. She hadn't expected him to bring *that* up, though she supposed she shouldn't have been surprised. "I am healing in God, and that's about the best I can do," she said. "I am not always or even often miserable. Some days, it's a dull ache—like a shadow that never quite leaves. Other days, it feels as if I can't breathe for the weight of it. It comes and goes. That said, Peter has made me very happy—after I let God work on my heart and began to let Peter love and understand me. And he has learned how to comfort me and make me feel safe. So that has given me a great deal of security, which is what we all need to rest and grow. I really don't mind talking about it, so you needn't look so uncomfortable. I'm fine. We're fine. Really."

Kirk nodded, his jaw tightening. "I was so scared for you ... back then. When—when Mr. Knight brought you to the stables after ..." He trailed off.

Oh. Alice hadn't even thought of that. He would have been at the stables when Father rode back with her, after she'd tried to take her own life. "You remember that?"

"Of course I do." Kirk's voice had a rough edge. "You were unconscious, soaked through, and so pale. I thought you were dead. I didn't know what to do. I couldn't do anything, except pray, and hate Parker for what he'd done to you. I knew it must be that, Alice. I knew it." A darkness passed over Kirk's face. "I've never been so afraid in my life. I thought maybe I should have told you when I knew—but I wouldn't have been able to soften the blow. I honestly didn't think you'd come back from it. But you did. You're stronger than I'll ever be."

Alice shook her head. "It wasn't strength, Kirk. It was grace. God's grace. I can't live in that past. I've told you that before. Peter never would have let me, anyway—he pulled me back from the edge. But you couldn't have, so I don't want you blaming yourself. There's been enough of that—blaming the wrong people in our lives for our misfortune."

Kirk went silent. When he spoke again, he'd lowered his voice slightly. "I have often done so. God's been teaching me about that. I have some repenting to do, and I've been turning to Him. But I don't know how anyone can avoid being angry when they have to watch a man destroy their lives."

"Is my life destroyed, Kirk?" Alice looked around the kitchen and laughed. "This is not Pearlbelle Park, but I'm happier here than I would have been in a giant mansion, living against God's will. I have experienced loss, but much of that, no one could have predicted. I believe that everything has happened as it was supposed to happen. I believe that God loved and chose me. I have a husband who loves me, a beautiful home, and my own sort of family. God has provided for us so abundantly through Peter's work that we never have to worry about money. And you—you'll have a new job in Kentucky, and if you just could be a little more impulsive, you could have a wife—"

"Leave it," Kirk said, but it was said with good humor and a slight grin.

"I will." She shrugged. "Though my point stands. God has never been far from either of us. Parker hasn't won. He caused pain and destruction, but God is in control, and 'destruction shall be to the workers of iniquity,' to quote Proverbs."

Kirk nodded solemnly. "You're right. I hope you appreciate me saying that."

"I do," she said airily. "But really—God is in control. He has planned our paths. We have only to trust Him. And I would never say that Parker ought to be allowed to continue behaving as he does, but if we are unforgiving in our hearts, it is our relationship with God that could be damaged. 'And when ye stand praying, forgive, if ye have ought against any: that your Father also which is in heaven may forgive you your trespasses.' Mark 11:25."

Kirk smiled. "It's true what they say about spouses becoming like each other. I've never heard you quoting Scripture before."

"You just must not have listened," she said, though he was probably right. Peter had taught her a lot over the years.

Kirk cast her a skeptical look before finishing his tea and setting the cup down. "Could I ask you another invasive question?"

Alice did narrow her eyes this time. "All right, you're one to talk about people changing when you want to ask me two questions in a row."

He grunted. "I just know I won't talk to you for a while. I'm not going to write."

"You are. But go on."

Kirk seemed to struggle for a moment before asking, "Do you ever think about adoption? I know that's not a nice question to ask, but I wonder. With what happened with you, and me as well, to a degree, I thought perhaps ... perhaps you might think of it differently than others would."

Alice pressed her lips together. "Yes. We've talked about it. We've prayed about it a lot, too. We're just not sure yet."

Kirk hesitated, then shrugged. "I don't know. I guess I've always been afraid of how people see me—as illegitimate. There's a certain ... There are beliefs about orphans, or people conceived out of wedlock, as we were, and I wondered if you—"

"Kirk." Alice did something entirely unlike herself then. She reached across the table and took his hand. "You don't believe them, do you?"

Kirk cocked his head. "I try not to. But you know how people are treated ... I mean, or you can guess."

"No one even knows—about either of us."

"Yes." He sighed. "But I know."

"That seems like something God could help you with," she said. "I won't pretend I always believed I had worth. I mean, you know I didn't. I was so angry and confused and ..." She bit back the tears and shook them away with a jerk of her head. "I didn't do what I did lightly. I felt like it would be better if I did. Oh, don't say anything. I don't want to talk about that. I've gone over it and over it with Peter and Nettie and others, and I've come to peace with it. The truth was, I had been made to feel that people like us—who weren't born in wedlock to two loving, Christian parents—were worthless. Immoral. But those thoughts weren't from God, and a society that encourages that kind of cruelty is hardly worth engaging in. That's another reason I'm glad I'm where I'm at. I couldn't stand living in the society I grew up in! I barely survived the one season I had. I'm not cut out for society. I can't stand the judgment that inevitably comes when a group of people decides on what the mark of perfection is. I never was perfect—and I hated myself for it, and I hated others for not being perfect, too. But you won't be like me, will you? Bitter and foolish, almost losing everything to conform to the stupid ideas of those who didn't have my best interests at heart?"

For a long moment, Kirk held her gaze. "I can't say you're right two times in the same day. It'd be embarrassing."

Alice felt the tension leave her shoulders, and she nodded. "I understand. But still, I hope you'll think about my words."

Kirk offered a slight smile. "I will indeed." He shoved the chair back and stood. "Thank you. Really. For everything."

"Oh, I think I've made you pay more than enough," she said, nodding toward the door. "Go on out and help Tommy, why don't you? Maybe it'll remind you that God has let you have a chance to rescue someone like you were never rescued. Maybe it'll give you a little insight on grace." She winked.

Kirk groaned. "Not everything is a lesson. You're worse than Nettie now—a lot worse, as you are only right maybe a quarter of the time."

Alice shoved him toward the door, and this time, he went.

December 1886
Clairdelune
Eleanor, Virginia

The snow in Virginia was deep and wet, and Alice didn't want to stay out in this miserable weather any longer than she had to.

Unfortunately, according to Riley, it was perfect sledding weather, and he knew the perfect hill.

Also unfortunately, Riley had failed to mention that the hill was approximately a mile from the mansion of Clairdelune, where they'd started out.

At least he made their Christmases memorable, one way or another. Was it just his way of removing himself from his mother's household as long as humanly possible? Absolutely. Did Alice blame him? Not at all. Mrs. Farjon was as cold as she was bitter, and it was far better to brave the weather than her glares, so the young people inevitably found ways to entertain themselves and their children out of doors.

Alice wasn't going to be left behind watching her mother-in-law try to chat with her prickly sister while their respective husbands looked on in awkward silence.

Alice laced her fingers through Peter's and tugged him along. His first response was to match her quick steps, but as they passed by the still, cold lilac bushes that circled the Farjon family graveyard, he slowed, his steps becoming steady and deliberate.

She frowned. What madness was this?

"You know, I wish I could believe you were holding my hand because you wanted to," he commented, his tone more amused than censorious, "and not because I was walking too slowly."

He stopped, and she halted with him, allowing herself to be pulled into an embrace. "Peter, we are never going to get anywhere—" she started in frustration.

He kissed her, and when he withdrew, he still kept her by his side, refusing to let her pull away or run to catch up with the others. "I have a secret to tell you."

She barely restrained herself from rolling her eyes. "Yes?"

"I'm in love with you."

She laughed. "I'm rather fond of you, too. Now can we—?"

He kissed her again.

This time, a shout came from up ahead: "Penn! Get off her and keep up!"

Alice drew away swiftly, feeling suddenly rather flustered—had she truly half forgotten they were in public? "We should go."

With a sigh, Peter took her hand again. "I'm not in a hurry to get to whatever Riley has planned, and I want to talk to you."

Alice sighed too but didn't argue. If Peter wanted to walk at his own pace, she supposed she'd let him. After all, he wasn't wrong about Riley's plans—suffering and Riley went hand in hand. It was easier to indulge Peter than to try to drag him along at the energetic speed Riley seemed to expect from everyone.

"All right, what do you want to talk about?" she asked.

Peter's expression shifted, his smile fading. He glanced over Alice's shoulder, as though making sure the rest of the family was out of earshot, and then turned his attention back to her. "This is going to be an … interesting Christmas."

Alice grimaced. "When is it not?"

Peter shook his head. "More than usual. It's about Aunt Georgiana."

Alice's frown deepened. "You think she'll say something to Flick?"

"I don't know. I wouldn't put it past her," Peter admitted in a low voice. "She's still furious about Essie running off. She'll never forgive Essie, but she comes from the oldest school. To her, it's a woman's responsibility to keep her husband from straying." He seemed to catch Alice's expression, because he nodded in agreement. "I know. It's wrong to blame a woman for her husband's sin, but you understand how cruel people can be. It wouldn't matter what she believed, though. Flick ... well, other than Riley, who will doubtless be scolded, too, Flick is the easiest target left."

Alice squeezed his hand. "It'll be all right."

Peter cocked his head and regarded her with a mix of suspicion and affection—or so she hoped. "How can you be so sure?"

"Because I won't let Aunt Georgiana hurt Flick." Alice's tone was as firm as she could make it. "Flick has enough to deal with, without Aunt Georgiana adding to it. If she says anything—*anything*—"

Peter's lips twitched, a hint of a smile returning. "You'd go toe-to-toe with Aunt Georgiana for Flick?"

"Absolutely." Alice didn't hesitate about that. It was a fact, plain and simple. "I'll defend her just like I'd defend you."

His smile grew, and he leaned over to kiss her cheek. "I am honored to have your protection."

"Penn!" Riley, up ahead, had once again noticed the pause. "Can you keep it in the bedroom and actually walk at a normal human pace?"

"You're lucky I'm here at all!" Peter shouted back. "If you don't want me to turn back around and march back to the warm house, you can be quiet."

Thankfully, Riley was too distracted by various other members of the sledding party to reply.

"Come on," Alice said, tugging Peter forward. "You'll survive. It's just sledding."

"It's never *just* sledding with Riley," Peter muttered, but he allowed her to pull him along.

"Don't be such a baby."

"Ah, yes, now see, I've tried that mentality." He gave a halfhearted tug away from her. "I've tried that, and I ended up with multiple broken limbs, and I almost drowned. Twice. Not to mention the amount of times I suddenly found myself having to escape a situation I certainly didn't want to be in."

She was the one who stopped them this time, putting both of her hands on his arms, and gave him what she hoped was a very firm look. "This is sledding, Peter."

"You'd be surprised how many people are injured sledding." Peter's voice dropped into a conspiratorial tone. "Especially when Riley's involved."

Alice couldn't help but laugh. "You'll survive. And besides, we have the babies to protect us if things get too wild. We can offer their parents' arms a rest, and that'll keep us out of the fray."

"Oh, brilliant. Use the infants as human shields." Peter made a sound somewhere between a laugh and a groan, but he offered her his arm, and they trudged onward, catching up with the others as the group reached the crest of the sledding hill.

The scene was chaotic at best. All the children were still quite young; three were infants, and Caroline's second-youngest was barely a toddler. Nonetheless, Riley had his two daughters and Caroline's two eldest assigned sleds and was shouting instructions to organize an ill-designed race.

"See?" Peter murmured, already easing them over to where Flick and Caroline had settled on a log and were chatting while trying to keep their babies warm. Unfortunately, the outdoors was far more hospitable than the inside of Clairdelune. "If any of my nieces or nephews are injured—"

"It'll be fine." Alice patted his arm. "We should see if we can help. Barnaby can't manage their three by himself."

As if anticipating this, Riley waved her over. "Alice, you take Maudie down. No, honey." This was said to his wife. "Polly should go down by herself. No, no, she's too old to be coddled. So is Susie for that matter, but I'm willing to—" And then he got distracted instructing Barnaby, who looked like a man being slowly tortured to death, on how to properly hold his younger son while sliding down the hill.

Barnaby protested that he wouldn't be joining any race with Howie, who was barely a toddler. Furthermore, his oldest son could manage alone; if Alice took Maudie, he would much rather go sit with his wife. Riley disagreed. Peter politely suggested he be quiet, and Riley lobbed a snowball at Peter's head and then grabbed Susie and positioned her sled, explaining that she was the princess of racing sleds and would win—must win—as

Polly had apparently rebelled against this competitiveness.

At last, though, there was a race of sorts, with Dahlia, who apparently could not be kept down despite having given birth not quite two months ago, being declared the winner.

After this, the spirit of organization was gladly lost, and Alice took Maudie and Susie down the hill several times each—and Howie once, after Barnaby grew tired of hauling sleds and children up and down.

At last, exhausted, they all began the trek back home, thankfully soon discovering that apparently, someone at the house had anticipated the folly of their expedition and sent sleighs with warm blankets to meet them.

Alice was just ashamed she hadn't thought to request it herself.

Chapter Twelve

"Do you remember?" Riley asked, looking around the tiny shed, "the wondrous lives we had planned for ourselves here?"

Peter, in the act of trying to lift a sled up onto the hooks suspended on the wall, paused and glanced around the cramped space overflowing with mismatched items—gardening supplies, an axe, tools, and the old sleds. "I suppose I do." The shed had inevitably been less full in the summer, as implements were removed by the gardeners, and it was the perfect fort for two little boys. "I never wanted to be an adventurer like you, though."

"No, you were always going to write great books." Riley grinned. "And of course you have."

Peter laughed. "You're an expert of literature now, are you?"

Riley paused and blinked, as if he'd not considered that he might not be. "You're *my* favorite author."

Peter rolled his eyes. "Remind me what *other* books you have read this year?"

"It's called *monogamy*, Penn," Riley said with great dignity. "I am faithful to the author of my youth."

Peter attempted to throw a loose gardening glove at him; it flapped to the floor like a sad green bird.

Riley looked at the glove then at Peter. "Still got that same throwing arm, I see."

"'*Monobiblio*,'" Peter said after a minute. "'*Gamos*' means *marriage*. *Monogamy*—single marriage. '*Monobiblio*'—single book."

Riley laughed. "Greek is not my native tongue."

"My grammar is wrong anyway, and I don't remember the word for *author*." Peter grunted and lifted a second sled onto a peg. "Anyway, you didn't go to China or even California, and you never learned to walk a tightrope or invented any interesting machines."

Riley chuckled. "I might some day. But I suppose I've been happier without any of those adventures—I don't think it would've meant much without Maddie and the girls. What's the point, really? It sounds glamorous, but I can't imagine it'd be all that fulfilling. Not to mention I couldn't live near you if I were running around the world doing whatever 'adventuring' entails. I presume a lawyer both makes more and loses less money, too. Though I think my quarterly earnings don't *quite* stack up to one of your royalty checks these days." He grinned and winked. "Perhaps you should have been the adventurer."

"No, it's far too expensive, even for me. One might even say it's not a legitimate career." Peter hung the last sled and turned to Riley, who was fiddling around with a wooden hoop that had somehow gotten twisted out of shape.

"I bet I could fix this," Riley said.

"But would you?"

"Maybe."

Peter grinned. Riley was notorious for picking up projects that involved some form of carpentry and then dropping them. "I'm sure your parents wouldn't miss it."

"I'm sure it *was* mine." Riley hefted the hoop onto his shoulder. "I'll fix it up, and maybe we can teach Polly to roll it."

Peter wasn't sure Polly would be up for that—she could be such a sedate little thing—but he nodded. "I think she'd like that." She'd like anything Riley did for her; she adored her father.

It struck Peter that he'd never truly pictured Riley as a good father. That is, not until he'd first seen Riley with Polly in his arms.

He remembered Riley, coming out of the bedroom back in Philadelphia. A crisp January morning had been brightened by Polly's presence, after a long night where Peter had watched Riley pace and pretended he wasn't scared out of his mind, which he was—they both were. Polly had been a tiny thing tucked in Riley's arms, all red and wrinkled and angry, and Riley himself had been a mess of laughter and tears, telling Peter that Maddie was all right, that it was a girl, that she was perfect.

Peter shook his head to dislodge the somewhat foolish smile on his face.

"What's that about?" Riley smacked him with the hoop as they exited the shed—though that might have been an accident, as it was somewhat unwieldy.

"Oh, nothing." Peter shrugged, reaching up to rub his shoulder. "It just seems as though it was only yesterday that we were running around Clairdelune—remember that summer? Playing in the creek, talking about El Dorado and the Mississippi and Lilliput as if they were all equally mysterious."

Riley laughed. "You mean that summer your mother brought Maddie down, and I threw her book in the creek, and you tried to kill me?"

Peter had forgotten that. "That might've been the one."

"I said we didn't need another girl around here, and you insisted I give her a chance and called me some mild, hardly offensive name, and I pushed you into the creek."

Now Peter remembered. He stopped, standing in the snowy yard, and frowned. "You knew very well I couldn't swim."

"That's how you learn, Penn," Riley called, walking on ahead.

"I could've drowned."

"What's that?" Riley cupped his free hand around his ear. "Do I hear the faint voice of my cousin Peter? Surely not. He died at eleven after a fatal creek accident. They never knew *why* he went into that water ... You see, the poor lad was a coward who couldn't swim."

Peter rolled his eyes and followed Riley. What would he do? He wasn't about to even try starting a snowball fight. He would inevitably lose. "You know—"

"Sometimes I can still hear his voice ..." Riley continued as he disappeared into the house.

Christmas Eve

The trek to collect the towering evergreen Riley had hunted out the year before had been miserable, with snow flying and temperatures dropping; but at last the tree was placed in the largest drawing room at Clairdelune, and Peter, ignoring Riley, was hanging ornaments wherever he thought best.

He knew his best friend's enthusiasm was a mask for his nerves. Aunt Georgiana had never been kind to her younger son. Riley, who by all accounts had made something of himself without his parents' help, would always be a disappointment to her. Simply put, Riley wasn't CJ, his brother who had died in the war. There was nothing Riley could do to change this—and yet, somehow it continued to be held against him.

As such, Aunt Georgiana reigned over the decorating process, eyes always slightly narrowed as if she were never without a headache and the cause of it was her family, her only living son being the primary target. Her husband, Uncle Colin, lived in a different world, one where he perhaps didn't have to feel so much—which Peter could understand, but it meant that Aunt Georgiana must be very alone the other eleven and a half months of the year.

Usually, Peter's mother did a good enough job keeping Aunt Georgiana entertained, allowing everyone else to have vestiges of a merry Christmas. Unfortunately, Mama had never had to deal with the way her older sister acted when confronted with one of her children running off with a married man, especially given said man's abandoned wife and infant were staying at Clairdelune for the duration of the holiday.

Peter draped a garland and stepped back to admire his handiwork. It wasn't perfect, but it was far better to do than listening to Aunt Georgiana's clipped commentary or watching Riley pace like a caged animal. Alice reached around Peter and adjusted the garland with deliberate care. Fortunately, he had long ago decided not to fight her "small tweaks" to any decorating he did. It seemed to soothe her, and usually the changes were miniscule.

Riley circled the tree again, Susie on his shoulders so she could spot the places that needed to be evened out. "I don't know, Miss Rosey. What do you think?"

"It's not right, Daddy," she told him.

"Everyone's a critic," Riley said, and laughed. "I'm just about to ask Polly and not you. What do you think about that empty spot up there? Do I need to move the garland up a branch?"

"Let Aunt Alice do it," Polly suggested, tugging at his trouser leg.

Riley's eyes flew wide in faked shock. "Maddie! Did you hear your daughter?"

"*My* daughter?" Maddie asked mildly, continuing to rummage through an old crate that was mostly empty. "At least listen to Peter if he tells you something's wrong."

"He's never listened to anyone before," Aunt Georgiana said. "It'd be a miracle if he started now."

Peter glanced at Riley, catching the flicker of anger behind his friend's eyes. But Riley merely exhaled sharply, adjusted Susie on his shoulders, and stepped back so Alice could "fix" the garland, which was perfectly acceptable.

Peter knew without asking that Riley didn't mind Alice, not really. It was his mother who drove him mad.

"I think those are the biggest pieces. Here, Susie," Riley said, holding a candle clip up to her. "Make sure it's nice and straight, or the wax will drip."

Susie nodded eagerly, her little hands taking the clip and carefully placing it where Riley directed. Peter thought the branch was sagging slightly under the weight, which could prove troublesome later, but he wisely kept his mouth shut.

Meanwhile, Aunt Georgiana leaned back in her chair, her expression as impassive as ever. "At least one of you knows how to follow instructions."

The room fell silent for a beat, save for the soft crackle of the fire. Lilli was the first to break the silence, her tone overly cheerful. "That's a lovely spot for it, Susie! Doesn't the tree look nice, Colin?"

Uncle Colin startled slightly. "Hm? Oh, yes. Very nice." He returned to staring into the fire.

Peter exchanged a glance with Alice, who gave him a small, helpless shrug. She moved to adjust another garland, but he could see the tension in her shoulders.

Riley took a step back. "What do you think now, Polly? Are we ruining things?"

Polly shuffled over, her thumb in her mouth. Peter noticed Aunt Georgiana's lips tighten slightly at the gesture but, thankfully, she said nothing.

"It's ... good," Polly said after a moment.

"High praise from a tough critic," Riley said with a grin, though his tone carried an edge now. He turned back to the tree, muttering under his breath, "Not the toughest one here."

"Riley," Aunt Georgiana said sharply, her voice cutting through the room.

"What?" His expression was tense, his smile gone. "We all know nothing I do will ever please you, so you'd be foolish to believe I'll keep trying. I understand; I'm the disappointing son."

Aunt Georgiana's eyes flashed. "Don't bring your brother into this."

"CJ, is it?" Riley's laugh was short and bitter. He shook his head with a small smile and lowered his daughter to the floor, though all Susie did was wrap her arms around his leg and hold tight. "It always comes back to him, doesn't it? Funny how he's the only one who's ever done anything right in this house, and he's been dead for over twenty years."

"*Riley*," Peter started, his tone placating, but Riley waved him off.

"No. I'm tired of pretending this is normal. Every year, we come here, and it's the same thing. CJ was perfect, CJ could do no wrong, and the rest of us—" He gestured around the room, his voice rising. "The rest of us will never live up to his massive shadow, will we? But would he really have lived up to your standards if he were with us today?"

"That is enough." Aunt Georgiana's voice was still sharp, and her composure didn't waver. "You will not speak of your brother that way."

"I'm not speaking of CJ in any sort of way," Riley replied, his shrug halfhearted. "I'm speaking of you. Of the way you've spent your life stuck in the past, holding the rest of us to an impossible standard that even he couldn't have lived up to—because no one could. It's not based on any reality. It's based on an idealized but untrue narrative of a world that never really existed. And look where it's gotten you. Eleanor won't come home for Christmas; Essie ran off with Terry; and you sit here blaming everyone but yourself."

"This has nothing to do with Essie," Aunt Georgiana said, her voice colder than ever. "Her disgrace is no one's fault but her own. I'm ashamed of her."

"Oh, of course." Riley's voice dripped with sarcasm. "It couldn't possibly have anything to do with the fact that she grew up seeing a Christianity with no grace and hardly any truth, bent on maintaining appearance and mourning a past that's long gone. She never had a chance. If it weren't for Penn, do you think I'd be here now?"

"Now, see here, Riley—" Aunt Georgiana's voice raised another notch. "I won't be hearing that in my own home. You can—"

"And Flick?" Riley continued. "You want to blame her, too? For not keeping Terry in line? Terry made his choices, just like Essie did. And if you keep trying to pin their mistakes on everyone else, you'll drive away what's left of this family."

Aunt Georgiana's lips thinned, her hands gripping the arms of her chair. "You don't understand—"

"No, I do understand." Riley lowered his voice, every word quiet and deliberate. "Your bitterness is keeping you from having a future with the family you do have. If you've ever said one kind word to my wife, I haven't heard it. I know you've never cared about me, except to scold and berate. One day, you'll wake up and realize it's too late."

The silence that followed was absolute. Aunt Georgiana's gaze didn't waver, but Peter saw something flicker in her expression—something fragile, almost vulnerable, that he had never witnessed before. Uncle Colin shifted uncomfortably in his seat, but said nothing.

Riley didn't move for a moment, his shoulders still tense, but eventually he exhaled. "I don't want to ruin Christmas for everyone, especially the children. Let's drop it."

Stiffly, Aunt Georgiana rose and exited the room. After a long moment, Uncle Colin followed her.

And everything felt a little lighter.

Hours later, when the house was quiet and their respective wives were tucked in bed, Peter and Riley sat in the parlor before the glittering Christmas tree, drank coffee, and talked.

In truth, Peter was worried about leaving Riley just yet. Riley had never really spoken to his parents that way since becoming a Christian—and Peter felt it had been long overdue. If he could do anything to encourage Riley to, calmly and respectfully, stand by what he had said, Peter would do so.

"I knew it had to be said," Riley was explaining as he drummed his fingers restlessly on the arm of his chair. "I've known for a while, though I wasn't sure I would say anything at Christmas. But in truth, Maddie and I had a long talk about my parents, and some of the things they said about her, and I knew it was past time to confront them."

"Oh?" Peter said carefully. Riley and Maddie had clearly had some ups and downs in the last few months, ever since Terry left Flick, but it seemed things had finally begun to level out. However, Peter hadn't wanted to pry.

"Yes." Riley picked up his mug, which was half full. "A few times, actually. We've had some long talks lately, about our family and what we want for the future. Remember what we talked about? Last summer, I mean?"

"Yes." How could Peter forget?

"I think we're in a much better spot. I can't share everything without breaking Maddie's privacy, but she helped me understand some of what she's been thinking and feeling, and I believe she heard me when I expressed my own concerns. We'll be all right." Riley took a sip of his coffee. "And if any of this comes back around, at least we'll know how to address it better."

"Sometimes knowing what went wrong in the first place can be the first step to avoiding it happening again." Peter stared into the blackness of his coffee and thought of his own marriage. "I hope it means I can avoid my past mistakes as a husband and better anticipate what Alice may be feeling when we experience certain things. It's no guarantee—but I know God will help me if and when we navigate more rough patches in our relationship."

"What went wrong with you?" Riley said after a long silence. "With you and Alice, I mean?"

Peter laughed wryly. "You know most of it. We didn't talk about anything we should have, and I didn't listen to what she was trying to say when she did talk. I was not a good husband to Alice. It's a miracle she's managed to forgive me."

Riley shook his head and set his cup down. "No man but you would take on all the blame, Penn."

"I don't feel that pointing fingers does any good; but I knew she was lost and wounded—I knew that before I married her, really—and I looked past it because my pride and my idea of logic were more important to me than my wife. I told myself it was all right, and that surely the past would not follow us into the present. I should have read between the lines and understood how deeply she was feeling about … everything. I let her be insecure about Maddie when I could have eased her mind by setting a few simple boundaries. I let her feel like she wasn't good enough when I could have seen the reason behind that and addressed it at once. If you think I'm forgetting that any time soon—if you think I'm *ever* forgetting that—you're wrong."

"No … no." Riley shook his head. "I don't think I could either, in your place. Alice was so tightly wound when you married her, Penn; I should have warned you. But she was so young, and I thought …" He shrugged. "It doesn't matter. You wouldn't have taken advice from me."

"No." Peter winced. "I wouldn't let you tell me anything, would I?"

"And I have such good advice!" Riley waved his hand, which was still holding his cup. Thankfully, it was mostly empty. "I could have told you to be careful with her, but you would have been *too* careful. There's a balance to such things, Penn," he added with an air of ancient wisdom. He rubbed at his chin with his free hand, as if stroking a long beard, though the effect was ruined by his clean-shaven cheeks. "Regardless, I'm not letting any more of my innocent friends 'discover things on their own.' That plainly doesn't work."

Peter rolled his eyes. "How many innocent friends do you have now?"

"None that I am close enough to talk to on such subjects." Riley shook his head. "It's more a note for the future. I plan on lecturing my sons, though discreetly. Despite what you think, I don't believe in interfering with the sacredness of marriage—you're right that some people make too light of it—but no one should enter an intimate relationship thinking they know everything because they understand the basic mechanics. Too many men and women suffer in the marriage bed in a way that is nearly blasphemous to God's intentions for the act. Now, don't you argue with me, Penn!"

Peter had absolutely opened his mouth to protest his past self's complete ignorance. After all, he had *some* pride, even if Riley was essentially correct. No amount of desire and willingness could have altered his mistake, especially with Alice so tormented by her own thoughts.

Riley continued, "That's water under the bridge, but I'm glad things are where they are now—for both our marriages."

"Yes." Peter could feel nothing but contentment for where they were. "I don't always expect it, but more and more, I see so much joy and happiness in life, and a great deal of it is purely because God gifted me Alice. Not that we can't find joy in any circumstance in God. 'Thou wilt shew me the path of life: in Thy presence is fulness of joy; at Thy right hand there are pleasures for evermore.'"

"Psalm something?" Riley guessed.

Peter nodded. "16:11."

Riley stood and stretched. "Speaking of our wives, I'd best get off to bed before Maddie sends out a search party. I'll see you in the morning."

"Yes. Good night, Rye."

"Good night, Penn."

Chapter Thirteen

March 1887
Cincinnati, Ohio

THE REST OF WINTER and the beginning of spring were largely uneventful. Peter and Alice briefly visited Boston in February to attend a wedding, but they could only stay a few days before they returned to Cincinnati. Peter kept busy with his writing, and when he wasn't working, he enjoyed every moment with his wife. Alice was more and more occupied these days, but she kept her evenings largely for him; and it was nice, for a change, to be at home, just the two of them—with the dog and the cats.

One evening, when the snow was finally starting to melt, Peter made his way to Riley's house after supper. Earlier that day, his cousin had sent a note, scribbled in haste and almost illegible, asking Peter to come by to help him sort through some papers. Riley's knack for getting himself buried in disorganized stacks of letters, receipts, and random doodles was legendary, but Peter couldn't help laughing at the idea that Riley thought *Peter* would be the one to impose order on it all. After all, *Alice* organized Peter's random papers for him. But the note had been unusually insistent, and Peter suspected there might be something more behind the request.

Peter knocked on the door, which was flung open almost immediately. Riley stood there, his sleeves rolled up and his hair in its usual state of disarray. He grinned broadly, stepping aside to let Peter in.

"Come on in, Penn. Don't mind the chaos—Maddie's resting, and I bribed the girls to play upstairs so we can get some actual work done."

Peter chuckled. "I didn't know sorting papers qualified as 'actual work,' but I'll do my best." He stepped into the warm home. A small stack of mismatched boots cluttered the entryway. *Odd.* "Is Maddie ill?"

"Uh … what?" Riley said, sounding distracted. He was already halfway to his study—or what passed for one. Peter followed him, surmising that Maddie *was* ill, and Riley was running on too many cups of coffee and however many hours of sleep the girls had allowed him.

Papers were scattered across the desk and spilling onto the floor.

Peter raised his eyebrows. "This is quite the collection."

Riley shrugged. "What can I say? I thrive on a system no one else understands."

"'System,'" Peter mumbled, but settled into a chair by the desk without further complaint, Riley taking the other one. The two of them began to sift through the chaos, Riley occasionally making jokes about his own messiness and Peter shaking his head in amusement. It wasn't long before Peter noticed Riley seemed a little distracted. He kept glancing toward the door, tapping his fingers on the desk when they weren't busy sorting.

"Out with it," Peter finally said, dropping a stack of papers. "You didn't ask me over just for this."

Riley looked sheepish for a moment, then his grin returned, wider than ever. He leaned forward, lowering his voice as though sharing a secret with a conspirator. "You're right."

Peter frowned slightly and waited.

Riley leaned back in his chair, looking uncharacteristically serious for a moment. Then he slapped his knees and grinned again. "Maddie is expecting. October, if all goes well. We wanted you to know before anyone else."

Peter stared at his best friend for a long moment, processing the words. Then a smile spread across his face. "Riley, that's wonderful news. Congratulations."

Riley waved a hand. "Thanks, thanks. But listen—I know you and Alice

… I *know*. I didn't want her to find out whenever Maddie is ready to tell everyone else. So I thought maybe you'd tell her when it feels like the right time."

Peter felt a lump rise in his throat. He should have expected Riley to be that thoughtful, but he sometimes forgot how well Riley knew him—and by extension, knew Alice. He nodded, swallowing hard. "Alice will be thrilled for you both. And Polly and Susie—they'll love having a little one around."

"They're already campaigning for names," Riley said. "Susie thinks it should be *Rosey* if it's a girl. I tried to explain how that could be confusing given that we often have called her *Rosey*, but that didn't seem to penetrate."

Peter chuckled. "She wants a namesake?"

"Yes." Riley grinned. "Maddie hopes it's a boy, but you know I don't care for that much. But if it is a boy, I think I'm a little more ready now to have a son than I was when Polly and Susie came along." For years, Riley had resisted the idea of raising a little man. For whatever reason, he'd tensed up at the thought and been infinitely relieved when his first two were daughters. "It doesn't matter, though; God knows what's best, and we're trusting Him."

"Yes, God certainly does know what's best. Thank you for telling me. Maddie's not feeling too well, I take it?"

"Yes, see, I've been sitting here trying to figure out how you knew that."

"The shoes by the door."

Riley threw back his head and laughed. "She is fastidious about her home, but I can hardly blame the woman. She has to put up with me; some part of her life should have order. Anyway, she takes such pride in it. I wish I could get her to rest sometimes." He shrugged. "But like I said, it pleases her."

"Right." Peter wasn't about to sit down and analyze the other man's wife, though, much as he did have some thoughts on *why* Maddie felt a need to organize her house so. "Was that all, or should we finish up here?"

"No, no." Riley stood, knocking three papers and a folder to the floor as he did. "As I said, I have a system."

"Very well." Peter rose, went around the desk, and embraced Riley. "I'm happy for you. Truly."

"Thanks, Penn. Will you tell Alice that I wish it were her?"

Peter hesitated, squinting at his cousin. "That's not what I wish, Rye. I wish for God's will to be done."

Riley gave Peter's arm a light shove—likely not going so far as to punch him only because Peter had repeatedly told him not to. "We are never asked *not* to pray for what we cannot achieve ourselves. I have faith! Don't you? Or do you think that you know what God has planned?"

"I admit, it can be easier not to hope," Peter said, his voice quiet. "Grief teaches you to hold things loosely."

"Right." Riley grinned. "So I suppose I'll do all the hoping for you."

"Prayers would be more appreciated."

"'Rejoicing in hope; patient in tribulation; continuing instant in prayer,' et cetera. I know *some* of the Bible, Penn." Riley winked. "I can both hope and pray at once." His grin softened. He leaned forward, his elbows scattering a few receipts onto the floor. "And sometimes, Penn, prayer needs feet. Look ..." He turned to the chaotic pile on his desk, not with his usual haphazard energy, but with a specific goal in mind. He shuffled a legal brief aside, lifted a stack of letters, and pulled out a single, folded sheet of paper covered in his nearly indecipherable handwriting.

"I took some ... unfortunate liberties," Riley began, suddenly looking a bit sheepish again. "I know we've talked about possibilities, and with my work, I hear things. I asked a colleague who has had dealings with them. I just wanted to know what the actual process was. In case you ever ... Here." He pushed the paper across the desk toward Peter.

Peter looked down at it. At the top, Riley had scrawled: "Cincinnati Orphan Asylum."

"It's the Protestant one, on Mount Auburn," Riley said quietly, all trace of his earlier boisterousness gone. "It's a formal, complicated affair, Penn. It's run by a 'Board of Lady Managers,' and from what I gather, they are very particular. You can't just go for a visit. You have to submit a formal application to their 'Committee of Admission.'" He tapped a section of his notes. "It must be accompanied by a letter of recommendation. You need someone of good standing who can vouch for you. I would write one, but I'd also ask Brett or the pastor. But you know there's any number of men and women in Cincinnati who would vouch for you."

Peter stared at the paper, the ink blurring as he tried to process Riley's words. "You found this for me?"

Riley nodded. "I know it's a lot, and maybe the timing is all wrong. But I couldn't stand the thought of you and Alice wanting to take a step and not knowing which way to turn. I wanted you to have the facts. Here's a proper door to knock on, if you ever choose to."

Peter finally lifted his gaze from the paper and looked at his cousin. He rose from his chair, his movements slow, and went around the desk to embrace Riley again, clapping him firmly on the back. His throat was too tight for speech, so he cleared it—once, then twice. "Thank you, Rye," he finally managed, his voice thick.

Riley gave his arm a light shove as they parted. "I'll pray for the decision, too."

Peter nodded, carefully folding the already crinkled paper and slipping it into his coat pocket. "Thank you. That'd be appreciated."

Alice was at the kitchen table trying to understand the irritating process of darning socks.

Oh, it wasn't truly difficult. She was just remarkably inept at it for someone who performed the task so regularly.

Which was why, when she'd fixed one sock, she tossed the rest into a basket and kicked it aside. It was too late in the evening to do something that inevitably gave her a headache. She decided to fill out the lines of a sketch she'd made of Polly the other day. So when Peter entered the house by the back door, she was rummaging through his office for her pencils, which he had moved.

"Peter?" she called. "Where are my pencils?"

Her husband appeared in the doorway of the office and glanced around. "What do you mean?"

"They were in the bottom drawer of your desk, which is now mysteriously filled with a single glove—that I don't recognize, by the way—and a scattering of papers, all apparently pertaining to edits of your novel in some way." She placed her hands on her hips. "And Riley called you over to help him organize *his* desk?"

Peter shuffled over to a shelf by the only window in his small office and moved three large books, withdrawing the small bag containing her pencils. "In my defense, I was trying to reorganize."

Alice took the bag. "I'm sure. You're back early." She picked up her drawing pad and preceded him into the kitchen, where she sat at the table.

"Riley and Maddie are expecting," he said softly. "This October, if all goes well."

Alice stilled, then nodded. She didn't have to force her smile—she wouldn't deny Riley and Maddie another child, certainly, if she had the choice. "I rather suspected that. She was by turns wan and glowing when I saw her the other day. Mrs. Engall, too," Alice said, absently flipping through her sketches. "This summer, I'd say."

"Oh, really?" Peter cocked his head. "I hadn't known they'd announced anything."

Alice shrugged. "She's hinted, more than anything, but everyone at the ladies' Bible study *knows* even though we don't really *know*."

"Oh, so it's gossip," Peter said with a slow smile. "Alice, you should know better."

She laughed. "It's *very* founded gossip about a *very* good thing! And Mrs. Engall has as good as confirmed it to Flick, though don't say I said anything."

Peter placed a hand over his heart. "And you're repeating a private confidence? *Alice*!"

"I'm happy for her, that's all."

He reached across the table and took her hands. "Riley wanted to tell me before anyone else, so I could tell you. He wanted you to know that he's still praying things will change for us."

"You'll have to thank him for me next time you see him." Alice would have handled it, but she wouldn't have liked to find out such news in a public environment, if it were at all avoidable. Somehow, being watched and pitied made everything so much worse. She sucked in a breath as a thought occurred to her. "Does Riley hope that we will conceive—or that we will adopt?"

A small smile passed over Peter's face. "Both, I think. He wants to see us be parents."

Alice started to withdraw her hands, then stopped; she was surprised by how often she needed a physical connection with Peter to cement herself in a moment. "What did he suggest? Don't tell me there's anything you and Riley *haven't* discussed."

"We have discussed it," he confirmed, "and I think Riley would like to see us raise a child, regardless of how it comes to be. We did talk about that tonight. Apparently he's looked into our options for us. That's part of what I wanted to talk to you about. You know Riley—he'd do anything to see us happy, and he's nothing if not proactive."

Alice raised her eyebrows. "You make it sound like kidnapping is a viable option."

"For Riley, maybe—but I like to avoid illegal activity where possible." Peter smiled, then his expression softened. He reached into his coat pocket and withdrew a folded sheet of paper covered with a messy scrawl, placing it on the table between them. "He simply told me what we would have to do, practically, if we were interested in pursuing adoption here in Cincinnati. Beyond the financial considerations, which he says we more than meet. He spoke to a colleague who has had dealings with the Cincinnati Orphan Asylum, which would be where we go. He wanted us to understand the proper channels, should we ever decide to … to proceed. But what about you?"

Alice was half listening to him and half trying to decipher Riley's handwriting. "What about me?"

"We haven't talked about adoption in a while."

Peter was the one who let go and drew away. She didn't like *that.*

"We've been busy, and I didn't want to …" He paused and then shook his head. "What are you thinking?"

"I'm much more open to the idea." She swallowed. "I admit I haven't thought about it much. I've kept myself busy. In some ways, I think I needed to prove to myself that I could be content and fulfilled as we are, and I believe I can. But neither do I feel strongly that God is leading us away from adoption."

Peter nodded. "I didn't want to make you think I'm not happy as we are, nor do I want to rush you or ask you to ignore your convictions. I have no doubt in my mind that if we adopted a child, we would love him or her as our own. We already love so many children who are not ours, don't we? Our nieces and nephews?"

"Yes. We do." But it was one thing to love a child, even deeply, and then always return them to their parents—and quite another to have a child who was always one's sole responsibility. As much as Alice wanted that, she could admit there was a healthy dose of fear within her at the idea, too. "But I know that process involves evaluations and … and telling people about our intentions. Doesn't that scare you a little, darling?" She swallowed again. "The truth is, I'm not at all sure I'd be a very good mother."

"Don't say that!" Suddenly, he was fierce, his eyes alight with passion. "You are *already* a mother—the only woman I would want to be the mother to my children. Don't you dare say that you wouldn't be a good mother, darling."

She avoided his eyes and fought back the heaviness in her chest. "Heaven knows I'm not the most tender woman, and I've never thought I was terribly good with children. I like them—and yes, I love our nieces and nephews. But I wasn't even the type of person who offered to watch her younger siblings except because I thought I ought to. My mother says I'm domineering. Nettie told me once that I tend to lead more by fear than love."

"When you were what? Eighteen?" Peter reached for her hand again. "Don't you think you've changed a little since then? I am sure you have."

"Perhaps. But if God has not willed that we have a child, there may be a reason for it. Obviously, that reason is not you."

"That's not reality." Peter shook his head. "We're past that, Alice. Far past thinking like that. Did Terry leave Flick because she was not deserving of a husband? What of my parents? Did they deserve to lose their children? Were you conceived because Nettie did not deserve to be loved and cherished—or treated like a human, for that matter?"

"No—no, that's just the sin of the world." She knew better now than to blame the victims—she had fought back those thoughts for so long, even though they'd become so ingrained that they felt like a part of her. "But it must sometimes be true that our actions have consequences, even ones we cannot directly control. King David's child died because he took advantage of Bathsheba and murdered Uriah. We are to follow God, and when we don't—"

"Alice." Peter gave her hands a determined squeeze. "Look at me. We all sin. I know that, and I'm not saying you're perfect, or that we deserve to have a child. But nothing that happened is because God is punishing us. He grieves with us for the loss of our sons. We have no reason to believe that those losses were the result of our sins. It would be as sinful to live in fear and undeserved shame—when we are meant to embrace God's hope and grace—as it would be to ignore our true convictions. Come here."

She let herself be tugged to her feet, around the table, and into his lap, where she could rest her head on his shoulder and pretend everything was all right.

"Would you be open to at least starting the process?" Peter's voice was quiet and hesitant. He tapped the paper on the table. "It's not as simple as walking in, I'm afraid. The Cincinnati Orphan Asylum—where Riley has connections—is run by a board of Lady Managers, women from the city's best families who have the final say in all these matters. He says the first step is to submit a formal application to their committee of admission. It must be accompanied by letters of recommendation." Peter looked up at her. "Riley said he would write one for us in a heartbeat, if we allow him."

Yes. Yes, Alice could start the process. "I would be open to that." What she didn't say is she would be open to submitting to Peter making the decision, but he would never accept that. Peter had grown a lot—maybe as much as she had—but he overanalyzed decisions.

If she admitted doubts, he would never move forward. Was it possible what he needed was to be forced to decide what direction their family would take next? She wasn't sure, but at least, she did feel peace in one thought: Peter was trustworthy. He would never willingly lead her astray.

"This puts it out of our hands, in a way," he whispered into her hair. "But from what Riley said, this could be a legitimate route forward for us. And Alice ... you *are* an excellent mother."

Suddenly too tired to argue about it, Alice simply nodded.

After talking it over between themselves, and then with Riley, Peter and Alice came up with a plan. Unfortunately for Alice, the first step of that plan involved her talking to Mrs. Engall about writing a recommendation to the Cincinnati Orphan Asylum.

According to Riley, Mrs. Engall had served on the Board before Cecelia's birth made her duties at home more extensive, and she was still involved enough to know the current Lady Managers.

"She'll know what they want to hear," Riley had said. "I'll write you a recommendation, too—but connections are everything here. Having that recommendation from Sarah would smooth the way for you."

Of course, Riley couldn't have picked another woman, with the exception of his own wife, whom Alice was more loath to ask a favor of. Mrs. Engall was a kind, to-the-point woman who had loved and advised Flick devotedly through Flick's pregnancy and continued to be a dear friend to her. She was the effortlessly genuine hostess of the weekly Bible study and prayer meeting that Alice attended. But even with all this, and even though she had been nothing but friendly to Alice, she was a dear friend of Maddie's—who knew what impressions Maddie may have given Mrs. Engall, to Alice's detriment?

But Riley had insisted, and he knew more of such things than either Alice or Peter did, so here Alice was, arriving at the Bible study a quarter of an hour early in hopes of catching Mrs. Engall alone.

The Engalls employed several servants—Dr. Engall seemed devoted to making his wife comfortable—so it was a maid who answered the door and encouraged Alice to wait in the parlor.

"Mrs. Engall should be with you in a moment, Mrs. Strauss," the maid said, then slipped out of the elegant room that somehow smelled of lavender. The decorations were simple and modern, but tasteful. Alice sank onto a chair near the window and waited.

Mrs. Engall appeared minutes later, smiling broadly.

"Mrs. Strauss, you're the first to arrive! I'm grateful to see you here early—we never get a moment to chat. How are you?"

"Very well, thank you, Mrs. Engall. Your home is lovely, as always." Alice swallowed and pushed her nerves to the back of her mind. "I confess I came early because I hoped I might have a private word with you, if you don't mind."

"Of course!" Mrs. Engall took a seat opposite and gestured for Alice to speak.

Alice took a deep breath and rushed through the speech she'd played in her mind over and over again. "As you know, my husband's cousin, Riley Farjon, is always looking for ways to be of service. He took the liberty of making some inquiries on our behalf regarding the Cincinnati Orphan Asylum. He mentioned that you had once served on one of their committees, before Cecelia was born, and suggested you would be the perfect person to offer counsel to my husband and me as we navigate this next step for our family, and perhaps, if you felt led, a letter of recommendation."

Mrs. Engall nodded along, but she gave little indication of her feelings. "I'm glad you came to me with this. I was on the board for several years, and I know the women who are still Lady Managers quite well. In fact, I was at the asylum earlier this week with my husband. I will admit I can't say I'm terribly surprised you've come to me with this—Maddie has mentioned something to that effect." She paused, and Alice thought she saw her wince, as if something about what Maddie had said was unpleasant.

Alice wondered what it was but said nothing.

"A letter like that is a serious undertaking. I would need to speak with my husband and pray on it. I hope you understand." Here, Mrs. Engall's shoulders moved in a slight, elegant shrug, the type Alice had become so adept at herself when she was in society's eyes.

"Of course," Alice said quickly. "I only wanted to reach out and see what is possible. This is not a decision we are making lightly. It's been a subject of serious prayer and consideration for my husband and me for well over a year."

"I understand." Mrs. Engall cocked her head. "May I ask you a question?"

"Yes." Alice was relieved they wouldn't sit in silence until the other women arrived, or attempt to make meaningless small talk while her heart pounded in her chest and the weight of the question she'd asked continued to taunt her.

Mrs. Engall nodded. "What brought you to this decision now? I only ask because I know the committee will want to understand your heart on the matter."

"It has been my husband's wish for a long time." Alice paused, searching for the right words. "I was slower to agree. I admit that at first, I wasn't sure. I needed time to grieve. You were there—when Daniel—" Her voice broke, and she dropped her eyes, surprised to find tears rising. But she forced herself to push through. "I barely remember the months after we lost him; we were both devastated. You must be aware of how deeply this loss was felt. It was cruel, especially as it had always been our desire to have a child. What you may not know is we had suffered a miscarriage the year before. Since then ..." She let her voice trail off, collecting herself. "I won't state the obvious. The last five years have been difficult, and God hasn't blessed us with another baby. However, we want to be parents." She wouldn't tell Mrs. Engall how unsure she still felt. "I understand this is not a simple process, nor will it be easy to raise a child who is not our own. But you've met my husband." Most women naturally understood how nurturing Peter was, and he'd certainly interacted with Mrs. Engall's children often enough at church or at Maddie's house. "If you were his wife, would you deny him a child, if it was within your ability to give him one, any way you could? I cannot deny my husband the chance to be a father, not if there is any path, any possibility at all, that lies within my power to explore for his sake."

Mrs. Engall made a soft, humming sound, and Alice wondered if the desperate edge of her voice was too much.

"Speaking of Mr. Strauss, how has his next book been coming along? We've been so delighted to see his success—Maddie has bought me several of his books. He's very talented. Surely that must bring him some notice."

Now that was a question Alice understood and could answer ably. It was not "tell me about the plot of his next novel." It was "are you able to support a child?" and she searched for a way to answer delicately. "Yes, Peter is talented," she agreed. "He is contracted for several novels with his publisher, and he's never without offers. He is doing well for himself. I am proud of him, and so happy that he's able to support us doing what he loves. And if he ever decides to step away from writing for a time, he could teach or return to work at the newspaper offices he's worked for in the past."

"I'm so glad to hear that!" Mrs. Engall glanced toward the door. "Another thing I'd love to know—"

Before she could finish her sentence, there was a commotion from the hallway. Shortly after, a nursemaid walked in, her face flushed and two-year-old Cecelia, wailing inconsolably, on her hip. Behind them trailed six-year-old Annabelle, who looked unrepentantly pouty. Alice took in the sum of the situation at once.

"Mrs. Engall, I'm so sorry to disturb you," the woman said, her voice raised over Cecelia's cries. "Miss Annabelle took the dolly's bonnet and won't return it, and now Miss Cecelia cannot be soothed."

Mrs. Engall rose and stepped toward her daughters, then she paused and slowly turned back toward Alice. For a moment, she met Alice's eyes, then she turned. "Oh, heavens—and the other ladies will be arriving at any moment. Alice, could I impose on you terribly to help Myra with the girls? Just for a moment. I must step into the kitchen and ensure the tea service is ready. Would you mind? Please?"

She didn't even give Alice a moment to reply before sweeping out of the room, leaving Alice with the maid and the two small children.

Alice swiftly stood and crossed the floor. She took Cecelia from the maid and gestured for Annabelle to approach, which the child did, scuffing her shoes along the rug.

"Belle," Alice said with as much patience as she could muster as Cecelia quietly whimpered in her arms, "why did you take Cece's dolly's bonnet?"

Annabelle's scowl only seemed to deepen. "Cece's had it all day long on her dolly. It's my turn."

"There's only one bonnet?" Alice turned to Myra, who shook her head.

"No, there *were* two, but I lost mine." For the first time, a flash of guilt crossed the little girl's face. "I guess the bonnet is Cece's."

"Yes," Alice said softly. "Should you have taken it?"

"Nooo ..." Annabelle let the word trail off. "But now my dolly is cold!"

"Surely there's a way to solve that problem." Again, Alice glanced at the maid, who nodded.

"Yes, Annabelle," Myra said. "I could help you find a way to keep your dolly warm."

"There you go! Myra will help you." Alice shifted Cecelia on her hip; the little girl was heavy, but her weight wasn't unpleasant. "Cece, Annabelle is going to give you your bonnet back."

Cecelia hiccuped and raised her face from the crook of Alice's neck. "Bonnet?" she asked in a demanding voice.

Alice laughed and lowered Cecelia to the floor. "Annabelle, what do you say?"

"I'm sorry," Annabelle mumbled, and from the pocket of her dress withdrew a crumpled white piece of lace and extended it.

Cecelia immediately snatched the bonnet.

"Cece." Alice put her hands on the child's shoulder. "Say 'thank you.'"

Cecelia mumbled something that might have been "thank you," and Alice caught a sigh before it escaped. She knew from experience that these situations could be much worse, and the last thing she wanted was Myra reporting back to Mrs. Engall that Mrs. Strauss had been unable to handle the quarrel of two small girls.

Alice had just returned Cecelia's hand to the maid, sharing a brief, knowing look of solidarity with the young woman, when the front door opened again. It was Flick, baby Allen on her hip.

"Glad to see you here, Alice," she said, just as Sarah Engall glided back into the room, now the picture of a calm and collected hostess.

"Flick, dear, welcome," Mrs. Engall said, her eyes moving from Flick to Alice and the now peaceful children. "Let me take him, won't you?"

Flick nodded and carefully transferred Allen to Mrs. Engall's arms. "You'll notice he's a pound heavier every week," she said, rolling her eyes. "He's growing far too fast."

"He is stout," Mrs. Engall said in a tone that was definitely complimentary. "It seems you've missed all the excitement."

Flick glanced at the girls, then back at Alice, with quizzical eyebrows. "Drama?" she suggested. "Does the infighting start that early? I'm glad I didn't have a sister."

"The Great Bonnet Crisis of 1887," Alice murmured back with a faint smile, feeling the tension finally leave her shoulders.

"Oh, it's always a bonnet, isn't it?" Flick rolled her eyes again.

Mrs. Engall crossed to Alice with a smile on her face. "Mrs. Strauss, would you walk up with me while we settle these little ones into the nursery?"

Alice nodded, taking Cecelia's arm. Myra and Annabelle walked ahead, while Alice trailed alongside Mrs. Engall.

"Can I call you Alice?" Mrs. Engall asked in an undertone.

"Yes, of course."

"And you must call me Sarah," Mrs. Engall added. "I wanted to take a moment to think it over, but I would love to write a letter of recommendation for you, Alice. Consider it done. Not only will I write a letter, but I will make a point of speaking personally with Mrs. Albright, who's on the admissions committee."

Alice paused on the landing, dropping Cecelia's hand out of shock. Cecelia scurried ahead to catch up to the maid. "Why?" Alice said.

Sarah straightened Allen's skirt. "Because you are not the type of woman to hesitate to mother a child who is not your own. I knew that was true when it came to Allen, but then, you have loved him and Flick both so dearly—surely, he is as good as your own child. I wasn't sure if it was universally true."

Alice opened her mouth, then closed it.

"Don't ask me to say what gave me that impression, Alice." Here, a flush colored Sarah's cheeks, and she ducked her head slightly. "I think we both know what I've heard about you and from whom. And I'm sorry."

The sound of Maddie Farjon's laughter drifted up the stairs—she had arrived and was greeting another woman in the foyer.

Alice met Sarah's eyes and smiled. "You are readily forgiven. Thank you—from the bottom of my heart."

CHAPTER FOURTEEN

PETER HEARD THE FRONT door open and shut, and set his pen down. He hadn't been writing anyway. Before him sat his cousin's letter of recommendation, freshly typed on the stationery that bore the name of Riley's law firm, but Peter hadn't opened it. He knew what Riley said would be accurate and kind and genuine. It would also, most likely, be reasonably appropriate.

But much as Riley was respected in Cincinnati, this recommendation was only one piece of the puzzle. However, if Mrs. Engall wrote something similar—or her husband , even—it would make all the difference. According to Riley, it could cut months off the process and guarantee that Peter and Alice's application was received positively.

And much as Peter had called their initial application "putting out a fleece," he wanted this to go through.

Unfortunately, Alice had not been exactly optimistic about the chances of Mrs. Engall giving her a stellar recommendation. Peter wasn't sure why. The Engalls were kind, generous people, and Mrs. Engall was close to both Flick and Maddie, so surely there was no reason for her to deny Alice.

He rose and walked to the front of the house. Alice had just finished hanging up her coat and was unpinning her hat. She turned to him—and nodded.

He felt his shoulders relax. It was going to be all right. "So she was receptive?"

A small, genuine smile graced her lips as she hung up her hat. The smile didn't quite reach her eyes, which were shadowed with fatigue, and the careful way she moved spoke of a deep-seated weariness. He wanted to rush to her, but he held back, sensing she needed a moment.

"Yes," she confirmed in a quiet, firm voice. "She's agreed to write the recommendation—*and* she told me she would speak personally with the head of the committee, a Mrs. Albright."

"That's wonderful." He paused, searching Alice's face. "Was the conversation as difficult as you feared?"

"In a way, yes." She bridged the distance between them and slipped into his arms. "I told her about us, a little—as much as I could while maintaining the thin veneer of politeness I've always been so bad at. You know I'm not one for subtlety, but I tried. But I could tell there was something holding her back, something making her wonder if she'd be damaging her own reputation by vouching for me—and I know why now."

Peter's brow furrowed, and he gently eased Alice back to see her face. "What was it?"

She opened her mouth, then seemed to think better of it. "Let's just say there are impressions of me circulating that are not entirely … flattering. I believe Sarah needed to see if they were true."

"What do you mean?"

"She tested me," Alice said simply. "Her daughters created a fuss, and she stepped away, leaving me to handle it."

A hot flash of anger went through him. "She *tested* you? You're not a potential employee, Alice—she had no right."

"It wasn't cruel," Alice insisted, perhaps seeing the look on his face. "It was necessary for her. And Peter, afterwards, she apologized. She apologized for having listened to the gossip, for having believed, even a little, that I was not a kind woman."

Protectiveness rose up in him. "Who is gossiping about you?"

"I don't know for sure, and I don't want to say."

He started to protest, but Alice gently cupped his face in her hands.

"Trust me—it's easier to not know. I'm all right. If anything, I think I made a new friend today."

Peter wanted to press the issue, but perhaps she was right—he wouldn't understand the dynamics without a full breakdown, and it might be better to just know that Alice and Mrs. Engall were friends now. "Then we're ready. I collected Riley's letter this afternoon—I have it in the office."

Alice nodded. "Did you read it?"

"I didn't; I wanted to wait for you." He hadn't feared what Riley had written, but he worried that opening it alone would feel like taking a step without her. Every part of this journey, fraught as it was, had to be theirs together. He needed her beside him. He offered a small, nervous smile. "Shall we?"

"Yes," she said, her own smile returning, the exhaustion momentarily forgotten. "Let's go read it."

April 1887

The bright spring day was meant to be lived in. Peter was already thinking ahead to a quiet meal with Alice after they arrived home from church, then perhaps an afternoon in the garden. She'd been pouring herself into weeding and snipping and planting lately, and Peter was eager to help.

He suspected half of the reason was because, since they'd mailed in their application, they'd both been on pins and needles—but Alice taking it in her stride ... more or less. Though the Cincinnati Orphan Asylum was never far from his mind, she was content and peaceful, perhaps even more so than normal.

Peter wasn't sure if her peace was a brave facade or something genuine, but he found himself watching her as she dropped his arm right outside the church and ran to Flick to coo over baby Allen, who was impossibly stout and had a big grin, complete with a few teeth now. Peter took a step to follow, only to find his path gently blocked by Mr. Tremain, whose beaming face was the very picture of Sunday morning cheer.

Peter returned the smile, preparing for a pleasantry.

"Peter, forgive the intrusion." Mr. Tremain didn't sound apologetic; he sounded happy. "My wife tells me you and Alice are embarking on a truly blessed path. I simply wanted to say how pleased we are for you. It takes a special kind of heart to do what you're doing."

Peter blinked. He forced a slow, deliberate nod, his mind racing to catch up.

"Mrs. Tremain and I have seen firsthand the kindness your wife has shown to our dear Flick. It came as no great surprise, then, when we heard you were extending that same Christian charity toward the children at the Asylum."

"Ah," Peter managed, finding his voice. The news was out then. There was no sense denying it. "Yes, Mr. Tremain. We are taking the first steps. Your prayers are most welcome."

"Have you heard from the board?"

"Not ... yet." Peter struggled to gain his mental equilibrium. "But I expect we will soon."

Mr. Tremain nodded wisely. "A piece of advice from an old man who has seen a few things—the ladies on that board ... they are good women, but they are prudent. When you speak with them, don't just speak of love and faith. Speak of stability, of your prospects. They need to know that a child will be provided for in all ways, not just with affection."

Stability. Prospects. As if Peter had thought of anything else for the past month. A flash of irritation went through him, which he immediately suppressed. The man meant well, and Peter knew he didn't always come across as the most practical sort; but he had nothing to prove. He had a practically ironclad multibook contract with his publisher, regular royalty checks that he still marveled at, and a bank account that could support a dozen children without strain. It was Alice he worried about, not the contents of their ledger. "That's wise counsel, sir. Thank you." He offered a tight smile. "Truly, your prayers are what we covet most."

"Naturally! We'll keep praying for you." Mr. Tremain gave Peter's shoulder a final, friendly pat and moved off to rejoin his wife.

Peter remained rooted to the spot, the polite smile fixed on his face until it felt like a mask.

Of course everyone knew. He should have expected that. All news spread quickly through their circles, especially at church. It wasn't as if everyone wasn't aware that Peter and Alice had lost Daniel, and that they longed for another child. This wasn't that different. It felt invasive, but that was a ridiculous reaction. After all, almost everyone meant well, even if they weren't precisely helpful.

He watched Alice across the churchyard. She was bouncing a delighted Allen in her arms, her head thrown back in a moment of pure, unguarded laughter. *How will she bear it—the constant, well-meaning scrutiny?* he thought, a familiar ache tightening his chest. She had built her peace so carefully, brick by painful brick, over these last few years. This public journey could tear it all down.

And what if they were rejected? What if something went wrong in the process? It would be far harder to bear disappointed hopes with the world looking on. Peter knew that from experience.

Alice caught his eye and sent him a radiant smile, a slight inclination of her head calling him to her side. He forced a smile in return and crossed the yard to join her and Flick. He slid his arm around Alice's waist, his grip a little tighter than usual.

"We were just admiring Allen's new tooth, which is a miracle in and of itself," Flick said with a wink.

"A fine tooth indeed," Peter said, his voice sounding distant to his own ears. His smile felt stiff, a poor imitation of the joy on his wife's face. He was there, beside her, but his mind was already calculating, already building fortifications against the whispers he knew were just beginning.

The last thing he wanted was to make Alice's life harder, especially since she had suffered so much from society's poor opinions in the past.

Alice carefully tucked her hair back behind her ears as she rose from a kneeling position in the garden. For a moment, she surveyed the flower bed, then she gathered up the weeds she'd removed and dumped them into the wheelbarrow that stood between her back garden and the Farjons'. Riley would haul off anything she and Maddie left there later that week.

"Auntie Alice!" Susie came through the gate, running into Alice's skirts and almost upsetting her.

"Miss Rosey!" Alice exclaimed with a smile, kneeling to kiss her niece's cheeks. "Have you come to help me? I'm almost done, but perhaps we can think of something to do."

Susie shook her head. "No, but I saw you from the window. Mama's lying down, and she said not to bother her; and Polly is reading." Susie's brow furrowed in annoyance; apparently neither of these activities suited her. "Do you think there are cookies?" she added in an undertone.

"I am not sure," Alice said thoughtfully. "Why don't we check my pantry?" After all, wasn't it the chief office of an aunt, even an honorary one, to provide treats?

Susie readily agreed and followed Alice through the back door into the kitchen, where there were no cookies; but with Susie's help, it only took half an hour to get some into the oven.

"There." Alice brushed flour off her hands. "Now we should clean up while we wait for those to bake."

Susie was less interested in cleaning than she'd been in baking, but she made a nominal effort. However, as soon as the treats were done, and she delivered a napkin full of cookies to "Uncle Penn" in his office, she sat at the table, legs swinging and mouth lined with milk, and enjoyed the bounties of her hard work.

"Aunt Alice?" she said thoughtfully, after her second cookie disappeared.

"Yes, my Rosey Girl?" Alice barely looked up from the sink where she was washing the few remaining dishes; after all, it was certainly a request for yet another sweet.

"Are you getting a baby from the orphanage? Like in a book?"

The dish slipped from Alice's soapy fingers, clattering softly against the bottom of the sink. She stilled, her back to her niece, before resuming her scrubbing, her movements suddenly stiff. "I'm not sure yet."

"All right."

"It depends on what the board says," Alice added. "We have to be approved."

"Oh." Susie paused, considering this. "I think you'll be."

"Be approved?"

"Yes."

Alice smiled at the sink water and placed a clean plate at her side. "What makes you think that?"

"Because ..." Susie drew the word out indefinitely. "Because maybe you will bring me a friend? There's no one my age on this street."

"It would probably be a younger baby," Alice said. Or at least, she hoped so. Sarah had given Alice the impression that usually babies were a much scarcer commodity, but surely, it would be an option—or even if it wasn't, they could surely find a child younger than five. "And it'd be a boy, but boys aren't so bad."

Susie made a sound of abject disgust. "I don't want a boy."

"Well, I do," Alice said simply. Surely that amount of preference could be considered. Alice wasn't sure she knew what to do with a little girl. Oh, she loved Polly and Susie, and she'd become affectionate toward her other nieces, but she yearned for a son—a strong, healthy, loud, boisterous boy like the one Daniel would have been. She'd always been closer to her younger brothers, especially Caleb, as she grew up—and though she understood her youngest sister a little better now, that had not been an easy lesson to learn.

The truth was, Alice wasn't quite sure she was up to navigating the challenges of raising a girl to be a woman. Her own mother had tried, yes, but Alice had such deep scars, and some of them still tugged, ached, told her that she was not womanly, not tender enough, not important enough. Her opinions were too strong, her reactions too loud. She felt damaged, and though the voice of God claimed this was not the truth, it was hard to dismiss deeply held feelings.

It would be harder still to manage the growth of a young lady knowing that she herself didn't feel all the way "grown" yet.

"Maybe your mama will have a girl, when the new baby comes," Alice offered, turning to her niece. "Isn't that what you want?"

Susie shrugged. "Mama wants a boy, too. And Daddy says he doesn't care, but he already has two girls, and he won't let me name the new baby Rosey, so I guess I don't care."

Alice smiled. "I'm sure you'll love your little brother or sister, no matter which it is."

Susie seemed unconvinced, but she gulped the last of her milk and jumped off her chair. "I guess I should go home."

"Yes, it's about time." Alice picked up Susie's glass off the table. "Here—wash your face and then go."

Susie did as she was told then disappeared through the back door. With a sigh, Alice finished straightening up the kitchen and began working her way through the last few chores she had before starting supper. As she passed through the living room, she saw that the postman had slid the mail—several letters—through the slot in the door. She paused, and collected them, then froze as she glanced at one of the envelopes.

The script was crisp and formal. The return address in the corner was embossed, not merely printed: *The Cincinnati Orphan Asylum, Mount Auburn.*

"Peter!" she called without thinking.

Her voice must have sounded more urgent than she intended, for he entered the room mere seconds later, pulled from his usual preoccupation. "Are you all right?"

"Yes, I'm fine," she said quickly. "Just—look." She held up the envelope.

Peter took it and turned it over in his hands. "Well, this is our answer." He turned, and she followed him to his office, where he picked up his letter opener. The sound of paper being sliced was loud in the still room. He wordlessly scanned the page first, his expression unreadable. Alice held her breath, watching his face for any flicker of emotion. The silence stretched, thick and heavy. Finally, he met her eyes, then looked back down at the page and read aloud:

"'The Committee of Admission has received and reviewed your application. You are hereby requested to attend an interview at the asylum on Tuesday, the tenth of May, at two o'clock in the afternoon. Sincerely, Mrs. Beatrice Albright, Committee Chair.'"

They stood quietly for a moment before Peter spoke again.

"Six days from now," he said. "I suppose we're as ready as we'll ever be."

"Yes." So why was terror filling her chest, tightening her throat, narrowing her vision?

"Hey." Peter set the letter down on his desk and reached for her. "Come here. It'll be all right."

"How can you know that?" she asked, but she stepped into his arms nonetheless. "How can you know they won't just tell us we can't adopt? We're not like Riley or the Engalls—we aren't *truly* wealthy or well-known or connected. It seems that they have high standards."

Peter shook his head. "Alice, listen to me. You may not feel it, but we are well-known and connected—at our church, yes; but also, at the risk of sounding prideful, you know my books are in every shop in this city. And we are more than 'wealthy' enough to provide a wonderful life for a child. But even more than that, would Riley and Mrs. Engall really have recommended us if they didn't think we met the standards?" Peter kissed her neck and held her close. "God has a plan for us. I promise. Let me pray for us. We'll seek God in this, and He won't fail us. He never does."

Alice released a shaky breath but didn't pull away. She nodded against his shoulder, absorbing his strength. The terror was still there, a cold knot in her chest, but beneath it, something else was taking root: a fragile, fierce resolve. Peter was right. God had not failed them, and they would not fail each other. They would face the committee, and they would do it together.

Alice made sure they arrived a little early for the meeting with the committee. They'd borrowed Riley's buggy, and the ride to Mount Auburn was mostly silent. The asylum was an imposing, multistory brick structure set back from the road. Both outside and inside, as they soon discovered, it was clean, orderly, and institutional.

It didn't look like a home; it looked like a fortress of charity.

A maid directed them to a formal waiting room. It was furnished with dark, horsehair-stuffed furniture; even before she sat on it, Alice knew it would be stiff and uncomfortable. Stern portraits of past benefactors lined the walls, their painted eyes judging all who entered.

It was eerily silent. Alice found herself listening for the sounds of children—a distant shout in the yard, the clatter of a dropped toy, even a cry—but there was nothing. The quiet was more unsettling than noise would have been. She glanced at the portraits on the wall, feeling the weight of their gazes, and clasped her hands tighter in her lap, her palms suddenly damp.

"It's clean, at least, and neat," Peter murmured.

Alice nodded but added nothing else. She already knew that she wouldn't want to say much. She felt awkward and strange in her own skin today. Though she was willing to do this, for Peter, her sense of unease had not faded. Adopting an orphan had never been an option growing up. She'd never heard of anyone doing so. Children who had no parents, or whose parents were unable to care for them, were taken in by relatives—or not at all. It was unfortunate that so many waifs crowded the streets, but Alice had always considered orphanages to be the solution for that. Social reforms ought to be made, yes, but she hadn't really thought about couples adopting a child, even if they had no children of their own. She'd even heard people speak about how it went against the natural order of things.

Now? She disagreed. Very much. Her understanding of what was right and wrong had changed, and more than that, her understanding of herself.

But old habits often died long and painful deaths, and she still felt as if she were doing something wrong. She still wasn't sure how she would explain this to Mother. Upper class families in England didn't take in children who weren't in some way related or obligated to them, and the status of a ward was inevitably different from that of one's own child. It had to be that way, for inheritance purposes, perhaps; but there were laws in America that dictated differently.

The door to the waiting room opened, and a woman with kind eyes and a soft smile nodded to them. "The committee will see you now."

Peter rose, offering a hand to Alice. His fingers were ice-cold in hers. They followed the woman—who must be Mrs. Gable—down a short, silent hall and into a formal parlor.

The air smelled of old paper and lemon oil. A large, severe mahogany table dominated the room, and the three women seated behind it looked less like a charitable committee and more like a panel of judges. Peter and Alice took the two stiff, straight-backed chairs placed before the group. The click of the door closing behind them seemed to seal them in.

The woman in the center, dressed in imposing black silk with a cameo at her throat, was clearly in charge. Her gaze was sharp and missed nothing. This had to be the chairwoman, Mrs. Beatrice Albright.

Introductions were stiffly issued, then the questioning began.

"Mr. and Mrs. Strauss," she began, her voice crisp and cold as a January morning. "Thank you for coming. We have reviewed your application and the letters from your sponsors." She did not elaborate on whether the letters were satisfactory. "Your file states you are members in good standing of First Baptist Church. Tell us, what is the nature of your service there?"

Peter cleared his throat slightly before responding. "We attend services regularly, of course. My wife is part of a weekly ladies' Bible study and prayer meeting, and we both contribute to the church's benevolence fund, particularly its outreach to widows and orphans."

Mrs. Albright made a small, noncommittal "hmm" and made a note on the paper before her. Her gaze then shifted fully to Peter.

"Mr. Strauss, your profession is listed as 'author.' While a noble pursuit, the committee must ask, is it a stable one? A child requires consistency above all else."

"It is, Mrs. Albright," Peter answered respectfully. "I am blessed with a long-term contract with my publisher in Philadelphia, and my books have fortunately found a steady readership. My current path is quite secure, but should circumstances ever change, my past experience as a journalist would provide more than adequate means."

At this, the woman who had led them in offered a small, encouraging smile. "Your novels are very popular in my reading circle, Mr. Strauss. They bring a great deal of joy."

"Thank you, Mrs. Gable," Peter said. Alice could sense the relief in his tone.

Mrs. Albright seemed unimpressed by the compliment. Her focus shifted to Alice. "Mrs. Strauss, your household is a small one. Are you prepared for the considerable increase in domestic labor a child brings?"

Alice wasn't worried about *that* question. After all, it wasn't as if she had much to do. "I am," she said, her voice quiet but clear. "I find great fulfillment in managing my home. Should the need arise, we are certainly in a position to hire whatever help is required to ensure a child would receive my full and undivided attention." The words were true, though a part of her bristled at the thought of hiring more help. After years of public life, she cherished the privacy of her own small household. But she knew this was the language the committee understood: the language of position, of means, of having resources in reserve. It was the language Mother spoke—a dialect of assumed power and capability that Alice had spent years trying to forget. Now, she summoned it with a detached precision. It was a part she must play.

Mrs. Albright set down her pen and folded her hands, her sharp gaze pinning them both. The preliminary questions were over. This was the heart of the matter. "We have read what your friends have to say about you. Now we wish to hear it from you. Why do you desire to adopt?"

The silence in the room was heavy, broken only by the ticking of a tall case clock in the corner. Alice felt Peter's knee press gently against hers.

"My wife and I have long wanted a family, Mrs. Albright," Peter began. "We have found that ... that path has not been open to us in the way we had prayed for." He paused. Alice could hear how rough his voice was, but he seemed to collect himself. "After a period of grieving, we have come to feel that God was not closing a door, but rather directing our steps onto a different road. We believe He is calling us to build our family through adoption. We have a great deal of love to give, and a stable, Christian home in which to give it."

His words hung in the still air. Mrs. Gable looked down at her hands, her expression one of deep sympathy. The third woman continued to write, her face impassive. Mrs. Albright simply watched Alice and Peter, her own expression unreadable.

After a long moment, she glanced at the clock on the mantel. The interview was over.

"Thank you for your time, Mr. and Mrs. Strauss," she said, her tone as crisp as it had been at the start. "The committee has several other applications to consider. You will be notified of our decision by letter in due course."

It was a clear dismissal. Peter and Alice rose. They each offered a polite, "Thank you," and turned. The walk back across the Persian rug felt a hundred miles long. Mrs. Gable opened the door for them, offering one last, small, compassionate smile that was the only crumb of hope they had to cling to.

Then the parlor door clicked shut behind them, and they were alone again in the silent, echoing hall.

Chapter Fifteen

May 1887

The weeks that followed passed with painful slowness.

The fragile hope Alice had felt after the initial interview began to fray, replaced by a familiar, heavy dread. Every day followed the same tense ritual. The sound of the postman on the lane would cause Peter and Alice's conversation to halt mid-sentence. An anxious look would pass between them. Then Peter would go to the door, returning with a handful of envelopes that were never the one they were waiting for. They stopped speaking of the interview after a few conversations during which they worried about every word, but it was a constant, silent presence in their home, a verdict hanging just out of reach.

On a Tuesday afternoon, as a cool May shower misted the windows, it finally came.

Peter had gone to the door as usual. Alice remained in the parlor, her hands still over the shirt she was trying to mend in her lap, listening to the familiar shuffle of envelopes. But this time, the silence from the hall stretched on. It was a different kind of silence—not the quiet of disappointment, but the stillness of discovery. She set her sewing aside and rose.

He appeared in the doorway, holding a single, thick, cream-colored envelope of the same style as the one that had held their invitation to the committee interview. He didn't have to say a word. She knew from the embossed seal in the corner, and from the guarded look in his eyes.

"Well, at least we have an answer!" She tried to imbue cheer into her voice, but it came across a little false, she knew.

He just nodded as he opened the envelope. He unfolded the single sheet of paper and scanned it silently. Alice watched his face, not the letter, searching for any flicker of emotion. She saw his jaw tighten, then, just as she was bracing for the worst, she saw the tension in his shoulders release in a subtle, almost imperceptible slump.

He looked at her, his eyes full of a profound, exhausted relief. He cleared his throat and read aloud, his voice steady.

"'Mr. and Mrs. Peter Strauss,'" he began. "'After careful consideration, the Committee of Admission is pleased to inform you that your application has been approved. We have deemed you a suitable family to be entrusted with the care of a child from this institution.'"

Alice's hand flew to her mouth, stifling a sound that was half sob, half gasp. *Approved*. The word echoed in the room, chasing away the ghosts of doubt and fear that had lingered there for weeks. "'Weighed in the balances' and found worthy," she said, a little jokingly, but in truth, she meant it.

"There's more," Peter continued, his own voice thick with emotion. "'To discuss the practicalities of placement and the next steps in this process, we invite you to a private meeting with Mrs. Gable on the afternoon of your choosing next week. Please send word of which day is most convenient. Sincerely, Mrs. Beatrice Albright, Committee Chair.'"

He lowered the letter, and a heavy silence fell, filled only by the soft drumming of the rain. The relief was so immense it was dizzying, but tangled within was a new, complicated feeling. The "it's really happening" kind of nerves that tightened Alice's throat.

"Mrs. Gable," she said, unable to stop a smile. "The kind one."

"Yes." Peter nodded, coming to Alice's side. "Not the whole committee. Just her."

Alice sank onto the sofa, the strength leaving her legs. "So we must go back." It wasn't a question. The thought of returning to that imposing brick fortress, even for a friendly meeting, sent a chill through her despite the wave of relief she'd just experienced.

"Yes," Peter said softly. He knelt before her, taking her hands in his. "But we'll go back differently this time, Alice. We'll go back as a family they have already chosen. Besides, I think Mrs. Gable's sympathetic to our cause. Mrs. Albright does seem a bit ... difficult. But Mrs. Gable certainly does not."

Alice held his eyes for a long moment. "You're going to help me through this, aren't you?"

Peter smiled. "When have I ever not? But Alice, this is a sign. God has cleared the path for us. We can accept this blessing."

Alice leaned forward and rested her forehead against Peter's. She agreed—that she must do this. Peter deserved to be a father; the committee had been right to approve them for his sake alone.

But oh, was she afraid she wouldn't be up for the challenge!

Less than a week later, they returned to the asylum. This time, there was no tense wait in a formal room. A maid led them directly to a small, private, quiet office, a world away from the intimidating boardroom. It was clear Mrs. Gable had been given leave to put her own touch on the space, which was simply and elegantly decorated. A large window overlooked a walled garden where a few early roses were beginning to bloom, and the shelves were filled not with ledgers, but with books.

Mrs. Gable rose from behind a modest oak desk as they entered, her smile warm and full of a sunshiney joy that hadn't been there when they met her last. "Mr. and Mrs. Strauss," she said, making an immediate gesture toward the chairs in front of the desk. "Please, come in. Sit down. I am so very pleased to be meeting with you again."

Alice forced a polite smile and sat, her posture as straight as she had been taught to keep it, and twice as stiff. She smoothed the fabric of her skirt, a small, repetitive motion to occupy her trembling hands. "Thank you."

"Yes, thank you," Peter said, as he, too, lowered himself into a chair. "We were very grateful to receive your letter."

"The committee was in unanimous agreement," Mrs. Gable continued, her gaze kind. "We were all very moved by your testimony—yes, even if it did not seem so, Mrs. Albright is not all thorns. We truly believe you will make wonderful parents."

Alice felt a flash of surprise. Affirmation was not what she had girded herself for. She offered a small, stiff nod in response, hoping it looked gracious and not as stunned as she felt.

"Now then," Mrs. Gable said, leaning forward slightly. "The next step is to discuss the practicalities of a placement. To that end, have you and your husband given thought to the child you feel your home is best equipped to welcome?"

Without attempting a response himself, Peter looked at Alice. She knew why, of course; she was the one with a preference. Peter wanted a child; Alice wanted a son.

But she couldn't just say that. So, instead, Alice clasped her hands in her lap and slowly, carefully, felt her way through the next sentence. "We have discussed it a great deal," she began, her voice steady. "But before we speak of our own hopes, perhaps you could tell us ... what is possible? To what extent are parents able to state a preference? Is it simply a matter of accepting whichever child is deemed a good fit, or are we allowed any say?" The rigid formality of the board seemed to say no, but Alice couldn't help hoping for more—that maybe, just maybe, they could have the child she wanted: the little boy who would make their life feel just a little more whole and normal.

Was that too much to ask?

Mrs. Gable smiled. "That's a wise question." She took a deep breath, seeming to consider her words. "In short, yes, there is a degree to which potential adoptive parents can make a decision, and certainly, no one will force you to take a child whom you feel will not be suited to you. That said, the children here are not made to order, and that means that, should you wish for a child who fulfills specific parameters of any kind, the wait may be long. I must be candid with you—the vast majority of requests we receive are for healthy children under the age of two, particularly boys. An infant placement is the rarest of all. They are few, and the waiting list of good families is very long."

Peter glanced at Alice; she avoided his eyes. After all, he had told her that, hadn't he? "We had suspected that might be the case," he said, his voice quiet.

"I'm afraid so," Mrs. Gable said in a tone that indicated she was not entirely unsympathetic. "The children who wait for a home the longest—the ones who most desperately need a mother and a father—are often those past the age of three. The older they are, the harder it is to find a placement."

Alice avoided meeting Peter's eyes; he had said something similar was likely the case, and perhaps she had known that; but it felt unfair to ask them to be the ones who did what no other couple would do. "I see," she said, her voice thinner than she meant it to be. "Thank you for your honesty." But that didn't mean she had to settle, did it? She wanted a child who could grow up, for all intents and purposes, *hers*. If so many other couples desired the same, and were willing to be relegated to a waitlist, why did it have to be seen as selfish or insecure for her to want it, too?

Mrs. Gable must have seen some of this flickering across Alice's face—or perhaps she hadn't; but her next words addressed Alice's specific terms. "Mr. and Mrs. Strauss, may I tell you about a little one who left us just last month? It might help you understand the nature of our work here ... the nature of the need."

Peter answered for them both. "We would appreciate that very much."

"His name was Amos," Mrs. Gable began. "He came to us when he was three, after losing both his parents to influenza. When he arrived, he was utterly silent. He didn't cry or rage; he simply disappeared within himself. His only real possession was a small wooden horse his father had carved for him, and he held it so tightly his knuckles were white."

Alice's own hands tightened in her lap. She pictured the little boy, small and solemn, his entire world shrunk down to a piece of carved wood.

"For weeks, he would not speak," Mrs. Gable continued. "Then one of our ladies began to visit him. She never pressed him, of course. She would sit beside him and pretend to talk to his wooden horse for hours, until at last, one day, something she had said to him—or perhaps the kindness in her tone, or the simple fact that she had given him her time—prompted him to speak. After that, he became the brightest, chattiest child in his group. We all loved him dearly, but we all hoped he would find a family of his own—and in due time, he did."

Alice was surprised at how tight her throat was, how deep the welling grief felt. She understood that silence ... and she understood the release of leaving it behind for better things.

"He didn't need a family to start his story," Mrs. Gable continued. "He needed a family who was strong enough to help him continue it. A couple—a professor and his wife—adopted him. The wife is a gardener, if I remember correctly; she understands that some things require patience and quiet care to bloom again. I know she had wanted a little girl—there was a lost child many years ago, and I think many women see adoption as a second chance to have what they were deprived of to begin with. It's a human impulse, and I do understand it; I would feel the same, at first. But I knew this couple would be a good fit for Amos, so I made sure they were introduced. Amos was so dear; of course he won them both over. The last I heard, he has started to call her *Mama*."

Alice nodded. She had received the message clearly—perhaps imperfectly, but she did understand. Though there was choice in the matter, reality meant that the chances of adopting an infant was near impossible. Besides, Mrs. Gable was right that that was perhaps not the healthiest response to grief. After all, what was lost could never be replaced. This child would have to be something new.

Peter knew that, but it seemed Alice could learn no lesson easily.

"Thank you for telling us that story," Peter said, filling in the silence Mrs. Gable left. "With this in mind, do you usually introduce prospective parents to a child—or children—who you feel would be a good match? We would be willing to trust your wisdom."

Mrs. Gable inclined her head. "Yes. I did not want to presume, but that is definitely something I can do. Generally, I will only arrange a meeting after significant interest has been expressed. However, I know some couples can be ... eager to see the children. Which I entirely understand. Many of the little ones are quite dear. Before you leave today, perhaps it would be helpful for you to see a small part of our world here? We won't interrupt the children's lessons. But to simply walk the halls, to understand the life within these walls, can help clarify what to expect."

Peter looked at Alice, once again leaving the decision to her.

She gave a small, hesitant nod.

Mrs. Gable led them from the quiet of her office into the main corridor. The halls were wide and immaculately clean, but the sounds were muted, institutional. From behind one closed door came the rhythmic murmur of a classroom recitation; from another, the distant clatter of pans from a kitchen. As they walked, Mrs. Gable pointed out various rooms.

"This is our main dining hall. The children eat in two shifts, the younger ones first," she explained. "And through there is the sewing room, where the older girls learn a trade that will allow them to support themselves."

They approached a large, arched doorway leading out to a walled garden, where the rain had stopped and the late afternoon sun was beginning to break through the clouds. The sounds of shuffling feet and childish whispers outside spilled into the hall. A caretaker with a weary but patient face was attempting to get a line of about six small children, all around four or five years old, organized for their walk.

"Hats on, children. Quickly now," the woman urged.

Just as the line was about to move, one little girl with cropped brown curls, which had probably been brushed and neat at one point but were now flying every which way, darted out of the line and took a determined step back towards the building's interior.

"Olivia, do not start," the caretaker said with a long-suffering sigh. "We are walking on the path. You will be perfectly safe."

The little girl, her face a mask of solemn conviction, muttered just loud enough for the adults to hear, "The path has puddles. Frogs live in puddles. And frogs," she finished with an air of irrefutable logic as she took yet another step toward where Alice, Peter, and Mrs. Gable stood, "are *wicked*."

A smile touched Peter's lips. Before Alice or Mrs. Gable could react, he took a small step forward, catching the little girl's eye. He crouched down slightly, bringing himself closer to her level.

She met his gaze boldly, with a hint of rebellion, as if she feared he, too, would drag her into the outdoors against her will.

"Are they now?" he asked, his voice full of gentle humor. "I've always found them to be more afraid of us than we are of them. They are noisy, though. It is hard to get a word in."

The girl—Olivia, Alice supposed—looked at him, her dark eyes wide with surprise. She seemed taken aback that a grown-up would engage with her on the particulars of her fear rather than simply dismissing it. Alice was adjusted to Peter's ways. She waited patiently for him to step back and allow the tour to continue.

Olivia gave him a long, serious, appraising look. "I am Ollie," she said after a moment. "Who are you?"

Peter extended his hand with a slightly crooked grin. "Mr. Strauss."

Olivia gave Peter's hand another long look before fastening her eyes on his face and taking his hand. She shook it, solemnly.

And Alice held her breath, because Peter looked *smitten*. Which wasn't fair. They knew nothing about this child—except that she wasn't where she was supposed to be. *Peter, be careful. We don't know anything yet.*

They weren't looking for a girl, anyway, were they? The idea was to adopt a little boy. She wasn't sure why that was the idea, but it was, and Alice didn't like to change her plans.

The caretaker reached Ollie and managed to coax her back into line. The small troop of children shuffled out into the garden, and the moment was over. The hallway was quiet again.

Mrs. Gable sighed as she turned away from the garden. "That's our Olivia," she said absently. "She's been a bit much to manage lately, so you must excuse her. Let's continue on with—"

But Alice hardly heard her. She was watching her husband. Peter hadn't moved. He was still looking at the empty doorway where the little girl had disappeared, his expression one of dawning certainty.

And in that moment, Alice felt a profound and terrifying shift in the air, as if the future she had so carefully planned had just been erased and was now being rewritten before her very eyes.

Peter hadn't believed in love at first sight until that afternoon.

The clatter of the buggy's wheels on the street was too loud, intrusive after the charged silence of the asylum. That—and steering Riley's flashy gelding through the streets of Cincinnati—gave his brain something to focus on other than the simple fact he'd just learned, but still, he managed to be so far into his thoughts that Alice repeatedly called him to the present with a light press to his arm.

He still didn't believe in *romantic* love at first sight, not for him. He hadn't had a lightning bolt moment when he'd realized he was in love with Alice; it had happened gradually, layer by layer. He had been wild about her before he quite knew how he'd gotten there.

But he might very well believe that different loves could happen at first sight. After all, that was how parents felt after meeting their child for the first time, wasn't it? Granted, that was generally after the rush and the fear and the intensity of childbirth, but this could not be so very different. At least, to Peter, it wasn't.

He replayed the moment in his mind for the tenth time. The line of children, the exasperated caretaker, and the small girl with the solemn face, stepping back from the line. *Frogs are wicked.*

He'd known as soon as he saw Ollie standing in that doorway that she was going to be his daughter.

It had hit him like a thunderclap. She'd seemed so small and so helpless, yet there was an unbreakable strength in the way she held his eyes. He could still feel the phantom weight of her small, cool hand in his own. As far as his heart was concerned, that was his child.

Peter risked a sideways glance at Alice. Her profile was turned to him, her expression closed. She was no doubt thinking of Mrs. Gable's words, of the infant son she had been asked to relinquish from her dreams only moments before this little girl had appeared. He couldn't possibly tell her what he was feeling. Not yet. It would be too much. She would think he had lost his mind.

As they turned onto their own street, the quiet in the buggy became heavier and heavier. Alice sat perfectly straight, her hands clasped tightly in her lap, her gaze fixed ahead. It was the posture she adopted when bracing for something unpleasant. Peter understood why; it was because Alice knew him well and even without him sharing what he thought, she knew, and that was ... well, it was a lot.

Yes, it was strange to feel so strongly attached to a child, as if he was her father, when they'd only just met and had one brief conversation. He'd been struck by her intelligence, her complete self-possession, for someone so young ... her wounded innocence. He felt the hurt in her, and somehow, he believed she could see a similar pain in him.

Alice might be another matter. Yes, yes, he'd respect her wishes, but he found himself praying that Alice would be struck by the same lightning bolt he had been—and soon—for he couldn't bear to leave Ollie at the asylum for long.

"You haven't said a word since we left." Alice spoke simply, calmly, and unaccusingly.

Peter brought the horse to a stop in front of their house. "I know," he said. "I am ... thinking."

"About what Mrs. Gable told us?" She said this almost as if she *hoped* that was what he was thinking about—and not about Ollie.

He shook his head. "No," he said simply. "I'm thinking about that little girl."

He said nothing more, simply looped the reins and climbed down from the buggy, turning to help her down. Alice took his hand; he could practically see the gears turning behind her eyes, but she walked up the path without a word, leaving Peter to return the horse and conveyance to Riley.

Back in the quiet of their own parlor, Peter removed his coat and draped it over the back of a chair before dropping onto the sofa. Alice moved about the room, tidying things that didn't need tidying—plumping a cushion, straightening a book he'd left on the mantel. The silence that had filled the buggy now seemed to fill the house, thick with unspoken questions.

"Do you want tea?" she asked. "Or I could make coffee, I suppose."

He shook his head. "No, thank you. If you want to sit, I could make you some. I'm sure I can manage that much."

She laughed. "No, that's not what I was hinting at. I suppose we ought to ... talk about it." She sank into her chair by the barren fireplace and watched him. "You liked her." It was not a question.

Peter's eyes flickered over to her. "Yes."

The simplicity of his answer, the weight behind that single word, made her press on. "I always thought ... I understand about infants, Peter. I do. It's not practical, and perhaps it's easier this way." She paused. "But I was so sure we would end up with a boy."

Peter's brow furrowed slightly. "A boy? Does it truly matter that much?"

She twisted her hands in her lap. "I don't know why, exactly. I suppose I just imagined it that way. A little boy running around this house, causing mischief, and ... and he'd ..." Her gaze dropped to her lap, her voice failing her.

"He'd be like our sons," Peter finished quietly.

Alice's lips tightened, and she gave a sharp, pained nod. That was the heart of it, Peter thought—the secret hope she had barely admitted to herself, let alone him. A son would feel like a continuation, a restoration. A daughter felt ... like uncharted territory. A reminder of her own complicated, painful path to womanhood.

Peter sat back, studying her closely. "I understand that," he said, his voice gentle. "I've thought about it, too. Truly. But today ... when I saw *her* ..." He shook his head, searching for words that were big enough for the feeling. "I don't know what it was. There's just something about her. The way she stood up for herself, the solemn look in her eyes. I can't explain it. I know it makes no sense, but when I saw her, I felt ... I felt as if I already knew her. It was as if a part of my own heart, a part I didn't know was missing, was standing right there in that hallway."

"Peter, she is a stranger. A little girl. We know nothing about her, except that she has a fear of frogs."

"That's not all we know," he countered. "We know she's bright, and brave, and she's ... she's *ours*. Or she's supposed to be. I can't explain it."

Alice took a deep, steadying breath. "Do you really feel that strongly about her? Already?"

Peter nodded, his gaze unwavering. There was no hesitation in him. "I do. I know it's sudden, but I can't stop thinking about her. Right now, in this moment, I couldn't consider adopting a different child. It would have to be her."

He saw the panic flicker in Alice's eyes, but what could he do?

"I just don't know," she said, her voice small. "It isn't what we planned. And what if ... what if we are not what she needs? I don't know the first thing about raising a little girl."

Peter rose from the sofa and crossed the space between them, kneeling before her chair. He took both of her hands in his. "That's why we take it one step at a time," he said, his voice an earnest plea. "I am not asking you to agree to adopt her today. You're right that we don't understand the situation yet. All I am asking you is to not close the door. Will you do that for me? Can we write to Mrs. Gable and request more information? That's all. We will pray about it, and we will allow God to lead us in every step after that. Just ... don't dismiss her out of hand. Please."

Alice looked down at him, and after a moment, the fear in her face eased into affection. "You are not a man given to wild whims, it is true," she said, placing a hand on his cheek. "I suppose I can trust you to be sensitive to God's leading—if it is that. I envy you your sureness. I am not."

Peter nodded. "I understand that. I am perhaps asking too much of you."

She shook her head. "Not too much—but a lot."

For a moment, they remained there in silence, then Peter leaned back. "Please pray about this, at least. I don't want to do anything without you, ever, but this has gripped my soul. It does not feel like an inclination. It feels real to me."

Alice released a long breath, her eyes now fastened on a distant point somewhere behind him, then she relaxed, slowly. "All right, Peter. I'll trust you. But you're going to have to help me along the way."

Peter smiled and pressed a quick kiss to her lips. "I promise I will not pressure you, but I hope you will come to feel as I do—and soon."

"I hope so, too." She sounded less than convinced, but *hope* was something Peter could work with.

Chapter Sixteen

A few days later, Peter and Alice returned to the asylum for the third time. The building felt familiar now—no less intimidating, but at least not unknown. Alice found herself more at ease, especially as they had primarily dealt with Mrs. Gable, who had been nothing but kindness. They had written to her, and she had confirmed that they could indeed consider the girl, whose full name was given as Olivia Muller, a candidate for placement and had arranged a private meeting for them in a small, quiet library off the main hall.

Mrs. Gable met them there, settling herself in a chair by the window. "Olivia will be along in a moment," she said. "I wanted to speak to you first, to discuss the situation, and the possibility of placing her with you. You saw Olivia only once, and not in a formal setting—and normally, I would have allowed for a much longer period of consideration before arranging a direct meeting of this nature." She paused, her eyes moving between them, assessing. "However, the connection you shared with her—or rather, Mr. Strauss, the one you seemed to form instantly—was noteworthy. I have learned to trust such moments. But I must be certain. Can you tell me what it was you saw in her?"

"I'm not sure I can explain it in a way that would satisfy a committee," Peter admitted. "It wasn't a logical decision. It was a recognition. I saw a little girl who was trying so hard to be brave, who stood up to a world she believed was full of 'wicked' frogs. There was a strength in her, and a deep well of hurt beneath it. I simply felt that I knew her. This is not the type of thing I would say without having prayed about it; I understand it is unusual. However, I cannot deny that I feel God is leading us toward Ollie."

Mrs. Gable nodded slowly, accepting this not entirely rational explanation in her stride. Her gaze then shifted to Alice, her expression softening with empathy.

"Mrs. Strauss, from what I understood, a child like Olivia—a four-year-old girl with a strong will—might not be exactly what you had in mind. It is very important for Olivia's sake, and for yours, that you are as certain about this as your husband."

This was the question Alice had been dreading. She could not lie, or at least, she did not want to lie, and she could not profess a feeling that wasn't there. She took a deep breath. "My husband … is not a man given to whims," she said, choosing each word carefully. "When he feels God's leading so strongly, I have learned to trust him, even when I do not understand it. I cannot say I feel what he feels, not yet. But I can say that I am willing to. My heart is open to learning what he already seems to know."

Mrs. Gable nodded. "Then that is all we can ask for," she said. "Now, before she comes in, let me tell you a little about the child you are about to meet. Olivia is an observant child. She is cautious with her trust, and it must be earned. She has a very strong sense of justice, and she does not care for things she deems illogical or unfair." A faint, fond smile touched Mrs. Gable's lips. "She feels things very deeply, even if she does not always show it. Do not be discouraged if she is quiet. Her silence is not emptiness; it is observation. I believe she is deeply intelligent, and that she understands both the thoughts and emotions of those around her in a way most four-year-olds fail to. She is usually fairly biddable. However, she can also be stubborn and impossible to lead where she does not want to go." Here, she paused. "Really, once she's decided on something, I have never seen her shaken."

A description, Alice thought wryly, that could have been applied to her own girlhood. *Comforting*. She resisted giving Peter an "I told you so" look.

"No child is going to be easy, though," Peter said, as if anticipating Alice's thoughts.

"No," Mrs. Gable agreed. "Especially not here."

The door opened, and a caretaker led Ollie into the room. She was wearing the same uniform pinafore, her cropped brown curls looking neatly brushed for the occasion. Her dark eyes scanned the room, landing on Peter with a flicker of recognition before she looked at the floor.

"Olivia, Mr. and Mrs. Strauss have come to visit with you for a few minutes," the caretaker said, giving Ollie's shoulder a gentle nudge forward before quietly exiting and closing the door behind her.

The girl stood in the center of the room, her hands clasped behind her back, a small, solemn statue.

Peter rose from the settee, took a few steps forward, and then knelt so he was on her level, just as he had before. His voice was soft and even. "Do you remember me?"

"Yes," was all Olivia said, her gaze firm. "Mr. Strauss."

"That's right," Peter said, a warm smile touching his lips. "And this is my wife, Mrs. Strauss. We wanted to meet you properly—just so we could talk. I hope you don't mind."

Olivia shook her head once.

"I've heard," Peter began, his tone conspiratorial, "that you don't like frogs very much."

Olivia gave him nothing in response to this comment. She simply nodded gravely, her expression suggesting that this was a self-evident truth, like the sky being blue.

"Why do you dislike them?" Peter asked.

"I don't dislike them," Olivia said, with a barely perceptible arch of her tiny eyebrows. "I *hate* them."

"Why do you *hate* them?"

"Because," she stated, then stopped. It was a complete sentence.

Peter gave the subject an appropriately long thought before nodding solemnly. He changed the subject. "I like your hair. I was told you gave it a bit of a trim yourself once."

Olivia's eyes immediately filled with a nearly tragic guilt. "They fixed it."

Alice's heart gave a small, unexpected pang of sympathy. The guilt in the girl's eyes was so profound, so out of proportion for a childish act. How harshly had she been scolded?

"Why did you want it short?"

There was a long pause. Olivia looked down at her shoes. "I don't remember."

"Fair enough," Peter said. "Do you have friends here, Ollie?"

"Yes. Some." She squirmed, and before Peter could ask another question, she blurted out, her own curiosity finally winning over her shyness, "Why are you here?"

Peter glanced at Alice, a silent invitation for her to join in. She gave a tiny, almost imperceptible shake of her head and a slight shrug. *This is your conversation*, she thought, feeling a wall of glass rise between her and the two of them. *In some ways, this child is already yours, not ours.*

"My wife and I are hoping to ... add a child to our family."

Olivia's eyes slid over to Alice—a quick, appraising look—before returning to Peter. "Why don't you get one from upstairs?"

"Upstairs?" Peter asked, confused.

"To get a baby," Olivia clarified, as if he were being unreasonably foolish. "The babies are *upstairs*."

A pained look flashed across Peter's face, so fleeting Alice almost missed it.

He recovered quickly. "We wanted to meet you, first."

"If I were you," Ollie confided, her voice dropping to a whisper, "I would get a baby from upstairs."

"Olivia," Mrs. Gable said gently from her corner, "I'm sure Mr. and Mrs. Strauss are prayerfully considering their decision and do not need your help."

Alice wished she and Peter were as unified as Mrs. Gable made it sound.

"You look like my picture," Olivia said suddenly.

"Your picture?" Peter asked, leaning forward slightly.

"Yes. Of Papa."

A stunned silence filled the room. Peter glanced at Mrs. Gable, whose brow was furrowed in confusion.

"You think Mr. Strauss looks like your father, Olivia?" she asked.

"Yes."

"Oh," Mrs. Gable said softly. "She has a photograph—from her parents' wedding, we believe. It is her most treasured possession. I confess I don't see the resemblance, but I understand that Olivia may."

Alice felt the blood drain from her face. *No*, she silently protested in her mind. It was a *coincidence*. A child's fancy. But she looked at her husband's face—surprised but rapt and filled with a look of profound awe—and she knew it didn't matter what she thought. Ollie's single sentence had sealed the business. For him, this was no longer a decision; it was destiny. And what power did her own careful plans have against a force like that?

His words came back to haunt her. *You don't have to beg me for anything that lies in my power to give you.*

If she wanted to love him as he did her ...

"Are our faces the same, Ollie?" Peter was asking.

Olivia squinted, studying him intently. "Your hair is. And your—" She gestured vaguely at the rest of him. "Rest of you."

"She's trying to say, politely, that he could have lost a stone and not missed it," Alice said, the words slipping out before she could stop them. Her own voice sounded strange in the quiet room.

Peter shot her a look, his eyes twinkling for a second, but he hid his laughter so as not to confuse Olivia. "Maybe so," he said to the girl. "You'll have to show me your picture someday."

Olivia nodded. "I wasn't born yet," she told them. "My papa was a train man. What kind of man are you?"

"She means he worked for the railroad," Mrs. Gable translated. "And what is your profession?"

"Ah. I write books," Peter said.

"I am a very good reader, for being only four," Olivia offered, obviously parroting someone else's words. "I'm bright."

"Humility is a virtue," Mrs. Gable said gently.

Olivia blinked. "Then why did Mrs. Jones *say* it?"

"Because—" Then Mrs. Gable paused and shook her head. "You must allow those who know you to do the bragging."

Olivia frowned. "But Mrs. Jones wasn't here."

"That's enough, Olivia."

Olivia opened her mouth, as if to argue the point further, then closed it and turned back to Peter. "Someday, you will come back and see me again, won't you?"

Peter's eyes seemed drawn to Alice as he replied. "I hope so, Ollie—if God wills it."

Olivia gave him a long look, as if taking in the sum of him, then nodded. "Everyone always is saying that," she said, "but I don't like it, because it's not a promise."

"No," Peter agreed, "it's not."

Peter's quiet admission hung in the air between them. Olivia seemed to accept it as a simple fact, a shared truth. She gave a single, solemn nod, as if he had finally understood the rules of the world as she saw them.

Mrs. Gable rose gracefully from her chair by the window. Her movement broke the spell.

"Ollie," she said, her voice gentle but firm, "it is time to rejoin your group. Cook will be serving supper soon." She came forward and placed a light hand on the little girl's shoulder. "Thank you for speaking with our guests."

Olivia looked up at Peter one last time, her dark eyes holding his for a long moment. It was an old soul's look, full of questions she didn't know how to ask. Then she turned without a word and allowed Mrs. Gable to guide her to the door, where the caretaker was waiting to lead her away.

They were alone again in the quiet library. Peter slowly rose from his kneeling position, a muscle working in his jaw.

"She is a remarkable child," Mrs. Gable said softly, returning to her desk. She wasn't looking at them, but rather giving them a moment to collect themselves. "A challenging one, at times, but she has a kind heart."

"The photograph ..." Peter began, his voice rough. "Is that ... common?"

"No," Mrs. Gable admitted. "A child's fancy, perhaps. A way to make sense of a loss. Or perhaps," she added, finally meeting his eyes, "it is simply the truth as she sees it." She folded her hands. "I will not press you for an answer now. Please, go home. Take a few days to pray and discuss this between yourselves. Whatever you decide, you have only to send me word. As I said in my letter, there is nothing to prevent Olivia being placed—but it would be a labor of love to learn her ways."

"Thank you, Mrs. Gable," Peter said. "We will consider it."

Alice could only manage a nod, her throat tight with a tangle of emotions she couldn't begin to name.

The walk back down the silent hall and out the heavy front door felt different. The first time, they had left with crushing uncertainty. The second, with a cautious hope. This time, Alice felt utterly unmoored.

They climbed into the buggy, the sounds of the city—a distant streetcar bell, the call of a vendor—rushing back in. Peter took the reins but didn't cluck to the horse. He was still looking at the imposing brick building, his face full of a quiet wonder.

Alice watched him, not the building. She had come here hoping for clarity, for a sign that she could do this. She had received one, she supposed, but it had not been for her. It had been for Peter. The ground she had so carefully prepared for herself had been washed away, leaving her standing on the edge of a precipice, with her husband already a step ahead, calling for her to follow.

The silence in the parlor was a living thing.

They had been home for nearly an hour, moving through the familiar motions of the evening—lighting the lamps, stoking the fire against the cool May night—without speaking a word. The encounter at the asylum hung in the air between them, unresolved. Alice went about the room, tidying things that didn't need tidying as she always did when she was worried about Peter. Her hands needed an occupation while her mind raced.

Finally, she could delay no longer. She sank into her armchair, and Peter, who had been staring into the flames, turned to her. His face was etched with a searching seriousness that made her stomach tighten.

"I cannot stop thinking about the photograph, Alice," he said, his voice low. "A coincidence feels too simple an explanation for what happened in that room."

Alice continued to pleat a fold in her skirt with her fingers, focusing on the repetitive motion. "It is a child's fancy, Peter," she said, her voice tight with forced reason. "Mrs. Gable said as much. Olivia sees a man of about your build with a kind face, and her grief makes a connection where there is none." Alice was trying to build a wall of logic against the tide of feeling she saw on her husband's face.

"Perhaps," he conceded, but he didn't sound convinced. He moved closer, his gaze so direct it felt as if he could see straight through her defenses. "But it was a connection to *me*. Which is what truly worries you, isn't it?"

Alice greatly disliked at times how logical Peter could be—and how he could see things that she never saw herself. She looked up, the careful wall crumbling. "Ollie looks at you, and she sees her father," she whispered, the words a raw rasp. "A beloved ghost, someone she already loves and yearns for. Who will she see when she looks at me? A stranger. An interloper. The woman who is not her mother. Where is my place in that story? I will be an outsider in my own home."

Peter didn't give Alice platitudes. He didn't say, "Of course Ollie'll love you." Though at times he knew just what to say, Alice understood he would never willingly lie to her—and how could Peter know what would happen with the girl? How could he really know? Instead, he rose from his chair and crossed the space between them, kneeling on the rug before Alice and taking both of her hands in his. His grip was firm.

"No," he said, his eyes locked on hers. "She won't look at you that way, because she will look at you as *Alice*. And you will look at her as *Ollie*. You will have to build your own foundation, from the very first stone. It will be harder for you; I know that. I see it; I won't try to deny that this may be easier for me simply because Ollie has connected with me in this way. That would be a lie."

The admission sent a strange shiver through her.

"But you will not be building it alone." He squeezed her hands. "I will be there, mixing the mortar for every single brick. Don't you know that? I will not let you be an outsider in our family. *Ever*. That is a promise I *can* make."

"But if—"

"No, Alice. I love you far too dearly to even hear 'ifs.'" A smile flickered across his face. "So we have a choice," he continued softly, his gaze intense. "We can walk away. We can leave that little girl in the asylum to wait for a father she believes she has already met ... and I will have to spend the rest of my life wondering what became of the daughter I feel I was meant to have. We can say no, and be done, and let this journey end. Or we can ask Mrs. Gable to introduce us to other children. Or," he paused, and Alice felt the weight of his next words, "we can say *yes*. We can step into this messy, complicated journey, and trust that God will give us the grace to see it through together."

Alice looked down at their joined hands. It would be much easier to say *no*. Safer. It would preserve the quiet, manageable peace of their life. But she looked up at his face, at the fierce, certain love shining in his eyes—love for her, and a new, shocking love for a child who was not yet theirs—and the thought of extinguishing that light felt like the heaviest burden of all.

"Now you are pressuring me," she whispered, joking to hide the fear that squeezed like a cold stone in her chest. "You're not giving me a choice at all."

"I'm sorry." A wry grin appeared across his face. "I hadn't meant to, but I feel so strongly. I promise I won't say more, and I promise this decision is yours."

"What you have said," Alice began, her voice quiet and clear, "is that if I deny you this, you will always look at me as the woman who took away your chance at fatherhood. That's a heavy burden for a woman to bear for the rest of her life—especially when I had already felt that way."

His face crumpled. "Alice, that is the furthest thing from the truth. Listen—if you don't want to do this, it would be insanity to pursue it. I know that." He dropped her hands; she missed his warmth. "You're right; what I said was unfair and wrong. But here's another truth: even in spite of all that, I will not raise a child without you. I don't want to be a father if you are not my child's mother. I *cannot* be. I refuse. This isn't about capability; I know that. It lies within your power to say 'yes, I will mother Ollie,' but if you feel any uncertainty—Alice, you are as capable as I am of spiritual discernment. Whatever happens will be God's will. I'm not afraid. Are you?"

Alice released a slow breath. "You will not let me fail?" she whispered, the question a final, desperate plea.

"I will not," he answered, his voice thick with an emotion that matched her own.

She let out a long, shaky breath and finally met his gaze without reservation. "All right, Peter," she said. "I know you would never ask something of me that you did not truly believe I could do. Write to Mrs. Gable. Tell her we wish to proceed."

A wave of profound relief washed over his face. Without speaking, he lifted her hands to his lips and kissed her knuckles.

The next meeting was simple—at least, for Peter.

"We would like to be formally considered as adoptive parents for Olivia," was all he had to say as he sat across from Mrs. Gable once more, Alice at his side. "What is our next step?"

A genuine, radiant smile broke across Mrs. Gable's face. "I am delighted to hear that," she said. "I confess, I had rather hoped that would be the case." She withdrew a slim file from the drawer of her desk but did not open it. "I come prepared. There are, unfortunately, a few more steps. Before we proceed down the path toward formal adoption, it is my duty to ensure you understand everything. You know that Olivia is a true orphan—but it is vital you understand her background. Before we begin, do you have any questions?"

Peter watched Alice; there was a small, thoughtful frown on her face. He had no idea what she would ask.

"You mentioned Olivia can be ... stubborn," Alice said carefully. "I was wondering about her life here. How is she disciplined? What are the expectations for her behavior?"

Of course. Peter mentally kicked himself; it was exactly the sort of practical information he should have thought to ask for.

"An important question," Mrs. Gable said. "Our approach is firm, but rooted in kindness. What Olivia needs most is consistency. She must know, without a doubt, where the boundaries lie."

"And her schooling?" Alice asked. "She seems so bright, and she mentioned reading, but I know she's quite young."

"She is bright," Mrs. Gable confirmed. "She has lessons here every morning, and she excels at them, when she chooses to."

Alice winced. "How often is that?"

Peter chuckled. "At four, you can't expect regular excellence, Alice."

Alice cast him a fond look. "I know that, but it doesn't hurt to ask."

Mrs. Gable laughed softly herself. "Oh, you never know with her. From what I've heard, she tries hard at reading, but refuses to learn even simple mathematics. At her age, it's hardly a concern."

"A child after my own heart," Peter commented before Alice shushed him.

Mrs. Gable simply smiled. "Yes, well, I have those papers, and I will make sure you have an opportunity to speak with the caretakers and the teachers before you leave. The other part you must understand about Olivia is ... You understand that a child like Olivia has a complex background."

Peter nodded. He had expected that, and it didn't frighten him. Alice might not feel the same. "Naturally. Go on."

"Olivia is precocious and endearing, as you know. But she is not an easy child, and her path here was difficult. Her father was a worker on the B&O Railroad. He died in an accident when she was quite young. Her mother passed from childbed fever after giving birth to Ollie's sister, Emma. The girls had no relatives and therefore came to us together. Olivia was nearing three, and she was ... difficult."

Peter's heart ached for Ollie. Already, he saw the writing on the wall—there had been no mention of Emma thus far, not by Ollie or by Mrs. Gable. The child had died ... or she had been placed in a home without Ollie. Either option was devastating.

He heard Alice's soft, sharp intake of breath beside him. "Oh, how awful," she whispered.

"You can guess how deeply Olivia felt the loss," Mrs. Gable said with a slight shake of her head. "Olivia was nearly three, and she was grieving and angry. Sometimes she took this out on our caretakers. It could make her difficult to manage."

"Was she violent?" Peter asked.

"Oh, no, never. Fiercely protective. She saw Emma as *her* baby to care for." A small, sad smile flickered over Mrs. Gable's face. "She adored her sister. She spent most of her time in the nursery, and nothing short of physical force could prevent this. She could be stubborn and would often choose not to speak, but she was always gentle with Emma. Unfortunately, even though there are many couples who would love two small daughters, we didn't trust Olivia outside the asylum at that point. Perhaps that might have changed with time, but she was increasingly irrational." She sighed. "Unfortunately, Emma was never a strong baby. She passed away just over a year ago."

Another baby, lost. Peter felt Alice's hand find his under the desk, her fingers cold and tight. He squeezed back, offering what comfort he could. He ached for the little girl who had lost not two family members, but three. A grief he and Alice knew all too well.

"That is when the true difficulties began. The nightmares, the withdrawn spells. There have been incidents. A few months ago, she found a pair of sewing scissors and cut off her own hair, as you saw. She is not unwell—mentally or physically. I have had a doctor confirm this. But she is a little girl with a deep, deep well of grief inside her."

"That poor little girl," Peter murmured.

Mrs. Gable nodded. "In truth, I have not recommended Olivia to be placed yet, because I have feared she would simply be returned. But it seems it is time. In the last few months—since the hair-cutting incident—Olivia's behavior has improved. This does not mean all of the struggles are gone. When she gets an idea in her head—like her fear of frogs—it is nearly impossible to shake. She does not need parents who are merely kind or loving. She needs parents who are strong, patient, and prepared for the ghosts she will bring with her."

Mrs. Gable leaned forward, her hands clasped on the desk. "So I must ask you both, plainly," she said. "Knowing all of this, can you be those parents for her?"

Peter knew his own answer; it was a fire in his chest. But this was not his decision alone. He turned to Alice, holding his breath, trying to read the complex emotions warring on her face—fear, sympathy, doubt. Her lips pressed into a thin line, but she gave a tight nod.

He turned back to Mrs. Gable, his voice firm and clear. "Yes. We can be those parents."

Chapter Seventeen

Late May 1887

THE HOUSE WAS QUIET except for the sound of Ollie's sobs, muffled but persistent, drifting down the hallway from her room. Alice couldn't bring herself to sit or rest. Things had seemed so simple this afternoon, when she and Peter had finally been allowed to take Ollie home. It had not taken long—though the official adoption process was complex, the girl had been released into their custody almost immediately.

Peter was ecstatic, and over the course of the month, more and more, Alice had realized Ollie was eager, too. And Alice had tried to get to know Ollie—really, she had. But it was always Peter who led the way. Generally, when Alice was there, Ollie was quieter—with Peter alone, she said more, talking about her sister, whom she missed quite fervently.

Alice wondered if perhaps part of the reason she didn't understand Ollie was because she saw herself in the girl. Alice hated mirrors; they never failed to show her angles she didn't like.

Ollie had more than once proffered the concept that Alice and Peter would be better off taking a baby—because "that's what I would do." She had immense sympathy for their plight; she was able to understand that sometimes babies didn't live, and that it caused a deep grief, and that perhaps, despite the loss, the love could be gifted elsewhere. She seemed almost shocked at the concept that Peter could give that love to *her*.

Now, Alice paced up and down in her bedroom, her hands clenched at her sides, her thoughts a whirl of doubt and guilt.

What have we done?

The night had been interrupted several times already by Ollie screaming in panic, unable to sleep for more than a few moments without jerking awake. The first time, when Alice had gone to Ollie, she had been pushed away.

Only Peter would do. Even now, Alice could hear, through the wall, the low murmur of his voice, a steady current meant to soothe Ollie's fears. He'd been there for hours, trying to comfort her through the nightmares that seemed to consume her small frame. Her cries would quiet for a moment, then start up again, sharper and more desperate, like she was being torn from sleep by something terrible.

Alice wrapped her arms around herself and stopped by the window, staring out into the moonlit yard. She had known this would be hard. She had known Ollie might struggle to adjust. But somehow, knowing hadn't prepared her for the reality—the helplessness, the fear, the overwhelming sense that she wasn't enough.

No, she had never really connected with Ollie, but she had thought, once Ollie was settled into their home, once they had made her their own, once Ollie's name was "Olivia Strauss," that would change.

Ollie would come to love her; Alice would find a way through to her; it would all become natural and make sense in some magical, beautiful way, if it were meant to be.

That moment had yet to arrive.

"Lord, help us," she whispered. "Comfort Ollie. Give Peter the words he needs to reassure her. Give her peace from whatever haunts her. And help me. I don't know what to do."

At last, she heard Peter's footsteps traverse the small hall from the bedroom they'd carefully prepared for Ollie to their own room. He slipped in, closing the door softly behind him.

"She's asleep again." He ran his hands through his already rumpled hair.

"I can't tell if it's something specific or simply being in a new place. She isn't completely awake when she cries. This is something like what the caretakers said has been happening in the last year. I think she sees her sister dying and is trying to save her. She was crying for Emma, sometimes, and other times for her mother."

Alice swallowed, her throat tight. *Of course… Ollie wants her* real *mother. No wonder a poor substitute is unneeded.* "You've been with her all night," she said. "You should try to get some sleep."

Peter lowered himself onto the edge of the bed. "I'll get a few hours here and there, and nap tomorrow. You should have been trying to sleep yourself."

"I don't know that I can." Alice turned back to the window, unable to meet his gaze. "I'm not sure I can do this, Peter."

She heard the bed creak as he rose, and then he wrapped his arms around her waist. "It's been less than a day since we've had her here," he said softly. "It's going to take a while, darling. Come on. We knew it wouldn't be easy. You wouldn't be distraught if we brought a puppy home and it cried all night."

Alice laughed; the sound was watery. "She's hardly a puppy."

"Right." Peter kissed the back of Alice's neck. "She's a human soul trying desperately to cope with a pain she can't understand. She doesn't *know* she's safe here yet, even if she understands the truth of it when she's awake. She's only four, and she's seen a lot of death and suffering in her time—to people she loved, but also, every child in that asylum had a similar story, and she must have heard horrible things. That's a lot for a child to try to reason with. We understand each other, I think, Ollie and I. But it's going to take some time for us all to be a true family."

"Why is this so simple for you?" The words sounded so little and bitter that Alice winced, but Peter didn't reprimand her. She felt him shrug instead.

"I don't know. Some day it'll be simple for you, too."

Alice narrowly avoided an unladylike snort. "Oh, I'm sure."

"I *am* sure." He kissed her shoulder then drew back. "Everything seems bad at this time of the night. Let's see if we can't sleep."

Knowing she'd have one ear tuned to Ollie's room all night long, Alice nodded and went to lie down. The lamp was extinguished, and she'd just started to drift off to sleep when she heard Ollie's heart-wrenching shriek, followed by a series of soft hiccuping sobs.

She started to sit up, but Peter placed a hand on her shoulder before rolling out of bed and picking up his robe.

"Stay here; I'll handle it," he said.

Alice rolled onto her back and began to pray once more.

Ollie was sullen and stubborn the next morning. Peter had decided about an hour into the night that he would not be working that day, and he was glad he wasn't even trying.

Instead, he took Ollie outside, where warm spring sunlight and soft, damp spring grass and bright, fragrant spring flowers in the large yard between the two houses were sure to soothe any damaged soul.

Ollie also loved the cats, and Juno; and though Cassius and Ophelia had become wary of her and found some secret hideaway, Juno followed her about the garden, sitting whenever she paused, dark eyes intent, as if Ollie were her sole charge and she the fearsome protector.

Ollie told Peter about her schooling, which had been delayed for the time being. Thankfully, the asylum had not made any specific requirements for her to immediately start school. Peter wanted to keep Ollie for the rest of the spring and summer and perhaps take some of her teaching on himself for a time. It wouldn't be good for her to be away from home for most of the day, not until things were more settled.

By late morning, Susie appeared in the yard—as Polly was off at school—and Peter brokered an introduction. Ollie roused herself at the sight of another child and soon she and Susie were rambling away at each other while Peter gave them their distance.

Then Susie was called home for lunch, and Peter took Ollie inside. All through the meal, she recounted her conversation with Susie and much more besides, and Peter found himself relaxing. Surely, such a sweet and social little girl couldn't be lost for long. If there were phantoms that taunted her while she slept, in time, with love and care, she must overcome them.

And if she couldn't? Well, that was a bridge Peter would cross when he came to it. After all, she was their daughter.

Then there was also Alice. Peter found himself watching her as much as he watched Ollie throughout the meal. She ate mostly in silence, only responding in soft murmurs to Ollie, letting Peter do most of the talking. That wasn't like Alice. At least, Peter always thought she was the brightest spot in every room. She was certainly not what he would call quiet.

"After we clean up, will you take Ollie to Riley's stables?" Peter asked as he helped clear the table. "I thought I might lie down for a few minutes, and Ollie will like to meet the horses."

Indeed, Ollie perked up at the mention of horses. "You will take me?" she said. The words were, unfortunately, directed at Peter.

"You could take her and then come back and nap afterwards," Alice said quickly, "or you could take her after dinner when Riley is home."

Why are these two women trying to work against me? Peter thought, and agreed that they would see the horses after Riley got home that evening. He had promised to properly introduce Ollie to his friend as well, so it wasn't as if that didn't fit into their already established plans. But he had wanted Alice to interact with Ollie more.

How would they ever get along if they didn't spend any time together?

But how will Alice spend any time with Ollie while feeling that she's not wanted?

He knew Alice so well. If this were Polly or Susie, she'd be in the thick of the action, laughing and directing their play. But this was different. This child came with the impossible title of "mother," and Alice was terrified by the weight of it. She couldn't see the little girl for the enormity of the role she was being asked to play. Peter was convinced that Alice's uncertainty here was all due to the fact that she was supposed to step in as Ollie's *mother*.

And she is, everything in Peter shouted. *She just needs to know it. That's all. If she just knew it, and acted on it, Ollie would come around in no time.*

It honestly would have been easier if Ollie had been inexplicably attached to Alice instead of Peter. He wouldn't have minded, really, but Alice *did* mind. Not that she was aware of how much Ollie's rejection bothered her, but Alice tended to lean on her internal sense of what was "rational" in times of stress, and her own feelings often led her astray. Unfortunately, such thoughts were rarely ever rational, and in fact, sometimes struck Peter as bordering on insane.

That evening fell softly, gently even, and Peter carried Ollie out of the house with one arm beneath her knees—more for fun than necessity, though she did not protest. He set her down when they neared their destination. She darted ahead as soon as her feet hit the ground, her short hair already askew and her small feet flying over the grass, and Peter followed at a more measured pace.

Riley was already in the yard, sleeves rolled, shirt unbuttoned at the throat, brushing down one of the horses that stood tied near the little stable. His head came up at the sound of Peter and Ollie's approach, and he grinned broadly when he saw Peter, then gave a mock-theatrical gasp upon spotting the child barreling toward him.

"Saints preserve us," he said, stepping back and lifting both hands as though in alarm. "It's the fierce little general Susie warned me about! Have mercy, won't you?"

Ollie stopped just short of him, blinking, uncertain.

"She said you fell off your horse," she said in an accusatory tone, as if evaluating a crime.

"I did, at that," Riley said gravely. "The other day my Chief must've sneezed or something, and he sent me flying right into the fence. Hit my nose on a post."

Ollie gave him a long, squinting look. "Did it bleed?"

"Like anything."

She nodded, seemingly satisfied. "Good."

Peter couldn't help but laugh at this verdict. "Ollie, you must be kind."

"Oh, don't bother her, Penn. I like her already," Riley said, crouching down. "Ollie, is it? I'm Riley, and these are my horses, though I confess they don't always do what they're told."

Ollie, already craning her neck to look past him, stepped forward without fear. "Susie says you have five horses. That is *too many* horses. Which one is Chief?"

Riley gestured with a tilt of his head toward the tall bay gelding. "That's the culprit."

Peter stood back, watching the two of them. Ollie had inched closer to Chief, one hand extended, and Riley murmured his encouragement.

Behind them, Alice had come over and stood just far enough away to not be part of the action, her hands clasped in front of her. Peter noticed her at once, and so did Riley, who straightened after a moment and tipped his head in her direction.

"Evening, Alice," he called before Peter could say a word. "Come to see the latest equestrian?"

She gave a small smile. "I thought I might."

"If she's anything like you, she'll take right to it." Riley patted Chief's neck. "I've started Susie—I could put Ollie on Cinnamon tonight if you don't care. You know I'm careful with little ones, and Cinnamon is more broken in than even your horse."

"I know," said Alice simply. "You'll have to talk Peter into it."

Peter caught the way Ollie glanced back, noted Alice's presence, and then turned her attention back to the horses as if nothing had occurred. He felt the ache of her disregard in his chest. "I don't mind, if you're very careful," he said. "What do you say, Ollie? Do you want a ride?"

Ollie scooted back a step or two. "I don't know," she said reflectively. "I haven't thought about it before."

Riley nodded solemnly. "Well—oh, there's my Dolly Girl."

Peter glanced over his shoulder to see Polly scurrying out of the house, Susie at her heels.

"Ollie," Riley said formally, "you know my daughter Susie, but this is Polly, the older of the two. I'm sure you'll get along because your names rhyme."

Ollie wrinkled her nose and Polly gave her a cursory glance before walking over to her father.

"Did you get the sugar cubes I asked for?" Riley asked.

Polly reached into the pocket of her dress and withdrew a handful, which immediately caught Chief's attention.

Riley grinned. "It's your job to show her how to feed him those without losing a hand, Miss Dolly. And you, too, Susie. You've got to teach Ollie to be a good hand with horses, like her mama, all right?"

There were eager cries of agreement. Riley came to stand beside Peter a few moments later, brushing his hands off on his trousers. "She seems sharp," he said. "I think she'll be a lot of fun for you."

"She is," Peter replied. "But I don't care if she's sharp—I'm just glad she's home with us."

Riley didn't look at him, only gave a slight nod toward Alice, who now stood nearer the fence. Peter didn't know why she didn't just walk over and take charge of the situation. She loved horses. It was so odd to watch her being pensive and withdrawn in a situation she'd previously have excelled in.

"She's trying, Penn," Riley said in a low voice, as if reading Peter's thoughts. "That's why she's here; don't be too hard on her. You know Alice and I haven't always gotten along, but I can tell when a woman wants to do something and can't let herself. She should just throw herself into mothering Ollie. The rest will come. You ought to talk to her."

"I have. This is only our first full day, but Alice wants to rush things."

Riley shrugged, shifting his attention back to the girls. "It's going to take a little time."

"I know that." Peter sighed. "I know that more than anyone. But you know Alice."

Riley chuckled. "A bit. Come on. I'll get that girl of yours on a horse yet." He turned towards Chief with a whistle. "Dolly Girl, let's get Cinnamon out. I want the saddle but not the bridle, and a lead rope, too."

Polly, quick to obey when horses were involved, disappeared inside the small stable without a word. Susie lingered near Ollie, who watched raptly as Riley tossed his grooming supplies into a bucket and then led Chief through the wide door. Ollie waited, holding onto Susie's hand as if they were lifetime friends, which made Peter smile.

Ollie wasn't timid, Peter thought—not in the usual sense. She was cautious with her trust, and she studied things with the intensity of someone determined to memorize them. There was a kind of carefulness to even this, as if she desperately needed to understand the world around her.

Alice was a bit like that, too.

Riley came back out with a saddle on one arm and Cinnamon's lead rope in his other hand. He worked quickly and surely, humming as he fitted the tack to Cinnamon's head and then to her back. She stood quietly throughout, ears flicking forward now and again at the rising chatter of the girls. Polly, who had ridden Cinnamon many times, patted her neck, and Cinnamon lowered her large head for a scratch behind the ears.

Peter stepped back next to Alice. "You could walk beside Ollie," he said softly. "You know that mare as well as Riley does. Or you could take your own horse out and hold her; that would make her feel safe."

She didn't look at him. "Riley knows what he's doing. I saw how he taught Polly and Susie to ride; he'll be just as careful with Ollie."

"I know he will," Peter said. "But so would you."

Alice's fingers flexed at her side, but she said nothing.

By the hitching post, Riley took Cinnamon's lead rope and patted her flank. "All right, Miss Ollie," he said, "if you want a ride, now's the chance."

Ollie cocked her head. "Is she a good horse?"

"Oh, she's a saint," Riley said. "I've done just about everything one could think to her so she won't toss one of my babies; you can be sure of that. You have to crawl all over a horse you want children on, and tie things to them, and make loud noises. I didn't let Polly or Susie near her until I'd done all that and more."

Ollie very solemnly held out her arms, and Riley carefully lifted her at the waist and set her on the saddle.

"Now," he said. "You can hold onto her mane or this—" He patted the front of the saddle, which was slightly elevated. "This is the pommel. Someday, you'll have reins, which are used to guide the horse, but I'm going to hold on to Cinnamon myself this time. All right?"

"All right," said Ollie. She had a determined expression.

They circled the yard in a slow loop. Ollie sat straight, not stiff, her eyes wide but unafraid. Riley, with a steady hand on the reins, kept up a running commentary of nonsense about Cinnamon's grand adventures, all of which Peter was fairly sure were fictionalized.

By the second lap, Susie had taken to marching alongside them like a pageboy escorting a queen, and Polly gave up her older-sister aloofness and offered soft but firm instructions like a stablemaster: "Sit straighter! Keep your knees bent, not locked! Watch her ears—she talks with those!"

Peter glanced sideways to see Alice watching too, her expression unreadable.

"I wonder if she'll like to ride," she murmured.

"I don't know." Peter smiled and placed a hand on Alice's waist. "I suppose we'll find out."

Alice crossed her arms, then uncrossed them. "She's not like I imagined, Peter."

"She's better than anything I imagined," he said gently.

Alice blinked, then gave a faint nod. "It's worth it then," she said in a low voice. "I'm sure it's worth it."

Riley drew the horse to a stop. "How was that, Ollie? Do you think you'll be an equestrian?"

Ollie squinted.

"A horse-riding person," Riley clarified.

"I don't know." Her eyes flew over to Peter, who stepped forward to the horse's side. "Are you a horse-riding person?" she asked in a low tone.

Peter shrugged. "I can ride, but—" He gestured back to Alice. "You shall have to talk to her about horses. She grew up with them, and she loves to ride. It's her favorite thing. Maybe you can go together some time—on a longer ride—and she could teach you."

Ollie gave Alice a quick glance and nodded. "Maybe." Again, she reminded him of Alice—Alice's "maybe" was never particularly close to "yes." They were pacifying remarks to keep those around her from putting up too much of an argument.

Soon, the light grew dim, and it was time to go home.

Alice watched as Peter set the oil lamp on the bedside table in Ollie's room. Its golden light filled the small space, chasing away eerie shadows that the dusk had brought. Alice went to the window and drew the sprigged floral curtains, blocking out the last of the evening light.

"Wash your face and hands, Ollie," Peter was saying. "The water is cold, but it'll feel good. Do you need help pouring it?"

Alice turned in time to see the disdainful look Ollie cast him. "I know how," she said regally.

"I know, darling; I was just checking."

The bed had been made earlier that day, and the little pitcher of water sat full beside the basin for washing. Peter gravely observed both Ollie's washing and then the brushing of her hair. If it were any child but Ollie, Alice would have banished him and tended to the girl alone, but it *was* Ollie, and Alice wasn't sure if Ollie would like being alone with her.

Alice stepped forward, feeling the stiff resistance of her own hesitation as though it were something stitched into the seams of her dress. "Shall I help you change?" she asked. "Your dress has buttons."

Ollie gave Alice a long look and then turned and dropped her head, waiting without a word for said buttons to be undone.

Peter took a step back. "I'll leave you to it and fetch a book I want to show you, Ollie. I'll be right back."

Alice approached the dresser and drew out one of the white nightgowns she'd placed there earlier. It was plain but the fabric was soft as silk. All of Ollie's things were fine and well-made—at least that was something Alice could provide for her. It was the best money she'd ever spent. "Arms up."

Ollie hesitated, then obeyed, remaining silent as Alice helped her out of the dress. The asylum had taught Ollie independence—Alice remembered that from the night before—and she seemed uncertain about why Alice wanted to help her with every facet of life. In truth, if Alice had even one other child, she'd have been glad of Ollie's capability, but Alice only had Ollie.

And I don't even have her, *really.*

She pushed away the thought, guiding Ollie's arms through the night-gown's sleeves with care.

"There," Alice said when the child was dressed again. "All ready."

Ollie climbed onto the bed herself. She didn't need help for that either.

Peter returned a few minutes later with a book with illustrations of animals, which he must have borrowed from Riley's girls. Together, they looked at several pictures and chatted about the exotic animals there were in this world.

And Alice watched, lingering in the middle of the room, until Peter put the book away and prayed with their daughter.

He kissed her brow as he tucked the blankets securely up to her chin. "God keep you, Ollie."

Alice crossed to the bed then. She bent, the movement deliberate but unsteady, and placed her lips to Ollie's forehead. "God keep you," she whispered.

Ollie didn't respond, but she didn't pull away either.

Peter doused the lamp. They left together, the door creaking faintly closed behind them.

At the top of the stairs, Alice paused, her hand on the banister. "She never says anything to me."

Peter's voice was low. "She's learning us. You know that."

Alice gave a small, humorless smile. "She already knows you, then."

"She trusts me because I look like someone she lost," he said. "She doesn't know what to make of you because you're here *now*, and that's harder."

Alice nodded. "I'm trying, Peter."

"I know."

They went down the stairs together in the dark, side by side, the echo of her whispered blessing still lingering on her lips.

God keep you, Ollie. God keep you.

Downstairs, the parlor was cool and still, a window cracked open to let in the faint breath of evening. Peter lit one of the table lamps and turned it low. The soft light flickered against the walls, warm but not what Alice would call cheery.

We are both too tired for cheer, Alice thought.

They both sat down, but it wasn't too long until Alice couldn't bear the silence. It pressed in on her, forcing her to speak words that did no earthly good. All she could do in her current frame of mind, she knew, was make Peter uncomfortable, crush his joy, and ruin something that was meant to be perfect.

But she said it anyway.

"I'm not sure Ollie cares if I'm here or not," she said in a low voice. "She doesn't seem to dislike me, no, but she's indifferent."

Peter sighed. She heard a deep exhaustion in him, and winced, for she was surely adding to that.

"She's trying to make sense of what you are to her. It might take her longer than it took with me, but that doesn't mean she won't love you."

Alice exhaled slowly. "I don't think I'm very easy to love."

Peter's brows drew together. "Alice, I am the last person on earth you could ever convince of that."

"You loved me before you knew the worst of me."

"And I love you now."

Alice gave a short laugh, but it was more tired than amused. "She doesn't even call me anything."

"Yes." Peter frowned. "But we aren't trying to force her to call us anything, if that feels unnatural to her."

They had offered options. Peter had suggested "Aunt" and "Uncle" might be gentler, at first. But Ollie, with the swift, unthinking cruelty of a child, had immediately chosen "Papa" for him—and no name at all for Alice. For someone so small and talkative, Ollie was stunningly careful with the words she used.

Alice didn't say that, though. She just nodded. "She's new here, and she had a rough night," she said like a mantra. "I'm being premature. And maybe tonight will be better."

It probably wouldn't be, but she hoped Peter might get a little sleep in.

At least Ollie was a sweet, kind girl, and she had not been particularly disobedient thus far. That was something to be thankful for.

As Alice prepared for bed, she found herself thinking of the careful preparations she had made—the clothes she'd purchased or sewn herself, the books and toys she'd bought, the way she'd cleaned the little bedroom from top to bottom and prayed over every inch of it. It was easy to love a child in the abstract, to perform the duties of a mother. The terrifying part was the silence that followed, waiting to see if that love would ever be returned.

Chapter Eighteen

It was early morning when Alice began the process of wringing out yet another pile of wet clothes. Breakfast was long finished, and Peter had retreated to his office with a kiss on Alice's cheek and a whispered assurance: *You're doing fine.*

Alice wasn't so sure.

She'd set Ollie up at the table with her paints, which had seemed to initially delight the child, but due perhaps to exhaustion or perhaps to pure stubbornness, she hadn't responded to any of Alice's comments. Alice had gotten more enthusiastic responses from the dog.

So now she worked in silence, only speaking occasionally.

For a while, this seemed to function. Alice occasionally glanced over her shoulder to see Ollie painting careful strokes of red and blue across the paper. But, after maybe half an hour, when she turned around again, Ollie was no longer at the table.

A quick scan of the room found the little girl in the pantry, standing on tiptoes to reach one of the higher shelves. A jar of preserves had somehow been nudged carefully toward the edge, and Ollie almost had her hand around it.

"Ollie!" Alice's voice was sharper than she intended, and Ollie froze. "What are you doing?" She rushed over to lift the little girl off the pantry stool Ollie had dragged over.

Ollie squirmed in Alice's arms with surprising strength for someone so small. "I wanted to *see* it," she said.

"That jam isn't for playing with," Alice said firmly, setting Ollie down on the floor and moving the stool back where it belonged. "And you shouldn't be climbing in the pantry. You could've fallen, or broken the jar, or both. I wouldn't be able to forgive myself if you were hurt."

Ollie's face slowly slid from defensive to a pout—bottom lip out, eyebrows lowered. "I wasn't going to break it. I was just going to *taste* it."

At least she was honest.

"Ollie." Alice placed her hands on her hips. "You'd spoil your appetite for lunch if you had jam now. Anyway, it's just for special occasions." In truth, it was a jam Maddie had made earlier in the spring, and Alice had forgotten about it, but she wasn't going to lose ground to a four-year-old by admitting that. "You can go back to the table and paint, or if you're tired of that, we can clean you up, and you can help me, and then play outside until dinner. All right?"

Ollie looked up at Alice with what could only be considered a glare, then deliberately kicked her as hard as she could.

It didn't hurt. Ollie was so tiny, and the force she could manage, all concentrated on Alice's shoe, was minimal.

No, it was the intention that counted here.

For a long moment, Alice stared at Ollie, her thoughts racing.

Well. Was this how it was going to be? Was she going to let this child—her daughter, in every way that counted—throw a tantrum and kick her? In her own house?

Not likely.

"Olivia," Alice said in a low voice, "you will go to your room and sit on your bed until I call you down for lunch. When you come, I will expect you to apologize for kicking me. Do you understand?"

The muleish look only deepened. "No," Ollie said simply and clearly.

Alice took hold of Ollie's shoulder—not roughly, but firmly—and turned her toward the door of the kitchen. Three steps in, Ollie realized what was happening and went limp, but again, she was so small. Alice had only to bend, scoop her up, and carry her.

Which was the point at which Ollie began screaming. Alice ignored her, proceeding out of the kitchen and up the stairs.

She heard the door to Peter's office open and him calling to her, but she ignored him, entered the nursery, and set Ollie down on the bed.

"I don't want to catch you off that bed until I come for you," Alice said. "Do you understand me?"

Ollie, who had stopped screaming halfway up the stairs, stared at her with a look of unveiled dislike, but said nothing.

"If you want a sip of water or to use the necessary, that's all right," Alice amended. "But otherwise, you're to stay here."

It would only be half an hour, which was a pathetic fraction of the time her own mother likely would have exacted for such an offense, but it was the principle of the matter. She was not going to be *kicked* by a *four-year-old* for the great sin of asking her not to get into the cupboards in between meals.

Alice left the room, closing the door softly behind her. She met Peter halfway up the stairs.

"What happened?" he asked. "Was she hurt?"

Alice gestured for him to precede her down the stairs. "She kicked me, so I put her in bed for a while."

Peter turned back to her. "I understand that's not appropriate, but don't you think ...?"

Alice said nothing. She *thought* she'd done exactly what she'd ought. If anything, she'd shown mercy. Certainly, she hadn't lost her temper. She would not have been rewarded with the same treatment as a child, at least from her mother, she was sure. Nettie would have been merciful and gracious—but firm. Alice sought to be the same.

"It's only her second day," Peter said.

Alice cocked her head. "And how do you want me to start on her second day, Peter? As I intend to continue, or should I be easy with her now and give her the idea that I will accept that kind of behavior?"

"Yes, I understand that, but a certain amount of grace, perhaps, could be extended. She might not understand what she did is wrong."

"I'm quite sure no one at the asylum allowed that kind of behavior, either," Alice said, "but she's four, so she'll test boundaries. I want her to find that when she acts out in that way, there is a line, and when she crosses it, she will be pulled back, and quickly. Don't you see that?"

Peter stood still for a long time, then gave a single, decisive nod. He walked the rest of the way down, and Alice followed, breathing a quiet sigh of relief. She couldn't manage this at all if Peter wasn't on her side.

Back in the kitchen, she plunged her hands into the soapy water, scrubbing one of Peter's shirts with more force than necessary. The scene with Ollie played over and over in her head. No, she *was* glad of how she'd handled it. She hadn't yelled or fussed. Alice doubted she would always react so well, and certainly she hadn't thought through how she would behave if Ollie kicked her, so God must have stepped into the places where her own humanity would have otherwise rushed in.

She sighed, wringing out the shirt and dropping it in a basket of damp clothes to be hung outside. This wasn't how she had imagined motherhood at all. She'd have thought that by the time her child was four, she'd know exactly what to do and who that child was, but it was more than that. She'd always imagined that when she and Peter brought a child into their home, regardless of how that happened, it would feel like an instant connection—a natural bond that blossomed from the first moment. But reality wasn't like that, was it?

As she scrubbed another garment, she forced herself to take a deep breath. She couldn't expect everything to fall into place overnight. Ollie had been through so much in her short life—losing both parents and then her sister, living in an orphanage instead of a home with a family, and now settling into a strange house with people she barely knew. Of course she would act out. Of course she'd test the limits.

Alice straightened and dropped the second shirt into her basket. "Lord," she whispered, "help me love her the way You love her. Help me to give her the structure she needs, but not at the expense of showing her kindness. And if You could just scrub me free of human impulses, that would be appreciated, too."

She had to smile at that thought. Alice felt she had quite a few human moments ahead of her.

"If You could help me let go of whatever ideas I have in my mind of how things are supposed to be, and just embrace what is, that'd be wonderful, too," she mumbled.

After seeing that all the clothes were hung up outside, Alice climbed back up the stairs to Ollie's room. Her heart softened as she cracked the door open to see the little girl curled up on the bed, facing the wall, her arms clutching a stuffed animal Peter had given her yesterday.

Alice crossed the room and perched on the edge of the bed. "Ollie," she said softly.

The little girl didn't move at first, but Alice saw the slight twitch of her shoulders and knew she was awake.

"It's time to come down for lunch," Alice said. "I thought you could help me make a sandwich for Mr. Str—for Papa. But before we go, I want to talk to you for a minute."

Ollie slowly rolled onto her back, her brown eyes wary. Tear marks traced her cheeks.

Alice reached into her pocket for a handkerchief. "Listen, Miss Ollie. I put you to bed earlier because you kicked me," she said as she dabbed at Ollie's face. At least, Ollie didn't resist her, letting Alice finish and then tuck the handkerchief away again. "You knew better when you kicked me. I know you did. I know the people at the asylum would have taught you better. It's not what the Lord wants for us. Do you understand?"

Ollie's lips pressed into a stubborn line, but after a long pause, she gave a small nod.

"I want you to grow up to be a woman who loves God," Alice said. "That is why I will not let you act out in anger. I am your mother now, and helping you learn that is my job. But what is your job?"

Ollie said nothing.

"It's to obey," Alice said. "I had to obey my mother growing up. So must you. And I hope when we get to know each other more, you'll like me a little, and you won't want to kick me. But it's all right if you don't. You don't have to like me. But you do have to obey me."

Ollie's eyes darted to Alice's face, and a long silence hung between them. Finally, she mumbled, "I'm sorry."

Alice's heart gave a little leap, but she kept her tone calm. "Thank you for saying that. I forgive you. Come on." She stood and held out her hand. "Let's go see what Papa's been up to and have some lunch."

June 1887

Alice had the honor of watching Annabelle and Cecelia Engall while Sarah brought her third child into the world. From what Alice understood, Maddie was with Sarah now. Sarah had gone into labor early that morning, and the little girls had been dropped off by their father.

Flick had appeared a few hours later, with Allen in tow, and the two women had sat about, chatting and watching the four children interact.

Alice, for her part, was feeling fairly optimistic. Though Ollie still plainly preferred Peter, she'd become more and more open to Alice's presence in her life, and certainly, she'd become more respectful with every day. That was probably because Alice had resolved not to take any sass, and had acted accordingly, but she had also tried to be gentle with Ollie. Peter was right that Ollie had gone through a lot, seen a lot, for one so young, and mercy was a requirement.

That didn't mean Ollie didn't need boundaries. In truth, the more Alice came to love Ollie—it was a slow surrender, and in strange, quiet moments she could feel the full intensity of her heart being stolen—the more Alice knew that Ollie *couldn't* be allowed total freedom. Not if Alice loved her enough to give her any sort of future. Indeed, in some ways, Ollie's behavior was better for Alice than for Peter, though she was sure they'd iron out those wrinkles eventually.

Eventually, they would face an unannounced supervisory visit by one of the representatives of the asylum—and then, assuming they received final approval and were able to file a petition for adoption, they'd face a court hearing—but until then, they were simply focused on keeping Ollie safe and working out what their life looked like with her in it.

It was nearing midday now, and the house was lively but surprisingly manageable. Annabelle was sitting on the floor in the corner, cutting out paper dolls from old magazines. Allen was toddling around the room, holding a sock—neither Flick nor Alice knew where he'd gotten it—over his head and crowing.

And Ollie and Cecelia were settled on the floor with a pile of building blocks.

"No, no, Cece!" Ollie said, her voice full of the great concern of one small child for another. "You can't *eat* it. You must *stack* it."

Ollie put some effort into prying the damp block out of Cece's hands. Cece squawked, but before Alice had time to interfere, Ollie smoothed over the situation by showing her young friend the superiority of stacking to eating.

"See?" Ollie crowed in delight. "Now you put one down. It'll be a big tower."

Moments later, Allen had joined them, and Ollie got the tower several more blocks high before one or both of the younger children knocked it to the floor.

Ollie clapped a hand to her cheek with an exaggerated look of shock. "Nooo!" she cried, though her horror was clearly feigned. "You ruined it!"

Allen broke into gurgling giggles while Cece laughed uproariously.

"Now I have to do it again—see?" said Ollie. "You broke my tower!"

Allen only laughed harder.

"See how funny that'll be when he's thirty," Flick observed wryly without looking up from her sewing.

"I'm sure it can be trained out of him by then," Alice replied.

"Maybe even by the time he's twenty-five," Flick joked.

Ollie had paused in her stacking, looking between Alice and Flick in confusion. "He'll have a job when he's that old," she said in a voice dripping with condescension.

Flick laughed. "Well, don't you just know better than anyone, honey?"

Ollie frowned and went back to her tower.

Alice hid her smile by ducking her head.

Just then, Annabelle looked up from her cutting and asked, "When do you think Mama's baby will be here?"

"Babies come in their own time, Annabelle," Alice answered. "It could be a while yet. But you can stay here tonight if it takes longer."

Annabelle frowned. "I hope it's soon. I want to tell Mama I made her a doll. See?" She presented a cutout of a lady in a dress from one of the magazines Alice had set aside for that purpose.

Alice nodded solemnly. "I'm sure your mama will love it."

The hours passed in that strange mix of frantic activity and crawling time unique to a day filled with small children. By afternoon, Alice was glad of an escape to the kitchen. She was in the middle of rolling out dough for biscuits when the knock at the door came. She wiped her hands on her apron and hurried to answer, finding Mr. Tremain standing at the back porch, his face pale and drawn.

"Are you alone, Mrs. Strauss?" Mr. Tremain asked.

Alice glanced over her shoulder. All the children were in the sitting room. "Yes. Will you come in?"

"I just heard from the Engalls' house—the baby was born several hours ago. It's a girl."

"Oh." Alice's brow furrowed in confusion. She'd expected Dr. Engall to come for his children once the baby was safely born, or to send someone to collect them. "What—?"

"Mrs. Engall passed on afterwards. The baby is well, but—" Mr. Tremain paused. "Dr. Engall asked me to come and tell you, so you wouldn't wonder. It was all very sudden. He'll do his best to come for the girls soon, but you can understand—"

"Yes." Alice swallowed; a lump had risen in her throat. *Lord, comfort Dr. Engall.* "Yes, I understand. Thank you for coming. Please—if you see him, share our condolences. We can keep Annabelle and Cece as long as we need to."

"Thank you; I'll let him know. Mrs. Tremain and Mrs. Farjon are there, preparing Mrs. Engall for burial. I understand it was not an easy passing." He sighed and shook his head. "Such a horrible thing. She did live to see her baby, I understand."

When Alice turned around, Flick was standing in the doorway of the kitchen, Allen balanced on her hip.

"What is it?" Flick asked. "What did he want?"

Alice swallowed hard. "Sarah Engall's gone," she said. "She died in childbirth this morning."

"Oh, Alice ..." Flick's free hand flew to her mouth. "How awful."

Before Alice could say more, a sharp cry interrupted them. Annabelle had followed Flick to the kitchen door, a sheet of paper she'd been drawing on clutched in her hand. The little girl stood with wide eyes, her paper fluttering to the ground.

"Mama?" she whimpered, her face crumpling. "No! That's not true! It's not true!"

Alice stepped forward, but Annabelle stepped back, into the sitting room, eyes still wide with horror, and then turned and ran up the stairs.

"I'll go," Flick said quickly, handing Allen over to Alice. "I know her pretty well, and I knew her mother better. You stay with Ollie and Cece." Without waiting for an answer, Flick followed Annabelle.

Alice clutched Allen to her chest, trying to gather herself. Cecelia, too young to understand what was happening, tugged at Alice's skirt. "Belle cry?"

"She's sad," Alice said softly. She crouched down, setting Allen on the floor and guiding Cecelia to sit with her. "Mrs. Tappet is going to help her feel better. Could you show me the dolls Annabelle cut out for you?"

Cecelia nodded and toddled off toward the pile Annabelle had left on the floor next to her drawing materials, which she had been using to make houses for the dolls.

But as Alice stood, she realized Ollie was watching her intently, her brow furrowed.

"Is Annabelle's mama dead?"

Alice sighed. "Ollie, let's talk about it later."

"Is she in Heaven already?" Ollie pressed.

"We're going to have a talk about it later tonight, when Cece isn't here," Alice said firmly. "Not now, all right?"

"But what if she—"

"Olivia Grace," Alice snapped. "I said *not now.*"

Ollie's shoulders stiffened. She blinked up at Alice, her lips parting as if she might say something, but then she shut them. "I will help Cece," she said.

"Thank you, Ollie." Of course Ollie would be so perfectly sweet the moment after Alice snapped at her. And Alice called her *Olivia Grace.* Alice and Peter had only decided last week that they would be adding *Grace* to Ollie's name, making her full name *Olivia Grace Strauss*. It had been a long discussion, but not one they'd had with Ollie yet. Alice didn't think Ollie would object—she didn't have a second name yet, so it would be an addition, not a subtraction or a replacement—but it was still something they wanted to talk to her about, at least as much as she could understand.

The name *Grace* held a lot of meaning for Alice. She wanted to sit down with Ollie in a quiet moment, with Peter, and take time to explain the significance. She hadn't meant to snap at Ollie at all.

Thankfully, it didn't seem that Ollie had even noticed.

The day wore on. At last, Mr. Tremain came back to collect Flick and Allen and drop Annabelle and Cecelia off at the Engall home. As soon as they were on their way, Alice turned from the door and went in search of Ollie.

She found Ollie sitting on her bed, clutching her stuffed rabbit and staring at the ceiling.

"That was a scary day," Alice commented, placing her hand on the doorframe for balance. "It's always sad when someone goes to Heaven."

"Yes," said Ollie.

"Do you want to talk about it? I'm sorry I snapped earlier, but I'd love to answer your questions now."

"No," said Ollie quietly.

Alice stepped into the room and sat down on the edge of Ollie's bed nonetheless. "Sometimes we don't know why people die," she said. "But Mrs. Engall was a Christian, and she is with Jesus now. There is no crying in Heaven and no sadness. But her family is going to miss her a lot, and they'll have to figure out how God wants them to live now that she's not there to fill a very important spot."

Ollie still said nothing, but after a moment, she rolled onto her side and slipped her hand into Alice's. Alice let out a slow breath and began to stroke Ollie's curls—neat this morning, thanks to Alice's efforts, but now hopelessly tangled again.

"When Papa gets home, you can ask him questions," she suggested. Peter had gone with Riley to offer what support he could to Dr. Engall. "He has some good answers. But I think he'd just tell us we have to pray for comfort for the Engalls. Would you pray with me?"

Ollie nodded slightly and scooted a little closer so her head was resting on Alice's lap.

"All right," Alice whispered. "Dear Lord, thank You for being here with us today. We know how much suffering there is in this world, but we are thankful for Your love and comfort in those hard moments. Please comfort the Engalls, who lost their mother today. And please help us trust You, even though hard, awful things happen to us and to those we love. In Jesus' name, Amen."

"Amen," Ollie whispered into the fabric of Alice's skirt. "Mama, what will the Engalls do?"

The word, spoken so simply, so naturally, struck Alice with the force of a physical blow. *Mama.* A title she had grieved for, yearned for, and finally despaired of ever hearing. It was a name she had been certain she would have to earn over years of patient service, if she earned it at all. And here it was, offered up by this strange, solemn little girl. Her breath caught, and for a second, she couldn't speak. She could only look down at the tangle of brown curls resting on her lap, her heart aching so fiercely it stole her words.

When Alice didn't say anything, Ollie added, "Will Dr. Engall send Annabelle and Cece to the asylum?"

"Oh, Ollie, no." Alice shook her head. "No, Dr. Engall isn't like ... he isn't like some people who *have* to leave their babies because they have no way to take care of them or because they had to go to Heaven. I think he has a lot of people who would love to help take care of Annabelle and Cece and the new baby. They'll be safe and loved." In truth, Alice knew that Dr. Engall had a cook and a nursemaid, so he didn't lack for assistance, but he was also a good father.

All the same, the loss would sting. Oh, Sarah would be missed—not just by her family, but by everyone who had known her.

Before Alice could quite think about it, a tear slipped down her cheek. *Oh, Lord, I'll miss her, too.*

Ollie sat up and reached up to touch Alice's damp cheek. "I'm sorry," Ollie said, "because she was your friend. Friends shouldn't die."

"No, they shouldn't," Alice said shakily. She gave Ollie a tight hug. "But it'll be all right, Miss Ollie. Don't you worry about it."

Ollie pushed back from Alice. "What is *Olivia Grace*?" she asked sternly. "That's not *Miss Ollie*."

"Ah, well." Alice sniffed and reached up to wipe her cheek with the back of her hand—she had given her handkerchief to Flick an hour ago and hadn't gone to get another one. It had felt easier at the time to hold herself together than to think about it. "We had hoped that, when we sign the papers and say we want you to be our daughter, we would put down 'Olivia Grace Strauss.' Because you only have one name, and perhaps, if you had two, you would feel ..." She stopped and shook her head. That wasn't the right way to explain this.

But what was?

"Why do you want me to be *Grace*?"

"When I was very tiny—just born—I was called *Grace*," Alice said. "It's a pretty name, don't you think?"

Ollie's brow furrowed. "Why aren't you *Grace* now? You're *Alice*. And I'm *Ollie*."

Alice nodded. "Indeed, you are. And you will always be *Ollie*. And I am *Alice* now, not *Grace*. When I was very small, my mother named me *Grace*, but then she couldn't be my mother anymore—and like you, I had someone else I called Mother, who gave me a new name. But when I grew older, I was told that my name was *Grace*, and it's a special name to me and to Papa for that reason."

Ollie cocked her head. "Did your mama die?"

"No, not quite." Alice struggled for words. What could a child of Ollie's age understand about the situation Alice had grown up in? "She didn't die. But she couldn't be my mama, even though she loved me. Sometimes, people aren't treated right because of who their parents are, even if that's not fair. My mama wanted me to be treated like I had parents who ... who would mean I was treated better."

Ollie seemed to slowly digest this, her fingers clenching and unclenching in the fabric of Alice's sleeve as she thought. "So she gave you a new mama so you could be safe," she concluded. "Did you love her?"

"Yes, I did. It wasn't easy, but it was the best my mama knew to do. That's all most mothers can do—their best." Alice hesitated, then said, "That's all I'm doing for you, Ollie. My best. But you know I'd do anything for you. I love you very much."

Ollie's head snapped up, her eyes wide with shock. She stared at Alice for a long moment before dropping her head onto Alice's shoulder with a choked sob.

"Ollie!" Alice's arms came around her daughter. "Ollie, what is it?"

But Ollie could only cry and cry and snuggle into Alice's shoulder, and at last, Alice just let her, held her, and patted her back.

At last, having cried herself out, Ollie fell asleep, tucked into Alice's arms, so Alice shifted her so she rested on the bed, lay down next to her, and watched her sleep.

Somehow, Ollie seemed too precious to leave right now—too fragile, too new.

Alice wasn't sure when she would be able to leave Ollie again, but something in her had cracked open.

She couldn't bear to be parted from her. She couldn't.

That was where Peter found them several hours later. Ollie slowly woke up, and Alice rose with her and carried her to the wash basin, carefully bathing her face and whispering soft reassurances while Ollie woke the rest of the way up.

"Everything is settled with the Engalls, as much as can be for now," Peter said in an undertone, waiting until Ollie had separated from them to find her abandoned paper dolls. "It's a horrible thing, though. I'm sorry I wasn't here with you. How are you doing?"

"I'm all right," Alice said. "Ollie and I had a good talk. I hope you don't mind that I told her about calling her *Olivia Grace*."

"Ah." Peter raised his eyebrows. "No, no, that's fine. How did she take it?"

"Fairly well, I think," Alice said. "She had a few questions, but I explained, and she seemed to like it. We talked about Sarah a little, and I told her what I felt I could about Claire and Nettie—which wasn't much, but there's time for that, as she grows older. She'll know the full story some day, when she's ready."

Peter nodded. "Yes, that's good. Now it would be too much, but when she's older ..."

"I told her I love her." Alice swallowed. "And that I will always do whatever I can to take care of her. And that made her cry—she cried herself to sleep in my arms."

Peter hesitated, placing a hand on her arm. "Why do you think that was?"

"I don't know." Alice would perhaps bring it up with Ollie again later, but the little girl seemed better now, if a bit drowsy. "I've told her I loved her before, haven't I?"

"Yes, I think so." Peter squeezed her arm. "Maybe she needed to hear that assurance, in that moment, from you."

"Maybe," Alice supposed. "But either way, I think things will be better now. Or at least—I hope so."

Peter smiled. "Yes, I think so, too."

Chapter Nineteen

Mid-June 1887

THE DAYS HAD BEEN warm but mild, not too windy but not too hot, and Alice finally felt like her garden looked *decent*. Between introducing Ollie to her new home and supporting the Engalls through their grief, the last month had been a challenge, but somehow, the weeds were relatively at bay.

Still, that didn't mean Alice could slack off, and with Ollie at her side, and Juno carefully guarding them from under the big tree, she was pulling weeds and digging up the soil around the rosebush in the corner.

"Very pastoral, Mrs. Strauss."

Alice sat up slightly and reached up to straighten her straw hat, then paused, not wanting to get dirt anywhere near her head. "Good morning, Riley. You're home?"

"Just for a few more minutes. Mornin', Ollie."

"Mornin', Uncle Riley," Ollie said cheerily, from where for unknown reasons she was tying the longest stems of grass together. Somehow, as soon as *Mama* had come, so had a number of other titles—*Uncle Riley* and *Aunt Maddie*, *Auntie Flick*, and "*my* Baby Allen," though Alice was trying to discourage that last one.

"You're not at your office today?" Alice settled for brushing her hands on her apron.

"It would appear not."

He stood in silence for a minute, prompting Alice to add:

"Riley, *why* are you not in your office today?"

"I thought you'd never ask." He winked at Ollie, who giggled, despite the fact that she couldn't possibly understand the joke—if there was a joke.

Alice wasn't sure.

"Penn and I are going over to the Engalls'." Riley glanced at Ollie, who was once again consumed with her grass chain, and lowered his voice slightly. "We're going to help Brett move some furniture around. With the new baby, and Sarah gone, he needs to turn the nursery into a proper room for a live-in nurse. We're moving Sarah's old sewing room furniture out to make more space."

"Oh, Riley. He's changing her rooms already?"

Riley shook his head, his usual cheerfulness gone for a moment. "He has to. He can't manage a newborn and his practice without full-time live-in help, more than he has right now. But the house ... He says it feels wrong to touch anything, like he's erasing her. He needs us there to help him face it."

Alice bit her lip. "I miss Sarah. We weren't friends for long, but I have always admired her. She was such a bright spot in this world. Is he ... is he doing all right?"

"He's putting one foot in front of the other. The baby is healthy, thank God, but he's still afraid he'll lose her, too. It's an irrational fear, but I think we've all had one of those. He's doing his best, though. It takes a lot out of him to do the basics—but he's giving all his energy to his daughters, which is really the best thing he can do."

Alice swallowed against a lump in her throat. She looked over at Ollie, who was now meticulously laying her grass chain out in a circle. The child seemed oblivious, lost in her own world. "I'm glad he's at least trying. I don't know what I'd do if anything happened to Peter."

"No—of course not. I'd be pretty lost without him, too. And if Maddie ..." Riley shook his head. "I won't think about that. Not with another little one due in October."

"Maddie has never had a hard delivery, Riley," Alice said firmly. "She told me that herself." *Gloating, but it was probably true.*

Riley's smile was tight. "Neither had Sarah, Alice."

Ollie suddenly jumped to her feet, the grass chain forgotten. "There are no frogs here," she proclaimed. "Not at this house."

"Ollie, for the hundredth time." Alice turned to her daughter. "There are frogs here."

Ollie glanced around, a blank look on her face. "No."

"Yes, Ollie. There are frogs somewhere in this garden. And someday, you are going to see them. Frogs are a part of life."

With an incredulous wrinkle of her brow, Ollie shook her head.

"*Yes*, Ollie." Alice brushed a stray lock of hair back and looked up to Riley. "Will you help me?"

Riley shrugged. "It *has* been a while since I've seen a frog in your garden."

"Don't indulge her delusion," Alice said, frowning at him before turning back to Ollie. "Ollie Grace, you can *hear* the frogs out here at night. We had your window open yesterday evening—you heard the frogs!"

Ollie considered this. "No," she said firmly. "No ribbits."

"At nighttime, they make a different sound—a trilling one." Alice wasn't going to try to imitate it. "Or maybe it's a chirping, but it is indeed a frog sound."

Ollie's face blanched. "*Why?*"

"To call for their sweethearts," Riley supplied when Alice hesitated a beat too long. "But you're right; it's not a ribbit."

Ollie took a careful step backwards, toward the house. "You're sure?"

"Yes, I'm *sure*," Alice emphasized. It would do no good to comfort Ollie with lies when reality would prove the opposite.

Ollie turned and ran back into the house.

Alice sighed and went back to her weeding. She'd deal with that later—though more likely, Ollie had run straight to Peter. Alice hoped so—perhaps his frog philosophy would be better than her frog practicality.

Still, she rather doubted it.

"Have you thought about facing the fear head on?" Riley asked.

"Don't you have anywhere to be?"

"No, I'm serious. That's how I got Peter through most of his irrational fears." Riley crouched next to Alice; she ignored him. "There's a point at which mind triumphs over matter—or I suppose the matter forces the mind to behave—and the fear goes away."

Alice made an unladylike, incredulous noise at the back of her throat. "And how did that work for Peter? I assume you took charge of most of the 'exposure.'"

"I thought it worked pretty well. It got him over the worst of them. Horse-riding, falling off, gun sounds, swimming, deep waters in general …" Riley shrugged and grinned. "Talking to girls was an abject failure, but you have to admit that's a decent rate of success."

Alice bit back a smile and kept weeding. "If you need to see him, he's in his office—likely comforting a hysterical four-year-old."

"I'll go see," Riley said cheerfully.

Alice shook her head, a genuine smile finally breaking through. *Men.* They could be so ridiculously simple sometimes. She returned to her roses, yanking a stubborn thistle from the soil with a satisfying tug. The peace of the garden settled around her again—the warmth of the sun on her back, the drone of a nearby bee. For a moment, she forgot the tension of Riley's conversation, forgot the argument about frogs, and simply existed in the pleasure of the work.

A few minutes later, Peter and Riley emerged from the back door, Peter shrugging on a light coat.

"Ready, Penn?" Riley asked, clapping him on the shoulder.

"As I'll ever be," Peter said. He walked over to Alice, bending to kiss the top of her head. "We shouldn't be more than a few hours. I'll be back long before supper." He then turned to Ollie, who had trailed after Riley and Peter—the frog conversation must be over. "Be good for your mama, Ollie Grace. I'll see you soon."

He gave her a quick, warm smile and followed Riley to his stable.

Alice watched them go, then turned back to her work with a sigh, half of contentment and half of resignation. “Well, Ollie,” she said without looking up, “it seems it is just us girls for the afternoon. Shall we finish this last patch of weeds and then go inside for a story? I think we have time.”

She received no answer.

“Ollie?” she prompted, still tugging at a persistent root. “Did you hear me?”

The silence that followed was heavy and absolute. It was different from Ollie’s usual thoughtful quiet. A prickle of unease ran down Alice’s spine. She sat back on her heels and turned.

Ollie hadn’t moved. She was standing in the exact spot where Peter had left her, a small, rigid statue in the middle of the lush green lawn. Her arms hung stiffly at her sides, her hands clutching the woven grass chain so tightly her knuckles were white. Her face was pale, her dark eyes fixed across the gardens through which the men had disappeared. She wasn’t pouting. She wasn’t angry. She looked ... lost.

“Ollie, darling? What is it?” Alice rose, brushing the dirt from her knees, and walked over to her daughter. “What’s the matter? Are you still worried about the frogs?”

Ollie gave a single, violent shake of her head, her eyes still glued to the gate.

“What is it, then?” Alice asked, kneeling in front of her. “You can tell me.”

For a long moment, Ollie said nothing. Then her lower lip began to tremble, and a terrible, silent tremor seemed to shake her whole body. She looked at Alice, her eyes wide with terror.

“Ollie, what is it?” Alice pulled Ollie onto her lap, despite the child’s unwilling stiffness. “What are you thinking about so hard?”

“Mama?” Ollie whispered, her voice trembling. “Is Aunt Maddie going to die, too?”

Alice drew Ollie’s head against her chest and held her tight. Her eyes flickered to the Farjons’ house, which was thankfully still, and she quickly said, “Oh, my sweet girl, no. Why would you ever think such a thing?”

"Because of the baby," Ollie stated, as if explaining a simple, horrible fact. "Mrs. Engall got a baby—and she died." Her voice hitched. "My mama got a baby—and she died."

"That doesn't happen every time," Alice said. But again, she knew she could never lie to a child. That might be the wise thing to do—even the *motherly* thing to do—but she would tell the truth. "Sometimes that happens, and we can't predict it. But God is taking care of Aunt Maddie—and sometimes He ... sometimes people go to Heaven like Mrs. Engall ... and sometimes they don't. But Aunt Maddie is strong and healthy. We have to trust God—He knows best."

The words, meant as a comfort, seemed to land like stones. Alice felt the small body in her lap tense up, and Ollie's fingers began twisting frantically in the fabric of Alice's skirt, her knuckles still white.

A small, hiccuping sound, half sob, half protest, jolted her frame. She took a shaky breath, wrestling her terror back into words. "If He knows best—" Ollie made a hiccuping sound then tried again. "If He knows best, Mrs. Engall would not be *gone*. She would be with her *baby*. And then she could *love* her baby."

"That's ... that's how we see it." Alice struggled for words. "But sometimes it's not that simple. We can't understand. But do you remember what I told you before? Mrs. Engall was a Christian, and she is with Jesus now." As Alice spoke, she felt Ollie begin to shake her head against her chest, a small, persistent, negative motion. "There is no pain in Heaven, no suffering. You are happy all the time. It is safe and nothing bad ever happens. And we don't get to decide when we go to Heaven, or when the people we love go to Heaven, but even if it hurts, it is *right*."

"*No*," Ollie whimpered, the word muffled against Alice's dress. She pushed back a little, looking up at Alice with frantic, tear-filled eyes. The carefully constructed theology was meaningless to her. "No, I don't *want* her to be in Heaven," she sobbed. "I want her *here*."

Alice held Ollie still as best she could, kissed the top of her head. "I know it seems that way, and it definitely is painful. But things don't have to be good and happy and perfect to be *right*."

Ollie's quiet whimper turned into a choked cry of pure panic. She began to struggle in earnest, no longer just flailing, but pushing against Alice's chest with surprising strength, her small body rigid with the desperate need to get away. "No!" she cried out. "No!"

Realizing that her embrace had become a cage, Alice immediately let go.

Ollie scrambled off Alice's lap and stumbled backward, her face ghostly pale, her whole body shaking with panic. "Will *you* have a baby?"

Alice swallowed. "We can't make it happen." She decided now was not the time to communicate that *her* babies had died.

Ollie's breaths were heavy and uneven. "If you ever have a baby, do you promise not to die?"

Alice weighed her options. She could say "yes" and be done with the conversation. She could put Ollie off or offer more pat answers. She could fudge the details, say that she was healthy and strong and there was no chance of that. She could even say that she didn't believe she would conceive again—which, though true, would make explaining even more difficult if Alice and Peter were ever so blessed.

And Alice had already almost died in childbirth. An hour more of ceaseless labor pains, weak as she'd been, and she would have gone—she understood that now.

"Ollie," Alice said quietly, "though I cannot make that promise, I—"

Ollie screamed. Loudly. "Scatter birds from the trees" loudly.

And then she once again ran to the house, threw open the back door, and slammed it behind her with surprising force for such a tiny child.

Alice closed her eyes for a moment then took a steadying breath, rose, and followed her daughter into the house. She paused in the kitchen to leave her gloves, apron, and hat on the table before beginning her search.

She expected Ollie to either hide in Peter's office or run up to her room, but instead, she found her in the parlor, curled up behind the armchair so she was pressed against the wall, half-hidden from view.

Alice knelt a few feet away. "Ollie, darling?"

From the subtle movements, Alice could tell Ollie was rocking herself; she was whimpering, but at least she wasn't screaming.

"I'm sorry, Ollie." Alice took a deep breath. "Did I scare you?"

Ollie didn't reply, but she stopped whimpering and her rocking slowed.

"God loves us." Alice swallowed. "And here's a promise: I will always love you. I promise I will take good care of you."

Ollie began rocking again but the whimpering did not resumed.

"Will you come out so I can hold you?"

Ollie seemed to hesitate. "No," she mumbled and continued her back and forth movement behind the chair.

Just then, there was a knock at the front door.

For a single, selfish second, Alice thought, *I will not answer it. Whoever it is can go away.* But it could be important—so Alice rose, straightened her skirts, and left her daughter hiding behind a chair like a sad little sprite.

Alice opened the door to reveal a serious woman, middle-aged perhaps, with a gray dress and graying brown hair.

"Mrs. Strauss?" The woman held a leather portfolio in her hands like an ancient hero might hold a sword. "I am Mrs. Davenport from the asylum's visiting committee. I trust this is not an inconvenient time?"

Naturally.

Alice's life could never be simple, could it?

She quickly collected herself. "Please come in, Mrs. Davenport. I admit this is not the most convenient time, but you are welcome in our home," she said, her voice as smooth as she could manage. As Mrs. Davenport stepped into the house, Alice continued, "Olivia is currently upset because we had a death in our closest circles lately—you must know of the tragedy with the Engalls. It is a challenge for a four-year-old child to understand such loss. However, I hope she will come out and see you shortly." Perhaps this interruption was a strange sort of mercy. How did one explain the will of God to a terrified four-year-old? Alice had no idea, and she was grateful, for a moment, not to have to try.

"Come out?" Mrs. Davenport glanced around the parlor with slightly arched eyebrows. "Where is she?"

"Currently," Alice said, "she is behind a chair." She scrambled for her dignity and asked, "Would you like some tea?"

Mrs. Davenport hesitated, then nodded, seeming slightly ill at ease with this development. "Yes, thank you, Mrs. Strauss."

"Very well."

After gesturing for Mrs. Davenport to take a seat in the parlor—not in the chair that Ollie was hidden behind—Alice walked toward the door then paused by Ollie.

For a long moment, Alice hesitated. She didn't want to get into a pointless fight or be seen trying to drag Ollie from her hiding spot. Neither did she particularly want to have a challenging conversation such as this one in front of Mrs. Davenport. The weight of this visit began to settle over her, a heavy burden that threatened to make her knees buckle.

What if I lose Ollie over this?

Her heart began to pound, and she prayed desperately for calm—and for favor.

But here was the truth: Alice was not going to calmly make tea and chat with Mrs. Davenport while her daughter whimpered behind an armchair.

Another hasty prayer, and she knelt beside the chair, very aware of Mrs. Davenport's eyes on her. But it didn't matter; not really. Alice could only do the best with this present moment as Ollie's mother.

Even if it's not forever.

"Ollie," Alice said in a soft voice, "I'm sorry you're sad, and I'm sorry if I frightened you. It's going to be all right; I promise. Nothing bad is happening today, and I need you to come out. Right now, we're going to go into the kitchen to get Mrs. Davenport some tea." And wash Ollie's face, but Alice wasn't about to lead with that.

She held her breath for a long beat of silence, then slowly, Ollie eased out from behind the chair, thumb in her mouth, hair askew, eyes red. Alice immediately tugged her daughter into her arms with a big hug and a kiss before standing, Ollie on her hip.

"If you'll excuse us for a moment, Mrs. Davenport," Alice said firmly and turned, walking into the kitchen.

There, she set Ollie on the counter. The little girl's whimpers had vanished, but her breathing was still uneven. Alice picked up a washcloth and wet it in the cool water from the pump—the routine action a balm to her own frayed nerves—and began to tenderly wipe the salty tear tracks from Ollie's flushed cheeks. The child didn't pull away; instead, she leaned into the touch with a weary sigh. When she finished, Alice re-wet the cloth, wrung it out, and placed it for a moment on Ollie's too-warm neck before smoothing the little girl's hair and retying the ribbon from that morning.

"There." She removed the cloth and dropped it in the sink. Then she placed her hands on Ollie's shoulders and met her eyes. "Listen to me, Ollie Grace. I cannot promise that sad things will never happen, but I can make you this promise: I will always fight for you and do all I can to take care of you. I love you. Papa loves you. You are safe, and you are loved by us and by God."

Ollie threw herself forward; her weight momentarily put Alice off balance, but she caught her daughter and held her tight; she let Ollie be the one who let go.

"All right?" she whispered when Ollie's arms loosened.

"All right," Ollie agreed. "Now tea?"

"Yes, tea. And you can have some milk, if you like."

Ollie nodded and slid to the floor, running to the stove and waiting for Alice to join her.

Thank You, God, Alice prayed as she walked over to put the kettle on.

Tea tray in hand, Alice soon returned to the parlor.

Mrs. Davenport was seated exactly where Alice had left her, her posture erect, her hands resting on the leather portfolio in her lap. Her expression was neutral, giving nothing away.

"My apologies for the delay, Mrs. Davenport." Alice kept her voice soft and even as she set the tray down. Ollie took a seat next to her, as close as she could comfortably get, while Alice proceeded with the calming ritual of pouring and preparing tea. "We had a difficult moment."

"So I gathered," Mrs. Davenport said, her gaze moving from Alice to the child settled beside her. "Children have many difficult moments. It is the parental response that is of interest to the committee." She opened a small notebook. "I do have a few questions, if you can spare the time now."

"Of course," Alice said. She glanced at her daughter. "Ollie, why don't you run upstairs for a few moments and fetch your new dolly?"

Ollie nodded and raced off.

"Sugar and cream?" Alice said as Ollie thumped up the stairs.

"Cream but no sugar," Mrs. Davenport said easily. She waited to speak again until Alice had passed a cup to her, then she sipped once before setting it aside. "How frequent are these ... difficult moments?"

Alice swallowed. "They are less so as time goes on," she said honestly. "Ollie is trying her best to learn, and to become used to living here, and we are being patient with her as she adjusts."

Mrs. Davenport inclined her head. "I understand. How is the child's appetite? Is she eating well?"

"She is. She is not particular about food." Alice was thankful for that; her own upbringing had offered no training in the art of culinary negotiation. "We make sure everything she has is nutritious, and she eats until she is full."

"And her sleeping habits?" Mrs. Davenport asked. "Does she rest well through the night?"

Alice hesitated. How easy it would be to lie—to say there was nothing of concern to report. But to lie to the inspector seemed unwise at best. "No," she said simply. "The nights are very difficult for her. She has nightmares. She wakes up frightened, crying for her mother and the sister she lost."

"I see," Mrs. Davenport said, making a note. "And how do you handle these episodes?"

"My husband and I take turns sitting with her," Alice said. "We hold her, we talk to her until the fear passes and she feels safe again. It often takes time."

Mrs. Davenport made another note.

Ollie returned, the small doll Riley had brought her last week tucked under her arm.

Mrs. Davenport looked up from her notebook, and for the first time, her severe features softened. It was not a smile, but it was adjacent to one. "May I see your doll, Olivia?"

Ollie presented her prize for inspection.

"Very pretty. Is it a new doll?"

Ollie nodded. "From Uncle Riley."

Mrs. Davenport glanced at Alice for confirmation.

"From my husband's cousin, Mr. Farjon. We are very close, and he bought her that as a gift last week."

Mrs. Davenport turned back to Ollie. "It's a fine home you have here. Are you happy?"

Ollie looked at the imposing woman, then glanced at Alice for a split second before looking back at the inspector. "Yes, ma'am," she said.

"And what do you like best about being here?"

Ollie didn't have to think about that. "*Cookies* and *biscuits* are the same thing, and they are both good," she said with solemn certainty. "Papa reads books to me, and he lets me sit in his lap and sound out some words. Mama and I are *gardeners*. I am a *help*."

"I see." Mrs. Davenport nodded.

"Perhaps you could go put dolly to bed, Ollie," Alice suggested. "Mrs. Davenport and I must speak a bit more."

Ollie disappeared up the stairs at a gallop, and Alice took a sip of her own tea—and waited.

"She seems to be well taken care of, Mrs. Strauss," Mrs. Davenport said. "It surprises me that Olivia is calling you *Mama*. It is rather early. She seems clean and healthy, and she certainly lacks no intelligence. I am impressed."

Alice pressed her lips together. "Then ...?"

"I believe I have all the information I require," Mrs. Davenport said, rising from her chair.

Alice stood as well, her heart pounding. "And your report?"

Mrs. Davenport closed her notebook with a soft, final snap. She met Alice's gaze, all professional severity gone. "My report," she said, pulling on her gloves, "will state that this placement is not merely suitable, but that it appears to be a work of genuine providence. The asylum can provide shelter and instruction. We cannot, however, provide a mother who will abandon her own dignity to kneel on the floor with a heartbroken child. It seems Olivia has found that here. I see no reason why you should not proceed with the legal petition as soon as you feel ready. Good day to you."

Moments later, she was gone.

The front door clicked shut, leaving Alice alone in the parlor.

She stood there, numb and shocked, until she heard the pitter-patter of Ollie racing back down the stairs. The little girl sidled up next to Alice and leaned against her skirts.

"Was that a test?" she asked, sliding her small hand into Alice's.

Alice laughed, a real, full-throated laugh of pure relief. "Yes, darling," she said, sinking back onto the settee and pulling her daughter into a hug. "I believe it was. And I do believe we passed."

Early July 1887

The noise of downtown Cincinnati was suffocating—the rumble of carriage wheels on the cobblestones, the clang of a distant streetcar bell, and the shouts of tradesmen mixed together into a chaotic harmony.

But honestly, Peter barely registered the noise. His entire focus was on the woman whose hand was tucked into the crook of his arm ... and on the task that lay before them. He reminded himself once more that the judgement was over—and this was the time to act.

He knew Riley's law office well, but it felt different today. He was not here as a friend and a cousin, or even as a temporary assistant to Riley, but as a client filling out important paperwork. Vital paperwork.

The tall, dusty windows let in streaming sunlight that cut through still more dust. *What Riley really needs is someone to clean this.* Peter pushed aside the unhelpful thought, determined to focus.

Riley rose as they entered, and Peter noted the subtle shift in his cousin's demeanor. The usual easy grin was there, but it was tempered by a professional seriousness. Today, he was not just their family; he was their legal counsel.

Honestly, Riley was probably more responsible as a lawyer than as a cousin, but Peter avoided voicing that thought.

"Alice, Penn," Riley said, gesturing to the two sturdy chairs before his desk. "Glad you could make it. Come in, sit down."

Peter helped Alice into a chair before taking his own. It felt strange, sitting across from Riley like this, the great desk seeming like an entire continent between them.

Riley settled back into his own chair, but he was still *Riley* despite the formality of this moment; his hands drummed a restless rhythm on the edge of the desk. "As I told you, I received the affidavit of consent from Mrs. Gable and the asylum this morning," he began. "We have their official sanction, which is all we were waiting for."

Peter took Alice's hand and squeezed it. "See? It's done."

"Now," Riley continued, "there is nothing left to do but make our own declaration to the court." He gestured to a stack of papers, which were relatively neatly stacked, for him. "I have the petition ready for your review."

He slid the stack of papers across the polished surface of his desk. "This," he said, his voice taking on a more formal, lawyerly tone as he tapped the top page, "is the official Petition for Adoption for Olivia Muller. I've drawn it up according to the Ohio statute."

Peter pulled the document closer, his eyes scanning the dense legal language. He felt Alice lean in beside him, her shoulder brushing against his; he suspected she was skimming faster than he was and, as usual, comprehending more.

"It's a formal petition to the Hamilton County Probate Court," Riley explained, pointing to specific lines as he spoke. "It names you both as the petitioners and Olivia as the child to be adopted. It states that her parents are deceased and that her legal guardianship currently rests with the Cincinnati Orphan Asylum—their signed and notarized consent is attached as the second page. It also affirms that you are fit and proper persons to provide for her care and education, and that upon the court's decree, she will be, for all legal purposes including inheritance, your child."

Peter's gaze fixed on the paragraph. *Your child*. The words, written in the cold, precise language of the law, shook him to the core.

Riley tapped a different section of the page. "This is where we formally state the name change, from Olivia Muller to Olivia Grace Strauss. It's all part of the same petition. Once the judge signs the final decree, that will be her legal name. Double check the spelling here—I assume it's all as it should be, but I got in trouble last week. Elisabeth with an *S*. Who knew?"

Peter couldn't speak, so Alice was the one who said, "Yes, that's right. I don't think there's another way to spell Olivia or Grace."

Riley grinned, and his tone became teasing for the first time that day. "Perhaps you wanted to spell Strauss differently. Now would be the time if you wanted to Americanize it. Of course, that would rather complicate things."

A smile slid across Peter's face in spite of himself. "When are you going to Americanize Farjon?"

"If you must know, there used to be an *E* in it."

"Farjeon is English," Alice protested.

Riley rolled his eyes. "Please don't tell my parents—they are convinced it's French."

"I make it a point to never try to tell your parents anything," Peter replied gamely.

"All I really need is your signatures," Riley said, his professional voice returning. He picked up a pen and extended it to Peter. "Whenever you're ready, Penn."

Peter took the pen. He dipped the nib into the inkwell, the scratching sound loud in the quiet office as he signed his name—*Peter William Strauss*—on the designated line.

"And mine?" Alice murmured, a slight hesitation in her tone, as Peter blotted the ink.

"Yes," Riley said.

Peter noted Riley knew now was not the time to launch into a rant about England's "backwards ways." He watched as she took the pen from him, her knuckles white. She leaned forward, poising the pen just above the line, and then she stopped. Peter's heart caught in his throat. He knew what this signature meant to her—it was the final, irrevocable surrender of the dream she had carried for so long. It was the legal claiming of a future she still feared she was not worthy of. He saw the flicker of panic in her eyes, the deep breath she took to steady herself.

He did not speak. He did not move. He simply waited. *I trust you. I know you. This is right; you know this is right.* He didn't say it aloud, but he hoped she knew.

She lowered the pen to the page, and with a quiet scratch that sealed their future, she signed her name in a whirling, elegant swoop: *Alice Strauss*.

Riley took the document back, a warm, genuine smile finally breaking through his professional facade. He reviewed their signatures and gave a satisfied nod.

"Excellent," he said. "I'll have my clerk file this with the court this afternoon. The judge's docket is fairly clear for the summer, I understand, so I would expect them to set a hearing date for sometime in late August or early September."

"And the hearing?" Peter asked the question he knew Alice was thinking. "What will that look like?"

"It's a formality, really." Riley leaned back in his chair, tilting the legs dangerously. "With the asylum's consent and no one to contest it, it will be a private proceeding in the judge's chambers. Just us, a representative of the orphanage, and the judge. He'll ask a few questions, verify you understand the permanence of the act, and then he will issue the final decree. From that moment on"—he grinned—"she is your daughter in every sense of the word."

A beat of silence followed Riley's declaration. Peter cleared his throat, his mind shifting to practicalities. "What do we owe you, Rye?"

"Don't be ridiculous, Penn. Consider it my first official gift as an uncle. All it cost me was a bit of ink." He winked. "She's my favorite niece, you know."

Peter rolled his eyes. "You barely know Eleanor's children, so that's no great compliment."

"Nevertheless." The grin slid off Riley's face. "I'm glad to do this for you. Both of you—really. I can honestly say I can't imagine anyone more worthy."

Peter swallowed hard, a painful lump forming in his throat. He had to look away for a moment, blindsided by the fierce sincerity in Riley's voice. "Thank you, Rye. That means more than you know."

Chapter Twenty

July 1887

RILEY WAS ADJUSTING HIS hat in the mirror and rambling about something Peter wasn't listening to when Polly approached them, eyes only for her father. Peter held out his arms for a hug, and she gave him one, but she was suspiciously distracted in that "I absolutely want something" way. Still in her Sunday best, given that they'd only returned from church a few minutes ago, and looking cute as a button, she clasped her hands in front of her and looked up at her father.

"Daddy," she said seriously, "can I go on the walk with you and Uncle Penn? Please? I promise I'll be good."

Riley raised an eyebrow, glancing at Peter with a small smirk. "She's using the 'I'll be good' line. Must be serious."

Peter chuckled. "She's picked up a few negotiation tactics from you. With her, it may be sincere, so be careful."

Riley crouched to Polly's level. "How about some walking shoes then, Baby Doll?"

Polly hesitated, glancing down at her stockinged feet. "I can get them."

Riley pushed himself to his feet and nodded toward the stairway which rose from the entryway. "Quickly, if you want to come. Don't tell Susie."

Polly nodded and padded up the stairs, clearly making an effort to show her maturity through a hurried but not scattered pace. As her soft footfalls faded, Peter leaned closer to Riley. "We're not telling her where we're going, are we?"

"Not a chance on earth, Penn. Not if we want this to remain a secret until we leave the house." Riley folded his arms across his chest. "If we say 'a birthday present,' she's going to run and brag to Susie—which will ruin the fun of the surprise."

"Right." Peter had to smile at that. "This gift is for both her and Susie, so perhaps she'd know better."

"She's a clever one," Riley admitted with a wry smile. "Must take after you, because she's nothing like me. But when she figures it out, we'll deal with it then. I suppose letting the girl pick her own pony out isn't a half-bad idea. You're right that they must share it."

Polly returned a moment later, carefully pulling on her shoes and tying them herself. She straightened, smoothing the front of her coat with practiced precision. "All ready," she announced, her tone measured.

"You sure you're up for a long walk?" Riley ruffled her carefully combed hair; Polly reached up to smooth it down. "I'm not going to carry you if you get tired."

Peter rolled his eyes. Riley didn't mean that; he was a pushover when it came to his daughters.

Polly nodded solemnly. "I can walk a long ways with you."

They kept Polly between them as they left their quiet neighborhood and headed toward the main avenues. Though many shops were closed for Sunday, the streets still bustled with activity. Vendors called from market stalls, carriage horses clattered against the cobblestones, and the steady, insistent clang of a cable car bell echoed over the din.

Peter held Polly's small hand firmly as they approached the corner of Gilbert Avenue. The sight of the cable car rumbling down the hill sent a pang of unease through him. He wasn't sure he would ever get used to the sight of those things. It wasn't as if he hadn't ridden one, but he was uncomfortable with them. Hence why he and Riley were walking to meet the owner of several suitable ponies today. Riley had promised Peter that Ollie would also be a beneficiary, so Peter hadn't brought her or Alice along. Neither of them would have been much good at concealing their excitement.

"Stay close, Polly," he said, glancing down at her. Her solemn face tilted up to meet his, her brow furrowed in concentration as she stepped carefully over a puddle. "We'll cross together when it's safe."

Ahead of them, Riley moved briskly, his long strides already carrying him across the street. He turned back with an easy smile.

"Come on, Penn," he called, raising his voice over the clamor. "You're far too slow! You know we haven't got all day, don't you?"

Peter hesitated, his grip tightening on Polly's hand. The street seemed anything but clear to him. A dray rattled past, its driver shouting at a pair of restless horses who were prancing to the side, obviously uncomfortable with the scene around them; and the cable car—ominous and heavy—rolled down the hill with increasing acceleration, its bell ringing insistently.

"Hold on, Rye." Peter bent to scoop up Polly. "Come here, Dolly. Those horses don't look happy to me. We'll have to rush across the street after the car goes past. We should—"

The scene unfolded in a horrific blur. The cable car's bell clanged wildly, a sound of pure panic now; the grinding of steel on steel screamed as the gripman frantically yanked the brake. Riley, caught mid-stride, turned, a flash of surprise on his face.

There was no time to shout.

The impact sent him sprawling onto the cobblestones with a sickening, final thud. Polly screamed.

Peter lowered the child to the ground, swiftly, as men dashed about him, obscuring his view of the street—of his best friend. "Stay here," he said hoarsely. "Do not move from this spot. Do you understand me?"

He wasn't sure what Polly said in return, if anything. He couldn't wait another moment. He dashed into the street, his heart pounding as he reached Riley's side. A small crowd had already begun to gather, their murmurs blending into the chaotic noise of the city.

Riley lay motionless, his face pale and damp with cold sweat. His chest heaved with shallow breaths, and his eyes fluttered open as Peter gripped his shoulder.

"Riley," Peter said. He was surprised at how calm and clear his voice was. *Let him be all right, Lord.* "Can you hear me? Are you hurt?"

Riley's frantic eyes flickered about, as if looking for something in particular. "I've had better days." His voice sounded tight, almost too faint to hear. "Polly?"

"She's safe. Don't try to move."

"No," was all Riley managed.

"Fetch a doctor!" one of the men shouted to the onlookers. A boy darted off through the crowd, his feet pounding against the cobblestones.

There were other men there then.

"We could lift him to the side, and then make a decision from there," one said.

Peter nodded. Yes, yes, Riley shouldn't be here long, but moving him seemed like more of a risk. "I'm going to try to find where you're hurt, Rye."

"No," Riley said. "Ribs ... *ugh* ..." He swallowed and winced. "Maybe just ribs. I can't feel anything else. Don't touch, though."

"Right." It was just like Riley to have some idea of how he'd managed to almost kill himself. But he was here now—he was conscious. That was a good sign. "They want to move you."

"Yeah."

"All right."

Someone brought a large plank of wood, maybe from a nearby store. Relieved, as he never would have thought of something like that, Peter helped get Riley's body onto the makeshift stretch.

Riley groaned and lost consciousness.

But he was fine. He had to be fine. After all, he wouldn't have been awake if he were really hurt. Comforting himself with this notion and praying without ceasing, Peter helped carry the stretcher to the sidewalk. A doctor was there shortly, and Riley returned to consciousness long enough to answer a few questions and then faint dead away again.

The doctor's face was gray and pinched.

But even if Riley's injuries were serious, at least the doctor would take care of him now, wouldn't he?

"He's lucky to be alive," the doctor said grimly, pressing lightly against Riley's chest once more. This time, Riley didn't stir.

God, help us. Peter clenched his fists. "What can be done for him?"

The doctor shook his head then sighed. "I have an office just down the street. If we can get him there, I'll do what I can. But we need to move quickly."

Peter nodded, relief and panic warring in his chest. He clung to the words. *'Lucky to be alive.' Not dead. Just alive.* "Right. We'll take him. I should send for his wife. And would you welcome another doctor?"

"Who?" the doctor asked, briefly glancing up at Peter.

"Dr. Engall. Riley has always gone to him."

"Yes. We'll send someone for both of them. He should see his wife."

Peter ignored that comment. *Lord, help the doctor know what to do to save him.*

A young man from the crowd darted forward. "I could run for Dr. Engall," he said.

"Thank you," Peter said, relieved. "You know his direction?"

"I do."

After the young man was gone, someone else came forward who was willing to fetch Maddie.

The men who had lifted the makeshift stretcher before stepped forward once more, ready to carry Riley. Peter's gaze swept the crowd and landed on Polly. She was exactly where he had left her, a small, still figure, with a kind-faced stranger resting a steadying hand on her shoulder. She seemed even tinier amidst the towering adults. Her wide eyes locked onto Peter, and he felt a pang of guilt for almost forgetting her in the commotion.

"Polly," he called, swiftly going to her. "We need to take your daddy to the doctor's office. You'll have to come with us. The doctor's going to help him, sweetheart," he added, tucking a stray lock of blonde hair behind her ear. "But we need to hurry."

Polly nodded but said nothing, her eyes wide and stricken, and Peter scooped her up in his arms.

As the stretcher bearers began their careful march toward the doctor's office, Peter followed closely, Polly's arms wrapped around his neck. He could feel her fingers gripping the collar of his coat tightly, her head resting against his shoulder. She didn't say a word.

Honestly, Peter was glad of it. He wouldn't have known how to respond.

At the office, he had no choice but to leave Polly in the waiting room. It was better than having her watch her father slip in and out of consciousness, but he could scarcely bear to leave her alone.

When Maddie comes, Alice probably will, too, and she can watch her, he reasoned.

In the doctor's office, they transferred Riley to an examination table, and the doctor worked efficiently to remove or cut the clothes from the top half of Riley's body. Peter came to stand at Riley's side once more.

He could see the damage to his cousin's body as Riley lay there without his jacket and shirt. Peter forced himself to look away. *This is bad.*

Riley was in and out of consciousness for the next twenty minutes. It seemed like an eternity later when Peter heard the hurried footsteps outside the examination room. He turned to the door just as it opened and Maddie burst in, her face pale and tearstained.

"Riley!" Her voice was hoarse with emotion as she rushed toward the table.

Fearing she might fling herself on Riley, Peter caught her arm. "Easy—he's unconscious. Dr. Engall should be here soon, then they'll decide what must be done."

She turned her stricken face to Peter then. "What happened?"

"It was a cable car. It couldn't have stopped in time, and he wasn't watching for it. There was a wagon, and he had to walk around it to cross the street. I held back—I didn't go with him. I thought—"

"Why would he run in front of a cable car?" Maddie cried. "Why wouldn't he look first? Why—?"

"It all happened so fast." In fact, Peter wasn't sure of the order of events, only that it had happened. He glanced over his shoulder at the doctor, bent over Riley and muttering instructions to a nurse who had appeared a few minutes before. Riley's face was still pale and his skin clammy, but his breathing was steady now, if shallow. "Can you be calm?"

"I—I—"

"You can't stay if you're not calm."

Maddie looked at Peter as if he'd slapped her, but he refused to pacify her. There were some tough decisions to be made very soon, and he couldn't have her wailing and carrying on.

"Is Alice here?" he asked.

"She's with Polly," Maddie said, her voice fainter now as her eyes fixed on Riley. "I'll stay calm."

"All right." He released her and stood back as she walked, with at least some semblance of control, to Riley's side and took his limp hand.

Dr. Engall arrived a few minutes later and immediately began to confer with the other doctor in low, urgent tones. Peter moved to Riley's other side and whispered prayers. They weren't very coherent, granted—he wasn't at all sure what he said, but he believed God would work His will with whatever made its way out of Peter's lips.

"Penn?" Riley's voice was rough, and he didn't open his eyes, but he had spoken.

"Maddie's here now, Rye," Peter said quickly. "Dr. Engall is here, too, and they're trying to decide how to help."

"It's pretty bad, isn't it?"

"Riley, don't say that!" Again, Maddie's tone had an edge of hysteria and Peter cut her a sharp look. "You don't mean that. You're going to get better. You *have* to."

Riley's eyes fluttered open, briefly landing on Peter before fixing on Maddie. "Stay with me. Will you stay with me?"

"Yes, yes." To Maddie's credit, she did fight the panic in her voice. "But I need you to stay with me."

"All right." Riley swallowed. "Can't breathe. Ribs, right?"

"Yes, it's your ribs," Peter said. "The doctors are deciding—oh, here they are."

The doctors looked grave, especially Dr. Engall, whose eyes flickered from Maddie to Peter and back with something that looked like indecision crossing his face. Peter stepped aside so Dr. Engall could stand next to Riley and briefly examine him, nodding as he seemed to confirm the other doctor's findings for himself.

"Maddie, can I talk to you?" Dr. Engall said gently. "You and Peter step away with me for a moment, and we'll have a quick chat."

"No," Riley said through gritted teeth. "I'd better hear, too."

Peter opened his mouth to protest then snapped it shut. Riley would want to know the prognosis—even if it were bad. *Lord, help us. Help us find a way. We can't lose him. I can't lose him.*

"Riley, things look bad. It seems like internal bleeding. We're not sure where, and it would likely be almost impossible to stem. We can try to operate, but—" Dr. Engall shook his head. "We don't believe that would do much good other than to hasten the end and cause your last moments to be under ether rather than with your family."

Maddie wavered on her feet. Peter circled around the exam table and caught her arms. He couldn't think. He couldn't do anything but breathe and do the next thing.

Something shifted in Riley's eyes—a desperate realization. His head turned toward Peter. "Gonna keep her safe?"

Confusion was quickly replaced by a raw horror. "Rye—"

"*No*, Penn. *You're* gonna keep her *safe*?"

Peter pressed his lips together then nodded. That was an easy promise to make—for Riley's sake, nothing would happen to Maddie that Peter could prevent. "Yes. I will."

"Peter! *No*!"

He ignored Maddie's horrified voice. "And the girls and the baby," he promised softly. "It'll be all right, Rye. You have nothing to fear on that front while I'm living."

"Peter, Riley, you *can't*." Maddie's voice rose another pitch, and she jerked away from Peter, stepping back, eyes wide. "I won't let you. Riley, I need you. You can't leave me. I couldn't live without you. There must be something—"

"Oh, honey," Riley said, then fought back a cough. "I love you. Tell the—the girls—'*I love you*.'"

"No, *no*. We'll operate. You can't just give up. There must be a way. There must be—"

Perhaps not for the first time, Riley ignored his wife. "Can I go home?" he managed. "Can I be at home with my family?"

"Yes, Riley. You could go home—and have the next few hours." Dr. Engall stepped back. "I could arrange for your transport."

Riley managed a tight nod, and Dr. Engall disappeared.

"You don't mean that." Maddie's tone could have cut diamonds. "If there's any chance—"

"That was his nice way of saying there *isn't*, honey," Riley said. "Don't wanna talk. Wanna hold your hand and go home. Please, Mads. Can't go to sleep and not wake up." For the first time, fear darted across his face. "Wanna be with you. *Please*."

There were tears streaming down Maddie's cheeks, but she held Riley's hand and stood, trembling, next to Peter while the doctor arranged whatever he needed to do so they could take Riley home.

And Peter didn't think about anything at all.

Alice knew, with a cold certainty that settled deep in her bones, that this would be one of those days. One of the few so horrible that the memory of it, even years later, would never fail to make her shudder with revulsion.

Riley did get home. It was touch and go for a while, from what Alice understood, but he seemed determined to make it, to be at his house when he died—for that was what was happening. He was coming home to die. Peter had managed to communicate that much to her, despite an oddly stoic demeanor. Alice got Polly, Susie, and Ollie to the Farjon house, and Flick came over and sat with them—Polly near catatonic, Susie sobbing inconsolably, Ollie with wide eyes full of an understanding too deep—while Alice went up the stairs to Maddie and Riley's bedroom and stood by her husband outside the door.

His arm came around her, but other than that, he didn't acknowledge her. Riley was settled now. They could hear Maddie weeping, and it seemed they could do nothing but grant her these last moments to say goodbye in private.

"I wish she'd control herself," Peter said.

Alice's eyes moved to Peter's face, surprised. "But ..." But Maddie's husband was dying. Her husband whom she adored with all her heart. Her husband who had been hale and hearty not an hour ago.

But she knew what Peter meant. Maddie wouldn't truly get to say goodbye to Riley if she did all her mourning before he left. That said, could Peter really blame her? His unnatural calm was manufactured at best; surely he knew that. Surely adrenaline alone was keeping him on his feet.

The door swung open. Maddie left it and walked back to the bedside.

"Will you come?" Peter asked.

Alice nodded. "Of course."

But she hung back, almost nervous to step close to the bedside. Riley wasn't a small man, but he looked so delicate, his face gray, his breath shallow and uneven, and it frightened her. Yet for Peter, she would sooner die than leave this room.

"Gonna see the girls in a minute." Riley seemed to be forcing himself to get a few last words. "Sorry, Penn. Sorry. Should've been more careful. Should've—"

"No, no, Rye. It's all right." Peter's voice held the threat of tears, and Alice slowly moved toward him, coming to place her hand on his lower back. "It was an accident. I'm so sorry. I love you. I hate this; this shouldn't have happened."

Somehow, Riley managed a crooked smile. "Wise man ... always told me ... about God's will ... trust Him. Love you, too. The girls?"

"Right." Peter stepped away, but Alice gestured for him to stay and went to fetch the girls herself.

The next half hour was even worse. Riley was fading but also fighting to behave a little normally for his daughters.

Susie calmed at the sight of him and wanted to crawl all over him, and then was angry when she couldn't. Polly said nothing but quietly squeezed his hand then stepped back, eyes wide with fright. But Dr. Engall had made the right choice—it was far better for the girls to say goodbye to Riley, to have him say "I love you" once last time, than to never see him living again.

Susie had to be forcibly removed from the room, while Polly left with only one backward glance. Alice retreated to the girls' room, holding Susie until the little girl's sobs subsided into sleep, then leaving her in Flick's care. She moved through the house with a quiet purpose, asking a neighbor to send a telegram to her in-laws and writing another to be sent the moment the end came. Someone would need to tell the Farjons—and Alice felt it would come best from Lilli. She didn't know what else to do, and it seemed cruel to ask Maddie to manage that.

When she returned to the room, Dr. Engall was monitoring Riley's thready pulse, and at last, despite Maddie fighting it every step of the way, Riley, who was having an increasingly hard time drawing breath, asked for ether. Not a large dose—but enough.

And so Alice stood to the side, weeping silently, and watched Riley tell Maddie that he loved her—and then fall asleep.

When he stopped breathing, Maddie's keening cries echoed throughout the house.

Chapter Twenty-One

Peter didn't know what he felt in the next hour or so. But he did things anyway. He did a lot of things.

Maddie wailed until she fainted. He let her lie next to Riley—no, Riley's body—after making sure she was still breathing.

Dr. Engall said he would start making arrangements.

Peter didn't know what to do then, so he went to Riley's office, Alice trailing behind him. She had been crying for a while but had stopped and was watching him closely. He unlocked the safe, and took out his cousin's will and other documents. A few years ago, Riley had asked Peter to be his executor in case of his untimely death. Peter had laughed at the time, but he'd signed the papers.

Alice helped him sort through the most vital papers and told him she had sent messages to his parents.

That was good. That was something he'd have needed to feel something about.

He went back upstairs. Maddie had come to and was crying over Riley's body.

"I'm sorry, Maddie," Peter said quietly, but he wasn't really anything. He was just numb. "I loved him like a brother. I'm so sorry."

"It won't bring him back," Maddie whimpered. "It won't."

"No." What else could Peter say? There was a giant cavern inside him.

It kept getting wider and wider. If he thought about it, he'd break down, and he couldn't because ... because ...

Because the last time Peter had broken down, really broken down, to the point of incoherently sobbing over something that felt too big and horrible and unfair to comprehend, he had just lost his son, and Riley had sat with him. Comforted him. Made him want to live again, or at least forced him to believe that he must.

Without Riley, Peter felt adrift.

"What can I do for you?" he asked Maddie, because he wanted to do something else, anything else. "Can I send someone to you? Can I bring you anything? Dr. Engall will help us t-take care of the body. What else do you need?"

Maddie slowly turned to him, suddenly calm. "I need my husband back."

What was there to say to that?

"I can't live without him, Peter—I can't. I wish I were dead. There is nothing I want save him—nothing." She dropped back down on the pillow beside Riley with a wail. "Nothing!"

"Maddie—"

"No. Get out. Leave us. I can't stand this awful nightmare; I can't stand it. Leave us, please."

Peter left, closing the door behind him then standing in front of it. What else could he do? They were both grieving a man they had cared about deeply—a husband, a brother—but could offer each other no true comfort. Of all the women in the world, Peter was least likely to step up for Maddie in that way. Even though this was an extreme circumstance, it never left his mind that Alice had once been jealous of Maddie, had doubted Peter's fidelity because of her. When it had finally gotten through Peter's thick skull what Alice was talking about in regards to his behavior with Maddie, he had never been alone with or touched Maddie in any way. He had been so careful, and he would not stop even now.

Because ... *Alice*. Alice was what mattered.

He turned to find her behind him. When he held out his arms, she went to him, and he gripped her with all the strength of his body. She wrapped her arms around him and squeezed.

After a time, he realized he was crying—sobbing, really—and she was rubbing his back and praying softly with words not her own.

"'Yea, though I walk through the valley of the shadow of death, I will fear no evil: for Thou art with me; Thy rod and Thy staff they comfort me. Thou preparest a table before me in the presence of mine enemies: Thou anointest my head with oil; my cup runneth over. Surely goodness and mercy shall follow me all the days of my life: and I will dwell in the house of the Lord for ever.'"

Not two hours after she'd sent the initial telegram, Alice received notice that her father-in-law would be there in the morning—traveling all night to reach Cincinnati—while Lilli was going down to Virginia to travel back up with Riley's parents.

She could feel the relief in Peter when she told him. He wouldn't have to bear the next few days alone; someone else with sense would be there to help sort through the legalities and make sure everything was settled.

Despite knowing there was little that could be done that evening, especially given that Maddie had locked her bedroom door and was not responding to anyone, Peter didn't sleep much—nor did Alice. He sat next to Polly's bed, holding her hand until she fell asleep, and then went back to Riley's study and sat there, silent, for a long time.

Alice went home and brought Ollie to bed with her. The little girl was quiet, and even her usual string of questions were muted tonight. She kept asking after Peter—"Papa is so, so sad," she whispered over and over again, until she fell asleep.

Early the following morning, Dr. Engall returned.

"Has Maddie emerged?" he asked gently.

Peter didn't reply, so Alice did. "No, we haven't seen her since last evening. The door was locked last time I checked."

The doctor nodded gravely. "I understand. However, it's time to prepare the body. She will have to give him up."

Alice took a deep breath and turned to Peter. He set down the paper he had been trying (apparently unsuccessfully) to read for several hours, and nodded. "I'll go speak with her."

Alice rose and went to his side, slipping her hand into his. "What will you say?" she murmured.

"I don't know," he said. "Dr. Engall, please make whatever arrangements you must." Then he disappeared up the stairs.

She couldn't hear what was said when he entered the room, but her imagination filled the silence with fragmented images—Maddie's tears, perhaps even an initial stubborn refusal, and, likely, Peter's quiet persistence. Whatever he said, it wasn't long before Alice heard a door opening and soft footsteps. From the bottom of the stairs, she watched as what could only be the ghost of Maddie Farjon drifted across the landing and into the guest room. Maddie was garbed in a black dress that seemed from another decade, another era of mourning. Her expression was hollow and her hair unkempt, still in the style she had worn the day before. Her movements were measured, her face white; there was a shakiness about her, and her hand briefly caught the doorframe as she entered the room, as if to steady herself.

Then the door closed behind her.

Peter descended the stairs a few moments later, his face gray—grayer than it had been. He didn't speak as he crossed the room, only pausing briefly to brush his hand against Alice's. After saying a few words to Dr. Engall, he turned back to her.

"You need to rest," she said softly. "There's nothing we can do here. Dr. Engall will take care of things—darling, please. I want to go home."

Peter looked at her for a long moment then nodded. "Yes. Yes, we should go home."

They passed through the kitchen back door into the garden. Riley's woebegone Quip greeted them. Peter paused to pat the dog's head, but Alice slipped her arm through his and tugged him along.

"You're going to eat something and lie down," she said firmly. "You're going to let me take care of you, darling."

He nodded wordlessly.

Ollie met them at the door, still in her nightgown, and Alice sent her up to dress, after a firm assurance that she would "take care of Papa."

Half an hour and a bowl of warm leftover stew later, Alice led her husband to their bedroom and commenced undressing him. He made the unfortunate mistake of protesting, but she couldn't let him.

"I'm going to help," she said, carefully laying his rumpled jacket over the edge of a chair, "and that's final."

After all, what else could she do but mother him a little? She had no words to comfort him. She prayed, yes, both aloud and in her heart—she repeated Scripture, as she had all the night before—but she had nothing to do other than to plea with God to find a way through this pain to her husband.

Peter didn't allow her to remove his shoes—as if that crossed some unspoken barrier he felt was "too far"—but otherwise was remarkably pliable; she drew the curtains and lay down next to him on the bed in the dim room.

He pulled her close, and Alice waited, patiently, and rubbed his back, and bit down all the phrases like, "This is a part of God's plan." It might be true, but it wasn't helpful in this moment to think that a loving God would remove a vibrant man, in the prime of his life, from his loving, pregnant wife and young, innocent children. She knew Riley was in Heaven, with the Lord, but she wasn't sure how comforting that reminder would be. In a few days, or a few weeks, that might offer comfort—but now, her only thought was, "But Peter is here."

For the longest time, it had not consoled her to know that her sons were in Paradise. That feeling had come later—not in the initial pain of the loss, but after she had allowed God time to work in her heart.

The only platitude she could think of that wouldn't crush Peter was, "You'll see him again someday. That wasn't goodbye forever; you'll see him again." He nodded when she said that.

But what a long life it would be until that day.

Peter hesitated outside the door to the guest room. The soft murmur of voices drifted down the hall from the girls' bedroom—Alice talking quietly to Polly, who had not said a word and Susie, who had not stopped crying. Ollie was there, but she mostly held her tongue and listened to Alice. Peter hated how competent his child was at dealing with the facts of life and death. It was unfair, and even more unfair that they had brought her into a household that seemed saturated with death.

He winced at the thought. That wasn't true. There was life here, too—it was just hard to see in the midst of the grief.

Other than Alice speaking, the house was silent, as it had been when Peter, Alice, and Ollie had arrived that morning. As it had been every morning, every day, since Riley's death.

The past few days had been a blur. Papa had arrived the morning after Riley passed. Legal matters, funeral arrangements, even decisions Peter couldn't begin to think about—Papa handled them all with calm precision. Peter was grateful, but at times, he wished he'd been left alone to figure it out. It was too painful to just sit and do nothing. At least the confusion and difficulties of managing Riley's will would have given him something to do other than bearing the emotions of every member of the family.

That, Peter decided, was perhaps too much for any one man. He had

God; even in the darkest times, he'd felt the Lord's presence, comforting him. Then there was Alice, who had stayed at his side faithfully through every hard moment. He saw, not for the first time but perhaps in a more impactful way, that she had grown up from the girl he'd once courted into a woman who, while not without flaws, was more than capable of standing by him, come what may. Then there was Ollie, who loved him with such sweet innocence and trusted him to care for her. She gave both him and Alice a renewed purpose. Yes, Alice and Ollie were great comforts to him, but that didn't erase the pain or lessen the loss he felt.

Mama had arrived a few days after Papa, with Uncle Colin and Aunt Georgiana in tow. His aunt and uncle were staying at a hotel, while his parents had taken shifts watching over Riley's daughters and Maddie so he and Alice could rest. They'd been a lot of help and had kept Uncle Colin and Aunt Georgiana from bringing too many dramatics to the situation.

Though to be fair, he wouldn't blame Riley's parents. They had lost their only living son. He was honestly surprised they had been as composed as they were.

But Maddie ...

Maddie had gone silent.

She hadn't come downstairs since that night, hadn't seen the girls, hadn't spoken to anyone ... anyone except Peter. She had even refused to greet her in-laws, which was no surprise given the prejudice they'd treated her with over the years, but given that Mama had practically raised her after Maddie's parents died, Peter found it a little hard to understand why she couldn't see his parents. They loved her, after all, and always would.

But Peter wasn't about to question the logic of a grieving widow.

There were some tricky parts to that decision. It wasn't that she asked much of Peter, exactly, but her dependence on him and only him could be suffocating. Every time he knocked on the door to bring her food or check on her—as she had again and again reiterated that she didn't want to see anyone but him; that "no one else understood"—he felt like he was intruding, and yet he was unable to simply leave her alone. He wouldn't let her starve herself.

Riley had asked him to keep his wife safe. Peter would do that.

He'd seen listlessness and depression before. He'd felt that way himself, so many times. In fact, if he let himself stop for a minute, he might feel that way again. Not to mention he'd watched Alice behave similarly after the loss of their sons.

It terrified him, because even now, he didn't quite know what he could have done differently to help Alice. It was God who had done all the work—Peter had stood by, hopelessly inept and helpless.

Today, Peter knocked gently on Maddie's door. Though there was no answer, he heard the faint creak of the floorboards inside, so he opened the door. The room was dim, curtains drawn tightly against the cheerful spring sunlight. Maddie sat on the edge of the bed, still in that same awful black gown. Her hands lay limp in her lap. She didn't look up when Peter stepped inside.

"How are you today, Maddie?"

She didn't respond. The room smelled of lavender and starch—a testament to Maddie's usual fastidiousness—but a stale, airless quality was beginning to creep in. He wasn't sure if he should force her out. She'd been firm that she didn't want anyone to come help her—with altering or procuring dresses, with cleaning, with cooking, with anything. It had been hard to turn away an entire church, and Peter hadn't been as obedient to that order as Maddie probably would have liked.

But if she didn't leave this room, how would she ever know?

He moved closer, stopping a few feet from the bed, which was as close as he ever got. Promise or no promise, he couldn't bear to comfort her. When he returned to Alice, he would be able to report that he had given Maddie nothing of himself beyond what the duty of friendship required. "Polly and Susie are asking for you again."

At that, Maddie's head lifted slightly, though her expression remained unreadable. "I can't see them," she said, her voice toneless. "Not yet."

"They're worried about you." Peter's tone was firmer than he intended, but he couldn't help it. *Why is she doing this?* He had never known Maddie to not show every appearance of being a loving, even doting, mother.

"They don't understand why you won't come out. Why you won't talk to them. You know that, don't you? They're too young to know what's happening. I'm afraid if this goes on, they could be ..." He stopped himself before he could utter the words "irreparably damaged"—partly because he was convinced the damage was already done.

After all, much as he and Alice loved Polly and Susie, they could only do so much.

Maddie's lips pressed into a thin line. She turned her face away, staring at the curtains. "I can't, Peter. I just ... I can't."

He ran a hand through his hair, the frustration spilling out of him despite his best efforts to keep it buried deep. "They're your daughters. They need you."

"They are *Riley's* daughters," she said. "I can't—I won't—" Then she shook her head. "I won't."

Peter exhaled and lowered his voice a notch. "Maddie, they've already lost their father. They can't lose you, too. They need you now more than ever."

Her eyes filled with tears. "Every time I think of them, I think of Riley. I can't bear to see them, and be reminded, again and again, of what I lost." She placed a hand over her swollen abdomen. "And this little one, who will never know him. It's almost too much to bear."

"I know," Peter said, fighting to keep his voice steady. "God help me, I know. But you have to fight through that. Riley loved those girls more than anything. If he were here, he'd tell you to fight for them."

Her shoulders trembled, hands twisting in her skirts. "It's easy for you to say," she whispered. "Your whole life didn't revolve around him. I lived for him, from the time he rose in the morning until he fell asleep. You don't have to wake up in the night and reach for him and not find him there."

Peter could acknowledge that. "Yes. And I would be devastated if I lost Alice. I won't pretend that's not true, but I also won't pretend I didn't love Riley as a brother. I knew him as well as anyone, perhaps besides you, and I know he would want you to keep trying for Polly and Susie and the new baby."

Maddie's eyes flashed with a bitter anger. "I know you two liked to pretend you were thick as thieves. I know you liked to believe I didn't know all your stupid secrets, the things about his past and yours that you kept from me. But I was his wife, Peter. At the end of the day, your relationship with him was just a friendship, but I was his other half. How do you think it feels to suddenly and horrifically have him stripped from me? How do you think I feel right now? You say you would be devastated losing your wife of six years. We had loved each other for over twenty years."

Peter barely concealed a laugh. Perhaps it was because his nerves were fraying; perhaps it was because she'd decided to snap at what he held most sacred; but suddenly he saw comedy in Maddie claiming to have loved Riley since she was perhaps eleven or twelve. Yes, Riley had developed an infatuation with Maddie when they were both still young, but it was insane to act as if such childish emotions were the types that lasted, especially since as far as Peter knew, Maddie had been oblivious to Riley's feelings at the time, as well she ought to be.

"What have you got to smile about?"

Peter shrugged. He wasn't about to explain his thoughts. "I'm sorry. Perhaps you're right, and I understand you're hurting, so I won't argue with you about it." No matter how much he felt the rather wild urge to prove, in some way, that his feelings for Alice were deep and abiding. "If you think it's easy for me to watch you fall apart, and to watch Riley's daughters suffer, and to not fall apart myself, when I've lost someone I have also loved, far longer than you ever knew him, then you're wrong. I am no stranger to grief. It's not a competition; I don't need to prove to you that I am grieving Riley. But if I can stand up and keep moving, so can you. You can still live. You have to."

Maddie's face crumpled, and she buried it in her hands, sobbing quietly. For a long moment, neither of them spoke. Peter stood there, his gaze wandering to the heavy curtains, the framed embroidery on the wall, the empty teacup on the bedside table. He hated this room. *Hated* what it had come to symbolize.

He had to get her out of here, but unless he dragged her, that wouldn't be happening. He understood why she would not want to return to the room where so much of her life must have played out—and where her husband had died.

At last, he rose and left. What else could he do but remove himself, if he could not take her away with anything short of force?

When Peter entered the girls' room, he paused in the doorway, catching his breath and trying to shake the heaviness that clung to him. Alice sat in a rocking chair by the window, slowly pushing herself back and forth, Susie sleeping in her arms. Polly was sitting at her feet, beside Ollie, who was holding one of Polly's hands in a white-knuckled grip.

When he stepped into the doorway, Alice glanced at him and then rose and laid Susie on her bed. Peter hurried to her side, caught up a blanket that was draped over the foot, and carefully tucked it around Susie.

"She's exhausted," Alice whispered. "Lilli says she was up crying all night."

Peter lightly brushed the child's red curls then drew back. "Polly, sweetheart?" He approached the older of the two girls, who hadn't moved from her spot on the floor. "Do you want to come down with Aunt Alice and me? I hear Aunt Lilli in the kitchen; I bet she's making something to eat."

Polly looked at him with blank eyes, devoid of emotion. She blinked twice then shook her head.

"All right, sweetheart. But we're going to talk later." Peter was determined to get at least a few words out of Polly. He'd asked Dr. Engall to examine her briefly, but there was nothing physically wrong with Polly. She simply remained stoic no matter what was said to her. "Come on, Ollie. We're going."

Ollie rose and tucked her hand into Peter's.

"Maddie?" Alice murmured as soon as they were out of the room.

Peter shook his head. "No change," he whispered. His voice felt unexpectedly hoarse and he cleared his throat.

Ollie looked between them, her brows tight with concern. "She's sad," Ollie clarified, as if Peter and Alice might not understand.

"Yes, I know, darling." Peter ruffled Ollie's hair then knelt and scooped her up. "We're all sad, but it's going to be all right."

Alice placed her hand on his arm, drawing closer to the two of them. "She wouldn't come down?"

"She won't even consider it." It might be marginally less frustrating to talk to a stone wall, but he'd likely get the same results. "She's still ... just sitting there. She refuses to see the girls. She has eaten, a little, but not enough to sustain herself."

Alice's lips pressed into a thin line, her disapproval clear, but she didn't say anything for a long moment. She just stood there and frowned.

Ollie kicked free of him. "I'm going to go see Grandmama and Grandpapa," she told him, then dashed off down the stairs.

Alice remained at his side, her hand still on his arm. "Are you all right?" she asked, brow furrowed. "Honestly. Tell me. What can I do?"

Peter placed a hand on the floral-papered wall. "I don't know, but I'm glad you're here." Somehow, Alice made everything a little easier with her presence. And there was another reason he liked that she had come even the short distance across the gardens to the Farjon house. "I admit I'm uneasy with some of this. With Maddie."

Alice tilted her head, her gaze sharp and searching. "What do you mean?"

"Do you remember how you have said in the past that Maddie can be a bit ... clingy?" He swallowed. "A bit too presumptuous of my time, perhaps?"

Alice's brows lowered slightly. "I remember something to that effect. Perhaps even an argument or two."

"I apologized for that," he said hastily, "and I would again, even with the information I had before this current trial. But I admit now I feel as if I see more of what you were talking about."

Alice was quick about hiding the fierceness that flared in her eyes, but not quite quick enough that Peter didn't catch it. He bit back a smile.

"I feel as if she expects me to step up for her where Riley had always stood," he said in a low voice. "Not just with the girls, though that is a big part of it, but with her. I believe she wants me to act as devastated as she does and to allow her to grow closer to me in the process. I don't think she realizes what she's doing, Alice, really, I don't. But I want to be careful, out of respect for you and for her, as well. So I'm telling you now."

A smile twitched around Alice's lips. "My faithful man," she murmured, bringing her hand up to cup his cheek. "I trust you completely, but she *is* grieving, and that can make the mind do strange things. I know that as well as anyone; I cannot judge her for what I myself struggled with. I don't believe Maddie would go as far as to actually attempt to do anything inappropriate, but she may not know *what* she's doing, and if you're uncomfortable, you need to make it clear to her what you will and will not do and remove yourself where she crosses a line."

Peter nodded and leaned his forehead against Alice's for a moment. "I want you to know that I'm trying to make choices for us, too. I promised Riley I would keep Maddie safe, and I'll do that, but not if that endangers my convictions—or you or Ollie."

Alice kissed his cheek then placed her hands on each of his arms and looked him in the eye. "Just tell me if you need me to follow you into that bedroom and make it extra clear you're mine, because I would do so without hesitance."

"I know you would." He couldn't help but smile at her possessiveness; he much preferred that to apathy. "I'll tell you whatever happens."

Chapter Twenty-Two

Alice followed Peter downstairs, her arm linked through his. Her husband had lost all his joy and gladness in the last several days. Though she didn't blame him, it meant she was watching him closely and doing everything she could to comfort him.

Now, it felt as if shoring up Peter had a new purpose for her, too—it was to comfort Ollie. Though Alice and Ollie had a far closer relationship now, there were still moments when only Peter would do. Alice needed her husband to be strong for her child. She would be fine—but she would stand between Ollie and Peter while he grieved.

As they reached the dining room, raised voices spilled into the hallway, and Alice immediately stiffened. She glanced at Peter, whose jaw clenched.

Of course Aunt Georgiana was causing a fuss. *Of course.* What else did she have to do? Her only surviving son was dead—the last of the four children she'd given Colin Farjon, the only one still willing to visit Clairdelune with any regularity now that Essie was gone.

The air was thick with tension. Uncle Colin paced by the window, more agitated and simultaneously more energetic than Alice had ever seen him. She saw the hard lines of grief on his face, recognizing the strain of a man pushed nearly to his limit.

Meanwhile, Aunt Georgiana sat imperiously at the head of the table, where her son had belonged by right. Her expression was sharp as nails and hard as stones.

Lilli and Chris sat at the table as well; Ollie was curled up on Lilli's lap with her thumb in her mouth. Chris paused whatever he had been saying and turned when Peter and Alice entered the room.

"What's going on?" Peter asked, glancing about.

Chris sighed, running a hand through his hair. "I wish I could say nothing was, but unfortunately, we're arguing about where Riley should be buried."

Alice's stomach turned. How unfair to make that an argument when the choice was clear; he would be buried here, in Cincinnati, near his family. She stayed close to Peter, her fingers brushing the back of his sleeve.

"This isn't up for debate," Aunt Georgiana snapped. "Riley will be buried in the family graveyard at Clairdelune. It's where he belongs."

Alice saw the muscle in Peter's jaw tighten.

"He belongs where Maddie and the girls can visit him," he said, his voice sterner than she'd heard before. "That's *here* in Cincinnati."

Aunt Georgiana frowned. "Maddie and the girls won't need to visit him here. They'll be living at Clairdelune. It's the only logical option. Maddie will need assistance, and the girls will need a stable home. Can you imagine a single woman trying to support herself and two—soon to be three—children alone in this terrible city?"

Peter shook his head. "They have a safe home here," he said. "This is where Riley and Maddie built their life. Their friends are here. Their church is here. Riley wouldn't want his family uprooted."

Aunt Georgiana tilted her head, her gaze icy. "Maddie can't manage everything on her own, and she shouldn't have to. Those children belong at Clairdelune; they always have. Riley should have moved them there years ago, as we always wanted; we should have pressed the matter. If we had, none of this would have happened; he would be alive today. Burying him there is for the best."

Alice saw Peter's face darken. She could tell he was holding himself back, biting down on words that might make the situation worse. But when he spoke, his voice was unwavering.

"Riley didn't want Maddie at Clairdelune." Each word was deliberate. "He told me himself, time and time again. He knew how you've treated her—how you've made her feel like an outsider. Do you really think he'd want his wife and daughters living under your roof after all you've said and done to her and to Riley? If Maddie and the girls need support, they'll get it here, from the people Riley trusted. From me, Alice, their church, their friends. Not from you."

Alice tightened her grip on Peter's hand, prepared for battle herself as Aunt Georgiana's lips pressed into a thin line.

Then a quiet voice broke through the tension.

"Stop it."

Alice turned. Maddie stood in the doorway, her black gown hanging loosely on her frame. She looked fragile, made of glass; tangled blonde hair hung about her pale, drawn face; but her eyes burned with a quiet fury that silenced everyone.

"Maddie," Peter said, stepping further into the room to allow her to enter, and holding out his hand. "Did you hear—?"

Maddie raised a hand, halting him in his tracks. Her gaze moved deliberately around the group, landing on each person in turn. "I've heard enough, I think," she said, her voice calm but oddly hollow, apathetic.

Aunt Georgiana rose from her chair, her tone still icy. "Maddie, we were just discussing what would be best for you and the girls—"

"I don't care," Maddie said, her voice steady but stripped of emotion. She stepped further into the room, her hands trembling as they gripped the back of a chair. "Take him to Clairdelune. Bury him there, if that's what you want. It doesn't matter to me." Her voice cracked with emotion. "He's gone, and no matter where you put him, he's not coming back. Why would I care where you leave his body?" She let out a shaky breath and released her hold. "Do whatever you want," she said quietly. "Just don't make me listen to it anymore."

"But Maddie—" Aunt Georgiana circled the table as if to come toward her. "We ought to make a decision about the girls. We'll want to let the men make decisions about what Riley owns here—the house and any other properties he has—so we can move you down quickly, maybe even before the funeral. I—"

Maddie face was still pale but a fierce, cold anger had entered her brown eyes. "I'll not hear another word about that from you," she said. "I'll go down for the funeral, but after that, I consider our relationship ended. I only ever tolerated you for Riley's sake. You've hated me from the first day you knew I existed, and even when I married your son and gave him children and kept him on the straight and narrow, at no small cost to myself, you never hid that you despised me. Well, I can't hide that I despise *you* anymore. So you'll leave me and my children alone, you hear? I don't want to see you or hear from you ever again after this is all settled. If you'd ever been half-decent parents to Riley—either of you—he wouldn't have been the mad, reckless man he was. He might be here with me today."

Peter winced, and Alice stepped back. That might be taking it a degree far. After all, Riley's personality had always been larger-than-life, and the accident had been unavoidable. But before anyone could get a word in edgewise, Maddie whirled and fled back up the stairs.

Peter was quiet as he undressed for bed that evening, and Alice didn't speak. As on every night since Riley's accident, she didn't know what to say, how to offer anything but her silent support and love. Perhaps she ought to know exactly what words would comfort her husband, but all she knew was that he was suffering and she had nothing to give him but her presence.

Ollie was already tucked away into bed. She'd been full of talk that evening, but thankfully for Peter and Alice, who were both bone-tired, her new grandparents were more than willing to engage with her for hours.

They'd worn her out, and she'd gone to sleep easily enough.

Peter sat down on the edge of the bed with a sigh, glanced at Alice, then slipped under the covers without a word.

She waited a beat, then another, before placing her hand on his shoulder. "Darling," she whispered, not a question, just a statement. "My darling."

He turned to her, pulled her into his lap, and buried his face in her hair. "Alice, why ...?" He couldn't finish the question.

"Shush, shush," she murmured, stroking his back as one might a child. "It's all right. What do you need from me? I want to stand by you. You have always seen the worst in me, so if there are doubts or fears or any kind of suffering, I want to know."

Peter nodded, and for a few moments, they simply sat, holding each other. "Alice?" he whispered at last.

"Hmm?"

He gently pushed her back and cupped her face with his hand. "Alice, can we lie together tonight?"

She blinked. She had assumed that would be the last thing on his mind.

At her failure to immediately say anything, his face was instantly awash with guilt. "I'm sorry. How stupid of me—that wouldn't be appropriate, and you must be exhausted. Forgive me."

"No, no. I was surprised—I would have thought *you* exhausted—but you know I am yours."

"I just want to be close to you."

She could argue that this could happen simply by him remaining close to her, as he had been. Yet she didn't argue—not when he already seemed embarrassed. She acknowledged that if she came to him with her longing, and he critiqued her reasoning for desiring him, she would be crushed. "You are always welcome to me," she said softly. "You know you have only to ask."

"That's not precisely true." He paused and considered. "Or I suppose it is, within reason, as is true of me—but I would never desire you unless you first desired me."

She laughed. "Now that is not *precisely* true, either. You mean you are not interested in taking something that is not freely offered, without pressure or some misguided idea of duty—but for all we did endure, you have never asked me for anything I have not wanted to give."

"What I suppose I mean is, in case you need a reminder, there is no pressure." And he seemed to examine her face, searching for any sign she might not appreciate his touch.

But hadn't she already said she belonged to him? "I would love to be with you tonight, Peter."

If their marriage bed was not a safe place to rest, to find comfort, to find *each other* in the midst of chaos, what else would it be?

Some time later, as she lay in his arms, watching him doze off to sleep, she didn't feel anything but contentment, a deep sense of well-being and rightness. She *liked* that Peter was a good lover—she *loved* that he was her husband. Still, it did help that all things were so easy between them now. It had not always been so. She would hate to return to those awkward, horrible days when she'd been so sure something was wrong with her—unsure if it was her own desire, or her inability to receive pleasure from him, that was the source of the flaw. When she'd wondered if it was evil to long for one's husband in a way that was surely unwomanly and impure—or if her crippling shame and anxiety was the greater sin.

Yet how many women were blessed enough to have a husband who stole those questions away with a firm but loving answer, cemented by his actions? Surely not everyone experienced this sort of passion. There would be no unhappy marriages in that case.

No, this was their secret, their respite, their hidden world. She pressed a final kiss to his forehead, smooth in his sleep, and snuggled into his chest, marveling at the joy he brought her.

There was more grief to come, she knew, but in that moment, she was simply and profoundly thankful that God had given her Peter.

Clairdelune
Eleanor, Virginia

The heat at least was not as blistering as it could have been as Riley's coffin was lowered into the ground.

The crowd of mourners was not small. Though many of his friends, business associates, and acquaintances from Philadelphia or Cincinnati could not travel to Virginia on such short notice, Riley still had many friends in Virginia, and a few of the wealthier families had been able to make the trip.

Many people came up to Peter throughout the day, shaking his hand, telling him a bit of a story or repeating a facetious quote Riley had once uttered. It was comforting to know that Riley would not be soon forgotten, but Peter had never doubted that. His best friend had been a charming, intelligent man, and he certainly took up space in a room; few people forgot Riley, even those who didn't precisely love him.

Maddie had greeted a few friends and then disappeared through much of the day. In truth, Peter didn't blame her for that. A grieving widow was not expected to spend hours receiving visitors, and even if she was, Maddie hadn't been exactly amiable of late.

At least she had finally allowed Lilli and a few women from church to help her buy or create the necessary accessories and gowns a woman needed to enter full mourning. Peter was grateful he didn't have to think about that too much. Even though he had chosen to mourn Riley as a brother, not as a cousin, the changes he had to make to his apparel were simple.

Even now, Peter's fingers traced the black band of his hat as he spoke to an older gentleman he'd not seen since he was eleven or twelve, when his family went to Clairdelune for the first time after the war, only staying there briefly before more quarrels drove his parents back to Philadelphia.

That was when Riley had met Maddie. And yes, he'd been a child, but it was clear that his subtle tormenting of her was the result of an infatuation. Peter had known that then—had defended her with the fierceness of a skinny, bookish little boy who only knew one unrelated girl to whom he felt truly comfortable talking, thereby making her the most important girl in the world.

But Riley hadn't forgotten Maddie. Peter had assumed he had, as the years passed, and they met only at an occasional family event. But when Riley had visited Philadelphia with Peter every time they had a break from their schooling at Harvard, and had suddenly started fighting every one of his wild, reckless instincts to earn her attention, Peter had known Riley *hadn't* forgotten. But at the time, Riley hadn't been a Christian, and Maddie was devout. Even Riley wasn't foolhardy enough to approach her, to risk a rejection; and besides, at the time, Peter had admired Maddie—had thought that, with their years of history and their closeness, she would make him a good wife. He knew now that he hadn't loved her, not really, but he had felt all the agony and longing of a first and only infatuation.

The idea was laughable now. Maddie never would have suited him, not in a million years, and not just because Peter wasn't ready for a relationship at that point in his life.

But the idea that he could never have Maddie had made Riley even more reckless, if possible, during college and law school. The years had passed. Slowly, with God's help and Peter's support, Riley had risen past the haze of alcohol, gambling, and loose women and found his way to Christ—and then he'd set about creating a life that could support a wife.

Peter had never approached Maddie. Had never known how to, had never believed he was worthy of her. She was a perfect golden beauty, always sweet and gentle, giving to a fault, not too stubborn, easy to talk to—in his mind, the summary of all things a good Christian woman *should* be.

It was almost funny to look back on those days, when he'd felt himself a grown man but acted like a foolish coward. Yet in some ways, his cowardice had saved him from being married to a woman who would have exhausted him. That was what it was, he had decided not long after marrying Alice; Maddie wore him out. It had been romantic to suppose that having constantly heightened emotions, and feeling slightly off-kilter but not knowing why, or seeming empty whenever her smiles inevitably turned to another man, was all love. But Peter could not bear that for long. He wasn't ashamed to admit his heart was more susceptible to a beating than Riley's. It had torn at his nerves.

But Alice soothed him and provoked him in all the best ways. When she was on his side, it meant something because she was never afraid to clearly state her opinion if she felt he was in the wrong. In a similar way, her compliments held more weight, because he knew she meant them. He'd soon learned if she was angry or hurting, there was a good reason—even if it wasn't abundantly clear at first glance, even if she couldn't explain it clearly herself. He had become so tired of investing energy into trying to sort through Maddie's mercurial feelings and having abundant sympathy for what had seemed to him to be petty squabbles. There was none of that with Alice; the only problems they'd had resulted from Peter not listening to her when he should have. And there would never be a day when Alice tried to attract the attention of another man, because there was no one she wanted but Peter.

Regardless, it wouldn't have mattered, for Riley had finally approached, courted, and married Maddie, when the time was right, and they had been happy. Riley had a way with Maddie—and in truth, she had a way with him, too. He'd been remarkably tender with her; she calmed him down and made him rethink his priorities.

At this point, a Maddie who didn't have Riley to ground her, make her laugh, and keep her from following her emotions wherever they might lead wasn't a Maddie Peter knew very well. All he could think of when he looked at her was what Maddie had been like at twenty or so, when Peter had been at the height of his infatuation with her.

It scared him a little.

It oughtn't to. If Peter had grown up, surely Maddie had as well.

It was just that he couldn't see that growth in Maddie at the moment.

Alice tugged on his arm, forcing him to drag his brain back to reality, to the present, where he was being given platitudes by yet another well-meaning mourner. Peter didn't mind platitudes; they were the outreaching of one soul to another, both of which were not meant for the grief of this fallen world. How could he reject the honest attempt of another human being to explain away or soothe what could not be explained away or comforted?

The person moved on. Alice squeezed Peter's arm.

"You don't have to talk to everyone," she murmured. "Have you eaten?"

He shook his head. Not today. He felt nauseated.

"You should," she prompted. "People will be leaving soon. We should go down to the kitchen together, just for a moment."

Peter nodded and let her lead him away. That was the other thing he loved about Alice; as she'd grown into herself, she'd become more and more comfortable telling him what to do, but it never felt as if she were manipulating him or trying to force him to bend to her will. No, it was that she wanted what was best for him, and even if there was a time or two when he'd had to put his foot down, in general, he quite agreed with her conclusions. Their relationship had balanced out beautifully over time. She respected his role as the leader of their family, but he respected her goals of keeping him fed and well-rested.

He chuckled to himself at the thought of Alice's only motivation being to keep him alive, which was far from the truth—there was a lot more to her and to their relationship. He might be a little more dead on his feet than she thought. Alice glanced at him, and he could tell she thought he was acting strange.

Yes, he'd better eat.

When they arrived at the kitchen, they found Riley's elder sister, Eleanor O'Brien, had already slipped down and was sitting at the kitchen table nibbling at a sandwich. Her husband and children were elsewhere, but she was chatting with the Farjons' elderly cook, Miss Ruth. Peter hadn't seen Eleanor—Nora, as she'd been known as a young woman—since Riley's wedding. Riley and Maddie had visited Eleanor and her husband in New York a scattering of times, but other than that, she'd had little contact with her family, preferring to invest in her husband, children, and in-laws who, to quote a young, newlywed Eleanor, "actually seemed to love her."

But Riley's funeral had been incentive enough to pull the O'Briens down to Clairdelune. After all, many grievances were forgotten after a marriage or a death in the family.

Essie and Terry, either fortunately or unfortunately, were who-knew-where doing who-knew-what, so they had not received an invitation. Peter wondered if learning that, whenever she did, would show Essie a little more of what she'd done—and what she'd lost in the process. Years ago, Essie had been the rambunctious, tomboyish little sister trailing after Peter and Riley on every adventure. She'd been a happy child—sometimes mulish, easily angered even, but so willing to do anything to please Riley. In return, Riley had given his younger sister much of the love and attention his parents had failed to. Their relationship hadn't changed much in their adulthood.

How Essie would feel when she perhaps read about Riley's death in a newspaper, Peter couldn't imagine. Surely there was nothing crueler than discovering such information from the cold recital of facts in black and white print, but Essie must have known that she would risk such things when she ran away with Terry.

Peter and Alice took a seat across the table from Eleanor and were given matching sandwiches. Peter let Miss Ruth fuss over him and tut and reminisce about Riley. Certainly, she had known him as well as any of them.

"It's just such a shame," Miss Ruth said. "He was in the prime of his life, too. Just a shame. Peter, dear, you've got to eat that sandwich."

Peter poked at it and ignored Alice's "I told you so" look.

"Rye was down here a lot, wasn't he?" Eleanor drummed her fingers on the table. Peter could feel she was tense—she didn't like being at Clairdelune—but she seemed slightly more at home here than she had been standing in the parlor with her mother, who scarcely made eye contact with her. "I seem to remember an incident or two."

A wide smile spread across Miss Ruth's face. "Oh, yes. We couldn't keep his hands out of the cookie jar! He was forever snatching something he ought not to have—he or Essie. But you never would, Peter."

Peter forced a smile. "I can't say that I didn't benefit from the spoils of such exploits from time to time, though."

Miss Ruth nodded. "I remember that being the way of it. He was such a bright, energetic child. Everyone loved him."

"Much more than CJ," Eleanor put in. "He was such a nuisance. I can't remember a time when he wasn't causing trouble for me or Rye or Essie or one of the servants."

Peter decided now was the time to take an extraordinarily large bite of his sandwich. What did one say when a sister decided to insult her long-dead older brother who, in his grieving parents' eyes, could do no wrong?

Neither Alice or Miss Ruth said anything, either, so Eleanor continued. "But they'll worship him until the day they die, just as they worship the idea of the Old South. I understand why. I lost my childhood to the war and my youth to the aftermath. I don't believe slavery was righteous now, but I did when I lived here, and I know all the arguments. Throughout the war, I saw what Mother saw, and I know what the men experienced. I even flatter myself that I understand some of the politics a little. But Father and Mother were both hard, cold people long before all that, and they never wanted to escape that prison. Why should any of their children be punished every day of their lives?" Eleanor shook her head. "I'm glad of my escape. All of us escaped however we could—even Essie—and I'm glad of it. You shouldn't have stayed, Miss Ruth—there's no life left in this awful place."

"Mr. and Mrs. Farjon just do what they think is right, Nora," Miss Ruth said in a low, gentle voice. "I suspect I'll always be here to take care of them, while I'm alive, because I know they're still hurting over CJ and over all the other friends and neighbors and relatives they lost, so they don't really mean to be so cold. Especially Mrs. Farjon. You forget I was here when she came as a new bride, and she was always a little prickly—that's true—but you don't know how much hope even a very cold person can have until you watch it go out of them."

"But you'll never save her or Mr. Farjon from that, Miss Ruth," Peter said softly. "You know that?"

Miss Ruth smiled. "Only the Lord could do that. But they treat me fairly, and I've nowhere else I'd rather be than here."

Peter nodded and glanced at Alice. "Perhaps we'd better go up."

Alice glanced at the watch pinned to the bodice of her black gown—her only ornament. Upon being pressed, Peter had admitted he would appreciate it if she felt comfortable mourning Riley as a brother, and she had quickly agreed. If she regretted it, he wouldn't mind if she wanted to mourn him as a cousin or a more distant relative, which would be a shorter period of time in full mourning—he understood that it would be a great deal more burdensome for her than for him in these next three months—but Alice seldom agreed to anything she didn't fully intend to do.

Eleanor also rose, and Peter followed her and Alice up the stairs from the kitchen.

"Peter?"

Peter paused on the stairs and turned back to face the kitchen. "Yes, Miss Ruth?"

"Riley wouldn't want his wife and those sweet girls here."

"I know. Maddie doesn't want to be here, either."

"Did Riley leave them settled?"

"Yes, Miss Ruth. Riley had everything settled before he left, and whatever isn't, I'll take care of."

"Thank you, Peter." Miss Ruth heaved a big sigh. "That makes me feel a heap of a lot better. I hope I see you again someday, but God bless you and comfort you."

"Thank you," he said sincerely. "The same to you."

After all, it was only God who could take these present sufferings away.

Chapter Twenty-Three

August 1887

Peter needed to get back to writing.

Thankfully, last year he'd turned in two books—one published under his name, one published under his barely-a-pen-name. Riley had all but chosen that pseudonym for Peter.

Both of the novels had done well. *In Heart-Wrung Tears* was a romantic novel, inspired in style and tone by the Brontë sisters and set in Scotland, which Peter had been visiting when it was written. The other story, simply titled *Mankind*, was a slightly more brutal one inspired by the years of watching his mother fight to abolish slavery—and then for progress to continue after the Emancipation Proclamation.

But progress in that arena seemed to have stalled, and Peter didn't mind writing something a little incendiary.

In Heart-Wrung Tears by Peter W. Strauss and *Mankind* by P.S. Penn were his sixth and seventh books to be published, and though they were not his most successful, he was proud of them. His first, *War of Brothers*, continued to be reprinted; *Matins* had found far greater success than he'd ever anticipated; and *The Death Upon Her Eyes*, the novel he had completed after nearly losing Alice, had also sold better, though Alice still joked it was dramatic mush. Peter admitted it was Edgar Allan Poe in novel form, but with a touch more reality and a lot more religion.

Despite the fact that *Mankind* had only technically begun printing in December, Peter knew it would be wise to continue working. He could probably not publish another book immediately and live off the occasional newspaper article or short story and the royalties of his books for a while, but Alice always felt they ought to be moving forward, a sentiment he understood completely. Besides, he knew that when he was hurting, the act of writing could be more healing than simply moping about.

Finding those words—finding a story to put those words into—was the trouble, unfortunately.

He sat with a pen and paper, made ink blots on the page, and prayed. For inspiration, maybe, but mainly for God's leading. Should he even be writing now? There was more to do to manage things for Maddie. Riley had left his family well supported; he'd saved enough through hard work and careful trading to purchase several rental properties—a few row houses in the city—that brought in a comfortable income. They also owned their home and had a tidy savings account. Yet there were things to be done, even now that ownership was transferred to Maddie. Things Maddie would never learn to do. Someone had to manage them for her—and that someone was Peter, as the executor of Riley's will.

Lord, how far does the duty to protect a dear friend's wife go? he found himself praying. *How do I respect my promise to Riley while honoring a deeper vow—my covenant with Alice?*

He had sworn when he married Alice to be her protector and provider, to make their family the most important thing in his life, second only to God.

There were other things to think about, too. Peter had found a new lawyer at Riley's firm, a Mr. Jennings, to take over their case with the probate court. The hearing for Ollie's adoption was still on the docket for September, but the thought of facing a judge without Riley at his side felt like sailing into a storm without a captain.

Since the funeral, Maddie had slowly begun caring for the girls, and to a certain degree, the house, but she'd become cold to them—well, that wasn't precisely accurate. It was more as if she'd lost her interest in everything and anything. With the baby coming in October, she was tired, too, but it was more than that. Nothing seemed to cause any emotion in her.

Peter knew it was because she wasn't giving God an opportunity to heal her. He understood that grief took time even with God's influence, but it was so hard on the girls that Peter found himself, Alice at his side, over at the Farjon house almost every day for hours, taking care of Polly and Susie alongside Ollie.

So far, Polly hadn't gone back to school—she still refused to talk, so what could a teacher do with her?—and Susie was still too young, so Alice had poured much into entertaining and educating them. She devoted herself to reading to them, playing with them, and encouraging them. It suited her well enough, given that Ollie and Susie were so close in age and got along well. But Peter couldn't help but feel like Alice shouldn't have to do that, either, much as he knew she was glad to.

And at the end of the day, no one could hold Polly and Susie's heart and trust like Maddie did. Hearts and trusts that Maddie was rapidly breaking. How much longer would the girls have forgiveness rather than anger and bitterness in their hearts toward their mother if she refused to show them love?

So he sat, his pen dropping ink blots onto a blank sheet of paper, thinking and praying. Even if he had been more intent upon writing, potential words, potential stories, potential characters were far from his reach. A glimmer of one might appear for a moment and then be gone the next.

He leaned back in his seat and sighed. It was a beautiful day outside—he could see that through his small window. The sun was bright; earlier he had gone into the garden and smelled sweet flowers and fresh air. Birds were singing; in the distance, he heard Susie's laughter—followed closely by a string of words from Ollie, who liked to ramble—and he smiled.

He could see Alice with them in the garden. Dressed in the unrelieved black crape of deep mourning, her form was a stark contrast to the children's simple white dresses, accented with black sashes and hair ribbons.

Alice had a way with those girls. He had her to thank for Polly and Susie's ability to have these moments to rest their minds for a short period of time and just be children.

Riley would love that. Would love to think that his daughters would grow and flourish and be happy again, even after his loss.

There was a knock on the doorframe, and Peter started into a more upright position. Maddie stood in the door; her black dress was slightly rumpled but otherwise she seemed somewhat more put together than she'd been lately. Her hair appeared to be combed and pinned back, though Peter was no expert on such matters; she wore no hat, but often she'd walked through the gardens without one, so that wasn't too unusual.

She just hadn't been leaving home without a hat and a heavy veil lately.

He supposed the walk across to his house wouldn't require one—but Maddie had been so particular it almost surprised him to see her bareheaded.

"I'm sorry if I'm interrupting. Alice said you wouldn't mind terribly if I stopped by for just a moment."

Peter didn't, but he was surprised Alice had sent Maddie over. Still, he nodded. "Not at all." He gestured to the chair that he'd placed in the corner for his wife. "Would you like to sit?"

She stepped inside, tentatively, as if she expected him to change his mind any moment. "The girls are playing in the yard with Alice," she said, glancing at him as she sank into the chair . "Polly isn't, really, but Alice got her to sit on the swing and watch. It's ... it's quiet in my house."

Peter blinked, unsure how to respond. "I imagine so."

Maddie sat for a moment, not saying anything. "Are you working on something new?" she asked finally.

"Trying to," Peter admitted, glancing down at his collection of ink blots. One was shaped a little like a cow, fancifully enough. "It's slow going."

"It always is for you at the first, isn't it? While everyone else was out having fun, you'd spend hours tucked away, struggling to get the first words out, and then Riley would come in and say something ridiculous, and suddenly you'd be scribbling away." Her brown eyes were distant with memory. "You and Riley made such a good team. I can't imagine ..." She trailed off. "I couldn't imagine one of you without the other. Before, I mean."

Peter shifted uncomfortably. What was the point of rehashing what he already knew? His life would always be changed by the loss of Riley, like Maddie's, but certainly to a lesser degree. "His humor had a way of cutting through a situation. He put a lot of people on edge, but I always felt better when he was around."

"I did as well," Maddie said, her voice wistful. "Do you remember that summer we went to the coast, just after Riley and I married? You came with us. I'd only just learned I was expecting Polly, and Riley wanted to tell you right then. We bickered over it, and you had to play peacemaker. Riley used it as a way to let you know it was all just me being irrational—because I was with child. I had to forgive him, because he was so charming and sweet when he apologized."

Peter smiled and nodded. What was unsaid between them was that Maddie had been angry at Peter for his distance—for trying to step back from a woman he thought he'd loved who was recently married to his best friend. Riley had been within the bounds of reason to want to tell Peter, as he and Maddie'd planned on telling the rest of the family once they got home. Though Riley had been wrong to do anything of the sort without her full agreement. Peter fully agreed with Maddie on that.

"I suppose I was a little angry at you," Maddie said. "You never were as nice to me after I married Riley."

Peter had nothing to say about that, so he remained silent.

"We were friends," she continued. "Dearest friends. You were like a brother to me. I never would have even considered Riley, not that way, if it weren't for you. You loved him, so I knew I could, too. But I don't know if I would have married him, back then, if I'd known I would lose your friendship."

Peter didn't really like the direction this was going, so he felt it best to nip whatever she was going on about in the bud. "You didn't lose my friendship. We still spent time together."

"Not like we used to. The three of us were so close. Then—"

"Maddie, I don't want to talk about this. You can stop or you can leave."

She cocked her head, and the look of innocence that slid across her face was so swift that Peter knew it was feigned. "Why, Peter, I don't mean any harm. I am just trying to understand. It was confusing. I have never understood your distance, and I've done so much to try to earn your friendship again, but you treat me like I'll poison you if you look at me. Why? Was Riley jealous of us? Did he think there was something between us? You could've told him—"

"Maddie—"

"Peter, did you love me then?"

A silence descended between them. Peter stared at her for a long moment then slowly rose to his feet. "I think you'd better go home."

Something like triumph eased across her face, and slowly, for the first time he'd seen since Riley died, she smiled. "You *did*."

Peter shook his head. "Not in the way you mean. But it doesn't matter. Regardless, this is not a conversation I'm comfortable having with you, especially alone, without Alice here."

"See, that's what I never understood." Maddie, too, stood, but she made no move toward the door. "You went off to England and married the first girl you met. I thought it was foolishness at the time, and I knew it was when I met Alice. Perhaps there's a kind of man who could like her, but I don't understand why you married her. You could've married half a dozen prettier, nicer girls in Philadelphia. Girls whom I was friends with, who I liked. I'd have rather had any one of them here, instead of Alice."

Peter's jaw tightened, his grip on the edge of the desk so firm that his knuckles turned white. For a moment, he couldn't speak. He couldn't even look at her. "Maddie," he said finally, his voice low and steady, though he was surprised just how angry he sounded despite his best efforts, "you are grieving. I understand that. I understand how loss can twist things in your mind, make you look for answers or blame in places where it doesn't belong. I can understand that; I can be patient with it. But I cannot ever hear you speak about *my wife* that way again."

Maddie didn't move. She crossed her arms, her expression mulish. "I'm not blaming Alice. I'm simply saying I don't understand. She's such a hard creature, Peter. She can't make you feel cared for and loved the way a gentle, mothering woman would. I don't know how she manages with *that child.* God knows your life with Alice has been nothing but pain—surely that should show you a little what kind of mistake it was. I wonder how you can live with her."

The anger Peter felt in that moment was unlike anything he'd experienced in his lifetime. It wasn't loud or explosive, but it snapped deep inside his chest. "You want to know why I married her?" His voice rose, a rare and dangerous thing. "Because I *love* her. I have loved her since shortly after I met her, and that feeling has only grown stronger with every day that has passed since. And yes, because she loves me, and she challenges me, and she makes me a better man by seeing who I really am, with all my flaws, which I'm sure you could recount in great detail. She doesn't try to shape me into an idealized version of a husband or hold me to standards I can never meet. She doesn't leave me guessing. She doesn't manipulate. But beyond all that, the reason I married her is because God led me to her. Because He created that woman with me in mind, and He shaped our lives, and if you think that I'd rather hear what you think about my life than what God thinks, you are sorely mistaken. I don't care what you think about me or my wife. Your opinion holds no weight here. She is my wife. And you will respect her—or you and I will have nothing more to say to each other."

Maddie flinched. "And what about Riley?" she shot back, but some of the bravado was gone from her voice. "You promised him to take care of me. Does he mean nothing to you?"

Peter stepped deliberately to the door, gave it a shove so it opened wider. "Riley trusted me to do what was best for you and for your daughters, and I will do whatever I can. But I am *not* Riley. I can't be him. I won't pretend to be. That's not what he would've wanted, and it's not what's right. My first concern is always Alice and *our* family. I never can do anything if it's against her best interests. All you've done is convinced me to treat you as you said I already was—like you're poisonous. You need to lean on God—not me.

Not Riley's memory. *God.*"

For a moment, Maddie stood in the middle of Peter's office, then slowly, she walked past him, her face hard. "I see," she said, though her tone suggested otherwise. "Then, if I'm so *poisonous*, maybe it'd be best if you weren't around my children."

Peter closed his eyes. He should have known she'd wield Polly and Susie like weapons. "That would be your choice."

"An easy choice to make," Maddie said.

"I'll still need to manage your finances," Peter said. "But if you'd prefer—"

"I don't care about that. I just don't want to see you."

"Very well." He gritted his teeth together. "I know this is hard, but I need you to understand that I would do anything in Riley's memory save dishonor my vows to Alice. You must have known I wouldn't—"

"Do you ever stop talking?" Maddie said, half to herself, before hastily walking through the kitchen and out the back door.

He heard her calling Polly and Susie's names as she went through the gardens back to her house.

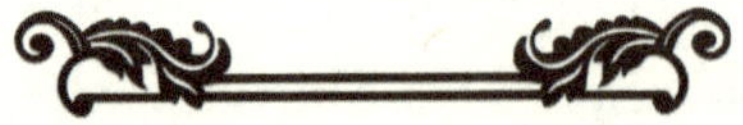

Alice crouched in the soft grass, her skirt spreading around her as she carefully balanced a crown of daisies on Susie's head. Susie giggled, tipping her head too far to one side and sending the crown sliding.

Alice caught the flowers before they fell to the ground. "You'll have to hold still if you want to be the flower queen."

"I'm not a queen," Susie declared. "I'm a *princess*. It's not fun to be queen. *Polly* can be the queen."

"No," said Ollie, adjusting her own flower crown with careful deliberation, "Polly can be my maid. *I* am the queen."

"No," said Susie, her brown eyes darkening. "*Polly* is the queen."

"Perhaps you are both the queens of neighboring countries," Alice suggested.

Polly sat on the swing a few feet away, listless, but now a spark of interest entered her eyes. Alice had been trying to get her to participate all day, but the little girl hadn't moved from the swing or spoken a word. Alice was scared to ask Maddie if Polly said anything at all, even in the privacy of her own home; she suspected the answer was "no."

Alice once again prayed in her heart that her eldest niece would recover from what she'd seen soon, that God would heal her, that Alice and Peter would know the right things to say. But what could she do? Polly wasn't her child, and even so, there was only so much humans, especially humans with little experience in such matters, could do. God must heal Polly—He must.

As Alice began instructing Susie and Ollie on good posture—something they were both sorely in need of, she was afraid—she heard the door to her kitchen slam. Her eyes flew up to see Maddie walking across the yard with more purpose and energy than she'd expressed since Riley's accident. She walked past Alice without a word.

"Polly! Susie! Come here this instant!"

All four of them turned toward the Farjon house, where Maddie had paused on the back porch. Her face was tight with some unreadable emotion, and her posture was rigid.

Slowly, Polly rose and gestured for Susie to follow her.

"I said now," Maddie called again, sharper this time.

Susie stood, brushing the dirt from her skirt. "Thank you for the crown."

"You're welcome, Rosey." Alice, too, rose and watched as the children disappeared into the house after their mother.

Ollie looked at Alice with wide eyes. "Is she mad?"

"Maybe so," Alice said vaguely. She wasn't sure. What could that be about? She couldn't imagine what Peter could have said to Maddie to put her in such a state, but there was only one way to find out.

After sending Ollie to wash her face and hands, Alice found Peter in his office, sitting at his desk with his elbows resting on the surface and his head in his hands. Papers were scattered about—which was hardly unusual—but for once, she could easily tell he was upset.

She lingered in the doorway for a moment, gathering her thoughts, before she spoke. "Peter?"

He looked up. His posture seemed to ease slightly when he saw her. "Alice," he said, his voice low. "I just had an interesting conversation."

She stepped inside, closing the door behind her, and lowered herself into her seat. "Maddie seemed to be in a state. She called Polly and Susie back to the house but didn't say a word to me."

"That sounds about right."

Alice offered a slight smile. "So does that mean it was less of an interesting conversation and more of an interesting argument?"

Peter winced and removed his spectacles, dropping them on the desk. "More or less," he mumbled, rubbing his hands over his face.

She opened her mouth to make a comment on that, something along the lines of "obviously it wasn't your fault and Maddie deserved whatever you said to her because you are perfect," but instead, she refrained and waited for him to speak.

He dropped his hands. "She said some things about you and about our marriage. They were blatantly untrue; there was no grounding in reality. I've been sitting here trying to think what her motive is. What could she possibly gain from saying cruel things about my wife?"

"What did she say?" Alice could guess at a few things, given that she'd made no secret of her own jealousy toward Maddie when Alice and Peter had first been married. Though that was a long time ago now, Alice wouldn't have forgotten, so she couldn't imagine Maddie had, either.

Peter shook his head. "Nothing that bears repeating. I just don't understand it. She started out talking about Riley, and how close we all were—the three of us, I mean—and I can understand why she'd want to reminisce with me. I'm far from the only one who remembers Riley fondly, but we shared a great many memories." He paused. "But then she asked me why I stopped being her friend when she and Riley married. I hadn't fully realized she understood it that way. You know I was just trying to ... I was immature, but my goal was to give them space and also prevent myself from becoming too close to her. Even then, it wasn't love—"

"It would be all right if it was," Alice said. After all, what did she care if Peter had loved another woman before he even knew Alice? Yes, it had driven her mad at first, but now that they'd been married, she knew that Peter was never going to experience the same things with another woman that he had with Alice. Any other relationship would be shallow and unimportant next to their marriage. He had an inherently deeper connection with her; what did she care if, before he even knew what it was to be married, he'd fallen in love with someone else?

"But it wasn't." Peter shrugged. "It's as simple as that. But you know all that better than anyone; you know that was a long time ago. I told her I didn't care to talk about it, but she wouldn't hear me, and she guessed that I had felt something for her. I denied it, because what she believed is not what really happened, and I think that annoyed her, so she insulted you. She went as far as to say that I should not have married you. I made it abundantly clear that I wouldn't tolerate that kind of talk in my house—not about you—and that led to an argument. In the end, she told me she didn't want me around Polly and Susie."

"Oh." Alice blinked. She certainly hadn't expected that. "Perhaps when she's not angry—"

"I'm not sure." Peter sighed. "She seemed determined. And the truth is, I don't want to see her again. Much as I'm committed to honoring Riley's memory, you're my first priority. I told Maddie that. If anyone threatens you—"

"Peter." Alice stood and circled the desk, placing her hands on his shoulders. "This is not a life-or-death situation. She may very well forget about this or at least forgive you. You only did what was right—and Maddie must know that. She's upset; she's grieving. She can't be thinking clearly. We'll be allowed to see Polly and Susie again. What does she think will happen?

That she can keep them from playing with Ollie, from visiting me? She cannot be so foolish to believe that will be easy."

He gestured vaguely toward the window, where the Farjon house was just visible through the garden. "This isn't what I wanted. Not for them."

Alice's throat tightened at the raw emotion in his voice. They'd come to love Polly and Susie so; it did seem unfair to separate them, especially given how little care Maddie was giving her daughters, and how Ollie adored them both. "I know." She hesitated, then said gently, "You need to talk to someone about this. Dr. Engall, maybe? He sees her regularly because of the baby. She used to be close to the Tremains, but I'm not sure now."

Peter frowned thoughtfully, then nodded. "That's a good idea. I'll think about talking to him—and maybe the pastor and his wife, too."

Alice squeezed his shoulders and kissed the top of his head. "You've done everything you can for Maddie and the girls, Peter. I know it doesn't feel like enough, but it is. God must do the rest. We're only mortal."

He looked up at her, his expression softening. "Thank you. You're right."

"I do like to hear that." She kissed him again, lingering this time, then drew away. "All we can do is pray."

Why did that feel like the anthem of the entire year?

CHAPTER TWENTY-FOUR

ALICE DUMPED A CUP of flour in the mixing bowl and then set down the measuring cup before reaching up to brush a hand over her forehead. The kitchen was warm; she'd had the oven hot all day, making bread and a pie and now biscuits. Across the room, Flick knelt on the floor, scrubbing out the baking pans Alice had used earlier that morning, and Ollie was "helping," more or less.

"Allen!" Flick called sharply as her baby crawled away. She shot out a hand and caught his leg just before he reached the stove. "That's not for you."

Allen let out a shriek of protest but quickly settled when Flick scooped him up and plopped him back down near a pile of various kitchen utensils Alice had given him to play with. He gave a happy squeal as he grabbed a wooden spoon, and Ollie scooted over to join him, forgetting her chores in her eagerness to play with the baby.

"He's keeping you on your toes today," Alice said as she added a pinch of salt to the bowl.

Flick rolled her eyes. "He's always like this now. Crawling everywhere, getting into everything. I can't even have him in the shop with me anymore, so Mrs. Tremain keeps him when I'm working. I don't know how one tiny person can cause so much chaos."

Alice laughed. "It's a gift, I suppose."

Flick grinned and returned to scrubbing. "What's next on the list?"

"Biscuits," Alice said, ignoring Flick mumbling "cookies" under her breath. "Peter's been asking for them—and my Ollie Girl has, too—and I thought I'd make a double batch to send some over to the Engalls."

At the mention of the Engalls, Flick went quiet for a moment. "I go over and see them when I can. Dr. Engall is heartbroken, but he's holding up."

"That's good." Alice glanced at Ollie, but she seemed consumed with playing with Allen. "It's such a tragic thing. I'm so glad that the church has been offering him so much support."

"Speaking of which, how's Maddie doing? Any change?"

Alice hesitated, her hands pausing over the dough. "Not really. She's as distant as ever. Dr. Engall has tried to talk to her, I think, and Peter met with the pastor about it because he's concerned about her—and also about Polly; we're very worried about Polly—but Maddie doesn't seem interested in hearing what anyone has to say."

Flick sat back on her heels and commenced drying her hands on the apron she'd borrowed. "She's a grown woman. If she doesn't want your help—unwise as that may be, given her current situation—she's within her rights not to accept it. That doesn't make it any easier, though." Flick cocked her head. "I know you love Polly and Susie."

"No, it doesn't." Alice kneaded the dough a little harder than necessary. "I understand why she's upset. She's grieving, and she's scared. But it's hard—so hard—not to see Polly and Susie. Especially with ..." She jerked her head toward Ollie. A four-year-old couldn't understand a forced separation from her friends because of a quarrel between two adults.

"I know," Flick said. "But Alice, at a certain point, you have to just move on. You and Peter have done everything you can. I know you, both of you, and this wasn't your fault. You've talked to Dr. Engall, the pastor—you've prayed, I'm sure. Beyond that, it's in God's hands."

Alice didn't answer immediately, unsure what to say. She stared down at the dough, her fingers working it into a smooth, even ball. Finally, she said, "If it weren't for Peter, I'd have given that woman a piece of my mind."

"Right—I would have, regardless of Peter. But I figure, what do I care what she does?" Flick shrugged. "I do miss Riley. But I know better than anyone that holding on to the past doesn't really help you. If Maddie's determined to make you miserable, well, don't let her. I think she enjoys getting so much attention. I've resolved not to give it to her."

Flick was true to her word, too. Though Alice had been somewhat polite to Maddie—who was cold and steely—when she saw her at church, Flick had cut her.

The look of rage on Maddie's face—Maddie, who had never liked Flick; who had treated her with barely concealed animosity for years and all but ignored her recently—had caused Alice an unchristian moment of delight. In church, too! She had quickly dampened such feelings and repented of them, but heavens, it had been satisfying.

One thing that couldn't be said about Flick was that she was disloyal. She'd decided that Peter and Alice were her friends, and this meant that Maddie's quarrel with Peter had earned Flick's anger—all of it directed at Maddie.

Alice sighed, pushing a stray strand of hair from her face with a flour-dusted wrist. "You're right. It's just one more thing to give over to God." She glanced at Flick. "You know the hearing is coming up."

"Right," Flick prompted, setting aside a pan she had just dried.

"For Ollie," Alice said, her voice dropping. "It's set for the second week of September. We have Mr. Jennings to help us, but I'm still nervous."

"Nervous? About what?" Flick's tone was practical, almost dismissive of the notion. "What could possibly go wrong? You have the asylum's glowing report; you have all the right paperwork. I know Riley would have prepared you. What is a judge going to say?"

"I don't know," Alice admitted, turning the dough over on the floured board. "It's a last hurdle that feels taller and wider without Riley. I never would have thought I'd miss him so much."

Flick paused then picked up another pan. "I miss him, too, and we barely spoke to each other. He was a light. But I know Mr. Jennings will push things through. There's nothing to worry about. Stop your worrying. That judge will take one look at the family you three have already become and thank God he gets to be a part of making it official. It will be fine."

At that moment, Allen let out a shriek of displeasure, having thrown his wooden spoon under the table, just beyond the reach of his hands. He was a little too plump to squeeze under the chair, and the simple solution of going around it hadn't yet occurred to him. Ollie had gotten distracted stacking bowls, and she only looked up at the same time as Alice and Flick did.

Flick laughed and scooped him up, spinning him around in her arms. "You're trouble, aren't you?"

Alice smiled faintly, her mind still turning over Flick's words.

Maybe it was just time to let Maddie go. After all, it wasn't as if they could force her to let Peter and Alice be around her children, if that was her choice.

Alas, for now, all Alice could do was wait and pray.

September 1887

The hallway of the Hamilton County Courthouse was cool and silent, the sound of their footsteps echoing off the marble floors. Alice held Ollie's hand tightly in hers, gripping it with perhaps a little too much strength. Ollie was quiet, her wide eyes taking in the imposing portraits of stern-faced men that lined the walls. She was wearing a new navy-blue dress Alice had finished just the week before. It was the nicest outfit Ollie owned by far; the matching hat was perched across carefully combed curls that still danced just above her shoulders.

Their new lawyer stood waiting for them outside a set of heavy oak doors, his expression professional but remote as they approached. Alice disliked that she never knew what Mr. Jennings was thinking; he was so unlike Riley, with his broad smiles and ready laughter. Beside the lawyer was a welcome sight: Mrs. Gable, who offered Alice a warm, reassuring smile.

Riley should be here, Alice thought, a familiar ache tightening her chest. He should be the one to clap Peter on the back and make a joke to cut the tension. He should be here to see this journey—which, in some ways, he had initiated—to its end.

"The judge is ready for you," Mr. Jennings said. "Remember, answer his questions simply and honestly. This is a formality, but a necessary one."

"Will Ollie need to speak?" Peter asked, glancing down at the little girl.

"Not much," Mr. Jennings said, "but he may speak to her to assess her general wellness. I am not concerned."

If only Alice could say the same. Ollie was well-dressed, healthy, and clean. She'd put on some weight in the last few months, and her smiles were easier to come by. But Alice still hated the thought of her daughter being *assessed*.

The clerk opened the door, and they filed into the judge's chambers. The room was a cavern of dark wood and leather-bound books. An enormous desk dominated the space, and behind it sat the probate judge, an older man with a fringe of white hair and spectacles perched on the end of his nose. He did not smile.

The judge gestured for them to sit. Alice, Peter, and Ollie took the three chairs placed before the desk, with Mrs. Gable and Mr. Jennings both taking seats slightly behind them. The click of the door closing seemed to suck all the air from the room.

Steady now, Alice reassured herself. Out of the corner of her eyes, she watched Ollie, who was sitting in a chair too tall for her, swinging her legs and looking around with an expression of mixed awe and curiosity.

Finally, the judge looked up, his gaze moving from Peter to Alice. "Mr. and Mrs. Strauss," he said, his voice a low gravel. "You have petitioned this court for the adoption of the minor child, Olivia Muller. Do you both affirm, before God and the state of Ohio, that this is your free and considered wish?"

"Yes, Your Honor. It is," Peter said.

Alice found her own voice quickly. "Yes, Your Honor."

The judge turned his gaze to Mrs. Gable. "And the Cincinnati Orphan Asylum gives its full and unconditional consent?"

"It does, Your Honor," Mrs. Gable said warmly. "With our most enthusiastic recommendation."

The judge gave a slight, satisfied nod. His stern expression softened almost imperceptibly as he turned his full attention to the little girl seated between her parents. He leaned forward slightly.

"Olivia, child," he said, his rough voice much gentler now. "I have one final question. These are good people, Mr. and Mrs. Strauss. They want to be your parents. Are you happy in their home?"

Ollie glanced at Alice, as if looking for confirmation that she could speak.

Alice nodded. "Go ahead, Ollie," she murmured.

"Yes," Ollie said clearly.

"*Sir*," Alice prompted.

"Yes, sir," Ollie mumbled, her voice suddenly small. Then, gathering herself, she added in that firm, decided voice of hers, "You have to let me stay."

The judge cleared his throat. He picked up his heavy fountain pen, dipped it deliberately into the inkwell, and turned to the final page of the decree. The scratch of the pen on the thick paper was the only sound in the room. He signed his name with a decisive flourish, then set the pen down. He looked directly at them over his spectacles, and for the first time, a true smile lit his face.

"Then it is done," he said. "By the authority vested in me by the state of Ohio, the petition is granted. In the eyes of the law, and with the blessing of God, Olivia Grace Strauss is your daughter. Congratulations, Mr. and Mrs. Strauss."

The front door clicked shut, and Peter stood in the entryway watching Ollie dance around the house, Alice's hand still in hers, questions flying from her mouth. She wanted to know about the decree, and if they would go see the judge again, and what Mrs. Gable's job was anyway, and if more ladies would come visit them and do "tests."

"We're done for good, Ollie Grace," Alice assured her, for perhaps the twentieth time since they'd left the judge's chambers. "You're home for good. You're our daughter."

Ollie squinted up at Alice and then, again not for the first time, suggested that she "should not cry about *that*."

Peter trailed after them to the kitchen, where Ollie had figured out that she could usually manipulate her way into a treat of some kind. Today, he didn't terribly mind, though they would have to be careful that every emotional moment didn't lead to a request for a cake-baking session.

He sat at the table and watched Ollie scurry back and forth, "helping" Alice in her unique Ollie way that led to spilled flour and a dropped egg. There could be no scolding today; neither Alice nor Peter had it in them.

"We'll sweep when we're done," was all Alice said as she knelt to clean up the egg. "Be careful, Ollie."

"I *am* careful," Ollie said with dignity. "It was slippery."

Peter hid his grin behind a cup of coffee.

"The egg was slippery?"

"Yes."

Alice gave Ollie a long look then turned back to the bowl with a slight sigh.

Once the cake was in the oven, Alice sent Ollie to change—something she probably should have done before the baking began, given how nice Ollie's dress was—and set about cleaning the dishes they'd used.

The room was suddenly quiet. The frantic, happy energy of the last half hour dissipated, leaving only the sound of the ticking clock and the hum of the oven. Alice stood by the sink, her back to Peter, gripping the edge of the basin. Her shoulders shook, and Peter swiftly rose.

"Alice?" he asked softly.

She turned, and he saw that silent tears were streaming down her cheeks. Without a word, she crossed the kitchen and stepped into his waiting arms, burying her face against his chest as a single, ragged sob escaped her. He held her tightly, stroking her hair.

"I don't know what's wrong with me," Alice whispered, her voice muffled against his shirt. "I'm sorry."

"Don't apologize," Peter said, dropping his face into her hair and breathing in the familiar scent of her. "It's been an emotional day. An emotional year. I don't blame you in the slightest." He held her for a long moment, simply letting her cry. When her sobs quieted into shaky breaths, he leaned back to look at her. "These are happy tears, aren't they?" he murmured. "It's the relief of it all. It's finally, truly over."

She gave a watery laugh and nodded against his chest. Relief, yes—but also so much more than that. Disbelief, and sadness for the years that had passed so painfully, and yes, still the old fears. But today felt like a bittersweet deliverance from all of those things.

There was a knock at the back door; Alice slid out of Peter's arms and opened it. Moments later, she was embracing Flick.

"Come in, come in!" Alice said. The moment of overwhelm had passed; she was smiling again. "All is well; she's ours."

"I knew she would be!" Flick exclaimed. She set Allen down on the kitchen floor where he immediately began trying to push himself to a standing position, though it was more an effort than a success. "Congratulations, both of you! I am so, so happy for you. Where is Miss Strauss?"

"Changing—albeit after I let her ruin a perfectly nice dress baking a cake," Alice said wryly. "I don't think I'm thinking clearly—my mind has been fuzzy all day."

"Well, no wonder." Flick stepped carefully around Allen. "I'd be fuzzy-headed, too. But it's over; it's done. She's yours."

"Yes, she is. Will you stay for dinner, Flick? And cake, too? We'd love it if you could celebrate with us." Alice knelt and took one of Allen's small hands, steadying him as he once again swayed on his feet. "I think Ollie would like that, too. You know she adores Allen."

"I'm a little concerned Ollie may steal Allen from me," Flick confessed with a twinkle in her eyes. "Now, don't worry, Peter—I'm not concerned that twenty years in the future, we'll have a wedding on our hands. Allen would be far too young for her. But I am worried that in the present, Ollie will petition to adopt him, and I don't know what I'd say."

Alice rolled her eyes and picked up Allen, swinging him into the air. "I fear I am too young to be a grandmother."

"That settles it, then." Flick sank into one of the chairs at the kitchen table. "We will stay, if you don't mind terribly, but you'd be honest with me if I were interfering with the private celebration of a new family, wouldn't you?"

Alice raised her eyebrows. "Have I ever been dishonest with you before?"

"No," Flick admitted. "Don't start."

Peter laughed. "I think that's the last concern I have about either of you."

Just then, Ollie appeared in the doorway, then ran forward and reached for Allen without pausing to greet Flick.

"Ollie, you must welcome Auntie Flick," Alice said, twisting so Ollie couldn't grab at Allen's leg. "Behave yourself."

"Good 'noon, Auntie Flick," said Ollie, who apparently had no time for the length of the word *afternoon*. "Can I hold Allen?"

"He is too heavy for you, but if you fetch a toy, you may play with him," Alice said, lowering him to the floor.

Allen let out a series of babbling noises and reached for Ollie, but Alice shooed her away, and Ollie raced off to find her doll.

"Alice?" Flick said in an undertone that Peter still caught.

"Hmm?" Alice had knelt again to hold Allen upright as he staggered through more attempted steps.

"This is far better than if you had taken Allen."

Alice paused then nodded. "Yes. That would not have been the right choice for either of us, Flick. But this—Ollie—is the right choice for Peter and me. She was meant to be our daughter."

"I couldn't agree more," Peter added. "And Allen is a blessing to you, too, Flick, and to all of us—as your son."

Flick cast him a genuine smile. "I agree—we are all incredibly blessed."

As Ollie ran back into the room, and extended her doll to Allen, Peter couldn't help but agree. Though life was far from perfect, it was also full of the Lord's immeasurable favor.

Chapter Twenty-Five

October 1887

Alice was up before the sun, as always, but for a slightly less pleasant reason this time. She went downstairs, and forced a piece of cold bread down. She checked on Ollie—still fast asleep, looking like a mischievous fae with her curls dancing about her increasingly plump cheeks—and then considered whether she ought to start breakfast.

It was perhaps too early to be rattling around the kitchen, and she knew that she wouldn't do anything useful until she spoke with Peter.

She returned to the bed and sat down beside his still form. "Peter."

He rolled over and reached for her, but she moved just out of his reach and remained there, hands folded in her lap, thinking.

"Peter, I haven't bled since August. Early August."

He blinked sleepily at her, then reached up to rub his eyes. After he spent a moment considering what she said, a sort of realization slid across his face before quickly being tamped down by a more neutral expression.

He doesn't want to think about it either. Aren't we a pair?

"That's happened before, hasn't it? So that'll be almost two months?"

"Sixty-five days today."

"That does seem a bit long." He sat up and caught her arm, and this time she let him pull her against his chest. "Alice, are you worried something's wrong ... or do you think you could be with child?"

The familiar nausea rose as if in answer to his question, but she pushed it down, determined not to let symptoms build into suspicions, nor suspicions into fragile hopes that could only be dashed. *Surely it's all in my head.* "It must be stress. It must be. I can't—I can't—" And she was ashamed of the sob that ripped from her throat.

"Oh, darling." He tightened his grip on her. "Symptoms?"

"Nausea if I don't eat, and exhaustion. But I've been so busy with everything, so happy with Ollie, I didn't think anything of it." She sighed. "If ... if ... well, it couldn't be worse timing, surely." She leaned back. "Peter, I—"

"No," he said firmly. He cupped her face in his hands. "It is not bad timing. It is always the *best* timing. And I am willing to hold this loosely, but don't you think for a minute that I don't believe this could be the answer to every one of our prayers."

"But ... but what about Ollie?" Alice tried to swallow the lump in her throat, to no avail. "How will she feel? And there's so much unrest right now, what with Maddie and the Engalls, and I wanted ... I wanted ..."

"God knows what's best, Alice. Whether we have a baby now or not, whether that baby is born living or whether it's lost sooner, He is still the Master, and we have to trust Him. So tell me the truth. Do you think we have a baby, or do you truly believe it's just stress?"

She pressed her face into Peter's shoulder and waited until she wasn't shaking to reply. Then, softly, she murmured, "Peter, I think we have a baby."

"All right." He shifted so she was sitting in his lap and then leaned against the headboard, rubbing the small of her back. "All right. I ... I suppose ..." Then his voice caught, and a soft chuckle emerged. "Wouldn't that be wonderful? Oh, Lord, please."

"Peter ..." It was better for him not to get his hopes up. She could bear her own broken hopes, but not his. "I'm not at all sure. I suspect. But ... but we can't really know ..."

"I understand."

Yet when she drew back and saw his smile, she was convinced he didn't understand at all.

"But if it is a baby, we have a baby."

"*Maybe. Maybe* we have a baby. Anything could happen."

"Even if we lose it, it's still a baby." His tone sobered as he spoke again. "I'm happy for whatever time we have, whatever dreams we are allowed." He placed a hand over her stomach. "I'm going to pray that you are with child, and that we get to keep this one. That this time, the Lord has a better use on earth for it than in Heaven. And I'm going to thank the Lord for whatever minutes or days or months we get. You would be due ... perhaps in the spring? April?"

"May," she murmured, for she had already counted in her head, despite her best efforts to do otherwise. "There would be a long winter between now and surety. Torture, if you ask me."

"A sweet sort of torture," Peter insisted. "Because we'll have him as long as we have him. All right? He's already ours. The amount of months he stays with us and whether or not he makes it into our arms doesn't change that."

And then she couldn't help weeping, and Peter held her while she cried herself out.

The only word that came to her in prayer was "please." Over and over, a desperate, simple plea. *Please, please, please.* It was all she had left to offer. She knew no promises of hers could offer a surer foundation. She could pledge her child's life to God; she could offer anything, her own life included, for its safe delivery.

But she could not do anything—not really. She could only plead that, for whatever unknowable reasons, this child was born healthy.

But she couldn't let herself believe it was real. Not yet.

Two days later, it was Peter's birthday—October 10th. He was turning thirty-four, which was an advanced age, Alice said teasingly—as she had every year since he turned thirty. He reminded her then that she would be twenty-six in December, or January, or whenever it was that she wanted her birthday to be (for they argued about it every year), and twenty-six was only four years shy of thirty. Practically an advanced age.

She was being cheerful because Peter was cheerful. Every day that passed her symptoms worsened—morning had become an irrational mix of sickness and hunger, and she needed a nap in the afternoon. Ollie had responded with cautious concern and a great level of clinginess, which she tried to mask as helpfulness.

Ollie was four. She was anything but helpful.

And Alice wasn't at all sure what kind of birthday this would be for Peter. She made him promise to leave paperwork behind and set aside his already-neglected work, and simply be with them both—for how badly they needed him, even if it was supposedly for his benefit. He spent a good two hours in the afternoon building a castle with Ollie out of pillows and blankets in the parlor while Alice snagged one pillow for herself and lay down. She did, however, rouse herself enough to nibble at some toast while she cooked—albeit nothing too particularly savory. It appeared that she was now at the stage where food could smell any way it wanted to, regardless of what it usually smelled like.

And again, "please" was the only word she had to offer the Lord. Anything more eloquent would have to wait for a time when she wasn't sure, at any moment, that her hope would be lost. If this pregnancy was anything like the one with Daniel, she wouldn't feel the baby move until at least Thanksgiving—and she wasn't sure she could be certain until the quickening. Not anymore.

The kitchen door opened, and Susie stood there, panting.

Alice's eyes widened. She hadn't seen Susie outside of the sporadic passing glance at church—which Maddie now only occasionally attended—since Maddie's falling out with Peter. Certainly, Susie had not been allowed to visit Alice.

"Auntie Alice," she said, her tone carrying a level of urgency that it seldom did, "Mama's baby is coming."

"Oh! I'll have Uncle Penn go for the doctor, all right, sweetheart? Come on in here. You'll stay with me while the baby is coming, won't you? And we'll get Polly." Alice said these words in a quiet, firm voice. Yes, Polly and Susie should be out of the Farjon house—she didn't care what Maddie said. They needed to be away while the baby was brought into the world. So much for Alice's dinner plans, and for Peter's birthday, but that mattered little in such situations.

She walked into the parlor and told Peter; they left Susie and Ollie to play and went over to see how Maddie was getting along.

Maddie was in early labor but progressing well. Peter went to collect Dr. Engall and alert friends of Maddie's who would be present during the birth, and after these people arrived, Alice sent Polly over to her house and went upstairs to fetch clothing for Polly and Susie, mentally calculating what it would take to stretch dinner. At least, she thought wryly, the cake she had planned was more than ample for the children. They would certainly be pleased about that. And truly, Ollie would probably be thrilled to be having an actual "party."

She met Peter in the hallway with a bundle of clothes and other miscellaneous items. He was pale, she thought.

"Is everything all right?" she murmured, glancing beyond him to the bedroom door.

"Alice, I can't stay with Maddie while she's giving birth. There is no world in which that's appropriate, and I just ... I can't."

"Oh." Alice's brow furrowed. "She asked you to?"

"Yes."

"Even though she hasn't ..." Alice's voice trailed off. "How could she ask that of you after refusing to see you for months?"

Peter shook his head, clearly as bothered and confused by this as Alice was. "She said she was sorry for how she's acted, but that she can't do this alone and needs me now more than ever."

"What did you say?"

"That she was well-supported—that I could be of no use. She didn't like that, but I said … I said she had the women there, and the doctor, for a reason—and to ask me to stand by her, to offer her comfort, was wrong. I just … I just don't think I can. Birth is an intimate thing, and I have never seen a child born before. I believe I would see more than I want to, and I know I would only get in the way. But even if neither of those were true, I know I am not supposed to. Not with Maddie. I just know it."

"Peter." Alice dropped the bundle, despite knowing it would be difficult to collect things in an orderly fashion once more, and took him by the arm. "Maddie can't ask that of you. She should know that that's a job for a husband, if any man not trained in medicine should be there at all—the Lord will have to give her strength to do without Riley. Birth is intimate, or at least, it ought to be, I think. You're not God; you can't provide comfort to everyone. And I … I can't have you there." She shook her head. "No. Come home. If no one else were able to be here, I would understand. If she were truly alone, I would understand. But as it is, *I* do not want you there."

He nodded, his shoulders relaxing. Alice knew that he had wanted her permission to escape this situation. "I'll pull Dr. Engall out and tell him."

From his office, Peter listened to Susie and Ollie chattering up a storm about a doll Susie had brought over—Peter silently reminded himself that for Christmas, Ollie ought to have a similar doll. That said, he wasn't sure where he'd be at Christmas this year. Perhaps, if they weren't going down to Eleanor—and before they'd stopped speaking, Maddie swore to him she would not, and it seemed likely the whole family was too fractured to keep up the tradition—he, Alice, and Ollie would stay here and have a quiet

Christmas, just the three of them.

He glanced through the open door of the office. Alice was sitting at the kitchen table, mending a hole in one of Ollie's stockings. *The four of us,* he amended silently. Alice was as certain as she could be that, if all went well, their baby would be arriving in the spring.

He dropped his pen in the inkwell and did another set of silent calculations. Ten weeks, perhaps, or slightly less. It could be as much as ten more weeks until she felt the baby move—though Alice hoped it would be sooner.

She believed she'd only been about seven or eight weeks pregnant, at the very most, with Zebedee when they lost him. Certainly, there was some security in being past that date. But there was still risk. There would always be risk.

God, give us courage and hope.

"It's almost time for bed, I'd think," Alice said, setting aside her work. "Do we want to—"

There was a knock at the back door.

Peter stood, gesturing for Alice to remain seated, and went to answer it.

When he opened the door, Dr. Engall stood on the porch, his medical bag in one hand and a weary expression on his face.

"Dr. Engall," Peter said, stepping back to let him in. "Come in."

"Thank you." The doctor stepped inside and removed his hat. His face was solemn. "Maddie is well; she delivered a son. She's named him *Colin Riley.*"

Peter glanced at Alice. *Colin Riley.* It was the traditional Farjon family name, passed down for three generations, and it seemed ... *strange* ... that Maddie would choose to honor that tradition now. Peter was almost certain it wasn't what Riley would have wanted. In fact, though he was never going to bring this up, the name that had been suggested, when Riley first began speaking of having another child, was *Peter.* He hadn't even told Alice that; it hadn't occurred to him since long before Riley died.

But the child was born on my birthday.

God had a sense of humor.

"The baby is healthy, and the pastor's wife is with her now, helping her rest." Dr. Engall turned toward Polly and Susie, who had rushed over to stand in the doorway of the kitchen. Both of them had wide eyes, and Susie was smiling. It was clear the baby was much anticipated.

Perhaps it feels like a return to normalcy.

"Girls, your mother will want to see you soon," the doctor continued. "I came to take you home. Can you get your things?"

Polly turned, gesturing for Susie to follow her. Susie had gotten good at reading Polly's subtle emotions and movements, Peter had noticed. He hoped Polly's silence wouldn't last forever, but what could he do? He'd spoken to Polly a few times over the course of the day, in between birthday celebrations and catching up with Susie—who had begged him to come see her more often in the most heartbreaking way possible—but he'd not gotten through to her. Nothing he said seemed to ripple her placid facade. It was terrible.

Ollie stepped forward then, skittering to Alice's side and clutching her skirt. She started to begin what was probably a barrage of questions about the new baby, but Alice stilled her with a hand on her shoulder.

Dr. Engall shifted awkwardly from foot to foot, his gaze flicking toward Peter. "There's ... one more thing. Can I talk to you, Peter?"

Peter glanced at Alice. There was nothing Dr. Engall would say that she couldn't hear, but Ollie was there.

"Ollie, go help Polly and Susie collect their things," Alice said softly.

"But Mama—"

"Ollie."

Ollie turned and left without another word, and Peter turned back to Dr. Engall. "Tell me."

The doctor cleared his throat, looking distinctly uncomfortable. "Maddie asked me to pass along a message." He hesitated, as if weighing his words carefully. "She's asked that I, along with our pastor, take over managing her finances and household affairs for the time being. She feels it would be best if someone else was in charge of such things. I'm sorry, Peter—I know you've done a lot for her. Maybe in time, after she recovers from the birth ..." He paused again and ran a hand along the back of his neck. "Grief does funny things to people."

Peter carefully schooled his reactions. Dr. Engall would know better than anyone how grief could confuse and frighten a person into doing things they normally wouldn't.

Unfortunately, Peter was convinced that this decision had nothing to do with grief. Well—it did, in a way. It was about Maddie wanting more from Peter than he ever could give her, even in the wake of Riley's death. It was about Maddie not being happy with boundaries he'd put in place to protect them both.

It was about Maddie not caring what happened to Peter—his marriage, his family, his spirit—as long as he prioritized what she wanted.

"I understand," Peter said. "We should meet soon and talk about what must be done. It isn't a terrible burden, but I can still explain it. In truth, if she were to apply herself, or care about it at all, Maddie could manage it herself." What he didn't say was that she would never choose to do so unless forced, but then, both he and Dr. Engall knew that, didn't they?

Dr. Engall nodded. "I wish I had better news. I know how much you care about Maddie, but I think she needs time. Perhaps when she's had some rest ..."

Peter took a deep breath. It was true that Maddie might be reasoned with. His promise to Riley still weighed heavily on his mind; he had done so little for Riley's family lately. Perhaps there was still a way that, at least, he and Alice could see Polly and Susie. "I'll give her a few days," he said, "and then I'll speak with her."

Moments later, Polly and Susie reappeared, Ollie trailing behind them.

"Are you ready, girls?" Dr. Engall asked.

Polly glanced at Peter one last time before nodding, and Susie followed silently.

"Thank you for watching them," Dr. Engall said as he ushered the girls toward the door.

"Of course," Alice said when Peter didn't say anything. "Give Maddie our congratulations. We're so thankful she and the child are healthy."

As the door shut behind the group, the house fell silent.

"Why don't we see them anymore?" Ollie asked, giving Peter's trouser leg a firm tug to draw his attention away from the closed door. "Why?"

It was always "why" with Ollie. That was by far her favorite word. Peter knelt and picked her up, swinging her into his arms so she giggled. "Someday maybe we'll get to see them again," he told her. "But right now, their mama needs them at home. We'll have the Engalls over again, soon, if you like."

Ollie hesitated then nodded. The Engall girls weren't as close in age to her as Susie was, but it would have to do, and Dr. Engall needed all the help he could get right now.

"Polly and Susie have a new baby brother," Ollie reflected, reaching up to remove Peter's spectacles, which he'd forgotten on the top of his head. She carefully placed them on his nose then gave a contented jerk of her head. "Can I see him?"

"Maybe someday." Peter set her down. "I don't know yet. For now, it's about time for bed."

Ollie seemed content with this response and allowed Alice to usher her toward the door.

"I'll come up when you're settled," Peter offered. "I can tell you a story before you go to bed."

"Of course," said Ollie without turning.

Alice gave him an amused look over her shoulder before they disappeared out of the room.

Chapter Twenty-Six

Dr. Engall arranged for Maddie and Peter to speak later that week, after she had had several days of quiet and rest. The timing still wasn't ideal—it was a vulnerable period, these first weeks and months after a new child was born, and Peter hated that he had to talk to her about things now.

He entered the Farjon house. After his banishment, being back felt shocking. He had spent so much of his life here, visiting frequently, spending evenings with Riley. For this once-familiar place to have become forbidden territory was a strange and bitter thing.

In truth, if it weren't for Polly and Susie, he wouldn't have minded.

The house was quiet except for the faint creak of the rocking chair in the parlor. Peter hadn't expected Maddie to agree this readily to speaking with him, especially so soon after the child had arrived, but plainly she hadn't wanted to wait either.

A soft voice called from the parlor. "You can come in, Peter."

Peter entered, finding Maddie in the rocking chair, cradling her infant son. Her face was pale, shadows etched beneath her eyes, but her posture was rigid.

Peter cleared his throat. "Thank you for agreeing to speak with me. I am so sorry this comes so soon after your son's arrival. There is no rush if you need more time."

"No. But I don't have much to say." Her voice was flat.

He hesitated. "I heard from Dr. Engall about your decision. I understand that you don't want my help anymore and would prefer he handle these things for you. But you and I *both* know that is not how Riley's will is structured. I am the executor of the estate. That is a legal duty I cannot simply hand off. However, I believe we can arrive at a practical solution that honors your wishes for privacy while allowing me to fulfill my promise to Riley and my legal obligations."

Maddie blinked, her lips parting as if she was about to argue, but she stopped herself.

Peter cleared his throat. "Dr. Engall has already graciously agreed to assist me in this duty. I will grant him a limited power of attorney to manage the day-to-day business of the rental properties and to provide you with your household allowance. We will meet monthly to discuss any issues or changes, and I will maintain final oversight. All communication regarding the estate will go through him. In this way, I can fulfill my duty as executor without needing to intrude upon your life here."

Maddie's jaw tightened. "So that's it, then? A business arrangement? You'll just manage Riley's money and be done with us?"

The bitterness in her tone made Peter's heart ache. "I made a promise to Riley," he said, his voice softer now. "On the night he died, he asked me to look after you, to keep you and the girls safe. I want to be respectful to that with the understanding that it is for Riley's sake, and for his children's. I care about you, yes, but only because I want to see you succeed. If we can't see each other, perhaps that's the best, but don't punish Alice for this. She's come to love Polly and Susie. It's not fair to ask the children to live so close and never interact with her." Granted, neither Polly or Susie seemed to play outside as much as they used to, but it was still painful to see them and avoid interaction, and Ollie couldn't understand it.

"Then put up a fence."

Peter flinched. "I'm not sure that's a real solution."

Maddie's grip on the baby tightened. "I know Riley believed you should take care of us, but I'm telling you this, Peter—you can forget about your promise. I'll feel *safest* without you here."

Peter flinched again but after a long moment of silence, he nodded. "I understand, Maddie. If that's how you feel, I'll honor that. We won't interact with your children, and I'll make sure everything else is handed off to some other person. But I need you to understand something—I'm not going to spend the rest of my life available for you if you change your mind. I can't be called back on a whim if it's convenient for you, and whatever decisions Alice and I make will be for our family."

Maddie blinked, her lips parting as if, again, she was about to argue, but she stopped herself once more. Instead, she looked down at the baby in her arms, her expression unreadable. "I understand."

Peter exhaled, relief mingling with sorrow. He glanced at the sleeping baby, who looked a lot like Polly had at that age. "Colin is beautiful, Maddie. Riley would've been so proud."

Maddie nodded stiffly, her fingers brushing the baby's cheek. "Thank you."

"We'll keep your family in our prayers. God keep you all."

She said nothing. Peter gave a final, formal nod and left the house behind, knowing it would be for the last time.

"There's Papa!" Ollie exclaimed when the kitchen door opened. Alice looked up from the sketch she was completing—another one of Ollie. Ollie jumped out of her chair at the table and ran to slam into his legs, which sent Juno barking and bouncing. Alice shushed her.

Peter picked Ollie up and gave her a tight hug. "There's my girl," he murmured before swinging her back to the ground.

"That was a short conversation," Alice said cautiously. She assumed this meant it hadn't gone particularly well.

"Yes." Peter's lips were pressed into a thin line. "It was that. Ollie, I need to have a talk with your mama. Will you go play in your room for a little?"

Ollie blinked, looking from Peter to Alice then back again. "No," she said at last. "I want to hear, too."

"Ollie Grace." Without really meaning to, Alice heard her voice lower a tone. "Run along."

Ollie seemed about to protest further, then she appeared to think better of it, and scampered off.

"What is it?" Alice asked once Ollie's light footsteps had faded up the stairs. "What did Maddie say to you?"

"Essentially what one would expect." Peter lowered himself into the chair Ollie had vacated at the table. His face was grave. "I will be giving Brett partial power of attorney so she need not deal directly with me. She wants nothing to do with either of us, but especially with me. She doesn't want me in any way involved with her life or in her children's lives. She told me that rather than finding a way for our children to play together despite our differences, we should endeavor to put up a fence."

Alice frowned. "That *is* rather what I suspected she would say. I'm sorry."

"I am, too." Peter rubbed his hands over his face. "I don't know what to do. The whole reason we moved here in the first place was to be with Riley and Maddie, because I considered them family. I feel as if I dragged you here, where you're away from our family, and for what? To share a garden with a woman who hates us, for no discernible reason? To be tortured with glimpses of our nieces and nephew, with whom we can never have a relationship? I feel like such a fool."

Alice reached across the table and took his hands. "Shh, we won't worry about that right now. We have Ollie because we moved to Cincinnati. Next year, perhaps—" She released one of his hands to place her hand over her still-flat stomach. "Next year, another little one, if all goes well. We've our church. We've friends."

Peter clung to the hand she'd left in his and looked into her eyes. "I want to go home, Alice. I want to go home to Philadelphia and be with our family. I know it's just an impulse—an emotional one at that. But Maddie doesn't want us here. Whether we have joy or tragedy, I want to share it with our family ... and though we have a community here, I can't help but feel that, with Riley gone, there's so much more for us in Philadelphia. But you must rein me in, darling—I know I'm a fool. Help me."

Her heart skipped a beat. How could she refuse an impulse she herself shared? Yes, she loved parts of Cincinnati, but they had faced so much tragedy here. The loss of their son, nearly losing their marriage, and now Riley's death. There had been joy in Cincinnati too, but it was interspersed with so much grief. And yes, they had a community here, but they also had one in Philadelphia. That was where Peter's family was. Where Cassie was. It felt closer to England, to the family Alice had left behind. That was where she had come as a new bride. Those days had felt so much more touched by happiness and hope than any in Cincinnati ever had. Now, with Maddie refusing to let them see her daughters, it seemed more likely than ever that peace and joy could be found in Philadelphia.

Yet Peter was right. It was an impulse guided more by feeling than logic. But what did feeling or logic matter when God was the One who guided their steps?

"We would have to pray about it," Alice said cautiously. "We would have to seek God and see what He thinks about this decision. But are you serious, Peter? Do you really think we could possibly move back to Philadelphia?"

Peter's eyes were serious, but there was a light of something like amusement in them now. "Don't tell me you've been dreaming of going back to Philadelphia this whole time?"

"I am happiest where you are," Alice said honestly. "But I have come to love your family, and that is where Cassie is. I felt at home at the church there. I even find it to be a more restful city for me. But I will always be where you are. I don't want to be anywhere where you aren't. If you live in Cincinnati, I will live in Cincinnati. But if you want to live in Philadelphia, I will pack my bags and be ready in an hour."

Peter laughed. "As quick as that?"

"Yes," Alice said. "As quick as that."

"Why did you not tell me?"

"As I said, this is our home. I did not want to leave for a variety of reasons. We have found a community here, and then there is always Flick to think about. We would have to ask Flick what she thinks, if this becomes a serious consideration. I would not want to abandon her without a word."

"I would not either," Peter agreed. "Still, I cannot discount that these are my emotions talking. We should definitely pray about this and see what happens in the next few weeks. I admit I am also loath to travel or move you with the baby coming. I asked you to move while with child once before, and I would not ask it again. It can be stressful. Especially so early on, I would fear; and later it would only exhaust you."

Alice nodded. "Yes. I can understand that. I believe if we timed it right, I could handle it. Especially since we will be going to your family and they would be sure to support us in any way we needed. But we do have a house here, a home, and there is much to consider. Fortunately, you are able to work anywhere. That is a blessing most couples do not have." Alice paused with a thoughtful expression. "The executorship is the biggest hurdle, but not an insurmountable one. Dr. Engall is a trustworthy man. With a formal power of attorney, he can manage the day-to-day business here perfectly well, and you can provide the final oversight from Philadelphia. That does not require you to live next door to a woman who causes us such pain."

"Yes—I suppose you are right." Peter sighed. "Here. Let's pray, and we'll talk about it later."

They bowed their heads together and sought the Lord.

Alice delayed telling Peter how bad the dizzy spells had gotten, but eventually, she felt compelled. In truth, she'd hoped they would just fade away or at least that she would find a way to manage them, but that hadn't proven to be the case. Flick said everyone who talked about pregnancy—and they did around her, to Flick's annoyance, because "apparently that's all these women have to talk about, Alice!"—always said that every baby was different. Alice was definitely feeling the effects of that—she'd not had much dizziness with Daniel.

She'd told Flick about the pregnancy, but no one else—not yet. Peter had agreed that it was right to wait as long as she felt she needed to. Besides, he had added, there was no one he really wanted to tell except family who lived so far away that it didn't make sense to announce it yet.

Alice was certainly more emotional this time than she'd been with Daniel; Peter's simple kindness about waiting to share the news had been enough to make her cry.

Honestly, she hated being weepy even more than she hated being dizzy, but neither could truly be helped.

At last, she had told Peter. He'd been predictably concerned, and wanted her to see a doctor.

It had taken him another week to talk her into visiting a doctor—someone with more experience with obstetrics than Dr. Engall, though Alice suspected that was also because Peter wasn't sure how to deal with news of Maddie and the girls just now. It still weighed on him to break his promise to Riley—she knew that.

But that felt like such a low priority to Alice just now. Much as she did love Polly and Susie, Ollie consumed all her thoughts and energy, not to mention the new baby.

If they were safe and well, nothing else mattered.

Yet because Peter would feel better if she saw a doctor, which she hadn't until this date, Alice agreed to do so. Dr. Beecham was a kindly older man who rambled about his granddaughter and asked Peter questions—probably because Peter clearly had more nerves than Alice did about this affair—about Ollie and Peter's work and their life, all while he completed a brief examination.

"You seem very healthy, Mrs. Strauss," the doctor said when he sat back. "Dizziness is not uncommon, but I do recommend rest. Sit down and take a moment if a spell does not immediately dissipate. Ensure you're eating nourishing foods, even if it's difficult, and sleeping as much as possible at night—and just try to do things a little *slowly*." He laughed. "Though I can't imagine the look I'd get if I told my wife that. In general, I wouldn't fear anything, though."

"We ..." Peter glanced at Alice, seeming to ask her an unspoken question. "Can I ...?"

Alice nodded.

"We haven't been able to conceive for several years now," he said, "and before that, we lost two children—one to miscarriage, and then our son was stillborn. And this time ..."

"You want to do everything you can to minimize the risk," the doctor said with an understanding nod. "There is little to do, except trust in Providence. But let me see—you are about three months along now, Mrs. Strauss?"

"I think so."

"Then I would say the risk of miscarriage is much lower than it was earlier on. And I hate to say this—trust me; I do—but sometimes these things happen for reasons we cannot know or control. It is unlikely either of you can do much to eliminate the risk of stillbirth or late miscarriage."

"Is there anything?" Peter pressed.

Alice placed a hand on his arm. "Darling—"

"Rest," the doctor said. "I won't pretend there aren't risks—every pregnancy carries them; we just can't always predict what may make a difference or if anything at all will—but you can help yourself by minimizing stress. Fresh air, plenty of rest, and avoiding heavy labor will be the best things for both you and the baby. Do you have family here?"

Alice's breath caught. Did they?

"We have a church," Peter said after a long moment. "My family is in Philadelphia, and my wife's is in England."

That was a fair assessment now, with Riley gone. There was Flick, but she had a life of her own.

"I wish we were closer to family," Peter added. "I would feel better if Alice had mine around her, and I'm sure Alice would as well."

That was an understatement. Alice would feel so much easier if she could just sit down with Lilli and talk things through. Lilli wasn't Nettie, but she was kind and understanding and so badly wanted for Alice and Peter to be happy. And Caroline and Dahlia had become sweet sisters, both offering comfort whenever Alice was able to see them. Not to mention Cassie lived in Philadelphia.

Oh, yes, Alice wished they lived in Philadelphia.

"I understand," said Dr. Beecham. "Work or other circumstances often take us away from family."

Alice glanced at Peter.

Was he thinking what she was?

If so, he didn't say it to the doctor.

After they'd bidden goodbye to Dr. Beecham and begun the short walk back to their house—Peter had only agreed to walk after Alice had specifically told him that a short walk in the fresh air wouldn't do her any harm, and in fact, might do her and the baby some good—Peter was the one who brought up the subject of moving once more.

"Why are we here?" he said bluntly. "What hold have we to Cincinnati, really, Alice?"

"You're asking me to defend a home I never wanted." Alice took a deep breath. "Ollie," she said. "She grew up here."

"Ollie can't have fond memories of the city." Peter shook his head. "Now that the adoption is finalized, we could take her with us. If you feel uneasy about it, we could leave word at the asylum if they need to contact us, but I doubt Ollie would object to moving somewhere where she'd be surrounded by loving family and friends."

"That's true," said Alice, surprised that she was rapidly becoming the voice of reason. She'd never had thought she'd be arguing for staying in Cincinnati. "But what of the house?"

"We can sell it," Peter said promptly. "Probably fairly easy. It's not a big house, but it's a nice one. With the city expanding, and what changes we have made, we'll make a profit on it. I know we could find somewhere to live in Philadelphia fairly easily, even if it means staying with my parents for a few months."

"But the baby, Peter. Can we really move with the baby coming?"

Peter pressed his lips together. "We can if you are willing. We would have to do so soon, before winter. If you think you would feel safer here, then we'll stay—and I won't discount that moving would do the opposite of what we want; it would *add* stress. But Alice, what if in the end, we are meant to be back in Philadelphia?"

Longing filled Alice's chest. Oh, to be near their family, to be near Cassie, to be where they would even be more likely to see Kirk.

Philadelphia was not a small city, but Alice was accustomed to visiting the quieter areas where Peter's family lived or Cassie's luxurious new neighborhood. Both seemed so wildly preferable to the booming river city of Cincinnati.

"This is our home now," Peter said as they approached their house. He paused at the front steps, placing an arm around her waist. "But I admit that, without Riley, I don't want to raise a family here. Philadelphia was always home for me. I want to go *home*, Alice."

"I understand," Alice said. "I feel much the same way."

Relief flashed across his face. "I know we've been praying about it, and we can continue to do so."

"We'd need to make plans," Alice added. God help her if Peter forgot that there was a lot to moving.

"Right. Right." He looked back up at the house. "We'd be leaving Daniel here," he said after a long moment, in an undertone. "Would that be hard for you?"

Alice hesitated. "Maybe. Maybe it would. But we wouldn't really be leaving anything but his body, and we've never lived near where we lost Zebedee." That had happened in a hotel in Buffalo, New York. "I wouldn't feel far away from him, not really. We've traveled away from here so much, and I know I carry him with me."

"As do I." Peter sighed. "Perhaps I should write to my father and ask his advice. I can do so without mentioning the baby—yet."

"Yes," Alice said after a long moment. "Yes, please do, darling. We need all the advice we can get."

Chapter Twenty-Seven

November 1887
Outside Philadelphia, Pennsylvania

"Arriving now in Philadelphia, Broad Street Station," the conductor called.

Peter put his book in the bag at his feet. "That'll be us," he said.

Alice immediately set aside her sketch pad, which she'd been bent over for the last half hour or so since she'd woken from an impromptu nap.

Ollie was still sleeping, so Alice gently shook her shoulders and then took the time to smooth her sleepy daughter's curls and replace her hat. Ollie looked adorable, but then, she always did. Alice had chosen Ollie's arrival outfit, a naval suit, with great care, only putting her in it about an hour ago.

Peter had protested that his family would adore Ollie if she showed up in a potato sack, but Alice took great pride in dressing her daughter, and his half-hearted reminders were probably more to reassure Ollie of her welcome than to deter Alice from her happy task.

"Remember," Alice said in what Peter called her "schoolteacher voice," "Grandmama and Grandpapa don't know about the baby yet, so it's a secret." They'd told Ollie about the baby before they left Cincinnati, and she had been nervous at first, asking dozens of uncomfortable questions, but after this initial burst of fear, she had been thrilled—and impatient to meet her new sibling. "But we don't need to talk about that, because they'll be so excited to get to know you more that nothing else will matter."

Ollie nodded solemnly. She had taken keeping their confidence with typical seriousness. Honestly, Alice wasn't sure if she was more thrilled to have a secret—or that the secret was she would have a younger sibling in the spring.

This had soothed Ollie when she realized that Cassius and Ophelia would not be coming with them to Philadelphia. Instead, an older couple who lived a few houses down had taken the cats, who'd never quite adjusted to Ollie's invasion anyway. At least Juno was able to travel; she was riding in the baggage compartment.

The train at last chugged to a stop. Soon, the three of them were on the bustling platform, the air thick with coal smoke and the hiss of steam. Juno was brought out on a leash, and Alice wished she had Ollie similarly contained. And then she saw Lilli, with Chris at her side, and Dahlia's husband, Elias, just behind, waiting for them right at the edge of the platform.

Peter wasted no time embracing both his parents and, after a pause, Elias, and Alice did the same. Chris and Lilli passed Ollie between them for firm hugs, crying that she had already grown so much in the last few months, and Elias greeted her with cheerful affection.

Ollie was beaming by the time they walked toward the street.

Most of their luggage had been sent ahead, and Chris mentioned he'd have it delivered. "Our train to Mount Airy leaves in twenty minutes from the local platform," he said. "We have plenty of time."

"You never did quite say why this sudden decision," Lilli said as they began the walk through the grand, echoing station. "Was it just time for a change? What with everything that's happened?" It was obvious Lilli had far more questions than that, but she was holding back her curiosity for Peter and Alice's sakes.

Peter glanced at Alice then began a long explanation of timing and their lives in Cincinnati and being near family and Ollie growing up with her cousins and on and on, and Alice found herself smiling like an idiot.

Peter stopped talking for a moment, and Lilli started to say something about how, of course, they were so glad Alice and Peter would be close, and they were so happy they would now be near Ollie, but Alice didn't need to hear the words to feel their joy.

Their family was simply happy to have them near.

And with that in mind, what right did Alice have to keep them from still more joy?

"And it's because I'm pregnant," Alice added. "We were waiting to tell you until we were sure—but I'm due in May."

"I knew it!" Lilli cried and drew Alice into a laughing, crying embrace.

The kitchen at the Strauss home smelled like rosemary and roast chicken, warm and savory and homey, and it was filled to the brim—not with guests; there was no need for that today; but with Peter's sisters and more laughter than Alice would've expected at the end of two travel-heavy days.

Caroline stood at the stove, sleeves rolled up past her elbows, whisking gravy with the same focused intensity she applied to all things. Dahlia, naturally, had taken it upon herself to taste everything in reach and offer commentary, invited or otherwise. Lilli was elbow-deep in a bowl of mashed potatoes, her cheeks pink from the heat and her light-brown hair curling about her cheeks.

Alice sat at the kitchen table, shelling peas into a cracked porcelain bowl, and watching. It was something she could do without getting in the way, and unlike Dahlia, she preferred not to constantly be underfoot. Dahlia would never quite outgrow being the youngest, despite being a wife and a mother to an adorable toddler.

"That smells like something we'll all regret eating too much of," Dahlia said, leaning dramatically around Caroline in an attempt to dip her finger in the gravy. "I already want thirds."

"You haven't had firsts," Caroline replied without looking up.

"But I will. That's the *point,* Caro—I shall be positively *stuffed*, like a Thanksgiving turkey, and then what shall you do with me? If I'm not preemptively miserable, what's the fun?"

"I'm planning to be smug about my restraint," Lilli said, wiping a bit of butter off her apron. "Which will last until the rolls come out of the oven, and then I'll disgrace myself."

Alice smiled into the bowl of peas. To be fair, Lilli's rolls were the work of legends—the recipe was Maddie's mother's, Alice had heard, but that never had dampened Alice's enjoyment of them.

"Alice," Lilli said suddenly, without looking up from the potatoes, "what would you say to a house with a big library and a lilac bush by the front gate?"

Alice blinked. "I ... suppose I would say it sounds lovely, for a theoretical house."

"Good." Dahlia beamed. "Because it's yours."

Caroline dropped the whisk, which clattered against the side of the pot with a sharp clang. "*Dahlia.*"

"Oh, bother. I wasn't supposed to say that yet, was I?" Dahlia looked positively tragic.

"No," Caroline said crisply, retrieving the whisk. "You weren't."

"Well, too late now." Dahlia shrugged, then turned to Alice with shining eyes. "It's true. We found you a house. It's close by, just in Germantown—on E. Penn Street; wouldn't that be hilarious? You could walk here in half an hour. It's perfect. Not too big, but plenty of room for the baby. And Ollie, of course. And other babies! And the *windows*, Alice! You'll love the light. Caroline said so, and she's terribly fussy about lighting."

"I am not—" Caroline began, then sighed. "Whatever. That's not the point. This was supposed to be a conversation we had with Alice and Peter a few days from now, when they were rested from their travels. We were *not* going to spring it on them the day they arrived. We were going to pace ourselves and tell them we found them a house *later*."

Alice paused, a half-shelled pea pod resting in her hands. "You … found us a house?" she repeated, voice thin.

Lilli finally turned, hands on her hips. "I'm sorry for the timing, but yes. The truth is, Elias found it."

"Elias?" Alice clarified, blinking.

"Yes!" Dahlia exclaimed. "You see, he helped build it. It's this gorgeous thing, with lots of bedrooms and a back yard already there with the lilac bush Mama mentioned—oh, you'll love it. It's so spacious! The previous owners, who had it built, are having to sell it unexpectedly, and the poor thing just *needs* a family! Why couldn't that be you and Peter?"

Lilli wiped her hands on a towel and dropped it on the counter. "I know it's sudden, Alice, but the moment you mentioned moving here, we started looking for a good place for you. You've had so much change all at once, and we thought—well, why not give you a soft landing? Somewhere with a bit of peace. A garden. A kitchen that gets morning sun. It'll smell of lilacs in the spring; I just know it will. That's my favorite scent."

Emotion rose in a wave, like it had been for these last few months, and Alice pressed her hand to her mouth.

"Oh, don't cry," Dahlia pleaded. "Unless it's in delight—in which case, carry on. I'd cry, too, if I were you."

Alice laughed despite herself, though it came out a little watery. "I don't know what to say."

"Say you'll let us take you to see it tomorrow," Lilli said firmly. "That's all. It's not a commitment. We'll figure that out together."

"I—of course. I'll see it, if you want me to." Alice hesitated. "Peter and I haven't even had a moment to discuss what we're looking for, or where we'd want to be. To have it all decided for us …"

"Don't worry about the details tonight," Caroline said gently, her tone softening in that way that always surprised Alice when it happened. "Just rest and eat. We'll talk through everything in the morning."

Dahlia gave a mock groan. "That's not how surprises work, Caro. You're supposed to say, 'It's yours!' and not ruin the magic with responsible conversations about 'making a decision as a couple.'"

Caroline rolled her eyes. "That's hardly practical."

Lilli stepped over and brushed a hand along Alice's shoulder, a mother's touch that made Alice's throat tighten. "It should be yours, dear. It *should* be. And it's nearby, so when you need help—because you will, all mothers do—you'll have it. You know I'll be here."

"All of us will," Caroline clarified.

Alice let out a slow breath. The peas in her lap blurred. "I think I might cry after all."

"Do," Dahlia said at once. "It'll make Mama feel accomplished."

Alice gave up and laughed again, properly this time, and Caroline set the whisk aside and reached for the ladle.

"Well," she said briskly, "since the surprise is ruined and the gravy's thick enough, shall we eat before someone else lets slip another secret?"

"I'm *not* pregnant," Dahlia announced cheerfully. "In case you were wondering!"

"Thank you, Dahlia," Caroline said dryly.

Alice had been up early the morning they were visiting the house, nervous to the point of nausea, though perhaps that was just the baby. The truth was, Alice was unaccustomed to hope, unaccustomed to things working out, unaccustomed to happiness—and it made her feel offish.

In no time, they stood before the house. It stood quiet and still in the dim late autumn light. From the outside, it looked solid—tall windows; clean lines, straight and proud; a neat fence encircling the front where a lilac bush stood, brittle now in the November chill.

Elias and Dahlia led Peter, Alice, Ollie, and Peter's parents in. Dahlia had taken on the saleswoman role, explaining all the benefits of purchasing this property while Peter and Elias teased her about her exuberance.

Only half hearing them, Alice moved slowly, through the wide front door into the foyer, her shoes echoing on the unfinished floorboards. The walls were paneled and completed with a rich, dark wood that reminded her of homes from centuries past. The large foyer featured a beautiful stairway to the right, and then a hallway and two doors—one of which opened to what must be a parlor. Though the door was leaning against the frame instead of being installed, she supposed the room to the left must be an office or library.

She walked into the room. Empty walls, bare floor, footsteps and voices echoing loudly. This must be the library Dahlia had mentioned. It was a massive room, with inlaid bookshelves lining every available wall.

She closed her eyes for a moment then opened them, mentally placing Peter's desk near the fireplace in the corner, and a chair or two for her and Ollie next to him. Would they spend long hours here in the evening, reading and talking? Would she slip in during the day to watch him work and look away every time he glanced up, afraid her open admiration would distract him from his writing? Toward the front of the house, it featured an alcove that would be perfect for placing chairs, the clean wavy glass of the windows letting in an abundance of light. Someone said something cheerful behind her—Dahlia, likely—but Alice barely registered it.

She turned back to the foyer, walked into the parlor, took in the larger fireplace, then passed on into the hallway. A smaller staircase rose to her left, and in front of her a large area for a dining room, which must lead to a kitchen, beckoned her.

She turned, leaving her family behind to argue about the finishing on the mantelpiece, and climbed up the steps. At the top, the stairway continued on to what she assumed was the third floor, but she stepped to the left instead, into an empty room with a tall window looking out into bare branches that reminded her of the ornamental cherry trees at Pearlbelle Park. A door opened into a small bedroom. Upon further investigation, she found there were two larger bedrooms to the right. She only glanced into them as she passed, turning to her right into another room.

She glanced around and decided this must be the master bedroom, though it was larger than any she'd been in since living at Pearlbelle Park. There was a stillness, a settling of sorts that she felt somewhere deep within. She walked to the far window and rested her palm on the sill. Would they wake to birdsong in this room? Would she nurse the baby in the early gray of morning, Peter still asleep behind her?

Was any of that to be? Could she risk it all on the hope that any of this dream would actually come to pass?

She stepped back, removing herself from the room she wasn't sure she dared to hope might be her own, and placed her hand on the door trim. The wood was cool, freshly sanded but not yet polished. This master bedroom appeared to have an attached bathing area and a fireplace.

A floor-length window opened onto a balcony; she pushed it open and found herself looking down on the lilac bush and the street. To her left, another door opened into the third bedroom. After a moment, the cold drove her back into the house, and she stood once more in the empty library.

She walked back into the second largest of the three bedrooms. She would put Ollie and the new baby here, once the baby was old enough to sleep on his own, and leave the other rooms open for guests.

Unless someday we have too many children for one room.

The thought was a strange one to Alice. Too long, she had not been able to think beyond a single healthy pregnancy, a single healthy child. Her dreams of a large family were scattered to the four winds, or perhaps it was more accurate to say they were tucked away safely, for her to take out when the time was right.

What if it was time to dream daringly?

After the loss of their sons, she had locked that part of her heart away. It had hurt too much to look at. But here, she could see them. A boy chasing Ollie down the hall. A baby toddling on unsteady feet. Another child—dark-haired, giggling, crawling beneath the table. Peter lifting them all in turn. Laughter spilling out, everywhere, through every doorway.

They could have bought a house in a grander neighborhood. Cassie and her family would be in her new Rittenhouse Square home, a world away in some respects, but the train from the station just down the road would have Alice on her doorstep in well under an hour. Close enough for real friendship. Close enough to not feel so *alone*.

"I could love this home," she whispered.

Behind her, the soft creak of a floorboard. *Peter*. He didn't speak, just came to stand beside her, one arm slipping around her waist.

She leaned into him. "I didn't know I still wanted this," she said, voice thick.

He kissed the side of her head, just above her temple. "I know."

Downstairs, Ollie's voice rang out in excited tones—Alice suspected that was the sound of a child discovering a yard big enough to run wild in. Someone—Elias, maybe—called out about the hinges on the back door, and how he would fix them, and Chris responded with a question about the kitchen—the stove, would it remain? Of course it would, Elias replied, unless they wanted a different one.

Peter smiled. "I'll talk it over with Papa and Elias to get their counsel on the particulars. I want to make sure the bones really *are* solid, as Elias says—we could always purchase a home that's a little more ... finished. But if we really want the place, Alice, we will make it happen."

"I do," Alice replied. Then she turned to him, quickly. "But you might be right that we're being hasty. If it's too much all at once—"

"Too much? *Alice*." He pulled her into his arms and playfully pressed his nose to hers, making her laugh. "Why do you think that anything I could possibly give you is 'too much'?"

"Because—" She pressed a kiss to his cheek. "I want to be a blessing to you and not a burden. I know—you would never say it—but with the baby, and this move, there is a lot to be sorted, and I don't want to be too hasty. If you think we're moving too fast, I'm willing to wait for a house that feels perfect. But this does feel perfect to me."

He kissed her then, silencing her stream of protestations, and something in Alice settled. She tightened her arms around his neck and kissed him back, hoping this could convey the gratitude for which she had no words. Peter was better at anything that required speech—he always knew what to say. Alice had to make it up to him somehow, and he'd never exactly protested.

"Papa!"

At Ollie's voice, Alice pulled away and glanced toward the door, where their daughter stood, arms folded across her chest.

"What is it, Ollie?" Peter said in that beyond-patient voice that said he would have liked to be left alone.

"You can kiss later," she informed them, just as patiently, as if they might not have thought of it on their own. "But now *I* am here."

"So you are."

"I waited," she said solemnly. "But that was *too* long a kiss, and I need you to come right now. I found my room upstairs. It is *very* big, and all the edges of the house are giving it a hug."

Peter opened his mouth, and Alice shushed him, mostly because she would prefer he not inform their four-year-old that was a very *short* kiss. "We'll be there in a moment. I haven't seen the third floor yet." Not that it was a selling point of the house to Alice, but she was glad Ollie was excited about it. She suspected that the "edges" and the "hug" referred to the sloping roof. No, Ollie would have much more space in this room; Alice wouldn't let her live upstairs.

Ollie turned, then paused near the stairway, watching them as if afraid they would go back to kissing and not follow her. "I will live upstairs," she informed them. "I will hang curtains."

"No, Ollie," Alice said, "if we decide to live here, and we're not sure yet, this will probably be your room." She gestured to the room behind them. "You'll like it. Look—it has the most beautiful windows, and we can decorate it however you like." *Within reason.*

Ollie frowned and then nodded. "We can discuss it."

Alice sighed; the tone and the words were a little too familiar. Peter shook with silent laughter, but Alice couldn't look at him. "*Ollie.*"

Ollie scuffed her shoe on the floor. “I should be able to say it, too,” she said, and then she turned and ran off.

“I see now that I should have been more prepared to raise a daughter of yours,” Peter commented. “I’m not sure I can negotiate room placement.”

“Then it’s a good thing I’m here.” Alice gave him a look then turned to follow Ollie up the stairs, calling her name.

Chapter Twenty-Eight

Early December 1887

PETER STRAIGHTENED, RUBBED THE small of his back, and surveyed the room.

The library was, in theory, finished. The walls had been papered in a subtle green stripe, the new hardwood floors polished until they gleamed. A thick Persian rug, one of their first purchases for the house, covered most of the floor space.

On Elias's recommendation, Peter had hired a master carpenter, who had spent the better part of a week installing the new, floor-to-ceiling oak bookshelves that now stood empty and waiting—their darker wood finish matched better with what Alice wanted, and the previous shelves had not been sturdy enough.

The furniture was in place as well: a handsome leather armchair, a smaller one upholstered in velvet for Alice, and a large mahogany desk positioned near the fireplace.

And yet, the room felt a world away from complete. The source of the remaining chaos was entirely Peter's own. His library, hundreds of volumes collected over a lifetime, still sat in dozens of wooden crates stacked against the far wall, alongside even more boxes of his papers and research notes.

He had insisted on this one task. The painters, the paperhangers, even

Alice and her whirlwind of female helpers had been given strict instructions to leave the books to him. Arranging his library was a private ritual, and he was not yet ready to begin. So for now, the grand new shelves stood empty, while the crates created a disorderly maze in the center of the otherwise perfect room.

The room was large and full of possibility. The boxes of books, which had so crowded his small office in Cincinnati, would look ridiculous here. But Peter had no problem collecting more books, and in time, when she was rested, he would let Alice help him arrange the shelves and add the miscellaneous objects that made a bookshelf look filled out. He had an abundance of Alice's sketches—perhaps he'd have some framed and placed about the room. Last week she'd shown him one that he loved of Ollie with her arms thrown around Juno's neck as the dog panted patiently.

Even the team of workers hadn't stopped the family from being involved. Papa and Elias had been over every day since Peter and Alice purchased the house to "oversee" things. Elias, with his builder's eye, kept the workmen on task, and Papa was never shy about sharing his opinions.

Meanwhile, the house was ever filled with Peter's sisters, their children, Cassie Hilton, his mother, and then other women, some of which he vaguely knew from church and some of which he recognized as old friends. They arrived with baskets of food for the workmen, offering their opinions on wallpaper samples, and turning the chaos of moving into a weeks-long, cheerful party.

There was still more work to do, but the worst of it had been taken care of, leaving Alice and Peter to purchase a few more things to fill out the space. Cassie, who was also with child, had been over most days and even stayed a night in one of their newly furnished guest rooms. Despite the interference of Cassie's nursemaid, Ollie had taken charge of Cassie's two sons like a tiny dictator, allowing Alice and Cassie to pore over the latest issue of *The Decorator and Furnisher*, circling imported armoires and debating whether the sitting room curtains should be cerulean silk or cobalt velvet.

But all that chaos had finally subsided. It had snowed throughout the day, and now through the window he could see the world blanketed with white, highlighted in the too-bright moonlight. He walked closer to the window and looked out at the side yard below. Ollie had made half a snowman before getting bored with it—that made him smile.

He heard the floorboard creak and turned to face Alice. She had a shawl wrapped around her shoulders. "Ollie's asleep," she said, dropping into her new armchair as if she had done so all her life. "At least for now."

"Is she still threatening to move herself to the third floor?"

"Of course." Alice smiled faintly, though a note of fond exasperation entered her voice. "I spend the last three weeks choosing that lovely, elegant rose-blossom wallpaper *especially* for her, and she decides her life's ambition is to live in a dusty, unfinished guest room."

Peter chuckled. "Perhaps it's her way of expressing independence. She will be five soon, as she has told us so many times."

Alice ignored that comment. "It'll still be colder than her bedroom. She told me before she went to sleep that truly *important* aesthetes—God only knows what she meant by that—live on the third floor, and she is going to be an aesthete when she grows up." Alice frowned. "At least, I believe that's what she said. Her pronunciation was none too perfect."

Ah. Perhaps there were some downsides to Peter's campaign to introduce a four-year-old to the details of the literary world. "That may be my fault. We were discussing the Aesthetic movement, and I was expressing some reservations, but I ended the conversation by telling her it was time for bed. I think she's getting back at me."

Peter had known Alice would be both exasperated and confused by this explanation, but she only looked at him for a long moment. "Why did you—never mind. This may be a battle we lose. I frankly don't care. She can shiver up there if she likes."

Peter turned back to the nearest crate, which was open, displaying a large collection of Shakespeare's works, interspersed with some Dickens and Brontë novels. "It won't be too cold, if she picks the room where the chimney goes up."

Alice glanced toward the ceiling. "So right above our heads?"

Peter grinned and placed a stack of books on the floor beside the crate. "I don't foresee Ollie stomping around too much at night."

"Mm. I'll think about it."

He watched Alice for a moment. The dark circles under her eyes spoke of the exhaustion of the past few weeks. This house was a blessing, but he was determined it would not become a burden to her. "Have you given any more thought to the kind of cook and housekeeper you're looking to find?" Knowing Alice, Peter's opinion on this matter would be considered, but she would make the final decision. Not only because it was her house, but also because Peter had no idea where to start with hiring servants. That was more Alice's world than his; it was strange to think that having servants would be a part of his day-to-day life. "I know Cassie gave you the names of a few agencies."

Alice shifted in the chair with a sigh. "I have. One woman I spoke with seemed very competent—but so stern. I don't want a dragon in my kitchen. Not with Ollie underfoot."

"Yes, I'm sure one dragon is enough for any household."

Alice picked up a throw pillow that had tumbled to the floor and tossed it at him.

He held up his hands. "I meant Ollie. But no, we do need someone kind—and someone who understands that this is a family home."

"Exactly," she said, a little of the tension leaving her shoulders. "And someone who won't mind living elsewhere. We might as well be back at Pearlbelle Park if we're going to have a live-in staff."

Peter smiled. He had honestly thought Alice wouldn't care; it amused him how protective she was of their privacy. "We have the means to be particular. Is there anyone whom you do like the sound of, then?"

A real smile touched Alice's lips for the first time that evening. "Actually, your mother mentioned someone," she said. "A widow from church, a Mrs. Peterson. Lilli says she is the soul of kindness and her scones are legendary, which would be lovely since my scones are slightly *less* than legendary."

They did somehow always come out a little tough, but Peter dutifully protested.

Alice waved his words away with barely a glance in his direction. "Anyway, she seems a good prospect for a cook and housekeeper. I'll interview her tomorrow afternoon. Cassie is going to help me go through resumes for a maid later."

"Good." He was worried about Alice being on her feet so much. This home was larger than the one in Cincinnati, and with Ollie and now the new baby, Alice simply couldn't manage all the household tasks on her own. They could have made do if they needed to, he supposed, with the help of family—but he was thankful they didn't have to. Hiring help gave Peter a simple way to channel his anxieties over Alice's health.

There was a long pause. When he looked over, Alice was staring into the flickering flames of the fire, her eyes distant, her hand on her rounded stomach. "Do you think it's a boy?" she whispered.

"I'd say we have about a fifty percent chance," he said, pausing his work and turning to her. "Do you want it to be a boy?"

"I don't know." Alice sighed. "In some ways, yes. But in truth, I want a *baby*."

"That's what I want."

Another long pause.

"What would we name a boy?" Peter asked. Might as well nudge her a bit if she was willing to discuss it. "We'd talked about *Benjamin*, once."

Alice shook her head. "I have since met a Benjamin I don't like."

Peter squinted. "Where have you met a Benjamin?"

"In Cincinnati. The Joneses' only son, from our church. He was two and ran the whole household. I've never known such a disagreeable child."

"Could that be because he was two?" Peter asked dryly.

Alice shrugged. "Let's just say *Benjamin* is not an option. I still like *David*. I always have."

Peter nodded. The choice had been between *David* and *Daniel* for several months before they settled on the latter for their son. "It's a beautiful name. And it sounds right with *Daniel*."

"Not so much with *Zebedee*, though," Alice said.

"Right. But children's names don't have to match."

"I have always liked when they do," she replied. "After all, there's a type of order to it."

"Your siblings' names are Ivy, Edmond, Caleb, John, and Rebecca. How do those names 'match'?"

Alice shrugged. "They're mostly family names. Well, *Edmond* and *John*; I think *Rebecca* was from *Ivanhoe*, and *Caleb* is from the Bible. Caleb is *Caleb Arthur*, and *Arthur* would have been my name if I was a boy."

Peter didn't bother to tell her it would have been *Ivy's* name if *Ivy* had been a boy. "Regardless, they don't match."

"I suppose not. And your parents almost *only* chose family names, except for Dahlia."

"I don't think my parents really intended to have Dahlia, regardless of what they say." Peter chuckled. "They were happy to have her, but it was a surprise. Do you want to use family names?"

"Not necessarily. Only if it feels right. I would name our son for you."

Peter shook his head. "I don't mind *William*, but I don't need a namesake. I prefer names with meanings. I have always liked *Elijah*—'the Lord is my God.' It feels joyful to me, too. Or what about *Isaac*?"

Alice tilted her head. "*Isaac* is nice."

"But?"

She gave a rueful smile. "He sounds like someone who might grow up to debate theology for fun."

Peter laughed. "And that would be such a hardship in this house."

"Perhaps not. We shall have to wait and see if he looks like a theologian."

"Or *she*, I suppose." Peter smiled. "We can't discount the possibility—"

Alice gasped and sat upright. "Oh," she whispered, and pressed her hand to her stomach.

Peter scrambled to his feet. "Alice?"

"It's all right," she said quickly. "He moved."

Peter took a hesitant step toward her. "You're sure?"

"Yes." Her voice was a little breathless, lowered, as if she suddenly felt she must whisper. "It was just a flutter, like a brush of wings. But he moved."

Peter approached and covered her hands with his. He knew it was too early for him to feel their child's kicks, but he still wanted to be close. "You've been waiting."

"I wasn't sure it would ever happen." Her voice broke a little. "He's all right then. I was so worried."

Peter brushed a tear off her cheek. "Thank God," he murmured. "He's being gracious to us, darling. We can trust Him with this, too. He loves us, and He wants to bless us. We must accept every precious moment as it is—an outpouring of His love. Look at how He has already blessed us! We must trust that He will continue to do so, and that His ways are best even when the sin of the world interferes. I want us to 'walk before God in the light of the living.'"

Alice leaned back slightly. "From Psalms, you mean? 'Wilt not Thou deliver my feet from falling, that I may walk before God in the light of the living?'"

Peter nodded. "David was so sure the Lord would rescue him from the Philistines and Saul that he wrote as if the rescue had already happened. Even in spite of the shadows, the dark places, the tears, the heartache, we can rest in His salvation; we can 'walk before God in the light of the living' because He has saved us. I am not afraid. Are you?"

Alice shook her head. "I am not afraid."

Their sorrows had not been wasted. Their tears had not fallen unnoticed—they were gathered in His bottle and kept and treasured. And He was not finished. The Lord had seen their suffering and heard their cries and answered them in their time of distress.

They would walk before God in the light of the living.

Epilogue

May 1888

THE NIGHT PETER HAD been dreading came. Alice's irregular contractions—which had only bothered her moderately throughout the day—began intensifying as the evening set in. By the time Ollie was tucked into bed, Alice had to pay attention to them.

And every nerve in Peter's body forced him to pay attention to them, too.

She didn't want to call his mother yet, but he stopped Mrs. Peterson, their new cook and housekeeper, to send a message for Cassie when she left, which Mrs. Peterson cheerfully agreed to do. It would be Cassie, his mother, and a midwife in the room during the birth ... and Peter. He was determined to be of use.

"I think we're counting this as hour three," Alice said around nine o'clock. "It's been easy so far, though. I understand I shouldn't worry until I can't ... oh." She paused and sucked in a breath, but then immediately resumed speaking. "Can't talk. I can still talk. I'm fine. I feel just fine. Peter, why don't you make yourself some coffee—you look miserable, and it'll be a long night."

He shook his head and reached for her hand, sitting on the edge of their bed. "No. Put me to work, but not for myself."

"I'm going to walk to the chair—no, no, unassisted; I'm *fine*, Peter—and let's change the sheets. There's a set in the cupboard I want on the bed."

Peter swiftly obeyed, waiting until she was settled in a chair by the window, rocking herself slightly and letting the evening breeze cool her, and then began stripping the sheets.

Their room was rather luxurious, in his mind—it had been from the start, but now it was a space that felt more like Alice than anywhere else on earth did. She had chosen everything: the willow-themed William Morris–style wallpaper; the heavy sage-colored silk curtains that muted the outside world; the dark, polished walnut of the furniture. Peter thought there was no place quite so pretty and peaceful.

The third floor, their last project, had been finished last week, along with the garden which Mrs. Peterson's nephew was helping with this spring. Peter hadn't wanted Alice to worry about anything once the baby was born, and it was nice to have the house and garden *finished*—at least for now.

Cassie arrived and helped him remake the bed and gather a few necessary implements that were not already in place. Then she made coffee—Mrs. Peterson had laid out the necessary tools before leaving that evening—and forced Peter to down a cup while she and Alice chatted casually about baby things.

Peter's hands were shaking, but it was Alice who would suffer. If she could bear this, he could bear to watch. That was all. He could be a steadfast witness.

Dahlia came over and collected Ollie from her bedroom, taking her back to her home for the night. Peter's mother arrived, but Alice didn't want the midwife yet. She wanted to walk about the room and fidget with things and talk to people. Peter didn't know how she was doing it. He was fighting off his panic constantly, and it was exhausting. He wasn't stupid enough to believe he was more exhausted than Alice was.

Towards midnight, Alice's sentences began cutting off during contractions, becoming stilted and harsh. She needed to grab a piece of furniture to remain steady or sit down. Peter watched and kept track of time.

Alice was fine, so he was, too. His whole world revolved around this woman, and around praying for her, trying his mightiest to surrender her and their child to God. God would make the final decision here, and there was nothing Peter could do about it. There were frequent prayers by the others, but Peter never stopped. He breathed prayers.

The night continued. Alice rested when she could, but the contractions kept waking her, and she kept wanting to get up, to talk, to move, as if she feared relaxing. Some time in the night, her waters broke; Mama said things might move quicker now and insisted they send for the midwife.

As they waited for the midwife, Peter thought perhaps Mama was wrong, as things actually seemed to slow down, Alice's contractions becoming irregular. The flash of fear in her eyes at this realization scared Peter, but moments later, resolve replaced it, and she rose again and moved around the room as if determined to pace her restlessness away, until Cassie forced her to sit and breathe.

The midwife arrived at the stroke of five. The mix of steady contractions, a nearly sleepless night, and anxiety were getting to Alice, and Peter could tell. As the pain grew worse, she clung to his hand, and when, a few more hours down the line, the intensity seemed to shift, her body bending under the strength of each surge, he felt her begin to shake.

"Peter," she gasped as another contraction waned. "I can't do this. I'm sorry. It's too much. Will you be all right? Please tell me you'll be all right. And Ollie. Peter, I can't ..."

"Darling, don't talk like that. You're doing so well."

She shook her head, fear and desperation on her face. "What if ... Peter, you said you'd save the baby this time. We agreed. And I just ..."

"It won't happen again. It might not have even—" But he stopped himself. Explaining the truth she already knew, that perhaps nothing could have saved their son in the first place, was purposeless. Instead, he'd focus on the now. "Just hold on, darling. Please. For me. Just one moment at a time. You can do that. You're doing so well."

As another contraction came, he held Alice through it, heard her deep, bone-shuddering groans, let her nearly break his hands off, and tried to believe that he had spoken the truth. She *could* bear this. He prayed, begging God for it to not be much longer.

When Alice repeated her fear that she couldn't go on, she asked his mother to "take care of Peter and Ollie—and the baby, if he lived." Mama, in response, simply commented that she was glad Alice was still coherent enough to speak, as if pleased Alice was thinking she was dying.

"This is the hardest part," he heard the midwife say in a chipper tone. "Once you're through this, pushing will seem easy."

The sun was high in the sky when it came time for that, and Peter decided firmly that midwives were insane. All of them, perhaps, but this one in particular.

This did not seem "easy."

The seconds, minutes, even up to what must be endless hours ticked on as Alice bore through wave after wave of intense pain, following the soft but firm instructions of the crazed midwife and the encouragement of his mother and Cassie.

This was ridiculous. This was terrible. This was so wildly unfair.

"He's crowning," the midwife said briskly. "You're getting closer, Mrs. Strauss."

Alice moaned and bent forward, gripping Peter's hand like a vice.

"We're nearly there," the midwife commented. "Now, again. It's burning, I know, but you need to bear down slowly. You've got a smart little fellow—big head, dark hair."

She babbled on, but Peter stopped listening as he knew Alice was the only one who needed to hear it right now. He was shaken. It was really happening. He knew she had never gotten this far with Daniel without intervention; the doctor had said her hips were too narrow.

Alice gasped. "Was that—?"

"That's the head," Peter's mother said. "Oh, Alice, my girl, he's beautiful. Just another push for the shoulders, and then he'll come fast!"

"Mr. Strauss, do you want to see?"

As if Peter was going to stop holding Alice's hand or remove his arm from behind her back, supporting her upright position. "No." If the baby made it, he'd see the baby then.

"Again."

There was a last effort, and the relief in Alice's breathing, and the midwife's soft chuckle as she caught up a small red thing that was the baby. Peter looked away. He wasn't sure why, though perhaps it had been to catch Alice's expression, her slightly pinched brow and the devastation in her eyes in what couldn't have been more than a few seconds as the midwife did whatever she was doing to the child. Probably trying to revive him.

Because he couldn't be alive. He *couldn't*.

If Peter were honest, he would acknowledge he didn't want to watch the last moments before they were broken all over again. Didn't want to see a limp, deformed body worked over in a vain hope, as if anything could be done ...

And then a raspy cry split the air.

He got to see, then, the change in Alice's face and features. The light in her eyes, followed by a sheen of tears—the shocked cry of joy—the outreached arms—the brilliant smile.

"Strong lungs, Mrs. Strauss—you needn't worry! Your baby is healthy and whole."

"Can I hold him?" Alice whispered, her voice shaking—only her tone was full of joy, not sadness or fear. "Please."

"Let me cut the cord." And then there was a baby in Alice's arms, wrapped in a white cloth. "Congratulations, Mr. and Mrs. Strauss."

Mama's teary-eyed face entered Peter's field of vision for a moment. "There, darlings. Take a moment and enjoy your baby. Peter, breathe, please. Don't faint on us."

He obediently sucked in a hasty breath, but he remained frozen, his arm still clamped around Alice's back, as she now relaxed against him. She tucked her head against his shoulder, giving him an unobstructed view of a tiny face, an abundance of dark hair, a wrinkled nose, a mouth opening and closing slowly, and a pair of eyes screwed shut.

Slowly, ever so slowly, his hand came up to brush a damp cheek, so soft and warm under his fingertips.

"Oh, God, thank You," Alice murmured. "Thank You. Thank You. Our son."

"Mrs. Strauss." The trace of humor in the midwife's voice caused Alice to look up. "You should look."

"What?" Alice swiftly brushed back the blanket.

It was as if a spell broke. Laughter bubbled up, and tears sprung to Peter's eyes. He clutched Alice closer, grinning into her hair, his eyes glued to his second daughter. "Now, Alice, even you can't control everything. Look—look, darling, you've given me another little girl. Alice, she's perfect!"

Some time later, after a lot of additional steps Peter had not known were part of the birthing process, Alice received a few stitches and was changed into a fresh nightgown. Then there was quiet, save the soft little baby sounds of his rather vocal daughter. He was able to hold her, after an hour or so during which Alice was unable to release her.

And Peter was in a dream—only it was real. He was really sitting on the bed next to Alice. He really had a perfect, warm, living bundle in his arm, containing his daughter, Alice's daughter. He really was able to press kisses to her downy head and rosy cheeks and button nose and tiny ears and precious fingertips—all ten of them carefully accounted for, along with a matching set of toes.

And she opened her eyes first to look at him—swirling grayish baby eyes, of any sort of color, but shaped like her mother's.

"Are you disappointed?" he murmured. "That she's not a boy."

Alice stirred sleepily. "Surprised. Not disappointed. I feel as if I've been given a gift I didn't know I wanted. She is ... everything."

He stilled, not sure that was the right way of expressing it. "More everything than Ollie?"

"Right now, yes. Tomorrow, no. Ollie is also everything. She's just her own sort of everything." Alice smiled slightly without opening her eyes. "I can't compare the two."

"I won't ask you to. I feel the same. But oh, to have *this*. This is ... indescribable. *She's* indescribable."

"What do you want to call her?" Alice stirred then, pushing herself up, a slight wince accompanying the movements. Peter had been strictly told not to let her attempt to walk for at least a week, and that she might need to have an extended lying-in due to the tearing, the blood loss, and the length of the birth.

After this, Peter would willingly have her on bed rest for the remainder of her life, but that probably wasn't practical.

"We can't call her *Elijah*," Alice continued. "Or *David* or *William*. We barely talked about girl names, actually. I hadn't realized what a mistake that was until this moment."

"I know. These are the situations where you end up with little Alice Jr." He grinned and winked. "I wouldn't mind it."

"No, absolutely not. Give her over so I can see."

"I barely got to hold her!"

"You'll have plenty of time while I sleep. But she deserves a name." Alice held out her arms, plainly not about to take no for an answer. "Our baby, please."

Grudgingly, he transferred the sleeping infant to Alice's arms.

"I admit, if I were to name my first child after any of the many incredible women in my life, I would choose *Nettie*."

"*Nettie*." Peter tried the name out on his tongue. It wasn't right, but he didn't want to say so. "She *has* had a large impact on our lives."

"*Anna*, then. That's Nettie's given name. I can't imagine having a little girl actually named *Nettie*."

Peter grinned. "*Anna* is beautiful. Our Anna. Our little girl. What then, *Anna Grace*?"

"Oh, no, Peter. You know that *Anna* means 'grace,' too."

It was still a beautiful name, but Alice did not like repetition, so he nodded. "Hmm. Speaking of names with meaning, then how about *Evelyn*?"

"*Evelyn*?"

"It means 'wished-for child.' I think that applies. Plus there's the matter of the child Claire lost—Flora Evelyn? I always thought that name was beautiful. Perhaps it would be a fitting tribute."

"*Anna Evelyn*? It flows well. Anna Evelyn Strauss. Miss Anna Strauss. Or would we call her *Evelyn*?"

"It's up to you."

"I quite *like* the name *Evelyn*." Alice cocked her head. "She certainly was wished-for. Never was a child more so. And *Eve* means 'life,' doesn't it?"

"Or something like it."

"Hmm." Alice clucked her tongue. "We can name her *Anna Evelyn* and call her *Evelyn*, I think. Unless you don't like it."

"I like it," Peter said. "And I think *Anna Evelyn* and *Olivia Grace* sound pretty together. They both have 'grace' in their name that way. Perhaps they will have an abundance of it in their lives."

"If only we could all be so blessed," Alice said with a soft laugh.

"Oh," Peter murmured, pressing a kiss to her forehead. "I think we are."

A Note from the Author

Dear Reader,

Thank you once again for trusting me with your time and your heart throughout this book. It's always an honor when someone reads through a novel all the way to the end—and still wants to read more!

I'd like to thank H.S. Kylian and Aimee Simpson for reading an earlier version of this story, back when it still involved St. Joseph's Catholic Orphanage. Thankfully, I was able to find enough resources to shift away from my less historically accurate initial portrayals of the adoption process. I'd also like to thank Katja H. Labonté for her lovely copyedits that gave this novel the polish it needs!

While Alice and Peter's story is fictional, I knew I wanted to portray the adoption process accurately. In this era, adoption was finally becoming a formal legal proceeding. The steps Peter and Alice took were guided by Ohio's 1859 adoption statute. In cities like Cincinnati, many prominent institutions, such as the real-life Cincinnati Orphan Asylum, were governed by a "Board of Lady Managers." (That said, all the "Lady Managers" in this novel are entirely fictional.) These women served as the primary gatekeepers, and their approval—often influenced by a family's reputation and social connections more so than their ability to love and care for a child—was just as crucial as the judge's.

While this was also the era of the famous Orphan Trains, a local, somewhat upper-class family like the Strausses would probably have instead gone through this more formal, institutional process. Plus, let's be honest—can you truly see Alice Strauss picking out a child at a train station?

On a related note, before writing this novel, I never had given much thought to how much money Peter and Alice actually had. I knew the Knights helped—a lot—and that potentially so did the Chattoways, but beyond that? All I knew was that they were never going to starve. I knew Peter's books sold well, but I hadn't given much thought to how well, and my initial estimates were based more on my modern understanding of publishing than a historical one.

That said, when I started thinking about them needing to buy another, nicer house—and, later on in my plotting, to be involved in an adoption process that required analysis of their current social standing—I found myself needing to find out exactly what their socioeconomic status was. As it turns out, the answer to the question, "Would the Strausses have a lot of money?" was simply, "Yes."

I love when things are simple. They so rarely are.

With contracts continuously renewing, his books in every popular shop, and so many books releasing in such a relatively short period of time, Peter doubtless was doing very well for himself. The choice to live within their means—and to spend most of their married life living with wealthy relatives where their expenses would have been few to nonexistent—would have meant their bank statements were looking pretty tidy by the time they arrived home in Cincinnati after yet another long absence.

I just had to let you know that for once in my author life, I didn't give my characters more money than they should have had—I gave them too little. Isn't that crazy? I must be growing as a person.

Finally, I wanted to once again thank every one of my readers for bearing through this massive family saga arc. Seeing Peter and Alice content, with children of their own to love, in a home they have truly settled into, has been healing for me. I hope it has been just as healing for you.

But the story isn't over yet! Book 8 of The Chronicles of Alice & Ivy is in the works, to bring you back to Ivy and Jordy's world—and beyond that, there will be a book 9 once again featuring Alice and Peter and their growing family.

If you'd like to follow along, be sure to subscribe to my email list to get regular updates about my writing process and cute border collie pictures:

kellynrothauthor.com/newsletter

May God keep you always,

TTFN!

Kellyn Roth

A Free Novella for You

Interested in a free novella, available only for subscribers to my mailing list?

January 1944

June Halsted moved her son to Hearthstone Cottage to escape the memories of her failed marriage and estranged family. A struggling artist in the midst of one of the coldest winters in Yorkshire, she finds herself seeking solace at church ... only to meet Mark Hayes, a kindly farmer with a limp and a knack for cheering up her son.

Inspired by The Tenant of Wildfell Hall, *this novella is a sweet romance with Christian themes.*

Go to *kellynrothauthor.com/newsletter* and subscribe to my email list to receive your free story!

Also by the Author

The Chronicles of Alice & Ivy

The Dressmaker's Secret
Ivy Introspective
The Knights of Pearlbelle Park (novella)
Becoming Miss Knight (novella)
At Her Fingertips
Beyond Her Calling
A Prayer Unanswered
After Our Castle

The Hilton Legacy

Like a Ship on the Sea
Like the Air After Rain
Like a Storm Against the Cliffs

Kees & Colliers

Souls Astray
The Lady of the Vineyard

Flowers in Her Heart

Standalone Short Stories

Esther Ashton's New Dress
Kind: a Christmas short story of post-WWII Munich
Eddy & the Tidepools

Anthologies

Springtime in Surrey
Novelists in November
Fingerprints in Frost
Voices of the Future: Stories of Courage & Compassion

www.ingramcontent.com/pod-product-compliance
Lightning Source LLC
LaVergne TN
LVHW041103080826
845145LV00007B/1679

* 9 7 8 1 9 6 2 2 2 2 0 8 2 *